BUTTL

BY

ASHLEY ANTOINETTE

www.thebooklovers.co

Designed by Joshua Wirth

ISBN: 978-1-7355171-4-8

Books may be purchased in bulk by emailing
aa.brandassistant@gmail.com

A caterpillar's old body must die inside the chrysalis...
before the beauty of a butterfly is born...

It's ugly...
It's painful...
It's necessary...

Ashley Antoinette

LETTER TO THE FANS

Dear Ash Army,

I can't even begin to tell you how thankful I am for this village. The support you all lend to me goes beyond books. Who knew that genuine connection could be established through my imagination? The power of words is incredible. I keep trying to get us out of Ethicland, but somehow, this rabbit hole just keeps getting deeper and deeper. It's a beautiful, complicated, erotic, and love-filled distraction from everyday life. We don't always like our people. They drive us crazy. They make loving them hard, but we love them all the same. The details of this world are intricate, and because of that, I cannot speed write through them. It's slow. It's purposeful. Why? Because growth takes time and changing a person's heart is not an overnight process. There is no winner, no loser, just lovers. Two men and one girl. Two beautiful twins. Some ghosts that require respect, and a whole lot of fearful people terrified to reveal painful truths. Thank you for indulging in these characters and for reading this series with your heart and not just your eyes. This isn't for the speed readers or action junkies. There are no glorified gangsters on these pages. We're diving into the hearts of men and letting them control the pen. Hold on tight. I wasn't ready. I envisioned a Butterfly 4 that is entirely different than what is on these pages. These characters took control and wrote themselves. We have no say-so. We just get to experience it. Happy reading, and thank you from the bottom of my heart for allowing my artistry to grow with every stroke of the keyboard.

-xoxo-

Ashley Antoinette

Special thanks to Lamia at Lethal Red Pen and Bianca at B. Edits for your hard work on this project. An author is only as strong as his/her editing team. You ladies are appreciated.

Butterfly 4 Playlist
can be found on the Book Lovers App

storm had come, and it was named Karma. She couldn't spend the night in this precinct. She tried to think of what he would want her to do, and she knew that wasn't what he would have wanted either.

Alani felt the betrayal of every step as she walked out of the building. She turned, staring up at the yellow lights that shone through the windows, casting a glow over the darkened lawn, and she wondered if he was up there staring down at her.

What the fuck am I supposed to do?

She was sure Eazy and Bella were losing their minds. She was barely holding onto her own sanity, so certainly, his children were terrified by the fear of the unknown and what-ifs. She didn't know if she should get them from Nannie's and bring them home or if she should wait until she had answers to give. She slid into the driver's seat of Ethic's Range Rover and pulled out her phone.

"Answer the phone, Mo," Alani whispered.

Morgan's phone had been going to voicemail all night, and she had half a mind to drive the hour to get her.

"Mo, this is Alani; please call me when you get this," she said. She tried to take the urgency out of her voice. She didn't want to scare Morgan. Picture that. Trying to lend bravery when she had none. It was laughable. She gripped the steering wheel and lowered her head, taking in deep breaths to still the anxiety crawling all over her. "Everything is going to be fine. Your daddy is not going to go to jail. He has to be here for you. For us all."

"Open the door, Mo."

Morgan sat on the floor of her twins' bedroom, knees tucked into her chest, gripping her phone as her eyes stared at the door handle. Bash kept shaking it, kept knocking, and she feared it wouldn't be long before he broke it down.

"My temper, Mo. It got away from me. I just want to talk. I just want to iron it out. The longer this door stays closed, the more you incite me... you love to incite me," he said, scoffing.

Did she? She knew she had. She owned that her actions had scratched away at the façade Bash had presented to her when they first met. She had disrespected him, had made a fool of him. No two men would react the same under those circumstances. Bash had become someone she didn't know in the blink of an eye. *Maybe I became someone he doesn't know too,* she thought.

"I just need a minute," she called out. Her voice barely worked. Pain could be heard in every broken syllable. Both physical and mental. Bash had broken something, or perhaps she had done that herself.

She could barely breathe without a sharpness piercing her entire center, and Morgan lifted her shirt to find bruises all over her stomach.

"Ethic and Messiah are both in jail, Mo. Police are on their way to pick the rest of your little gang up as we speak. No one's coming," he said.

CHAPTER 1

Ezra Okafor. His birthdate is 7-7-84. Check again," Alani said as she blew out a deep breath. The angst that pressed on her soul was almost worse than the baby that pressed on her bladder. She was in so much pain. Physically and emotionally. All she had left was her sanity and that was slowly leaving her too. She had no idea where her husband was...hell, she had no idea how he was or if he was even still breathing. Black men died in the back of police cars every day. Cuffs seemed to be the precursors to caskets for onyx-colored men such as the one she was fighting for, and the thought of it, even being a possibility, haunted her.

The cop typed in the information into his flat screen computer. "He's not here."

"Then where is he?" she asked. Decency was non-existent. The cop rolled his wide body around in the squeaky chair, reaching for a stack of papers behind him. He didn't even bother to answer her question.

"Can you check for Hendrix Outlaw? He was brought in with my husband," Alani asked. The phone beside the man trilled, filling the lobby with echoes of urgency. He picked it up only to put it back down, ending the call. Someone's emergency, someone's life, terminated possibly by a blasé cop who was on the end of a long shift. An indifferent man, there for a paycheck, but with no interest to protect and serve. This type of cop had her husband in custody, and Alani was terrified. She knew Ethic could handle himself but somehow, his dominance and natural kingliness worried her more. Certainly, they would feel intimidated, under his intense stare that they didn't understand, that they didn't know was his thinking stare would terrify them. His towering strength, his stern nature, would put the cops on edge, causing their hands to linger near their holsters. Her unarmed, Black king was a trigger finger away from death as long as he was under their care. Even if he did nothing wrong at all, someone entitled to the legacy of their whiteness, bound to the legacy of enforcing the law of slave-catching Black men, who dared challenge their authority would try to put Ezra in his place. It would end badly. She felt it. *I have to get him out of here.*

More ringing. Another emergency.

"They are both here, and I'm not leaving until you tell me-"

He answered the ringing phone, putting her on pause mid-sentence. Her urgency was not his apparently. Waiting was tonight's agenda. She had dressed as quickly as she could. She sped all the way to Nannie's house to drop Eazy off there for the night. Her car had been on E because she had forgotten to tell Ethic she needed it filled up earlier than his normal Sunday routine. That extra five minutes it took for her to pump enough gas to get them across town might have cost her dearly. Such a shame. A Black woman couldn't trust a Black man in the possession of the law for five measly minutes. So many what-ifs went through her mind, and this dismissive officer was lighting a flame he wouldn't be able to put out.

"Hey!" She said, slamming her hand against the high countertop. "WHERE IS MY FUCKING HUSBAND?"

"Sit down, ma'am, before I have you cuffed," the man said.

"Cuffed? I'm 36 weeks pregnant, and you'd rather cuff me than assist me with information? I would love to see you try so I can take your pension, your badge, and your reputation," she said. There had never been a fire in her chest quite like this. "Now look his name up again, and if you can't give me an answer, I need to speak to someone who can. You have me entirely fucked up if you think I'm walking out of this police station without the Black man who belongs to me."

A second officer, plain-clothed, and stern buzzed his way from the back to intervene.

"Ma'am," he said.

"Mrs. Okafor," she corrected. "Mrs. Ezra Okafor," she said, eyes burning with conviction and fear all the same. In that moment she wondered if she truly wanted another boy. She and Ethic had been at odds for months over the impending reveal of what she was carrying. He wanted a boy. Alani was team girl, but this night... this arrest... this raid of their home had changed her mind in the blink of an eye. She already had two Black men to worry over. Eazy and Ethic were already the targets of the world's hate. Could she protect another one? Did she have room to worry at night over whether some rogue vigilante or racist cop would villainize someone who belonged to her before they could make it through her door?

3

She had become team girl in the blink of an eye. These cops forced her to abandon any notion of another son due to fear.

"Mrs. Okafor, if you calm down, we can help you."

"Don't chastise me. Don't play good cop. There is no good cop, bad cop. Until every single one of you are held accountable, you're all bad. This is all a bad-ass dream," Alani whispered in disbelief. "How is this even happening right now?" She said that part more to herself. She didn't want to cry, but she felt it coming. She was so overwhelmed. Terrified. She had to turn away from the officers and pull air into her lungs as she rubbed her hands over her swollen belly. She could feel her blood pressure rising. Her heartbeat was like a drum in her ear, and the kicks in her womb were hard enough to take her to her knees.

"It's a Friday evening, Mrs. Okafor. No courts are open over the weekend. He won't see a judge until Monday, and he's not even pulling up in our system yet. There is nothing you can do for him right now."

Alani turned away from the man, not wanting him to see the emotion building in her eyes. She didn't know what to do. He was the king. He ordered her steps. Ethic lead and Alani followed, submitted— willingly. Now that he couldn't, she wondered, *can I?* She had known what type of man he was when she married him. Prison or death was always a possibility. She liked to tell herself that those days were behind him. That his maturity and excellence as a Black man and father had erased the ill deeds he had willingly indulged in the first half of his life, that karma wouldn't come, but here it was, charging at them with category five force winds. Their storm had come, and it was named Karma. She couldn't spend the night in this precinct. She tried to think of what he would want her to do, and she knew that wasn't what he would have wanted either.

Alani felt the betrayal of every step as she walked out of the building. She turned, staring up at the yellow lights that shone through the windows, casting a glow over the darkened lawn, and she wondered if he was up there staring down at her.

What the fuck am I supposed to do?

She was sure Eazy and Bella were losing their minds. She was barely holding onto her own sanity, so certainly, his children were terrified by the fear of the unknown and what-ifs. She didn't know if she should get them from Nannie's and bring them home or if she should wait until she had answers to give. She slid into the driver's seat of Ethic's Range Rover and pulled out her phone.

"Answer the phone, Mo," Alani whispered.

Morgan's phone had been going to voicemail all night, and she had half a mind to drive the hour to get her.

"Mo, this is Alani; please call me when you get this," she said. She tried to take the urgency out of her voice. She didn't want to scare Morgan. Picture that. Trying to lend bravery when she had none. It was laughable. She gripped the steering wheel and lowered her head, taking in deep breaths to still the anxiety crawling all over her. "Everything is going to be fine. Your daddy is not going to go to jail. He has to be here for you. For us all."

"Open the door, Mo."

Morgan sat on the floor of her twins' bedroom, knees tucked into her chest, gripping her phone as her eyes stared at the door handle. Bash kept shaking it, kept knocking, and she feared it wouldn't be long before he broke it down.

"My temper, Mo. It got away from me. I just want to talk. I just want to iron it out. The longer this door stays closed, the more you incite me... you love to incite me," he said, scoffing.

Did she? She knew she had. She owned that her actions had scratched away at the façade Bash had presented to her when they first met. She had disrespected him, had made a fool of him. No two men would react the same under those circumstances. Bash had become someone she didn't know in the blink of an eye. *Maybe I became someone he doesn't know too,* she thought.

"I just need a minute," she called out. Her voice barely worked. Pain could be heard in every broken syllable. Both physical and mental. Bash had broken something, or perhaps she had done that herself.

She could barely breathe without a sharpness piercing her entire center, and Morgan lifted her shirt to find bruises all over her stomach.

"Ethic and Messiah are both in jail, Mo. Police are on their way to pick the rest of your little gang up as we speak. No one's coming," he said.

Her eyes burned at that revelation. She rushed to open the door.

"Where are my babies?" she asked. "Messiah had them! If he's locked up, where are they?!" she cried.

"Our babies, Morgan," he corrected as he pinched her chin, manipulating her face left, then right.

"Bash, please. You can play with anything and anybody in my life except them. You can kill me in this apartment but please, please just tell me my kids are safe," Morgan pleaded.

"Likely they're with social services by now. They can stay there, or we can go get them. Depends on what we come to terms with," he said.

"Why are you doing this?" she asked. "What do you get out of keeping me around? Things end, Bash. Sometimes, things don't work out. I'm 21 years old. You're going to ruin my life because our relationship isn't what I want?" she asked.

"You don't even know who you are. Do you even know what you want?" Bash asked. "Because on those nights in London when everyone had given up on you and I was there, you wanted me."

For the first time, Morgan realized how dangerous this had become. She had allowed Bash to become a constant factor in her life. She had given him hope of a future that she was just trying to make it to. She had run from the remnants of Messiah but was so blinded by pain that she couldn't see that she was running towards trouble. Bash's eagerness to be a part of her life should have been a red flag, but instead, it had served as consolation for all she had lost. If she couldn't be with the one she loved, at least she had the one who loved her. What a grave mistake she had made. "We're done with the games, with your whims," Bash said.

Morgan was speechless. She had never recognized how intimidating Bash was until now. The way he loomed over her. The darkness in his eyes. This man was her friend once upon a time. He had made her smile. He had made her blush. They had laughed over biochemistry and popcorn. She had missed something. She had been too numb, going through life too agreeably, not noticing that Bash was no knight in shining armor. He wanted to trap her, with his status, his influence, and the formality of royal life in London. Morgan wasn't made for that life. If he forced her to live it, she was sure she would die there.

"Where are my kids, Bash?" she asked. Morgan's emotions were overpowering her. She wanted to cry but was too stubborn to let him see that he was winning this mental battle. She felt like a butterfly trapped under a glass dome. She just wanted to break free. "Stop playing with me about my kids! Where are they?!"

The knock on her door put a flicker of hope in her chest. She pushed by him, ignoring the pain that was erupting through her body with every step. Morgan rushed to the front door. She prayed that it was her babies being delivered back to her somehow. She couldn't even process what was happening right now. Her heart was torn in every direction. Ethic. God. Ethic was in jail. Messiah with him, but her babies tore her up most. Morgan pulled open the door, and when she saw Christiana empty handed, rage filled her.

Bruised ribs and all, she spun on Bash, swinging blows so vicious that he was unprepared.

"WHERE ARE MY FUCKING KIDS?!" She screamed. Everything good about her was wrapped up in her babies. They were the best parts of her. They were the pieces of her that still made sense. They made life better, the world better, and she had no idea where they were or if they were in good care. "I WILL KILL YOU!"

With strength she didn't know he had, he wrapped one hand around her neck and forced her against the wall. She was sure he would have broken her neck had Christiana not intervened.

"Sebastian, settle."

Bash released Morgan. "You're gonna learn how to act." He backpedaled and took a seat as Morgan stood heaving, gripping her neck and gritting her teeth.

Christiana pulled out a piece of paper and placed it on the living room table.

"Have a seat, dear," Christiana said.

"You watch your son put his hands on me, and that's all you have to say?" Morgan asked.

"I have more to say and you're going to listen," Christiana replied. She sat beside Bash placing a hand to his bouncing knee, seemingly turning down the heat on Bash's fiery disposition.

Morgan felt like she was in some twisted mother-son horror flick. How hadn't she seen this dysfunction before now?

"You're a mother, Morgan. As am I. Mothers are protectors of their children," Christiana said. "We have come to love those babies. We've helped raise them. We are their family. We are your family. We provided a haven for you when you were at your lowest. Our family's legacy won't be tarnished by your continued antics. It's beginning to look a bit unstable. We don't want discord in this family. All I've ever wanted was for Sebastian to be happy, and he's chosen you. We presented you to our world, Morgan. There is no leaving that affiliation. You won't make a mockery of our institution."

"I just want my family safe. Ethic, my kids, and Messiah because he shouldn't be in prison. I'll stay away from him. I'll go back to London. I just need them released, and I need my babies back in my arms. Please, Christiana." Morgan was desperate. More desperate than she had ever been.

"I want you to read these documents," Christiana said, passing Morgan a stack of papers. Morgan's heart dropped as she took in the words.

"I didn't sign this," she whispered. "How did you... what does this mean?"

"Well, when I helped you apply for dual citizenship for you and the children in London, you were so unfocused, so extremely withdrawn, depressed even," Christiana said. "You were just signing page after page without reading. As you can see..."

Morgan gasped as she looked at the pages. "You tricked me into this. I didn't..."

"Your children are legally adopted by Sebastian. We will take full custody of them and prove you unfit if you don't get your act together, Morgan."

"Bash," Morgan whispered. He had robbed her of her will to protest. Her children were pawns, and Bash would move them around the board, sacrificing them if it came to that. She shook her head, and her chin quivered. "Bash, this is too far."

"Isn't so fun when the rabbit's got the gun, huh, Mo?" Bash asked.

"What do you want?" Morgan asked.

"That's the difference between us. You measured what I could do for you. That made you stay, right? The convenience? The money? I only wanted you for who you are," Bash answered.

"That's not what happened!" Morgan shouted. "You wanted something I couldn't give you! I was broken inside, Bash. I could barely love me, and you wanted me to love you! How is that fair to ask? How is that possible?"

"And I understood that. I knew it would take time. I knew you had some things to heal first, but then you gave everything I had worked for to him," Bash said. "No healing required. No two-year wait period for him."

Ahmeek Harris. Morgan closed her eyes. She had needed no pre-heat period for him, and Morgan didn't know why. She just fell. She had fallen so hard and felt a love so glorious that everything that had hurt before him made sense because it was what led her to him. It was a slap in the face, and it turned Bash's understanding into contempt.

"I will do anything," Morgan whispered. She didn't even have to say anything else. She would sell her soul to fix this. If only she could rewind time and reverse-engineer the past two and a half years. Her tears could no longer be held back. Her back was against the wall.

"Yeah, you will," Bash agreed. He nodded his head and stood to his feet, extending his hand to Morgan.

Her skin crawled as she left it dangling mid-air.

"I just want my kids," she repeated.

"Whose kids?" Bash asked.

Her heart ached. She had gone along with this lie. She had let the world believe this story. Now, fiction had become fact. "Our kids," she whispered. For the first time, she realized how big of a mistake she had made by stripping Messiah of the title. Now, there was no undoing it. Morgan and her twins belonged to the Fredericks.

"Where is that man?"

Messari was a marvel to Bleu. His little hands signed the words he spoke so that his sister, the beautiful Yara, could understand.

"That man is your daddy, you know," Bleu said softly.

"I know that, silly. Him name is like mine," Messari said.

Oh, what Bleu would give to see MJ at this exact age. The inquisitive nature of Messari's stare. The softness of his tender skin as he grabbed her hand to pull her around the room to lead her to something he found interesting. The furrowed brow that was seemingly the only thing he had gotten from Messiah. He was both a painful reminder of what she had

lost and a beautiful reminder of the beauty Messiah could manifest. "I want my mommy," Yara signed. Bleu couldn't understand her need, but she knew fear when she saw it. Yara wasn't as easygoing as Messari. She was uncomfortable. She had been to two new environments and in the care of two strangers in the past 24 hours, and her soul was unsettled. "Hey, Messari, can you help me talk to your sister? What is she trying to tell me? I'm not as smart as you. I can't sign. Can you be in charge and sign for me?" Bleu asked.

"Me?" Messari asked. "Me is just a kid."

Bleu laughed at his confusion. She couldn't help but love him. Morgan and Messiah had created pure perfection together. It made sense. As potently as he had loved Morgan, she didn't expect anything less than these two beautiful rewards. If Yara and Messari were evidence of the power of love, no way could Bleu hold a candle to Morgan. The twins put a sadness in Bleu like nothing she had ever felt.

"How about you just tell her one thing, okay? Tell her my name and that I'm a friend of your mommy's and that I will take good care of you both until your mommy comes. She will be here soon," Bleu said.

Messari signed the words and Yara seemed to settle some, using distance as a coping mechanism, choosing the opposite end of the couch to settle into. Bleu had refused to hand Messiah's kids off to social services, but with them in her possession and Messiah in jail, it felt like she was in over her head. She hadn't had Morgan's phone number in years, and Meek's phone was going directly to voicemail. Even Isa was impossible to reach, leaving her to wonder if the entire crew had been arrested. Thank God she had stopped for Pull-Ups and pajamas, but even that had been a task. Wrangling two confused toddlers with no car seats into Walmart in the middle of the night had been a challenge. Between Yara's wails and Messari telling the cashier, "I don't know this lady," she was surprised she hadn't been arrested her damn self. An hour later, and a stop at McDonald's for fries and nuggets, then a quick bath, and they were fighting sleep. Bleu was exhausted. Terrified, worried, and motherfucking exhausted.

"I'm going to lay you down right here by Yara, okay?" she asked. She tucked them snugly beside one another, propping their heads up on pillows before placing a throw blanket over them.

She turned the television on Disney Junior, remembering that it had television shows Saviour used to love, and then she crept into the kitchen. Within fifteen minutes, they were out like a light, and relief flooded her.

"Come on, Ahmeek. Where are you?" She huffed as she redialed his number. No answer. A text. Green bubbles. What the fuck? He had an iPhone, so his bubbles should be blue. His phone was off, and panic was rising in her. In all her years of knowing The Crew, they had always been accessible to her. Even when they would make runs out of town, they made sure to always check in with Bleu. The only time communication had ceased was when she chose to pull away after Messiah disappeared. Hiding her pregnancy from the world had caused her to become distant. Things hadn't quite been the same since. Messiah's absence had shaken up all of their lives. She could only imagine what his incarceration would do. She and Morgan hadn't crossed paths in years. A girl she used to see as an innocent beauty with a healing love had somehow become someone she both envied and resented. Not because Messiah loved Morgan. She could live with that. When they had been at their best, Messiah had been happy. It was his despair that ate away at Bleu, and the cause was Mo. She had no right or no place to feel any type of way, but her feelings were her feelings. She couldn't unaffect her heart. He had already touched it.

Eyes to the ceiling, hands propped behind his head, pretty-ass bitch beside him, Ahmeek was silent. The rise and fall of his chest did little to ease his anxiety. He had never let anyone unnerve him like Morgan Atkins. His entire situation. Him and Mo. Mo and Bash.

Bitch-ass nigga.

Mo and Messiah.

Those fucking kids.

It was all an inconvenience. Distractions like none he had ever had. Ahmeek was torn between honoring a brotherhood he had experienced his entire life and the awakening of his soul by a girl he should have never known intimately. He hated that he was even involved. Messiah's return had added a layer of complication that hadn't existed before and witnessing Mo's lies, learning of Messiah's fatherhood, destroyed him.

Her ass been lying to everybody for years, he thought. *Doing that hood-rat-ass shit, yo. Keeping that nigga from his kids.*

He had been there for the era of M&M. He had witnessed the brutality of its end. It had been a war of emotions when Messiah and Morgan had ended, and there were causalities of war all over that battlefield. PTSD. Even being a witness to it, nobody walked away from that battle the same. He knew why Morgan had done it. Why she had felt the need to erase any trace of Messiah from her life afterward, but he was a man, and he just couldn't get with a woman playing with a man's legacy. At the end of the day, that was all a nigga had. His name. Morgan had even stripped the twins of Messiah's last name.

He felt Livi stir next to him. He shouldn't even be thinking of Morgan with available pussy beside him, but she was ever present, living in his mind like she paid rent there; nah, fuck that... like she owned the shit. He had walked away. The tears she had cried. The way that lip had trembled. Sad-ass eyes on her pretty-ass face, begging him for a little understanding. He had none. He couldn't lend to her what he didn't possess. Messiah and Morgan had children.

Those fucking babies, man. My babies, he thought. He had envisioned being something to them. He wasn't sure what. He just knew they were important. They occupied his heart but with the discovery of who they belonged to, he was realizing they wouldn't occupy his life. That shit hurt worse than losing Mo. He had lost Messiah once. He knew what life without him was like. Messiah's absence had forced them all to feel a faux grief that they had attempted to live through. It had hurt. It had put a hole straight through him and Ahmeek had been cold afterward. He had put his head down with Isa in the streets and ignored every single feeling of loss that threatened to break him down. He smoked his way through it, drank a little too heavily, partied, bullshitted, fucked. Time had moved him along, so he knew what it was like to have his brother removed from his world. To now have to adjust to another loss, the removal of the sun, he was fed up. Flint didn't even feel like home anymore because no way could he be so close and not bask in the glory of her rays.

"You haven't slept?" Livi's sweet voice interrupted his thoughts, then her hand to his chest, which he trapped with one hand.

"I'm good." The answer couldn't have been furthest from the truth. All they had ever indulged in was surface bullshit. A little fucking. A little shopping. A little eating. So, she didn't know to look for the answer behind his answer. He was grateful because she wouldn't like what she would have unearthed if she knew how to read him. When she had fallen asleep, he hadn't seen the harm in letting her stay the night, but now he wished he had sent her on her way. Solitude. Ahmeek was searching for a bit of solitude to accompany his thoughts. "I know I've been super weird lately. I'm not applying pressure, Meek, but I know what I want," she said.

"That's the topic of conversation at 3 a.m.?" he asked, brow denting. He looked down at her as she moved her head to his chest. "We shouldn't be doing no talking. You know what I'm trying to do."

He lifted, taking a dominant position as he rolled her onto her back. She wasn't even supposed to be in his loft. He was breaking all kinds of rules, making up rationale that made her presence okay. He reached for the nightstand, grabbing a condom and then trapping it between his teeth. She reached up to pull him down by his neck forcing connection, causing him to fumble with the condom. Body to body. Another nigga would slide in without thinking twice, especially the way she was reaching for his manhood, using the tip of him to rub her clit in circles. Livi was a freak. She gave Meek no limits in bed, and the way she took dick, she needed to teach a class.

"She's wet for you, Meek," she moaned.

"Yup," he said as he lowered his lips to her nipple, palming her left breast before slurping it into his mouth. "Hmm..." He took a handful, his full lips devouring her body as she squirmed beneath him. "Damn."

"Just fuck me, Meek. I want to feel all of you," she said.

He lifted, located the condom, and ripped it open with his teeth.

He didn't even speak as he strapped up then took both her legs, pulling them over his shoulder as he entered her.

"This dick is the besttt," she groaned as he gave her a moment to adjust to his size. He strummed her love, thumbing her clit. He may as well have been turning the faucet the way she flooded.

"Yo, this shit is a mess," he said, bottom lip trapped between white teeth as he went swimming in her waters. Meek's stroke was experienced, rhythmic. Cirque du Soleil-dick-ass nigga. He was hitting Livi so proper, all she could do was hold on for the ride. She should have been used to the ways he worked her over. She had experienced him many times, but she hadn't quite mastered the art of him. She came in minutes, shaking, clawing at the sheets. He wasn't mad. He knew she would climb back in the ring and go rounds with him as soon as the convulsions stopped. They had already gone two. He needed more, anything to take the focus off his focus because his focus was on a woman who belonged to his mans. Pussy was the world's greatest distraction.

He gripped the sides of her thighs, thumbs denting her thickness as he pulled her onto his dick.

"Tape me, baby. Play in this pussy and send it to me so I can cum later after I leave," she said. A bad fucking bitch. Livi knew what Meek liked. He was a hood nigga who loved nasty shit, and Livi let him have his way every time. She had no reservations about the ways he liked to fuck. She was the best kind of situationship to have. Good pussy, no headaches, her own bag, and a class act in public. It wasn't until recently had Livi begun to require more, and he wasn't mad at it. Surprised, yes. Mad, no. Her timing was simply off, because his heart was wrapped up in someone else; in a spoiled ass woman with an unexplainable vibe he couldn't seem to replicate. He didn't know what it was about Morgan Atkins but even in their disconnected moments he felt connected to her.

"You wild," he said, smirking as he reached for his phone on the nightstand.

It was on DND, but the message notifications that awaited him on the home screen told a story of alarm without returning one call. Morgan had called back-to-back for almost half an hour.

He had seen her go a little crazy before, so it wouldn't have been so alarming if it weren't for Bleu's calls around the same time. She never called. She would check in from time to time. Mostly texts. The fact that her name was on his phone six times made him abandon the bed altogether.

"Hey, we're kind of in the middle of something," Livi said, seduction and wanting dripping in her tone.

"Sum'n up. Give me a minute," he said. His sudden seriousness brought her up on one elbow, frowning. Ahmeek Harris was no longer in the room. He was Murder Meek. He slipped into hoop shorts and walked out of the bedroom as he opted to return Bleu's call first. If Bleu could fill him in, there wouldn't be any need to contact Mo.

"Thank God! Where you been?! Are you with Morgan?" Bleu shouted.

"Nah, man, that's a wrap. I ain't with her. What's up with you blowing a nigga line up, B?" Meek responded.

"The police ran in Messiah's apartment right after you left," she said. He heard the panic. He heard something else too. Worry…The kind a woman had for a man she loved. He recognized it because he had heard it before, from Morgan when she hadn't wanted him to make his runs. It didn't need addressing. It was clear as day and not his business.

"Ran in the crib for what? The nigga know better than to trap where he sleep so they ain't find nothing there. What did they say?" Meek asked, mind already spinning, thinking of the worst-case scenario. What the fuck had Messiah gotten into since being back? He had nothing to lose, so perhaps he had broken the rules that had led to this type of heat. Meek couldn't see it, but he couldn't be sure. The Messiah he used to know moved a bit different than the ghost that had returned. This one was reckless; an act first, think later kind of nigga. Still, his man being locked up didn't sit right on his conscience. The silk of Livi's fingertips against his neck reminded him of her presence. He gave her his attention.

"Yo, get dressed. Some shit came up," he said. "I'ma follow you to the crib."

She sucked her teeth, and Meek turned his back on her. Back to Bleu. Back to this revelation.

"Now, what else they say, B? What's the charge? Was there a warrant?

Where the kids?" Meek asked.

"I either had to keep them or let the police take them to social services. I didn't have a choice but to bring them to my house. I don't know if I'm the one who should be taking care of them, Meek. I don't know how to reach Mo. Isa isn't answering, so I'm not sure if he got locked up. Until you called, I thought they got you too."

Ahmeek's stomach knotted. "I'm on my way," he said.

"Fuck, man," he muttered.

"You really got a lot of nerve." Livi's voice over his shoulder held contempt. He turned to her. "That bitch call your phone and you just drop everything? Send me on my way in the middle of the night to go running to her?"

"It's a good idea for you to put your clothes on, Liv," Ahmeek said, patience non-existent after the news he had just received.

"Don't bother following me home. I'm a big girl. I know how to get there," she said. She snatched up her clothes. Meek lowered the phone to his side and sternly took the clothes from her hands. "Your feelings would be a lot less hurt if you stayed in your lane, Liv. I ain't on no phone with no bitch. You worried about the wrong shit," Ahmeek said. "Go shower while I take this call and come back out here with that attitude gone. I said I'ma follow you, didn't I?"

Livi rolled her eyes and looked away.

"You want the gangster or the gentleman, Liv? Cuz you riding the fence on my patience right now. Which side of the yard you hopping down on?"

"You're not the only one with two sides. I can be your bitch or a bitch. Respect me. Don't be answering no calls from no bitches while I'm in your face," she said. "You know what I want and..."

"...That ain't gon' happen overnight," Meek interrupted. "I ain't got no ill intentions with you, but I ain't good for you right now. Not for what you wanting. You come over here putting pussy on a nigga. We always been good at that. I'ma always know how to put that down on you cuz you been pulling up on a nigga for a minute. I been playing in that pussy for years," he said, pulling her hand, snatching her toward him, and then taking her neck in one hand. "You don't want what I'm giving right now. Shit's all fucked up. Some shit go down and a nigga need time to get his head back on straight. You a good woman, Sullivan. I'm not in it to ruin that, but this conversation is already too long and too hard on a night when I don't have time to have it. What a nigga supposed to do when he know what you want but ain't got it to give?"

She stood speechless, searching for a reply because she knew if she could give him the blueprint, he would follow it. Ahmeek was the type of man who would do all he could to get it right, but he had been wronged, and those wounds were too fresh to do anything other than fuck and blow bags. "She ruined you."

"Yeah, well, I helped ruin her first," he answered. "Get dressed. I got business."

Livi was stunned to silence as she made her way to the bathroom.

He couldn't deal with false assumptions right now. He wondered if the police would be knocking down his door next.

Fuck this nigga don' got hemmed up on?

He hit Isa's line, immediately bypassing the do not disturb because the Crew kept each other locked in on the favorites list.

"Nigga, I was getting some; this better be good," Isa said. Meek heard the phone fall and a subsequent, "Damn, Ali! Fuck! Hitting a nigga and shit!" He complained before retrieving the phone. Isa and Aria and their toxic love. Meek envied even their bond in this moment because out of them all, Isa and Aria were the ones who had endured. They had been solid for years, even when Aria thought Isa wasn't; Meek and everybody around him knew that Aria had his soul. Aria had never made him go without her presence, she had never disappeared, never pulled out. Getting Morgan to do the same was an anomaly, so yeah, he respected their bickering. He saw nothing wrong with a little sour with the sweet.

"Something happened with your bro," Meek said.

"Man, here y'all go with this bullshit," Isa groaned. Ever since they were kids, when Meek and Messiah would disagree, they would disown one another, "unclaim" the love. Messiah would become "yo' bro," and Meek would always turn into "yo' nigga." Two stubborn men unable to tell the other that they were hurt. They just held their ground until something brought them back to a commonplace. "Fuck that nigga do now, bruh?"

"I don't know what, but he on papers. They came to the spot with a warrant to pick him up."

"How you know? What the fuckkk?" Isa said, suddenly giving the conversation his full attention.

"I know," Meek said. "Bleu just called." Conflict filled him. Messiah was his brother, but he wasn't so sure they were friends anymore. This wasn't technically his problem, but the blood pact they had made as kids somehow burned in his mind. "To the top or to the grave but never to the pen. Money over bitches, brothers through it all." They had been so young then. Little-dick-ass kids with big dreams and growing egos. They were starting on their corner boy shit at 11 years old. He recalled the days of admiring the major players in the city. Benny Atkins and his team ran the Northside. He'd never forget the Deuce Deuce Benny used to ride around with, and

Justine Atkins had been a dream. Messiah, Isa, and Ahmeek would dream of the day it would be them mobbing through the city in dope cars with pretty girls.

"My bitch gon' be the baddest! Swear to God! And she ain't gon' never be fucking with nobody but me!" Messiah used to brag.

Never would Meek have predicted the daughter of Benny Atkins would be that girl for them both, the girl to divide them.

"How you want to play it?" Isa asked. "If they got him, they prolly got warrants for us. We can't walk in no precinct after him. We got to send Bleu in there after him."

"Nah," Meek replied. "It got to be somebody that they can't hit with a RICO charge. He in deep with Bleu. Been in deep. She don' spent some of this dope money. Can't send her in there; she might not come out."

"Nobody they can hit with a RICO charge," Meek said.

He heard Livi behind him, making her presence known as she brought the scent of BYREDO body wash into the room with her. He hated it. Her wearing it felt wrong. It was Morgan's scent. Girl soap. Fifty-dollars-a-bottle type shit because little Morgan was spoiled and accustomed to expensive shit. Now, Livi was walking through the loft, smelling like Morgan, and it all fucked him up. Just the night before, he had discovered the worst about Morgan. She was more underhanded than he ever would have thought. He had never anticipated deception from her, and he couldn't help but wonder if this was merely a fraction of what she had felt all those years ago when she had discovered the plot against her family. Ahmeek had juggled many hearts before but had never put his in the hands of someone else. His head hadn't been in the game. He and Messiah had been at odds. Somewhere, somehow, they had slipped up. Meek knew what it was like to do a bid. He had promised himself that he would never see the inside of a cell again. He had told himself that it was either come up or get out the game altogether because falling off wasn't an option, but with Messiah behind bars, it felt like a bad ending was near.

"I'ma call the lawyer. I got somebody to put the bond up," Meek said. "Get up and go to the spot. Don't take nothing major. No bags or no shit. Nothing that make it look like you running. Get your girl out that house, bruh. Never know when them folk will come through with a warrant for us too. I'll be there when I get Messiah out. Have Aria call Mo. Bleu got the twins."

"Hol' up. Bleu? Fuck Bleu doing with 'em?" Isa asked.

"She was with Messiah when he got popped," Meek informed. "Just have her call Mo. They don't know Bleu like that. They need to be at home with they mama. I should have took 'em there last night."

"Why you can't handle that?" Isa asked.

"It ain't mine to handle no more, bruh," Meek said. The silence that ate up the line was filled with sorrow, one so dreadful that even Isa felt it.

"Yeah, I heard. Real shit, though, didn't you ever think the shit? Like they don't look shit like that nigga, but no lie, when I hold Yolly bad-ass, it was like I could feel that nigga, man. And when I fought with Messari little soft-ass,

26

I would try to rough him up cuz in my head I was baiting him, just waiting to see that temper flare-up, just waiting to get a piece of bro, cuz if he was in that lil' nigga, it was gon' eventually come out. I knew she was full of shit, man, but I knew she had her reasons. The way we fucked her over, I knew why she was running from it, so I let her be. Are you really that surprised? I thought the way you loved them was because of him, low-key."

Meek couldn't get in too deep with the conversation, not with Livi hawking his call inconspicuously, but he wondered if he had ignored all the signs to make himself feel better. He hadn't asked. Hadn't questioned things that didn't make sense. He hadn't pegged Morgan as a liar, but she had told the biggest lie of all. In that moment, Meek had to admit that he had wanted to believe the lies, but he had felt it too…The connection Isa was describing. He had loved those babies from the moment he set his eyes on them because his heart filled some after the "death" of Messiah had emptied him. "I guess I lied to myself, my nigga," he replied. "Get out of there, though. Get off the grid and only make calls from the burner. Tell your girl to leave her phone too. I'ma get with you. If you don't hear from me by morning, head to Florida."

Meek felt a gloom fill the room as the line went dead.

They had prepared for this.

They had people in Florida, associates who they could get busy with until they figured out where the smoke was coming from. He looked over his shoulder.

"I need you to do me a favor, Liv. A big fucking favor, man. This nigga," he mumbled.

Ethic hadn't spoken in hours— at least it felt like hours. He didn't quite know because they had taken his hundred thousand-dollar Audemar during processing. He leaned over onto his knees, intertwining his fingers, head down, as thoughts of his wife and children raced through his mind. Something in his stratosphere was off. If he was sitting behind concrete and steel, someone had intentionally put him there. He rubbed his hands together, turning the wheels of his mind, temper lunging behind the invisible fence of his gangster. Niggas just wouldn't let him elevate. He was minding his business, loving his woman, taking care of his kids, and whomever had set off this chain of events was just begging him to hang up the family man act and end lives. Because contrary to popular belief, gangsters didn't mature into gentlemen; they masqueraded as such. All it took was the right reason to bring the wrong version of him to the surface, and he felt the façade slipping away.

Messiah stood across from him, leaned against the wall, hands clasped in front of him, head up. The blankest expression covered his face, and Ethic knew the young killer was beside himself. The finger rubbing told him that Messiah was in a murderous state.

"You gon' burn a hole through the floor," Ethic said. Hendrix had been pacing, back and forth, forth and back for hours, as his nerves ate away at him. "You never let a cop see you unnerved. That's how they want you. They want to break you. They'll do anything to pull you into desperation. Beat you, starve you, or just put you on a shelf and test your shelf life. They let you sit until your mind starts betraying you and next thing you know you telling shit that ain't even real just to get out of here. Find a seat and be still, young."

"Nigga don't know what still is," Messiah said, voice void of all emotion except malice.

"You be still too," Ethic stated. Back to the silence because Ethic wasn't talking about motion. He was talking about stilling their minds.

"Outlaw, on your feet!"

An officer came to the cell and buzzed it open, motioning for Hendrix. "Back to me, come back slowly," he instructed.

Hendrix's eyes had been full of emotion since the moment he stepped foot in the cell. Ethic recognized fear when he saw it. Hendrix was fighting it, but it was there, and the longer they sat down with no answers, Ethic could see it growing. He didn't judge him. Hendrix was just a kid. He pretended to be tougher than he was. At the heart of him, he was good.

"Hendrix," Ethic called.

Ethic sat up straight, squaring his shoulders, bouncing them a bit like he was setting an example. "Be still."

Hendrix sucked in a deep breath and stood up straight, lifting his chin as Ethic watched his eyes harden. He blinked away tears as the cuffs tightened around his wrists, wincing because they were so tight.

"Piece of advice," Ethic said to the cop. "Play it by the book. He ain't just anybody son."

The cop hesitated before dragging Hendrix from the cell and out of sight.

There was no shame in Bella's tears. She laid in Kenzie's old room hugging her pillow to her body as tears rolled out of her eyes. "Please, God. Please, God. Please, God." It was all she had to give. Pleas to a God she had learned had infinite power. Bella's heart felt like it was outside her body the moment she saw the red, white, and blue lights. "Please don't let my daddy go to jail. Please don't let Henny go to jail. God, please."

She couldn't sleep. She suspected she would never be able to sleep again because this felt like the makings of a nightmare.

Bella kicked the cover off as she grabbed her phone. Her mind wouldn't turn off. She didn't know why the police had taken her father, but she knew what they were holding Henny for. Bella couldn't just lay there guessing and crying. No one would tell her anything. Alani had promised to call, but she hadn't heard from her in hours, and Nannie had no answers. They were treating her like a child, but she was fifteen; she could handle the truth. All she wanted was information. Bianca's page was where all the gossip went down. She was always first to know anything on Susan Street and despite the fact that Bella had told no one, sure enough, Henny's arrest was hood news, headlined by none other than Bianca.

How does she know already? Bella thought, her heart thundering as she rummaged through the comments of the SCREAMING FREE HENNY posts. She didn't know why it bothered her that Bianca was championing for Henny's release, but a nagging pulled at her gut as she read the comments.

"Free Drix..."
"...Free my nigga Henny"
"Damn, that's fucked up..."
"...He's out of here for a minute!"
"He should have never been in GB..."
"...Trying to keep up with that bougie-ass girl got him caught up"
"He was only fucking with her to get next to her pops. That nigga, Ethic, the connect..."
"...Ethic will get him out"
"Heard they locked that nigga up too..."

The entire conversation was loud and wrong, but it hurt her feelings all the same and the way Bianca was threaded throughout the entire conversation annoyed her so much that she clicked out the app.

She tried calling Morgan again. The voicemail made anxiety shoot through her.

"Where are you? Daddy got arrested, Mo! Call me back!"

She heard the engine of her father's Range Rover as it came up the block, and she rushed out of the room, down the stairs, and onto the porch, before Nannie could even rise out of her La-Z-Boy.

Bella broke down before Alani even popped open the door because she knew her daddy wasn't in the car. No way would Alani be behind the wheel if her father was in the car.

"Oh, baby girl," Alani said as she took the steps slowly.

"Why didn't you get him out, Alani? They're not going to let him come home, are they?" Alani enveloped her in a hug as violent cries took over Bella.

"He's okay, baby girl. Your daddy is strong and he's okay. Everything is going to be okay. Because he was taken in on a Friday, he can't see a judge until Monday," Alani said, trying to explain something that made no sense to herself. That was parenthood, however. Making the world feel safe despite the malice that dwelled in it. Making waiting until Monday feel acceptable as if Saturday and Sunday didn't exist. She felt Bella's struggles. She had just finished crying the same tears, but she couldn't show Bella how terrified she was. She had to cover her from the uncertainty and make the fear disappear. She had to do for Bella what Ethic did for them all every day. She had never realized how hard his job as a husband, as head of their household, truly was. Today, it felt impossible.

"Shhh," Alani soothed, rubbing the back of Bella's head. "Come inside. It's late. We all just need to get to bed. Emotions are high right now. We'll all have a clearer head after some sleep."

She looked to Nannie, who stood in the doorway watching with worried eyes. Her tired bones barely held her up, so she leaned against the frame.

"Get in here before you drop that baby off on my front porch," Nannie said.

"Where's Eazy?" Alani asked.

"He's upstairs asleep, finally."

Alani lifted eyes to the voice descending the stairs and instant relief flooded her when Nyair came into her vision.

"Thank God you're here," Alani whispered.

Nannie placed hands on Bella's shoulders. "Let's get to bed, little girl. It's been a long night for everybody," Nannie said. "Help an old girl up the stairs, baby."

"I'm not a kid. Whatever is happening, I don't want to be left in the dark," Bella said, resisting.

Alani stepped in front of Bella and grabbed both her hands. "I won't keep anything from you, Bella. Nothing at all. You're my best friend. I don't keep secrets from you, but I need a little time to figure out how to get your daddy home. Just give me a little time. Okay? I know how much you need him. I need him too. Trust that I'm going to do everything I can to make sure he makes it home. Trust me, Bella, okay?" she asked.

Bella nodded, and Alani caressed Bella's cheek, wiping away her tears before planting a kiss on her forehead.

"Go upstairs and try to get some sleep," Alani said.

Bella nodded in submission. "Good night, everybody," Bella said. Alani had never heard her sound so defeated. It reflected exactly how she felt on the inside.

Nannie and Bella slowly ascended the stairs and Alani waited anxiously until she heard both doors close before she fell apart in Nyair's arms. She stifled her cries, his chest muffling them.

"They're gonna take him away from us, Ny. I feel it," she said. Nyair pulled out a dining room chair, and Alani took a seat. Nyair sat across from her.

"Word is somebody knows about Kenzie, La," Nyair informed.

"Oh my god," Alani gasped. "Oh my god," she repeated. Reckoning. This was reckoning. She had known that sins like the one Ethic had committed couldn't possibly go unpunished. She lived daily, awaiting karma that she could feel coming but one that she couldn't see. It was a constant state of anticipation, anxiety, and sometimes on days when the feeling felt like it would consume her, she would lash out. Ethic called her mean on those days, but he had no idea the things she battled within her heart. It felt like the war she waged within herself was being exposed for the world to see.

"How, Nyair? Nobody knows. The only person who knows that could threaten my family is dead," she whispered.

"I don't know," Nyair replied.

"Did you tell anyone?" Alani asked.

"What?" Nyair asked, frowning. "No, La."

"Then who? Because that secret should be buried. I married the man who killed my daughter." Saying it aloud. Putting it plainly made them sound so wrong. It made a mockery of what she knew to be pure because what the fuck had they done? Who did they think they were to defy right and wrong that way? How could she? She didn't have those answers. All she knew was that they had done it, that they were doing it. Loving one another and choosing that love every day over the pain that created their origin. "I love him.

ASHLEY ANTOINETTE

How do you think that's going to play out in public if this gets bad? That can't happen. I don't know what happens to us if that happens, Nyair."

"Then hire a lawyer," Nyair said. "A good one. I'm going down to the holding cell to tap in with him."

"They wouldn't tell me anything. Not until Monday," she said.

"I'm religious counsel. They have to give me access."

Hope filled Alani's eyes. Finally. A little relief. A small piece of progress. She nodded. "Okay, but I'm going with you."

"They won't let you come back with me, La. You're a thousand months pregnant. You need to follow your own advice. Go upstairs and get some rest."

"I can't. Morgan still doesn't even know what went down, and her phone is going straight to voicemail. I need to go tell her," Alani said.

"I'll go to Mo's afterward. You just get that lawyer. Whoever represents Ethic, call them tonight. If I know him at all, he has a retainer put down for situations just like this."

Alani nodded. "Make her come home. We all need to be in one place right now. I can't be worrying about Ethic and her and the twins all at the same time. I need to call Messiah and tell him to bring them to me as well. Call me as soon as you know something."

CHAPTER 2

Messiah fixed his eyes on the clock above the detective's head. Four and a half hours. That's how long he had been in police custody. He wasn't sure why it had felt like forever, but he was unmoved either way. A lifetime or a moment, Messiah was never going to fold. They could ask their questions a hundred different ways, and the answer would always be silence.

"We know a lot about you, Mr. Williams," the detective said as he opened the Manila folder he had in his hands.

"You skipped town a few years ago, but you're known for a string of robberies down the interstate. Your name has also come up several times in the disappearance of Lawrence Blake." The man removed a picture from the folder and placed it on the table. Messiah wondered if Lil' Henny had flinched. If he had been bothered by the image because he was certain the police had shown it to him. Messiah didn't even blink, but he knew the nigga. His temper flared at just the sight of the man who had raped Morgan. The second picture that was placed down made his heartbeat pound in his ears like a drum. Lucas Hill's picture was before him and Messiah had the urge to dig up a grave just to get his hands on the men who had hurt Morgan. That had been the start of a dark rabbit hole that they all had yet to climb from. Messiah held not one regret as he looked at the gruesome evidence before him. Not even the picture of Kenzie being placed before him evoked an outward reaction, but inside, he thought of the little people who had suddenly bombarded his life.

Damn, he thought. *They really have been through hell.*

His thoughts instantly went to Alani. He was mesmerized by her ability to stick by Ethic, to choose Ethic through it all.

That's a hell of a woman. Can't buy loyalty like that. She give up a lot of herself just to stand next to that nigga.

Messiah knew Alani had to struggle with herself. How could she not? Guilt filled him as he wondered if he was asking Morgan to do the same. To ignore a hurt she couldn't control just to be by his side. Alani handled it with so much grace that it was hard to remember how she had entered their lives, but Messiah recognized hurt in other people. He had been hurt enough to identify the victims of it at first sight. It was in her eyes. An ever existence of things she wished she had never seen lived in Alani's stare. It made him listen to her. It made Messiah see her. Trust her. Dare he say? Those eyes made Messiah love Alani since the moment he returned. He had fallen into her arms like a baby, and it was because she was like him. A damaged motherfucker, hurt by people you trusted most, and he just wanted to put the burden down. He wanted her to show him how.

Messiah sat unaffected. If he was a killer, he had to be. He couldn't protect her and be emotional. He couldn't wear his heart on his sleeve. Messiah had not one regret about how these lives had been taken.

Them niggas took something too. Took a little life from shorty too. I'ma always go to hell over her, Messiah thought.

"These photos are horrific. One man was beaten to death. Yet you don't flinch. Almost like you've seen this image before." The detective was baiting Messiah. Guilty men normally talked too much. They normally felt inclined to provide alibis, to talk themselves out of a trap before it was even set. Messiah felt like these niggas had murdered themselves. The moment they touched Morgan, they had determined their fates, so there was nothing for him to admit.

"When we finally dig a nail in you, Mr. Williams, it'll be in your coffin. You can change that. Save yourself. Tell us about Okafor's involvement in this little girl's murder. What was it? Some sort of sick way to make an example of Lucas Hill? He was pushing into your territory, right? You are Ethic's soldier? This order wasn't on you, right? Come on, Mr. Williams. We have the kid's father's statement on record accusing you first, then recanting and pointing the finger at Ezra Okafor for the murder of his daughter. Now, he's nowhere to be found. I can't see you killing a kid. That was Mr. Okafor, right? He killed the kid, then killed the father for snitching. Is that right? Just nod your head if he's behind this."

Messiah didn't move. Didn't breathe. Even the inclination of a nod they would run with.

"I want a lawyer," he said.

"Guilty men ask for lawyers, Mr. Williams. We're just talking here," the detective pressed. "We can have an easy conversation, get you some food, you've been in here for hours. You must be starving. Or we can take a ride and do this the hard way. Cut the cameras, and you know what happens then."

Torture. The police weren't above it, and they were the only ones on the planet who could get away with it.

Messiah gritted his teeth. He knew that shit was about to get ugly because he wasn't talking, no matter what they did to him. He mentally began bracing himself for the worst as the detective snatched him from his seat and handed him off to another officer outside the door.

"Take him for a ride," the detective said.

"Isa, slow the fuck down! What is going on?" Aria said as she watched Isa pull a large duffel bag from the top of their bedroom closet. He tossed it to Aria.

"Quit yapping and get the money out the safe. Clear that mu'fucka out and grab the two pistols that's in there too," Isa instructed. "We got ten minutes to break the fuck out of here."

"What is happening right now? It's the middle of the night," Aria protested.

"You wasn't just making that mouth move like that a minute ago, Ali," Isa said. "Less talk back, more action. Trust ya man, and go get the money."

Aria had never seen Isa this serious before. It was enough for her to backpedal from the room and rush to the basement where Isa kept his safe. She stuffed it so full she could barely zip it, and then she hurried to grab the matching duffel he had gifted her for Christmas. When both were full, she lugged them upstairs and handed them off to Isa.

"Call Mo. Can't nobody reach her ass. Laid up with that fucking square-ass nigga, she don't even know what the fuck's going down," Isa barked.

"Wait, nigga, walk lighter on Mo," Aria defended as she pulled his arm to stop him from moving. He was like a runaway freight train. The Crew had a protocol for shit like this. One gets popped, get the other two out of town. Not until the other two were safe did you send in the lawyers. "What is going on?"

"Messiah's locked up. Unless you want to be the one bailing your nigga out of jail, you need to move faster," Isa said. "And call her. Bleu got the twins, and can't nobody reach Mo."

"And she's not with Meek?" Aria asked.

"Nah," Isa said.

Aria felt a disruption in her body like nothing she had ever felt before. This was the moment, the moment when she knew everything was about to change. Choosing a man like Isa was more than adrenaline and dope nights doing dangerous things. This was the part her brother had warned her about. The gathering of dope money and living on the run with a man the police were looking for. She had just been in college a few weeks ago. How had it come to this? She retrieved her purse and her phone from the nightstand, but Isa quickly took both from her hands.

"What are you doing?" she asked as he dismantled the phone, removing the SIM card and the battery. He pulled out a burner cell and gave it to her.

"Call her from here and take every single bank card out your purse. Cash only until we figure out what's what and who got a target on our backs," Isa said.

Aria was glad she knew Mo's number by heart. She dialed it as Isa held her hand and practically pulled her out the house.

"Voicemail," Aria announced.

"And I guess you ain't leaving town without her?" Isa asked.

"She wouldn't leave without me," Aria answered. "And she definitely wouldn't want her babies with Bleu. They don't even know her. How the hell did she end up with them anyway?" Aria's mind began turning.

"Ain't none of that our concern, Ali. Morgan has Ethic. She ain't never at stake, and Bleu got the twins under control. You can catch up with Mo when we get where we going," he said.

"And where's that?" Aria asked.

"Low. We going low."

"You know what happens if anything happens to the baby in my wife's stomach because I'm here tonight?" Ethic asked aloud without looking up at the detective who stood at the

ASHLEY ANTOINETTE

entrance to the holding cell. He waited for Ethic to stand and turn around, then to walk backward to the door. A few awkward minutes had passed since he had given the order. Ethic hadn't even spoken, hadn't moved, he wasn't quick to rise, and the officer was hesitant to make him. Couldn't make him. Ezra Okafor moved when he wanted to. His question, however, was rhetorical. "Yeah, you know. I'm sure you know." He nodded.

"Okay, you want to do this right here? Your choice, Mr. Okafor," the detective stated. "What do you do for a living?"

Ethic scoffed but didn't answer. He had learned to do more listening than speaking. Especially, in a position of weakness where he found himself outside an environment he could control. He needed answers on why he was in bondage. There had only been one crime that could send him back here and he prayed for any other reason to be here beside that one. That one would strip of much more than his freedom but his life. "You ashamed to be a drug dealer? A cold-blooded murderer? You do this to children?" The detective asked, flicking out the picture that Ethic had been anticipating since stepping foot inside these walls.

Kenzie. The beautiful little girl who had become his greatest travesty. A face he often saw, in Alani's car, because her picture was taped to the mirror in the visor. He saw her in Alani's two-story closet, a beautiful painting he had paid a celebrated artist to commission was a tribute to this tiny face, and most of all, he saw that face every time he looked into his wife's eyes. She haunted him. The magnitude of what he had caused never left him, and now, seeing crime scene photos moved him to feel an emotion he couldn't show because if he did, they would convict him. Perhaps it was guilt that he deserved to be punished for. He would have no qualms about that if it were not for the family he had at home. Every time he left his home, he prayed to make it back to them. Too much went on in a world that didn't like him strictly for the tone of his skin, add in the gun he kept holstered on his hip, and the gangster he kept hidden in his soul, and he was a walking target. Any day could be his last simply because of the design of him, and that thought terrorized him.

If I make it out of here, it's time to start preparing them for life without me. If it comes to that, they need to know how to exist without me.

Alani eased some of that burden because if he never made it through their threshold, he knew she would raise his children well. They would know love and he had done his job well enough for generations who bore his last name to never know the struggle. Alani would keep his family safe and be a cornerstone of love in their lives, but who would be her rock? If he went away, who would remind her to breathe on days when grief weighed down her chest? Who would spread life through her with kisses at dawn? Who would awaken her soul with dick that stretched through her body, electrifying her heart? His wife would break and if she broke, his children would too, especially if Kenzie's murder was the reason.

"You have children. What if someone did this to them?" The detective's question brought Ethic to his feet, but he didn't backpedal. He approached the officer slowly, staring him in his eyes. The hand to the gun put the scent of fear in the room. Not Ezra's. The cop's intimidation reeked off him.

"Turn around, Mr. Okafor," the cop said with bass, and Ethic lifted his hands in front of him.

"If you're going to put a bullet in me or a knee in my neck, I want to see it coming," he said. "That's the type of shit you do, no?"

"I'd rather close the door on your cell and watch you rot for the rest of your life," the detective replied as he put cuffs on Ethic and then escorted him to an interrogation room.

"I don't answer no questions without my attorney," Ethic said.

"We're going to get him here. As soon as possible. We're going to be real patient first. We've got the other two. Your workers? Extensions of your criminal enterprise? We got them under questioning. Let's see how long before they break first. You just sit tight." The detective forced Ethic down into a hard chair and then connected his cuffs to the steel table before leaving him alone in the room. When the lights went out and the room cloaked in darkness, Ethic knew this was an off-the-books operation. They were going to play this dirty, and he knew no method was above reproach. They wanted him, and they wanted him bad. He knew the torture would come. They were trying to break him mentally first. Starve him out. Deprive him of light and when he heard the ventilation kick off, he knew they were trying to deprive him of air. He would be in this room for a while. Days probably. They had until Monday until a supervising officer came in and would have to bring him before a judge. It would be a long weekend, a hard weekend. He closed his eyes, disappearing in his mind to where they couldn't fuck with him, where his wife met him nightly, in his dreams because thinking of her would keep him strong. Everything he had built was in jeopardy. There was someone pulling strings behind the scenes, and that someone was powerful. He just had to figure out who.

Alani entered the castle Ethic had built for her, and she had never felt lonelier. Any other day it was filled with life, with noise, with Eazy running through the halls flying a drone nicking her walls, her fussing at him for it, Bella listening to music or watching Anime, and Ethic, her king, their everything, the most silent of them all, brooding because surely they were all too damn noisy for his liking. Today, it was a ghost town. She wondered if she had missed the moment that had been their last happy moment. If she had rushed through it. If she had appreciated it enough. Just the night before, she had made dinner and helped Eazy with homework. She had been too tired to hand-wash the dishes, so Ethic had pulled out a chair for her to sit and talk to him while he did it himself because Alani didn't believe dishwashers truly got dishes clean.

He's so patient with me, she thought. He had cleaned the entire kitchen while she told him her vision for their baby's nursery. *He's supposed to be putting up the crib right now. I'm supposed to be fussing about him not using the instruction manual, and we're supposed to be arguing over colors. How is he not here right now?*

Alani dared the path to Ethic's office. She never ventured inside without invitation. She didn't believe in going through his things because she had learned a long time ago that when you went looking for something bad, something bad found you. They had battled enough bad to last a lifetime, so she never looked. She didn't snoop, didn't go through his phone, didn't check pockets, although she knew women swooned over him everywhere he went, ~~and~~ she didn't pry. Alani existed in the comfort that Ethic had painted for her. Now, she found herself afraid to touch even one thing on his desk. Nervous about popping the bubble they existed inside of. Every man created that safe space for his woman, a realm where everything felt good, where it all made sense, even if no one else had the capacity to understand. If she found anything damaging, they would never get back to that place again. Trust, once fleeting, was impossible to chase down. Alani sat in the executive leather chair and pulled open the center drawer. Nothing. Nothing of importance anyway. A $700 Montblanc pen, some Tiffany paperclips. Only Ezra would buy an expensive-ass paperclip. A Louis Vuitton planner. Top-notch shit for a top-notch nigga. A mood. A vibe. An incarcerated-ass, yoga-doing, dick-slinging, pain-absorbing, kill yo' mama, fuck yo' bitch, grey-sweatpants-wearing-ass nigga. She just kept adding to that list. Such a multifaceted man.

The second drawer contained an expensive whiskey and nothing else. The third drawer was locked.

Alani stood and walked to the bookshelf, scanning the shelves with a finger until she stopped on Ethic's favorite book.

The Art of War, she thought.

She pulled the book from the shelf opening it to find the hollowed-out pages inside. A tiny ledger and a key were inside. She removed the ledger and opened it. Her eyes betrayed her as she read his handwriting.

Alani,

If you're reading this, it's bad, and I'm sorry I'm not there to protect you. I'm sorry you're feeling anything other than how much I love you. The ways I love you, woman. SMH. You are freedom in a world of enslavement. Life in a world of death. So, if either of those things has occurred, know that I am okay because neither death nor bars rival you. You are my heaven and my release. A blessing you are, Lenika. My legacy is in you. A queen carrying life is true power. You've always been the boss, baby. My fucking god, you're the source of everything I find worthy. I will always love you. Take care of our children, Alani. Take care of my queen. I'm okay. Breathe.

Yours in this life and every life thereafter.

Ezra

PS: Stop biting your jaw.

Alani immediately released the inside of her jaw and smiled timidly. Her eyes blurred as she fought unbelievable grief. He had prepared for this. Every day that he loved her, that he tucked their children in goodnight, every day of happiness she had thought the storm was over, and he had been anticipating its arrival. Her heart was so broken. Alani felt like her life was over, but he had left her with so much to live for she had no choice but to will strength into her legs. She flipped the page of the small notebook and found a page of numbers. Swiss bank codes, BAFTA codes, routing and account numbers, and...

Thank God, she thought.

The word *HELP* had been written down in bold Sharpie.

FOR *WHATEVER YOU NEED*...had been written afterwards. *DIAL FROM THE PHONE INSIDE MY DESK.*

+39-2349355

Alani took the key and opened the drawer to find a phone. A satellite phone that was untraceable and international. Very few people had access to secure lines like this. Alani dialed the number without hesitation.

"Something must be going extremely good or extremely bad for you to be calling, Ethic."

The woman's voice knotted Alani's belly, taking her breath away. The fact that it was a woman answering at all made her sick.

"This is Alani, Ethic's wife," she said.

"Oh!" The voice replied in surprise. "So, something bad has happened. Where is he?"

Alani blew out a breath. Certainly, her husband wouldn't walk her right into heartbreak. This woman had to be an ally to them, but the level of concern she heard in the woman's voice bothered her.

"Umm... before I answer that, I'm still not sure who I'm talking to. Ethic left instructions. Your number was there, but no name..."

"Alani, Ethic would never have you calling a woman who puts your emotions in jeopardy. If he was cheating on you, you would literally never know. He'd never expose you to any kind of hurt. In fact, I don't think Ethic would ever cheat on you, sis. Whatever you've done to him, you did it well. Teach me the game, Ghost."

Alani laughed, relieved as she took a seat in Ethic's chair.

"This is Zya," the voice revealed. "And it sounds like we need to talk more often, so you know who I am. I'm just a friend, and you're his queen, which means I'm your friend too. Now, tell me everything that happened."

"I need to charge my phone, Bash," Morgan said. "I really need my kids. I need Ethic. Sebastian, if you do this to me, there won't be anything left for you to have. No wife, no anything. I swear to God, I will marry you tomorrow if you just make all this go away. You have adoption papers on my kids, Bash. What else am I going to do? I can't do anything except what you say. Please!"

"I want you to understand, Mo, that you made it like this between us. All I wanted was a shot. I could finally get the girl, and you led us to this," Bash said.

Morgan lowered her head and squeezed her eyes closed. She had never felt trapped like this. The psychological warfare Bash and his family had over her was crueler than anything. Morgan couldn't leave. She wouldn't dare leave if the possibility of the twins being stripped from her was still on the table.

"Get up. I'll take you to get them. They're probably scared," he said.

"Of course, they're scared, Bash. You know them. That's what you got to remember. You've known them their entire lives. Everything you're doing hurts them." Maybe reason would bring Bash to a place of mercy.

"That's not what I want to do," Bash said.

This nigga is crazy, Mo thought. One minute he was vengeful and controlling; the next, he was remorseful.

She had seen these qualities before in a man, in Mizan, and she knew if she didn't break free, where this would lead.

"Let's go get them. We'll leave for London before Monday. Once we've landed, I'll make the call to get Ethic released," Bash said.

She wanted to ask about Messiah so badly, but she knew mentioning him again would only worsen the situation. She just needed her kids in her possession before she could think of what to do next, but her soul ached from every angle. She had always been on the receiving end of pain, but the fact that she had put people she loved in danger was something unlike she had ever felt before. It hurt. It was a runaway train that she couldn't stop, and the worst part was Morgan was at Bash's mercy.

"I never wanted this for us. I do love you. I've loved you for a long time. You got to learn, though. You got to learn to let me," he said.

Her skin crawled as he got on his knees in front of her, bending to kiss her knee and then opening her thighs so that he could fit between them.

"Let me, Morgan," he said.

Her back stiffened as he closed in for a kiss. Her lips didn't part. She was shaking. Her hands pressed against his chest to create some resistance.

"Bash, I can't, I can't," she said, panicking.

"Try, Mo," he said. When his lips connected to hers, she cried out as he pushed her back onto the couch.

"Bash, wait, I'm hurting," she said, wincing. He looked down at the way she was holding her stomach, and he lifted her shirt. Morgan's entire stomach was evidence of his harm. The damage was enough to turn him to steel.

"Fuck, Mo. Why do you make me this way?" he asked. Her eyes widened in alarm. "You made me wait so long. I thought about it. Night after night. I tried to be a gentleman with you and then you..." he paused. "I'm sorry, Mo," he said, kissing her skin, trying to soothe the pain he had caused, bruises he had given. "I don't want to be this way with you. I've tried hard not to be like this with you."

Morgan didn't know what to say or do. She was caught in a moment of indecision. She didn't know if she should be fighting or fleeing, but the moment felt so delicate that if she chose wrong, her entire life could end.

"I know I'm wrong," she said. "I did this to us. I promise I'll do better. We can just start over. I can go back to being that little freshman girl who walked into your class, and you can go back to being the guy who always stepped up to save me when I couldn't even see I needed help. We can be those people again, Bash."

Morgan was laying it on thick. She would say anything to change the look in Bash's eyes. It was like he was going back and forth between crazy and sane. The part of him that she believed loved her was vulnerable and understanding. The part that had been lied to and betrayed just wanted to punish her unsympathetically. She understood both parts. She possessed both parts. When someone hurts you, it's hard not to imagine causing them a pain that makes yours feel relatable. Morgan had wished pain on Messiah so many days because she knew if he could feel what he was making her feel, then he would stop causing her grief. Maybe Bash was doing that. Putting pain on her so she would know what it felt like to be in his shoes. Morgan was remorseful in ways she couldn't express, but she couldn't help but feel like she was being persecuted for finding love. Judged for following her heart. Condemned for believing that she could find healing after her life had been dismantled by loss. Messiah hadn't been the cause of all of it. He had just put more hurt on top of a lifetime that already existed. Morgan was a girl who was well-acquainted with a broken heart. Hers had been torn apart the moment her sister, Raven, left home all those years ago. She had missed her terribly, and that one decision had been the beginning of a generation of curses. After her father died and her mother's imprisonment, things were impossibly hard. Raven's murder came next. Then, Messiah came along, loving all of her wickedness, praising her spoiled ways, and making them worse because he said she deserved all that she expected from others. He had loved her so gloriously that she became addicted, and then he withdrew it all. She thought he was the answer to prayers she had repeated nightly since she was six years old. His letdown was the straw that broke the camel's back. Now, here she was hurting men because she was hurting, and there were consequences for that. This was her punishment. Forced connection. An unhappy union. Bash was going to force this marriage onto her whether she wanted it or not.

"I don't know if we can, Mo," Bash said. His anger seemed to be lessened because Morgan was appealing to his conscience. At their core, Bash and Morgan had started as friends. He had been the man wanting to save a young girl, so she appealed to that. She had turned down the temperature of his emotions. There was a mental war of manipulation being played, and for a long time, she hadn't realized she was a participant. Now that she was aware, she would act accordingly until she could find her way out of this situation. One thing Morgan was very aware of was the fact that she would never win a physical fight with Bash. The way her body ached told her that trying to fight him off physically would lead to her being seriously hurt. She had to use the beguiles of femininity to overpower the ego of his manhood if she wanted to break free of Bash and his mother. She saw it working, saw him breaking down, moving from anger to something less aggressive, less dangerous. Morgan's heart was beating so hard she could hear it as he caressed her face. "Get yourself together so we can get the twins."

She released a breath of anxiety and lowered her head, nodding while fighting tears. It was a small win, a smaller mercy bestowed by Bash, but she was grateful because she couldn't wrap her mind around anything, not Ethic, not Messiah, not escaping until her babies were safe.

Morgan stared at the red battery symbol on her screen until the phone came alive in her hand. Dark stretches of highway passed her outside the car window as Bash drove. Silence filled the car, and Morgan drowned in it. Her messages came through instantly, one after another. Everyone was trying to tell her about what had gone down, unknowing that she was the reason for it all.

"Be careful how you respond," Bash said without looking her way, eyes keen on the road before them.

"I have to call them back; Aria messaged me that Bleu has the twins," Morgan said. *Why would she have them?*

She begrudgingly gave directions to Bash until she was sitting in front of Bleu's home. It hadn't changed. It felt like déjà vu sitting there. The house, this moment, drudged up years of emotion in her. She had begged Messiah on this very lawn.

If he had just stayed...

She would never be here, sitting in this car with Bash, and he wouldn't be behind bars. She had wished a lot on Messiah over the years, but she had never wanted to see him in a cage.

She climbed out of the car, but before she could clear the door, Bash pulled her back into her seat. "Remember what's at stake here, Mo. The thing about me is my power don't really end with me. So, whatever you're thinking...whatever ways you think you can leave. You can't."

Morgan wouldn't be able to live like this, under a constant threat, in an anxiety-induced state. She had been numb before in Bash's care. Every part of her was awakened now, and the things she felt in his presence caused the hair to stand up on the back of her neck.

She pulled away and exited the car, taking hurried steps to Bleu's porch. She could feel her babies inside. There was something about motherhood that always told her when they were near. Her heart was like a metal detector searching for something real beneath the surface. She was so eager to get to them that her eyes prickled as she rang Bleu's doorbell.

"Mo!" Bleu said, shock revealing how unprepared she was for this face to face.

"Are they okay?" Mo asked, voice breaking under pressure. *SHE* was breaking under pressure.

"Are you okay?" Bleu asked, frowning as she pulled at the sleeve of her shirt to cover the tattoo on her hand.

"Where are they?" Morgan asked.

Bleu stepped aside and allowed Morgan access to her house. Bleu led the way, and when Morgan spotted her children, she immediately picked them up. She didn't care that they were sleeping; she cried over them violently, hugging and kissing them, scaring them so badly that they began crying too.

"Oh, thank God," she whispered. "You're okay?" she asked Messari as she rocked him in her arms. "Are you okay, Yolly? My sweet girl. Mommy's right here," she signed.

"The bad men came with guns, and they threw Meekie's fwiend on the floor!" Messari said.

"Did they hurt you?" Morgan asked frantically. "Did they touch you?"

Morgan hugged her kids so tightly they couldn't breathe.

Bleu stood there, speechless, as she absorbed the love Morgan had for her children. It was just an energy that filled the room.

"You were at Messiah's when the police came?" Morgan asked, finally turning her attention to Bleu.

Bleu took a deep breath. "Yeah," she admitted. "He was…" she paused. "He just needed help. Finding out he was a father was a lot."

"I know," Morgan said. "I know. I messed so many things up."

"Yeah, you did, Mo. I can't pretend like I don't feel a way about you right now. You didn't see him. He's devastated. You hurt that man so bad."

"*I* hurt *him*?" Morgan asked in disbelief. "Yeah, okay." She nodded her head, outdone at Bleu's audacity as she gathered her kids. One on her hip, one gripping her hand. She turned for the door but suddenly turned back. "You know, of course, you would take his side. You've always condoned his bullshit. I tried not to dislike you, tried to be understanding of your friendship with Messiah, but you know what? Fuck you, Bleu. You're just as much to blame for him not knowing he had kids as I am."

"Really? Queen Morgan. Everybody's guilty but you, right?" Bleu asked. "Girl, get out my house with that."

"You fucking kept him from me. I came to you. No pride, no worth. I begged you to tell me where he was. Begged you to just reconnect us, and you stood in my face, staring at me with fake sympathy like you were his fucking gatekeeper or something I was pregnant then. You're another woman. Don't tell me you didn't know. I needed him. My man. Mine! And you liked the fact that you had the power to keep me away. So, bitch, fuck you and your judgment. The nigga would have been here at my side, rubbing my feet, kissing my belly if it wasn't for you playing guard dog. Good job, best friend," Morgan said as she pulled her kids to the door.

"You are so selfish. Literally, the most selfish person I've ever met. You have no idea what anybody else goes through outside yourself. You tore him apart! All he's ever had was his crew, and little Miss Morgan Atkins strolls in and hops on not one but two Crew niggas. Had to have your cake and eat it too. Well, guess what? The table broke, Morgan. Their friendship will never be the same again, and now Messiah's locked up. How much you wanna bet it's behind something stupid he did over you?"

Morgan shook her head, but she couldn't offer a defense to that because he was indeed in this situation because of her.

"Do you even love him, Mo?" Bleu asked.

"Let me be clear with you, *B*," Morgan said sarcastically using the nickname Messiah called her. "I could hate that nigga a million different ways, and my hate will still be full of more love than anybody else can give him."

Morgan took her babies and turned her back to Bleu, walking out into the night.

CHAPTER 3

What the fuck, man!" Messiah shouted as the momentum of the turn sent him flying across the back of the van. He collided with the wall so viciously that he felt the taste of blood fill his mouth. He had no idea where the police were taking him, but he knew that this was bad. The speeds at which he was being driven and sharps turns, and hard stops were torture. The cops had left him cuffed and intentionally left his seat belt unfastened. It didn't matter how much Messiah tried to brace himself. The twists and turns sent him crashing into steel walls every few seconds. This ride just may kill him. With his hands behind his back, he couldn't even attempt to hold on. He was at their mercy, and they would show none until he gave them what they wanted.

The next turn sent him violently crashing into the steel bench and then snatched him clear across the space.

"Fuck!" He screamed as blood filled his vision, his forehead splitting open from the impact. By the time they pulled the police van over, Messiah was on the floor, conscious but groaning in excruciating pain.

"Get him up," the detective said.

Messiah was bloody as they dragged him out of the back

of the van. The deserted field was every indication of what would happen next. Now, it made sense why they hadn't processed him into the system all night. They hadn't taken one fingerprint, hadn't conducted one mug shot. They had just let him sit because they wanted no proof that he had been there.

"You should really start talking," the detective said.

"Whatever you planned to do out here, you gon' have to see that all the way through," Messiah said, spitting out a mouthful of blood, only for it to fill with more. He was leaking everywhere.

"You'll die for him? For a man who has poisoned women and kids and the community for years?" The detective tested.

Messiah tried to pick up his head, but he was sure one of his shoulders had been dislocated from the drive.

"On every day of any week. You gon' have to kill me," Messiah said. "I'm ready to die 'bout mine. Do what you got to do."

The history between them didn't matter. Ethic and Messiah were complicated, full of love and betrayal all in the same breath, but Ethic was the single most important man in Messiah's life.

He hadn't been able to betray him before, and the loyalty had only grown over the years. He wouldn't fold now. Even with the trust Ethic had lost in him, Messiah still couldn't fold. He was solid. A dependable lieutenant to a street king, despite a sordid history. The detective looked at his partner and nodded. "Tough guy," he said. "Should be fun. Make him talk. Let's see how strong that loyalty is."

Hendrix sat with his head resting on his stacked fists as he thought of everything outside these walls.

I know my smart girl mad as fuck, man, he thought. *I ain't never getting to that door with her.*

He had been thinking of ending things with Bella for weeks. She was simply too good for him. *She's hella smart. Hella loyal too. She going to do some dope shit, and I'm just a hood nigga that's going to hold her back. After this, Ethic ain't gon' let me near her anyway.*

Henny had been feeling inadequate lately, like the dreams Bella had him trying on were too big for him. It was the reason why he had stepped both feet into the game, copping product and making runs for The Crew to prove his value to their organization. The more money he got with them, the more he knew that he and Bella would end. She wouldn't understand his reasons, and he wasn't looking to explain them to her. They were from two different worlds, and although they had their eye on the same destination, they had to walk different paths to get there. His arrest was like a pin to a balloon; it deflated every dream he had imagined with Bella. There would be no evolving love story. With the amount of product they had caught him with, Henny knew they were going to lock him away. The thought made his eyes burn.

The growl of his stomach was overpowered by the sickness he felt at his core. He was terrified. He was trying his hardest to be like Ethic and Messiah. He watched them closely in that cell. He had seen no fear in them, not even a hint of it, so he had faked it too. He pretended to be okay, but he wasn't. Hendrix was a boy masquerading as a man, but in the eyes of the law, he was a menace.

He was shivering as the air conditioning flowed into the room. His clothes clung to his body, the wetness making the air conditioning feel like pure ice water running through his veins. They had waterboarded him for close to an hour. A soundproof basement, a single chair, a steel table that he was cuffed to, and one light bulb hanging from the ceiling. That's all that filled this dank room. He could hear mice scurrying in the corners of the room where the pathetic light bulb's glow didn't reach.

He was breaking down in this room. Fear and desertion made it feel like the cops were pulling him away from his pack, away from Ethic, and he was left to figure out survival on his own. Hendrix was a cub without the protection of a full-grown lion. He needed help. He needed someone to get him out of there. The way they had abused him first with phonebooks, then with tasers, and then with a burlap bag and what felt like an ocean's worth of water, Henny was broken. He just wanted to go home.

The door to the basement opened, and the detective walked into the room.

"I want a lawyer, man," Hendrix said. "You can't just keep me down here."

"You're your own way out," the detective replied. "Nobody took a mug shot of you, no fingerprints, technically we don't even have you in our possession. Think about that for a minute, young man. You don't exist unless we say you exist behind these walls. You can go home. I'd love to let you go home, but you got to give me something first," the detective said.

"I don't know nothing about what you talking about. I date Mr. Okafor's daughter. That's it. I was only over there to see her," he said, sticking to his story.

"Fucking broken record," the detective muttered in frustration. He pulled out a mug shot and placed it up to Hendrix's face, grabbing his hair with one tight fist, forcing him to look at the picture. "What about her? You know her?"

Hendrix's mother was before him. It had been a while since they had spoken. It had been even longer since he had seen her.

"She got picked up down there on Avenue B. High out of her mind. This is her third offense. Judge will probably give her a few," the detective said.

Hendrix's heart felt like it was split open. Avenue B was a known prostitute alley, and if she was arrested there, it meant his mother was selling pussy to support her drug habit. A mixture of shame and rage filled him, but the most overwhelming emotion of them all was helplessness. His mother had been breaking his heart for as long as he could remember. Promises of getting clean were always broken by her love for dope. Hendrix desperately wanted to know what it was like to be someone's first love, to be loved so wholly that nothing else came before him. A boy normally received that from his mother. Hendrix never had because crack and heroin always came first. He had learned that lesson the hard way over the years, and seeing her mug shot before him was only another stab to his ego as her son. He prayed nightly for a mother who was strong enough to beat addiction for him. He wanted to be a kid she could love enough to use as motivation to get her life straight, but he was never enough. The resentment he had built up over the years sat in the pit of him like bricks weighing down a sinking boat.

Hendrix's jaw locked as he fought the emotion building. It felt like hurricane force winds were blowing through his chest. He fought a good fight as he willed himself not to care. *Ain't nobody ever gave a fuck about you. That ain't even yo' mama. You don't even know the lady in that picture.* Only it was his mama. Despite the weight loss, the skin that had seen better days, and the matted hair on her head, the eyes were the same. Eyes he had always found beautiful, ever since she had held him to his chest as a baby boy. She was his mama, and she was strung out, and the shit hurt. The heaviest tear drops fell from his eyes as he fought his own psyche, trying to convince himself not to care.

"You tell us what we want to know maybe it could help your mother," the detective pushed. "You can take your mother and go home. Leave us to deal with the real bad guy in this situation."

Hendrix couldn't tear his eyes away from the picture.

"I don't know shit about what you talking," he said, voice wracked with disappointment and sadness.

"That's too bad, son," the detective said. "You sure he would do the same for you? Give up his life with his wife, with his children, with his blood family for you? Men like

Ezra Okafor use boys like you. You take all the risk for a little pocket money and status, while he sits upon the mountain top, sending his kids to fancy schools, unreachable and untouchable."

Hendrix stared the detective directly in the eyes and said, "Fuck you."

It was the last thing he said before he was hit with a taser to the neck sending his world fading to black.

"Little piece of shit," the detective spat.

"Please take me to Ethic's," Morgan said. "Alani's pregnant. She's been calling me all night. Bella and Eazy are scared. I should be there for them right now."

"How does that work, Mo? You run to your family and what? Tell them everything? Do you really think that helps? Getting rid of me doesn't get rid of your problem. I've taken precautions. If anything happens to me, this all gets worse for you," Bash said as he drove.

"I know what I've done and what's at stake." Hopelessness loomed over her. She wanted to ask for help. She wanted to tell it all, but every time she built up the courage to tell someone, Bash doubled down on his threats. First, it was her schooling. When she built up enough moxie to follow her heart anyway, Bash put Ethic's freedom on the table, and just to ensure she understood her position, he added her children in the pile of collateral damage. "I just want to be there for them."

"And pretend like you aren't the reason why their world is falling apart? You're going to go there and look that woman in the face and cry with her, all the while pretending like you don't know why he's in jail? You're a sick individual, Morgan," Bash snickered. "You don't even like her, do you? You tolerate her. You're so obsessed with Ethic that you hate his wife, and you chase anything that reminds you of the way he loves. Is that why you can't be happy with me? Because I'm nothing like him? Because you have daddy issues? Am I not street enough? Not damaged enough?"

She didn't expect Bash to understand. There weren't many who could fathom the bond Morgan and Ethic shared. She had put him in jeopardy, and if he lost everything because of her, Morgan would never forgive herself.

"Blackmailing someone so they can't leave sounds damaged to me," Morgan whispered. "If I don't show up for this, Ethic will know something is wrong. He'll think something has happened to me."

Morgan felt sick to her stomach when Bash didn't change course. They drove in silence all the way to her apartment.

"Grab some stuff for you and the twins. We're going to my family's estate," Bash said.

She nodded because she didn't know what else she could do but be agreeable.

Morgan didn't even want to leave her kids in the car with him while she packed. She shook Messari awake and picked up a sleeping Yara. Bash reached for her daughter, and she maneuvered out of his reach.

"I got it," she said, defensive, untrusting. Morgan's emotional pain overpowered anything physical she felt, but everything was battered. From her ribcage to her soul. Everything ached.

Bash didn't push as he followed her up the walkway to her building.

"Mo!"

The sound of Nyair's voice breaking through the silent night was like a lever to her tears. She turned toward him and practically ran into his arms.

"We've been calling you all night," Nyair said.

Morgan cried on his shoulder. It was the first time she had felt safe all night.

"Ethic's in trouble. Alani needs you home," Nyair said. "Get it out right here so when you get there you can be strong. You hear me? And if you ain't strong, I'ma be right there. I got you, Mo."

"This is all my fault," she cried.

"Nah, Mo. It ain't. Everybody has their day of reckoning. Nothing goes unseen, and nothing is left unaddressed before God. We gon' figure it out, though. That's my word. We gon' get him out of there," Nyair said, gripping her chin and bending his neck to look in her eyes. Morgan nodded and Nyair frowned as he bent to pick up Messari who was glued to Morgan's leg. "I know," Nyair said. Anyone who had ever spent even a second around Ethic could identify the love he had for his family. If anything happened to Ethic, so many people's lives would be left in shambles. "You're shaking," Nyair said.

"I just want to go home," Morgan said, finding solace in his presence, a safety that was elusive, and a trust that wouldn't flee. She knew if she left there with Nyair, she would be safe. She may even be able to ask him for help. He wouldn't judge. He wouldn't hate her for making a selfish mistake. "Ny…I need…"

"I'll drive them," Bash interjected. "We were just headed that way."

Nyair nodded. "I've got to go down to the jail, so that works." "We can ride with you," Mo pressed.

"I'll meet you back at the house. If I don't get down there, things can get rough for Ethic inside. They need to know the church is invested in this arrest," Nyair said. Ny shifted his focus to Bash. "Get them there safely, G. I don't really play about her." Nyair extended his hand, and Bash accepted it, shaking it.

"That makes two of us," Bash replied.

Nyair kissed Morgan's cheek. "I'ma call as soon as I hear something. Pick up your phone, Mo, and take it easy on Alani. She's trying to act like she's not falling apart, but she's hurting."

When he walked away, Morgan felt sick. Bash gripped her side, putting pressure on her injured abdomen, reminding her to play her role. "Get it together. You know what happens if you don't."

Alani sat on the couch holding her wedding album in her hands, fingers trembling as she flipped through the memories. Ezra was on every page, and every time she laid eyes on him, her heart skipped a beat. She didn't even know how they had gotten here. In no logical world should she exist in his space, but his space was the only place she wanted to be. Everything about their relationship was unconventional, but their love was a tradition that couldn't be more classic. They were like those old, black and white romance movies. They felt like a 90's R&B groove on a Sunday morning. Ethic and Alani had written a love story against all odds.

Please, she thought, silently begging for a resolution.

The Ring doorbell alerted her that there was movement at her front gate, and she opened the app urgently. Her heart ached in the seconds it took to pull up the footage. She was relieved to see Bash's car pulling onto their property.

Morgan and her babies would make her feel less alone tonight. She pulled herself to her feet and lost breath as she struggled to the door. The discomfort of her third trimester made her feel like she was sprinting as she made her way to greet them.

Opening the door, she waited as the car pulled to a stop in the middle of the circular driveway. Morgan's melancholy could be felt before she even stepped out.

As soon as she got out, Alani lifted praying hands to her lips. "Thank you for coming, Mo. You don't even know how much I need you right now."

"I can guarantee I need you more," Morgan said softly. She was shrinking by the minute, breaking down inside. "Have you heard anything?"

"Not yet. They couldn't even find him in the system when I went down there," Alani said. "Ny's going to see what he can find out."

"What does that mean?" Morgan asked, turning to Bash, who was pulling Yara from the backseat of his car.

"It means a lot of people have to do their job to make sure he comes home safe," Bash said. The hidden innuendo in the threat made Morgan breathless. Nothing had ever felt so cruel. Alani missed it because he was right. Lawyers, cops, judges, they all had to conduct themselves with justice in mind in order for Ethic to have a fair shot of being released. Human bias couldn't get in the way, but just from her interactions at the station tonight, she had a feeling that they were in for the fight of their lives.

"I thought the kids were with Messiah," Alani said.

"He was arrested tonight too," Morgan answered. "They took him away in front of them."

"This really can't get any worse," Alani whispered. "Let's get the kids in the house and in the bed. They've been through enough tonight." She went to retrieve Messari, who was sleeping in the backseat.

"I can get him," Mo said.

"I got him." Alani carried him into the house and laid him on the couch. "You can give me her too." She reached for Yara and then cozied up beside them. "I need all the energy my babies have to give right now. You two can head up and get some rest." She pulled the oversized throw over their bodies. "We all need it. Help is coming in the morning."

"Help?" Bash asked.

"Nyair thinks there is someone pulling strings on this from the inside. Probably a cop with a grudge or something. I don't know, but we have strings to pull too. They'll have to bury me before I leave him in there," Alani said. "The way they put those cuffs on him. The way they manhandled Hendrix…"

"Hendrix got arrested too?" Morgan's shock couldn't be hidden. So many people were affected by her decisions. People who didn't deserve it.

"Bash, can you excuse us?" Alani asked.

Bash hesitated and shot a glance at Morgan before ascending the stairs.

"I still don't know what they're holding Ezra for, but my gut is telling me it's about my baby, Mo. If it's about Kenzie and this goes to court, you'll have to relive a nightmare. We all will have to go back in time and relive it. If this gets bad, it's going to rip this family apart. You and I can't be at odds. We can't let anything or anyone take us back to the place we've grown from, Mo. I love you. I'm so sorry about what my brother did to you and how we entered each other's lives, but we're family now. I just want you to know that. No matter how ugly this gets or how bad it hurts when the past and our secrets are put on trial for people to judge, I love you, and we're family, and Ezra will need us to remember that."

Morgan nodded, eyes weighted with emotion, heart burdened with guilt. Alani hugged Morgan tightly, and Morgan winced, pulling back. "You okay?" Alani asked.

Morgan shook her head and then nodded, changing her mind in a milli-second about asking for help. Alani couldn't help her. No one could. The amount of power the Fredericks had was unequal to the amount of power Ethic had. Street politics couldn't measure up. She had to fix this herself, and the best way to do that was from the inside.

CHAPTER 4

I f my dad goes to jail, does that mean I'm the man of the house?"

Eazy's question cut through Alani like glass, and she had to take a moment to stop her eyes from tearing before turning toward him. She gripped the edge of the wooden seat before her as she waited anxiously for the court proceedings to begin.

"No, baby. You're a boy. Nothing's going to make you become a man before it's your time. Daddy is going to be okay. This is all a misunderstanding, and we're going to clear it up soon," she reassured.

Alani had wanted to leave Eazy home, but the attorney Zya had sent had insisted that his entire family be present when he appeared before the court. Eazy gripped Alani's hand and leaned his head against her body. Bella sat on her other side. Morgan sat beside Bella, and Bash capped off the end. Nyair sat in the row in front of them beside his father and Zora.

She was anxious to plant eyes on her husband. They didn't go days without speaking, without contact; it felt like a lifetime.

When the side door opened, Alani's heart stalled. Ethic walked in, wearing an orange jumpsuit, shackled at the wrists and the feet.

"Where is his suit? The lawyer told me to drop off a suit for him to wear to court," Alani whispered. His feet stopped moving when he spotted his family, and their eyes met. A thousand "I love you's" flew through mid-air just to reach one another. She could see the sorrow in him. The regret. The apology. No one else would notice the chip in his armor but Alani saw it clearly. She knew him too well to miss it. This was bad. She had known it was when the police had shown up to their home, but seeing him now, in police custody, she could tell that he was worried. Whatever storm had entered their life was far from over. "Ny, he looks like a criminal. Where is his suit?" Alani leaned forward, tapping his shoulder, and whispering in Nyair's ear.

"I'm sure that's on purpose," Nyair said. "They always want to make sure a nigga looks like a nigga."

"All rise. Court is in session. Honorable Judge Mitchell presiding," the bailiff announced. Alani lifted from her seat.

"Where's Henny?" Bella asked.

"The judge won't see them together, baby girl. We'll have to wait for his case to be called," Alani said.

"We're going to wait, right?"

Alani heard the worry. She grabbed Bella's hands as they stood side by side. "Yes, B, we're going to wait."

The judge entered the room and took his seat. Alani's faith dwindled when she saw the elderly white man. The fate of a Black man always somehow came down to being in the hands of a white man.

"You may be seated," the judge said.

Everyone in attendance sat, and Alani hoped Ethic would turn around. She just wanted to see his face one more time, but instead, he sat facing forward, focused on the front of the courtroom. Alani examined the attorney Zya had sent. She had studied his resume for hours the night before, reading about his unbelievable wins in prior court cases. His expensive suit and debonair persona were charming. The way he spoke was calming. She hoped it was a recipe for freedom, and she waited anxiously as he approached the podium to speak.

"Good morning, officers of the court, Jamal Bishop, lead counsel for the defense. I'd like to request that we waive the reading of the indictment against my client. Mr. Okafor has been provided with a written form of his charges. Due to the sensitive nature of the accused crime and the fact that his lovely wife and children are in attendance, we would like to bypass that part."

The judge looked down; a stern brow showed he was unmoved.

"Mr. Okafor, you've read the indictment, and you understand the charges that have been brought against you?"

Ethic stood, and Alani quivered. Even in state-issued clothing, his presence was felt. His authority. His dominance. It filled up the entire room.

"I do," he said.

The judge glanced back over at the family and then waved his hand.

"Straight to the matter of bail then."

The prosecuting attorney piped up. "The people ask for

remand. Mr. Okafor is a violent threat to the community and has the financial means to flee. It would be a grave disservice to the victim's families and the community."

"This is a witch hunt. If you read the indictment, Your Honor, it reads like a grocery list. The prosecution is shopping, throwing everything in their cart until they find the one thing they can sell to a jury to convict my client."

"We don't need your grandstanding, Mr. Bishop. This is a pre-trial hearing. Your showmanship is not required. Make it plain," the judge warned.

"Make it plain? Okay. The prosecution says, letting Mr. Okafor out on bail would be going against the wishes of the victim's family. So, let's let them speak for themselves."

"Come again?" Ethic interrupted.

"Mr. Okafor, you will not speak out of turn in my court. In here, I'm the master," the judge chastised.

"What was that?" Ethic asked.

His tone was deadly. He knew the games white men in black robes played with Black faces. This courtroom may as well have been a slave field because judges were nothing more than overseers, sitting up on their horses passing down punishments to Black men.

"Excuse me, Mr. Okafor?" The judge challenged.

"I need clarity on the way this master thing works. That will dictate what happens next," Ethic responded.

"Ezra!" Alani's voice was like an extinguisher to his emblazoned soul. She stood from her seat and made her way to the podium as Ethic turned to steel in his chair.

"This is the victim's family, Your Honor," Bishop said,

opening the swinging door that separated the audience from the lawyers. "The mother of Kenzie Hill and sister to Lucas Hill."

Shaky limbs carried Alani to the podium. She gripped the sides of the wood.

"I…I…"

She glanced back at Ethic. His elbows rested on the table in front of him; his hands were clenched, his head bowed on top of them. "I need you to look at me," Alani said, turning to the defense table.

When their eyes met, Alani felt her cheek go wet. This was the position they both had silently feared for years. The day when her mourning would no longer be hers to behold in the safety of her heart. Alani flipped through pictures of Kenzie in private every day, reminiscing alone so that her grief wouldn't bring a cloud over her entire household. Now, it was on a stage. This was the E&A show, and the crime of the week was murder. Her baby's murder. Oh, how her heart ached. She knew he felt it because the gloss of his stare revealed that he shared her distress.

He shook his head slightly.

"I need a second with you," Ethic said, turning his attention to his lawyer.

"We request a short recess, Your Honor. Ten minutes to discuss the course of action with my client," Bishop said.

"Court will recess for ten minutes."

Before Alani could utter a word to him, officers escorted Ethic away.

"Can I see him?" Alani asked.

"You're about to speak on behalf of the victims. It's not a good idea to make it seem disingenuous or coerced by having you speak with him beforehand."

"I'll go," Morgan said. "Please, I have to see him." Morgan stepped up. "I just want to make sure he's okay."

"It wouldn't be a good idea for you to speak to him either. The inciting incident surrounds you. This is a unique circumstance. If it looks contrived in any way, it could cost him his life." "I'll speak to Ethic," Nyair said.

"No," Ezekiel interrupted. "He's my son. I should."

Alani felt helpless as Ezekiel walked out of the courtroom with Ethic's lawyer. She was his wife. She was supposed to be by his side, but she could tell he didn't want her there. Before his wife, she was a mother, and her motherhood trumped all. It was one of the greatest qualities that had made him love her. One role was pitted against the other, and it made them enemies.

Ethic stood in the courthouse conference room, staring out of the barred windows.

"Son…"

The sound of Ezekiel's voice pulled his attention toward the door.

Discomfort filled the space between them. Their relationship was fickle. Ezekiel had been a terrible father to Ethic, but he was atoning for that in the grandfather department. They both knew it was too late for parenting for Ethic, but he acknowledged the effort to connect with Bella and Eazy.

"Everyone's on edge out there," Ezekiel said. "But we're all here, standing behind you. Especially, Lenika. That's some woman."

Ethic was silent as he stared at his father. It felt too little too late, but the boy in him was tolerant of Ezekiel's presence. The part of him that overcompensated with his children to make sure they never felt the inadequacy he felt from his father's abandonment was grateful for his presence.

"She's my wife," Ethic said. "She can't do this. I'll plead guilty before I make her get up in front of the world and defend me."

His lawyer entered the room and closed the door.

"You need her. If she vouches for your innocence, it's a strong possibility that the judge and jury will too." Bishop pushed his agenda strong. He was a shark of an attorney who would do anything to win.

"I won't play on her grief. I need to see her. I've got seven minutes left. They belong to her," Ethic said.

"You do realize the risk you take by not using her to speak on your behalf?" Bishop asked.

"It'll break her. I took my time putting that woman back together. I won't break her again and leave her with the pieces," he said. It was an adamant no.

"Mr. Okafor…"

"I speak, you listen, no? That is the dynamic of this arrangement. Get my wife," Ethic said.

Bishop nodded, biting his tongue, stopping himself from pushing more. He turned to exit.

"I need you to check on Messiah Williams and Hendrix Outlaw," Ethic said. "Whoever has been assigned to their counsel, their services are no longer needed."

"Amy Fisher has been retained for Mr. Williams," Bishop informed.

Ethic was stunned. She was one of the tastemakers in the legal system in Michigan. "Retained by who?" He asked, wondering who could have made the call to get her to take on a new client. She worked with a very select clientele.

"An Ahmeek Harris arranged that," Bishop answered.

Ethic nodded. "The nigga solid I'll give him that," Ethic whispered.

"I'll work on Hendrix Outlaw. He's being repped by someone from the public defender's office," Bishop said.

"Do all you can for him. Spare no expense. Tack the bill onto mine," Ethic informed. "And get my wife."

"He wants to see you."

The news eased some of Alani's anxiety, and she breathed a sigh of relief, releasing Eazy's hand.

"Can we come?" Eazy asked.

"You can't. Not right now, but I'll be right back, baby boy. I promise," Alani said as Bishop ushered her away.

"How long do I have with him?" She asked. "Only a few

minutes," Bishop replied. "We have to make it quick."

Alani followed him into the conference room, and as soon as she saw Ethic, her emotional dam burst. She rushed to him, and Ethic lifted his cuffed wrists to receive her, locking her inside his hold. He rested his chin on top of her head and closed his eyes.

"I'm terrified, Ezra," she whispered.

"I know, baby."

"I need you," she cried. "We all need you so much."

She couldn't foresee a life without him. The notion was preposterous.

"It isn't your place to defend me from this, Alani," he said. "I'll never compromise you in that way. It's my job to protect you, not the other way around. We don't speak about Kenzie often but know I'm eternally sorry, Alani. I'm a ruined man behind that night..."

"I know you are." She looked up at him, caressing his face. "How did this happen to us?"

"I don't know, but I'm going to find out," Ethic replied. "It isn't on you to defend me. You don't even have to be here. It took a lot of love to erase the way you used to look at me. Putting you in the middle of this will end us. You can't be here, baby."

"Where else would I be?" Alani asked. She kissed his lips, and he held her tighter before bringing his arms from around her. He dropped to one knee. Alani rubbed the top of his head, circling waves with manicured nails as he kissed her belly.

"I feel like I'm losing you." Alani's voice barely existed. She didn't even want to speak it into existence, but it was true.

Only two days had passed since his arrest, and she felt like he would never come home again. Like the last time, he had walked out the door had been the last time, and she hadn't appreciated it enough because she hadn't known she should be savoring it.

"I need you strong, baby. I need Lenika," he said, standing. "If I don't make it home…"

"I'm gonna die," she whispered. "Ezra, no." His thumb swiped at her tears.

"We have to talk about it, baby," Ethic said. Her face was in his hands now as he covered it with love. Her cheek first. The salt of the tears lingered on his lips as he moved to her chin, then her lips.

"I don't want to." Her lips stretched, and she lowered her head, defeated, as she sobbed.

"We have to," Ethic said.

"You're not a killer," she cried.

"I am," he answered. His answer was so matter of fact. She could tell he had prepared for this day, and it angered her. How had he prepared but left her unprepared?

"You're not," she defended.

"I am."

"So, do something. Kill everybody that's keeping you away from us," Alani sobbed.

They spent every second they had absorbing this moment.

"I don't want to give birth without you," she said. "You know what happened last time. I can't do it alone."

He took her hands in his and lifted them to his lips. "I'm gonna be there. I'm going to give you your entire birth plan, baby. In a nasty-ass pool in the middle of your fifty-thousand-dollar birthing room."

Alani laughed through her tears. "You gonna get in with me?"

Ethic groaned. "I'ma get in the mucus water with you, Lenika."

"You better be there," she whispered, holding him tighter.

"I wouldn't miss it," he promised. "Take care of my babies. Be strong."

She nodded.

When Bishop and the court officers entered the room, Alani and Ethic were forehead to forehead as Alani prayed aloud.

"The judge is waiting," Bishop said.

Alani held him tighter and she cried a little harder, blowing out a breath of angst as she attempted to gather her composure.

"I love you so much," she said. Her eyes were clamped shut.

"Look at me," he commanded. They fluttered open.

"I love you. You're the best thing that ever happened to a nigga, Lenika."

"Mr. Okafor, step away!" The officer said, reaching for Alani to separate them.

"You touch her, you die," Ethic said.

"Let's not keep the judge waiting further," Bishop said, stepping between the officer and Ethic. "Mrs. Okafor can walk with us back to the courtroom. I can't see that doing any harm. We know she has no contraband since she was searched upon entry to the courthouse."

The officer's temperament settled some as he took a step back.

Ethic was escorted back to the courtroom, and Alani walked behind him and the officers. She found her seat as the court proceedings resumed.

"Is the defense ready to proceed with the matter of bail?" The judge asked.

"We are, Your Honor," Bishop answered. "My client's wife is pregnant. She's due any day now. He is a doting father and family man. His entire family is here today on his behalf. He has young children. Certainly, you can reconsider letting this man go home to his family. He is no flight risk. To leave would be to leave them behind. He is a member of the community; as you can see, one of the most prominent officials in the city is here on his behalf. He has people who need him. It is a waste of taxpayer dollars to keep him locked up while the prosecution builds a shaky case against him. We request recognizance, Your Honor."

"Ezra Okafor may be an upstanding citizen. A reformed man, Your Honor," the prosecution said. "But Ethic, the man who has flooded this city with cocaine and violence is a criminal. The people ask you to keep our city safe and hold him on remand."

"I'd like to speak, Your Honor!"

Ethic's head whipped back at her, bewildered that she was changing the plan. He had said no; she had decided otherwise— the story of their entire marriage. Alani was the big boss. Because his heart beat at her command, it made her command, the only word that mattered. The judge motioned for her to take the floor, and she stood to make her way to the podium.

"My name is Alani Okafor…"

"Mr. Bishop, we don't take pleas of mercy from the defendant's family," the judge said.

"I'm the victim's mother," Alani said. Her voice broke. Ethic knew it would… knew she would. This was trauma on top of trauma. Alani's fists were tight as the pressure built in her. She felt like the worst kind of woman, the type who chose a man over her flesh and blood, over her child. She had judged women like that. Half-ass mothers, putting their sons out to keep boyfriends satisfied and feeling like the man of the house. Sorry-ass mothers who sided with abusive boyfriends when teenaged daughters screamed foul play. Alani would have been ready to slap a bitch like that, and here she was… a bitch like that. She wondered if other women gave the same excuses to make sense of the pain their men caused.

Ezra's not like those men. He's a good man. It was a mistake, she thought. She was sure all the women she had judged over the years had told themselves that very same thing.

Her throat was so tight she couldn't sip air.

"Breathe."

She turned to him. Just the sound of his voice, and it was like she had permission to exist again.

Many women may justify their men's misdeed but just staring in his eyes Alani knew her justification was true. Sad but still true.

"The victim's mother," Alani said more confidently as she turned back to the judge. "My brother and my daughter are the lives you're trying to find justice for. I want that but not at the sake of Ezra Okafor. He's my husband, and I am eight months pregnant. I need him home. We have three children and two grandchildren who need him home. My daughter lost her life. Do you think I'd be pleading on this man's behalf if I thought he was a bad man? Please grant bail so that if these are the last days we get to see him free, we'll get to be with him. Give him enough time to see his child be born into the world."

Alani made her way back to her seat.

"Bail is set at one million," the judge said.

"I'm coming to get you, Ezra!" Alani shouted as she watched the officers lead him out of the courtroom. "I'm coming to get you!"

CHAPTER 5

Morgan couldn't get Messiah off her mind. The thought of him locked up, for reasons undeserving, peeled back layers of her that had long been buried. Her heart pounded in anticipation as she wondered if his case would be called next.

"I have to get to the bank and then come back to process his bail," Alani said.

"What about Henny?" Bella asked. "We can't just leave. His mom won't come for him. I'm all he has." The passion in Bella's voice couldn't be mistaken. She was a young girl in love. Nothing outweighed that. There was nothing that would get her to leave Hendrix behind.

"Mo, can you stay here with her? We'll post his bond. I have to make it to the bank. I can't be in two places at once," Alani said. "Bash, you can take the twins home, can't you? This will be a long day for us. They don't need to be here."

"No, they can stay with me," Morgan interjected. The idea of him alone with her children terrified her. If he had changed with her, would he treat them differently? He had never hurt them before, but she had no way to know what he was capable of.

"That doesn't make sense. I'll take them to my family's home. You handle your business. We'll be there when you're done," Bash said. He kissed the top of Morgan's head, and she turned to ice.

"Can I talk to you for a second before you leave?" Morgan asked.

She scooped Yara into her arms and held Messari's hand before following him into the hallway.

"Bash, they can stay with me. After last night, I don't want to let them out of my sight," Morgan said. "Please, just leave them. I swear to God I'm not going to say anything. You don't have to use them as leverage. You have the power to take them; I heard you loud and clear. I don't plan to give you a reason to. Just let me keep my babies near me right now. I'm falling apart," she pleaded.

"Mo, you got to stop painting me as the monster. I've been here for them since the day they were born. You've got to know they're safe with me. You come with your bullshit, but *we* raised these kids, Mo. You're trying to convince yourself that you did it alone, but I was there. My family and I have been putting these babies first since they entered our lives. Let me show you something," Bash said. He pulled out his phone and passed it to Morgan.

There was a text exchange between him and an unsaved number. Only one short message appeared.

Grant him bail.

Morgan looked up at Bash in shock. Her fate was really his to toy with. The helplessness she felt was crippling. If she moved her piece across the board in the wrong direction, she would lose the game.

"I don't want to ruin you. This can get worst, or you can be better. You can get it right, and all this can go away. It can be simple, Mo," he said.

Her lip quivered. Bash had been the reason Ethic was granted bail. That type of power was scary. How was she supposed to escape that type of hold?

"They had a long night. Let me take them home, re-establish some normalcy for them. They're safe with me. They always have been. You on the other hand…"

"I'll leave with you," Morgan said. "Just give me a minute to tell Alani."

There was no way she was letting him out of her sight with her twins. She wanted to stay. She desperately wanted to be near her family. She wanted to wait for Messiah's case to be called. She needed to see that he was okay, but she couldn't let Bash walk out of this building with her kids.

She stepped over to her family.

"I have to go, Alani. The kids are restless, and Yara's clinging to me more than usual after last night. I should get them home. I'm sorry," Morgan said.

Alani was too consumed by her own turmoil to identify Morgan's. They were all just reacting to the possibility of life-altering change, trying to prevent the unfathomable from occurring.

"Okay, yeah, okay, Mo. I'll call you as soon as Ethic is released," she said.

"And Messiah," Morgan whispered. "Call me as soon as you know something about him."

Alani glanced over Morgan's shoulder, pausing long enough to stare Morgan in the eyes. "Of course," Alani replied.

Morgan turned to walk away, and Alani grabbed her hand. "Hey, are you good? We're going to get them all out of here. We just got to stick together and be strong until they're home. This trial can't make us lose sight of how far we've come, Mo. I love you. We're in this together. Don't put me back on the other side. I don't want to go back to being someone you hate."

Morgan nodded and placed a hand on Alani's belly. "I don't want to be someone you hate either. Promise you'll never go back to hating me," she whispered, growing emotional as her chin quivered.

Alani placed a flat palm beneath Morgan's chin. "Never, Mo. Like motherfucking ever. Okay?"

Morgan nodded and then walked out of the courthouse. She prayed to have Alani as the voice of reason when her treason became known. She was the most well-versed of them all when it came to forgiveness. Morgan would need her to salvage her relationship with Ethic because she could feel it in her bones. The fallout was inevitable.

Hours. Bella Okafor sat in the courthouse for hours, waiting for Hendrix's name to be called. Zora sat beside her, and they hadn't spoken very often. Bella was sucked into the trials and tribulations of the people who stood before the court, waiting to hear their fates.

"This is terrible," she whispered. Ninety percent of the people who came before the judge were Black, and Bella felt sick as she watched him hand down harsh sentencing or impossible bail amounts. "He's being way harder on the Black people who stand in front of him," Bella said, voice low and in despair. "Auntie Zora, none of this is fair."

"It never is, Bella," Zora said. "They may not arraign him today. Maybe we should head home?"

"I can't leave him in here. Look around. His mom isn't here. If I'm not here, he'll feel alone, and he's not alone. I'd never leave him alone," Bella said. "I know people think I'm too young to know what love is, but I'm not. I really love him. He makes me feel like it's okay to be different from all the other girls. Like, I don't wear a bunch of makeup, my clothes aren't always tight, and my hair isn't always perfect. I started to think I had to do something to fit in on Susan Street, but then he made it okay for me to stand out. I want to make it okay for him to stand out too. To be the first one of his friends to go to college and just do something different. This isn't supposed to be his life."

"That's beautiful, Bella," Zora replied. "Sometimes, life throws you on a different path, and you have to take a detour that makes it a little harder to get where you're going."

"He'll get there, though," Bella said, never taking her eyes off the front of the courtroom. "He has to."

When Bella saw Hendrix finally emerge from the side door, relief flooded her.

He was limping and dragging cuffed feet as he looked at the ground in front of him.

She just wanted him to look up at her, but he didn't. He kept his head down all the way to his seat.

Bella didn't hear anything the entire arraignment except that his bail had been set at fifty thousand dollars.

"So he can get out, right?" Bella asked. "That's what that means, right, Mr. Bishop?"

Hendrix turned at the sound of her voice. He was a shell of his usual self. No charm, no smile, no sparkle in his eyes like when he normally looked at her. He just spun the swivel chair forward and focused on the cops that were forcing him to stand. They escorted him out, and Bella's chest caved in.

"Auntie Zo, please get him out," Bella said.

"We will. Come on. Let's go," Zora said, easing out into the aisle.

"What about Messiah?" Bella asked.

"That was the last case of the day, Bella. I don't know why they didn't call him, but he won't see a judge today."

Zora approached Ethic's attorney. "Can you tell me when Messiah Williams will be arraigned?"

"Apparently, those charges have been dropped. I just got word. Makes me wonder what he gave up in return to be released."

"Fuck you doing here?" Messiah asked as he emerged from the city jailhouse, day's old clothes weighing him down as he stared Livi up and down, then up again. In her eyes. Her pretty-ass eyes. He might have been appreciative to see her if he hadn't known who had sent her.

"Just doing Meek a favor," Livi said.

"I don't need no favors, shorty," Messiah said.

"Yeah, well, how about a ride?" Livi asked. "He said you'd be difficult but that you would know what needed to happen next and where to go."

Messiah stalled because he did know. The Crew didn't slip. They had a plan for everything, and all three of them knew it was time to blow town until things cooled off.

"They really fucked you up in there," Livi said. "Come on."

Messiah reluctantly followed Livi to her car. Meek was smart. He sent unsuspecting pussy into the police station after Messiah instead of risking his arrest by coming personally. The cops were playing a dirty game by not charging him. He would have to prove he hadn't flipped on Ethic, and if he skipped town, he knew it would make him look guilty. The cops were banking on it. They were setting a trap for Ethic to suspect Messiah of treachery to incite Ethic's wrath. If anything happened to Messiah, all roads would lead back to Ethic and they would kill two birds with one stone. Messiah felt the pressure on his shoulders. He wasn't an indecisive man, but he didn't know what to do. He was silent as Livi drove him forty minutes down I-75, pulling over at a motel, one that took cash only and had no cameras. They had mapped this place out years ago for instances just like these.

He stepped out of the car and Ahmeek opened the door to the room in front of their parking spot. He sauntered to the driver's side of the car and slid Livi a healthy stack of banded bills. Payment for her time and services.

"Good looking," he said as he leaned down against her window so that they were eye to eye. "You don't know shit, a'ight? Last time you saw me was last night. You left the crib after a long night. The police come asking questions, you tell them everything we did until I got that call. Everything before that point is true; you won't forget it. You can recall that the same way, again and again, no matter how many times you're asked."

"And what if they ask me what happened after that?" Livi asked.

"You won't know because the cameras in my building caught you leaving in the middle of the night. You don't know shit else, and you ain't heard from me since you left. You understand?"

Livi nodded. "Where are you going?" She asked.

Ahmeek tapped her lips, signaling for her to stop. No questions. "Be careful, okay?"

"Yup," he replied. "Don't concern yourself with the bullshit, Liv. I'ma get with you soon, beautiful." He tapped the roof of the car and stood up straight as Livi reversed her car and drove away.

Messiah and Ahmeek squared off, standing in the desolate parking lot; the energy between them was foreign, resentful. Neither knew what to say, but they were silently grateful for their mutual freedom. Messiah was bloody. The joyride had done a number on him. His shoulder felt like it was out of socket. His right eye was swollen, almost shut, and blackened.

He had bruises everywhere, a nasty gash behind his ear that had yet to stop bleeding.

"You good?" Meek asked.

"The less you talk, the more they fuck you up," Messiah said. "I'ma be a'ight though. I don' been through worse."

Meek nodded. These men were at an impasse. They had too much love between them to fully hate one another, but too much had been done to fully love one another. They were stuck. Existing awkwardly, bound by loyalty that most wouldn't understand.

"Money's in the trunk. Miami been called. CJ say we can post up down there. They got the condos in dummy names, cars with new plates, all that. A whole new setup waiting for us until these mu'fuckas get the targets off our backs," Ahmeek said. "They handling some business in Houston, but everything's ready in Miami. They rolling out the red carpet. Isa's already on the road. I'ma go a different way, though. Miami ain't feeling like the move for me. But everything is set up. Ain't no risk down there for you or Isa."

Messiah knew Meek well enough to know that he no longer trusted him. If his freedom were on the line, he wouldn't put it in Messiah's hands. Not after the hit Messiah had called on his life. Time had truly changed their dynamic. Meek had elevated. He had bossed all the way up, secured the block, and gotten in bed with Hak. It was exactly what Messiah would have done had he been around to put the next job on the table. Meek had kept the Crew eating and the money flowing in. In fact, it was overflowing. His only misstep over the past few years had been to fall in love. Messiah knew how it had happened. He knew why it had happened. If there was ever a girl to love, surely Morgan Atkins was it. He still hated it. He still resented him for discovering the mystery of her love.

"I can't leave town again," Messiah said, breaking the silence. "I just found out about them. Last time I broke out, I lost everything. My kids here. Another nigga raising what's mine. I can't leave."

"I hear that," Ahmeek said.

Messiah nodded. "Cops trying to throw dirt on my name. They want Ethic to think I snitched."

"I don't know that nigga too good, but what I know is that he know you ain't talking," Ahmeek answered.

"Do he?" Messiah asked. "I ain't got the best track record of loyalty with homie."

"You wouldn't be alive if he thought otherwise. He left you with your life because he loves you. The nigga put a hole in me for less," Meek said.

Messiah nodded. "Po-po gon' put me back on that hook. They know about Lucas, the little girl, the nigga I stomped out at the club. They got every bone, man. If they can't get Ethic, they gon' bury me," Messiah said.

"So, move smart," Ahmeek said.

Ahmeek tossed Messiah a car key to the rental car he had arranged, and then he walked over to the rental secured for him.

"This the end of an era, ain't it?" Messiah asked before Meek opened the door.

Ahmeek shook his head. "Nah, I think it ended a long time ago when you left the first time. You just missed the goodbyes," Ahmeek said. A solemn they had never felt consumed them. "Keep your head above the dirt," Ahmeek said.

"And your body free," Messiah finished, both men uttering words they had said to one another many times. That had been the motto. Get money. Stay breathing. Ride free.

Messiah felt a heaviness in his chest that he couldn't contain as Meek climbed in the car and drove away.

"What's taking them so long?" Eazy asked. "Uncle Ny should be back with Daddy by now."

"It just takes a little time, Big Man. That's all. Daddy will be starving when he gets here. Why don't you help me fix dinner? Grab the green beans out of the bag and snap the ends," Alani instructed. She couldn't help but keep herself busy. She had spent too many days doing nothing but wallowing in the absence of her husband. She had to make use of her hands, of herself, because, with Ethic gone, Alani felt useless.

Eazy sat at the kitchen table and grabbed the bowl of beans, and began snapping. It was a routine he had grown used to while working in Alani's garden. Alani couldn't help but smile because Eazy's anxiety was tamed by the repetitive chore. She was able to manage what doctors had advised medication for with pure love. Eazy's ADHD was tackled in the hands of Alani because she refused to let anyone label him. A mother's love was all he had been missing, and she was so honored to provide that, but he needed his father too, and the thought that he may not be there was crippling.

"Bella, can you call Mo again?" Alani asked.

"Morgan is going to turn up when Morgan turns up. She knows Ethic is coming home. She'll be here for him," Nannie fussed. "If anybody loves him more than you, it's that narrow tail, hardheaded girl. So stop worrying yourself and get off your feet before you have that baby right here on the kitchen floor. Don't make me call your midwife."

"He's been away for two days, Nannie. If you think I'm letting him come in this house without a warm meal, you got another thing coming, old lady," Alani replied.

"He gon' want something warm alright and it ain't gon' be nothing you can put on the stove," Nannie said, snickering.

"What?" Eazy asked.

"Pie," Nannie said, finding amusement in her inside joke as she gave a hearty laugh. Bella looked up from her phone for the first time since arriving home and erupted in laughter. Alani blushed and shook her head, laughing.

"Stop it, old woman," Alani said, tickled to tears.

"What's so funny?" Eazy asked.

"Nothing, boy, you wouldn't understand," Bella said.

"And it bothers me that you understand," Alani said. "Come take this cornbread out of the oven."

"Yes, ma'am," Bella said, lifting from her seat.

"Can we eat?" Eazy asked.

"No, not until your father walks in this house. We fix his plate first," Alani said. They were words she would eat because two hours passed, and there was still no sight of Ethic. Even Nyair's phone was going to voicemail.

"Where are they?" Alani asked no one in particular. "Why don't we eat, let the kids go to bed..."

"We're not eating without him," Alani said. She was emotional, and the angst sitting on her shoulders made waiting unbearable.

"Kids, go fix your plates and take them upstairs. Don't leave them plates up there, you hear me?" Nannie fussed.

"Yes, ma'am," Eazy, answered. When Bella and Eazy were out of sight, Alani planted her face in her palms.

"I feel helpless, Nannie. They're asking questions I can't answer. Even when he gets home tonight, how long will he stay home? This is just bail. It's temporary. What if they lock him up? What if I have to testify? What do I say? Do I lie? Who do I protect? My baby or my husband? Do I do what's best for the baby I'm carrying or the baby I was forced to bury? Locking Ezra up doesn't feel like justice. I know he did it. I know I'm crazy for loving him anyway, but he's not a monster. Locking him up won't make it better. It'll just be pain on top of pain."

"I know you want me to give you the answers, baby, but I don't have them. You've got to give it to God," Nannie said.

"God be on that bullshit!" Alani dismissed. Her entire life she had been taught to trust God's plan, and often times, she strayed from Him because she couldn't understand why she had to endure so much as a young girl. This was one of those times of confusion. "Ezra asked for forgiveness. The man stood in front of an entire church and got baptized. He's repented. He's different. He believes, and still, he's punished. That don't sound like God."

"God's will ain't for you to understand, little girl," Nannie said. "And I know you love the man's dirty drawers, but Ethic can't change God's will either. Trust in the Lord, Alani, not to prevent the storm but to make sure you're covered while it rains. He won't ever put more on you than you can bear."

Alani shook her head. "That's laughable. I reached my breaking point a long time ago. I can't take any more."

"Well, baby, you signed up for this when you chose that man. All that 'breathe, Lenika' don't come without some heartache too. A man like Ethic bringing plenty of heartaches, one way or another. You knew what and who he was, so you have to endure his trials and tribulations. They were always coming. That's the one thing about the world; it always brings your crap back to you. Everything comes full circle."

Nannie arose from her seat. "Let me go wake Mr. Larry up so he can take me home," Nannie said, making her way to the living room.

"You don't want to stay?" Alani asked.

"I want to sleep in my own bed. You and Ethic like to pretend like I live here. I like my house and my own space. I love Eazy to death, but that boy too loud in the mornings. I need some peace and quiet sometimes. Nerves get bad when you get my age, all that racket will drive you to the madhouse." Alani scoffed as she watched Nannie make her exit. "Call me in the morning. I'm sure Ethic will be home by then. Try not to worry yourself sick. You've got to think about them babies over everything. As terrified as you are, they are feeling ten times that. Ezra doesn't need you to be his strength. He needs you to be theirs."

As the night grew long and the house stilled, Alani feared the worst. She laid on the couch, placing a pillow between her thighs to ease the pressure of her belly as she waited impatiently.

"Something had to go wrong," she whispered. She forced her eyes open for as long as she could before her exhaustion took her under.

CHAPTER 6

Mommy, where were you?" Yara signed as Morgan went down on her knees so that she was at eye level with her babies.

"Mommy just wanted you to spend a little time with your dad," Morgan whispered and signed.

"Him is Meekie's best friend. Meekie said him is cool," Messari said excitedly. "Him not cool, though. Him mean."

Morgan shook her head. "He only seems mean because you don't know him yet. He loves you, and he'll never be mean to you. He's going to save you from everything that hurts. He's your superhero. He can't save me, but he will save you and your sister one day."

"Why can't he save you too, Mommy?" Yara signed.

"He just can't, baby," she signed.

"It's cuz him got tooken, Yolly. Him can't come," Messari said.

"Shhh," Morgan said, swiping a runaway tear. "We can't talk about that right now, okay, baby?" Morgan said, looking over her shoulder as Bash's footsteps echoed off the tile floor in the hallway. They were getting closer, and Morgan desperately wanted to change the conversation.

"Why not?" Messari asked.

"We just can't. Tell Mommy a story, a really good one, the best bedtime story you can imagine," Morgan said. "Can you do that? It'll make Mommy sleep so much better." Her voice was shaking and her heart pounding as she tried her best to hide her trepidation from her kids.

Messari nodded, and his hands started moving. He signed beautifully, getting stuck on a few words that he was still learning, but Morgan had no worries; she knew he would eventually become fluent.

"Once upon a time, there was a princess named Mommy," he signed.

Morgan laughed. Her sweet boy always knew what to do to bring her joy. It was the absolute best perk of being a young mother. There were smiles that only Messari and Yara could pull from her because she could identify little pieces of love from Messiah in them. There were moments shared between the three of them that only DNA could explain. Like when Yara rubbed her thumb and pointer finger together when she was angry or frustrated. Or the way Messari's forehead wrinkled whenever he was focused on one thing for too long. Messiah came out of them in the most subtle ways, and even in her darkest days when she hated him, she loved him too because he had given her two babies that kept her alive.

"Oh really? I think I know someone by that name," she said.

"It's you, silly," Yara signed.

"No, I think the princess is you, baby," Morgan answered.

Bash cleared his throat behind her, and Morgan didn't turn to him. Her head bowed for a beat as she took a deep breath and squeezed her twins' hands. "Okay, in bed, Mommy's

Ssari. We can finish the story tomorrow. It's late," she signed. Morgan tucked her children under thousand-dollar sheets and pulled the duvet to their chests. "I love you, Messari. I love you, Yolly."

Morgan turned off the light and made sure to turn on the bathroom light before meeting Bash at the door.

"It's been a long night for everybody," he said.

She nodded. She was unsure of what to say or do. He reached for her face, and Morgan pulled back.

"I just need a minute," she said. She walked by him, closing the twins' door as she made her way across the hall into another room, where she would sleep. She prayed he slept somewhere else. The bathroom was her sanctuary, and as soon as she locked the door, Morgan felt safe enough to release her tears. She muffled her cries with one hand.

This is too much, she thought. She removed her shirt, wincing in pain as she looked down at her battered body.

It had taken all she had to pretend to be okay all day. Something felt broken inside her. Her heart. Her ribs. The pain was bearable but agonizing all at the same time. She ran a warm bath and poured bath salts inside, hoping to take away some of the aches. She slid inside the water, crying out in pain until she was submerged.

She didn't know if the bath was soothing or if she just needed it as an excuse to be away from Bash, but she spent an hour in the tub.

It didn't matter. Bash was waiting on the other side of the door for her when she came out.

Morgan noticed her bags had been brought up, and she rummaged through them, pulling out leggings and a t-shirt.

She turned toward the bathroom, but Bash's voice stopped her.

"Let me see your stomach," he said.

"It's fine," she replied. "I'm fine, Bash."

"I apologize. Let me just make sure nothing's seriously wrong," he said as he came up behind her. The kiss to the back of her shoulder made her cringe. "I could see you were in pain today."

Morgan turned to face him. "I promise I'm good. Can you just... I don't know. I'm just tired and afraid and overwhelmed, Bash. Can you just get me some water? I just feel like I can't breathe. Like I don't know you..."

"You know me. I'm the same person who was there the day you delivered the twins. The same one who massaged your feet when they were swollen, the same one who helped you study at 3 a.m. when you had tests to wake up to, and the same one who took night shifts so you could get rest, Mo. I only lost my way because you lost yours. This isn't how we have to be," Bash said. "Why can't you just give this a chance?"

She was crying, and her face was in his hands. Her stomach was twisted in discomfort and regret.

"I know I've done you wrong. I've done a lot of people wrong. I don't want people to hurt because of me. Not you, not anybody," she replied.

"Stop crying, Mo. I'm going to go get Tylenol for the pain. Then, we'll talk about how we come back from this," Bash said.

Morgan nodded, and as soon as he exited the room, she threw on her clothes and then went to her bag, searching for her phone.

"What the fuck? Where is it?" She asked. Bash came back into the room, and Morgan stopped searching, sitting on the bed feeling as if he had busted her red-handed. She had an eerie feeling that he had taken her phone, and she dreaded what was to come if he read her messages. Text threads between she and Ahmeek played back in her mind. Things they had said. Pictures they had sent. Morgan had exposed more than her heart in that phone. Her body and soul were within the text threads of their messages. If Bash read them, it would be like gasoline to a fire. Meek would be next to be arrested, and Morgan wasn't quite sure what threat Bash would make good on when it came to her.

"Here, Mo," he said. He handed her the bottle of Tylenol and a glass of orange juice, and Morgan took them, praying it would ease the throbbing in her mid-section.

"You don't get to leave me after everything I've done for you." He said it so plainly like he hadn't just shattered every notion of her future that she had built up in her mind over the past few months.

"Why would you want me after all this?" she asked. She was drained. All her fight was gone. She had done what the fairy tales had taught her to do. She had followed her heart. Not once, but twice, and it had led her here. So, fuck it. Why fight it? Why fight Bash when she knew how it would end? She would lose. She always suffered the greatest losses. This one didn't even surprise her. Perhaps that's why she had moved so recklessly, loving Ahmeek so boldly, so loudly without apology. Had she known all along that he wouldn't be someone she could keep? Had she known that about Messiah too? Had the greatest loves of her life been mere lessons?

Morgan didn't even recognize Bash. He hadn't always been like this. She had pushed him to this. One too many instances of disrespect had gotten them to this place. Morgan remembered the days of sitting with Raven, watching her cover bruises and pretend not to be hurt, pretend to be happy. Morgan never thought that would become her. Her head was spinning as Bash leaned over, sweeping her hair off her neck. His lips on the softest part of her neck, and Morgan jerked away.

"It's been two years. You think I don't want you. I think about it all the time, Mo," he said.

"Bash, stop," she said. Morgan stood, and the entire room rotated. She reached out, unable to steady herself. She grabbed nothing but air as Bash caught her.

It was like she was trying to get through a fog. She was moving in slow motion, and her legs felt like logs.

"Take it easy, Mo," Bash said, moving her to the bed.

"What did you give me?" Morgan asked. She could barely hold her head up as he accosted her. She felt the air hit her nipples as he lifted her shirt. They stiffened, and Morgan felt nauseous because she didn't understand why her body responded to him. The saliva he left behind felt like icicles when the air met her skin. She peeled his fingers off her body every time, pushing him away, trying to free herself of his hold. His grip was so tight it felt like he was digging holes in her skin.

"Relax, Mo," he said. Every place he touched felt dirty, like his fingertips were left behind, leaving evidence of this night behind.

"Stop, Bash." Her voice felt small, even though it echoed in her mind. She felt like she was screaming, but he barely reacted. Christiana was home. She wasn't interrupting, so she couldn't have been loud. Morgan felt like she was screaming for her life, but he wasn't stopping. Her arms felt numb, and she couldn't quite get them to move. She felt him, smelled his spit on her skin as he left trails of wet kisses along her body. Morgan was horrified. She had felt this before. The disgust. The shame. The feeling of filth that men left behind when they touched her without love. Lucas had made her feel like this. That night, all those years ago.

It was like she was frozen. Stuck in a time when she was misunderstood, when others couldn't understand her, and when she didn't even have a voice to say no.

Bash couldn't hear her. He didn't understand her no. Was she even saying it? Morgan couldn't tell anymore, and when he entered her, he may as well have detonated a mental bomb. She felt everything and nothing all at once. Morgan had known this moment would happen between them eventually. It had been two and a half long years of waiting, of patience, of her making excuses. He had been more than understanding. His tolerance had run out. It felt like she was watching this scene play out instead of living it, like she was out of her body and trying to fight Bash. Push him, pull him, punches flying, feet kicking, anything to get him off, but in reality, she laid paralyzed because her body didn't work. She felt trapped as her silence permitted him to keep going. His lips were everywhere, his tongue doing everything, hands staining parts of her body he had never touched. Those babies he wanted to make, the ones he had tormented Ahmeek with at the dinner table during her graduation, the ones she was sure would enslave her to this lifestyle and this man forever; she felt them spill into her. Tears melted out the corners of her eyes as he finished. *"You don't play with a man's emotions."* Ethic's voice echoed in her mind.

She had done exactly that, and now she was paying the ultimate cost.

He hovered over her, inside her, moving her hair out of her face as he realized she was crying.

"No, no, no, don't cry. You think I want to hurt you? I don't want to hurt you. The other men hurt you. I just want to have you. I just want to kiss you," he whispered as he pressed his lips to hers. "Just let me kiss it, Mo." Morgan pushed against his chest weakly, anger building in her that she couldn't let out.

"No, Bash, no please nooooo," she sobbed. "This can't happen to me again." He put his tongue in her mouth, and Morgan cringed. She moved her head to the side and felt tears leak out of her eyes as he initiated round two.

"I'm done waiting, Mo."

"Just give it to me, Mo," he moaned. "See. It's good, baby. It's so good. Damn, you feel good." Nothing. Morgan felt nothing. He stroked her slowly as he pinned her hands above her head with one hand. "Damn," Bash called out. "You owe me, Mo. You owe me. Damn, just let me get it." Another man with the power to take what he wanted. He put a hand around her throat and squeezed as he had his way again.

"Alli, you feel so good," he whispered.

Alli?

It was the look in his eyes that told her he wasn't even in the room. His mind was somewhere else, and the more into it he became, the tighter his grip around her throat became.

"B-ash…" Morgan could barely get his name out. He was squeezing the life out of her. His hands just kept tightening. He squeezed harder and harder the more into it he became. His hips dove so deep into her that the bed moved across the floor with every stroke. Air. There was none. Her vision blurred, transforming him into a distorted image of himself, like something terrifying. A monster. This was the boogeyman that would terrify her for nights to come. She didn't even recognize the man on top of her.

Morgan felt like bullets entered her when he came. He climbed off and began to adjust his clothes as Morgan struggled to lift her body weight. She couldn't do anything but roll onto her side. She hadn't felt this out of it, ever. A few drunken nights with Stiletto Gang had come close, but nothing ever this debilitating. Her mouth was dry, like it was stuffed full of cotton balls, and they were getting stuck in her throat.

I can't breathe, she thought, panicking.

"It isn't that bad, Morgan. Loving a regular man. Having a

regular life. What I'm offering is good for you. It's good for our kids," he said.

"Bash, please help me," she cried, lying there, watching him dress so normally as if he hadn't just violated her. She had never felt so naked. He had stripped her without even using aggression. Men like Bash were the worst. With their entitlement, their money, their manipulation. He didn't need bravado because he had bank and his big bank trumped her little bank every time.

Morgan felt numb as he squatted beside the bed.

"You're emotional right now. You need to sleep. You'll feel fine by morning. We both have done some things we aren't proud of tonight. You said some things you don't mean because surely you don't want Ethic to sit in a prison cell for the rest of his life, and you know that's what's going to happen if you leave me. We will get back on track, Morgan. You see Ahmeek or Messiah again and I'll make sure they share a cell right beside Ethic's. I give you my word." Bash spoke calmly and kissed the top of her head. "One thing about you, Mo, it isn't overrated."

He walked out, and Morgan passed out, giving in to the overwhelming urge to make everything go away.

CHAPTER 7

Men had a way of taking things for granted. Not the big things. Men neglected the little things, but as Ethic stepped over the threshold of his home, he took it all in. The shoes Eazy had left scattered by the front door. The smell of something unhealthy Alani had prepared. The lights that had been left on because his whole family was afraid to sleep in a completely dark house when he wasn't home. The little things were the big things. He knew that now more than ever because he had been taken away from his family for an entire weekend, and he had wanted nothing more than to walk back through these doors. Hendrix trailed him, and Ethic turned to him.

"We gon' talk that talk in the morning. You know that, right?" Ethic asked.

Hendrix nodded but was too somber to reply. They had ridden in silence the entire way to Ethic's estate. Not even Nyair had uttered a word. Just two men and a boy consumed by their thoughts.

"You can sleep in the basement," Ethic said.

"Can I just see her first, big dawg? Let her know I'm out? I swear to God I ain't gon' be on no BS, I just want to see her."

Ethic felt that. He had a girl he just wanted to see as well.

"You leave the door open or you leaving out the window, you hear me?" Ethic asked.

"Thanks, man," Henny said, voice cracking, shoulders hung in defeat as he kicked off his shoes because he knew better than to leave them on in Alani's house. That's how often he had come around. He was present enough to know the lay of the land. Ethic's soul was a bit weary because he knew Henny was about to become a stranger. Prison did that to a man, made him unfamiliar to those who had once been intimate. So, Ethic would bend his rules and allow Hendrix access to see the one person he had watched the young man agonize over for the last three days... Bella.

Hendrix disappeared up the stairs, and Ethic sought the woman he had agonized over while in police custody.

Ethic saw the silhouette of Alani as she laid on the plush couch. He knew she would be there. She didn't believe in going to bed without him. Even when he wasn't tired, he would have to let her lay beneath him until she fell asleep before he crept back out of the room to finish the remainder of his night. He went to his knees in front of the couch and bowed his head, nudging his way into her space and arousing her out of her slumber.

"Baby," Alani whispered. "Oh my god, I was so scared." Her hormones and relief overwhelmed her, releasing a flood of tears as Ethic wrapped his arms around her. He pulled her from the couch and held her in his arms as she soaked his shoulder.

She was a wreck but just being in his embrace brought her liberation from the sorrow and uncertainty that had plagued the last few days. None of their problems had disappeared, but his presence came with answers. He would know what to do.

"Are you okay?" she asked. "Did they hurt you?"

"I'm okay," he answered. "Stop crying for me, baby."

"I can't. I've been imagining my life without you. What if they have evidence? What if they take you away from us?" Alani had gone over the possibilities repeatedly. They all hurt. Anything other than Ethic's freedom would destroy her.

"Breathe."

She nodded, and he sat there with her in his lap, rocking her like a baby until her breathing calmed.

She kissed his neck.

"I got to talk to you, Lenika," he said.

He was serious, and she dreaded what was to come next because he only called her that when they were at odds. Or when he was solemn.

"I've tried to be the type of husband you want," he paused, choosing careful words. "The type of man you need." He cleared his throat. "But I got to be something else right now. I'ma have to get into something real different than what you're used to, and I need to know you're going to be here when I'm done."

She retreated, leaning back to look into his eyes. She placed his hands on her stomach. "I don't want to raise this baby alone. I don't want to have to stare into your eyes across a visiting room table or with bulletproof glass separating us.

Whatever it takes to keep you here with us is what needs to be done. I give no objections to that. I don't want to think about it or know about it. Just make it home to me."

"Always." It was a promise, and Alani had learned not to trust in men and their words, but Ethic never spoke prematurely. If he couldn't deliver something, the words never graced his lips. "I'ma make up for it all."

"Ethic, you can't make up for it, and I see you every day trying so hard to earn my love, to give me yours. You do everything I would want a man to do, but what you're trying to fix is something that will forever be broken in me. Kenzie was my world, and I know you didn't mean to hurt her, but she's still gone. I can still smell the scent of her hair at night when I close my eyes. She used to climb out of her bed and come sleep with me, so the monsters wouldn't get her," Alani scoffed and flicked away a tear.

"And a monster got her," Ethic said, voice low, shame-filled.

"You're not. I don't know how you're not a monster to me, but you're not," Alani said. "Why don't you ever say her name? Why don't we ever talk about it? About her? Sometimes, I just want to reminisce about when I used to have her. I want to share pieces of those memories with you so you can understand how much I love her."

"It don't feel like my place," Ethic admitted. "You pray for normal shit. For health, for happiness. You thank God for another day when you wake up. I pray for two things. The health of my family and that you don't wake up one day, look in my eyes and decide to leave. I try not to breathe her name, baby, because it's wrong to say it. It's wrong to have you, but damn I want you. And if this goes to court, they gon' say her name every day, and one of those times, it's going to be like the fingertips snapping to break a hypnotist's spell. On that day, you'll walk out, and I'll never see you again."

"Ezra," she gasped.

What kind of way was that to live? The constant anxiety. The anticipating the end.

"I'm going to die with you," she said. "I'm never leaving; even when it's hard, and these last few days were, I'll be right here. I don't know what else I got to do to make you believe that, but trust in me the way I trust in you. It doesn't have to make sense when it feels this good."

He rested against her forehead. Nose to nose. His eyes closed, hers remained opened, examining the texture of his face. Ezra Okafor was a perfectly imperfect man.

"You're my anchor, Ezra, and I feel like I can't talk to you about my baby and she makes up a huge part of who I am. I need to be able to acknowledge that out loud without feeling bad about it," Alani said.

"I'll try. I just try to be respectful, Alani. To her and to you," he said. "I haven't forgiven myself for that night, and somehow this whole thing, the arrest, the trial, if they find me guilty, it seems like the only thing that will give you the justice you deserve as her mother because you are still a victim in this. I hurt you."

"And you heal me," she added. "Come on. I know you're starving, and you haven't showered in days. I'll run you a bath and fix you food."

"Fuck the food," he said.

He stood and grabbed her hand, helping her up before leading her up to their room. He ran a bath, adding bubbles and bath salts, and then helped her into the oversized tub. His undressing was her undoing. She blushed every time because Ethic was a god. His body. His dick. He was just made to fuck women. Strong. Black. He was endowed to a heritage of royalty that was proven not just in the glorious dick he served but in the heart he gave to his family. He took responsibility for everyone under his care. He made them feel safe.

"I can't even count the ways I love you anymore, Ethic," she said. He lowered into the water, sitting across from her and taking siege of her ankles and placing them on his chest. He rubbed just the right spot.

"Four more weeks," he said. They had been bathing once a week together as they counted down until their baby's arrival. "We almost there." Instead of smiling this time, she frowned, concern wearing her, ruining her moment. She had wished this pregnancy would speed up many times; now, she wanted to slow it down. Too much was in the way of them and the finish line. She didn't want to finish this race by herself.

"Stop worrying. I said I'ma be here. You spoke to Zya?"

"I did. She sent the lawyer. I was expecting her to come to court. I'm not sure why she wasn't there."

"The day you see Zya in a courtroom, we're all in trouble," Ethic said. "If I'm ever not here, you call her. Only if the need is great. You understand?"

Alani nodded.

"About the other charge, Ethic? I know where you come from and what you've done in the past, but that's your past. You aren't still in the streets, are you?"

"What do your eyes tell you, Lenika?" he asked. "I'm here with you. Every day. I'm present. Ain't no late nights. No runs. I'm legitimate. They won't find anything that leads back to me. They can't prove these kingpin charges they're trying to stick me with."

Alani moved across the water and sat between his legs, her back to his chest. His hands found their rightful place. His seed was growing, and he rubbed her belly with such care that Alani released a soft sigh. She prayed he was right, but her gut was telling her something different. She anticipated the worst because her intuition never lied.

Hendrix sat at the foot of Bella's bed. Her breathing was so light he questioned if her chest was moving at all. She was the prettiest girl he had ever seen. He didn't know what it was about her. He had seen badder, had fucked sexier, he had definitely been with more experienced girls than Bella. Still, this baby-faced beauty with her standards and her intellect completely unraveled him. She had no idea how he prepared when they would spend time together. Henny made sure he followed her social media posts to see what her monthly book choice was so that he could secretly read it too. He just wanted to have something to talk about with her. He wanted her to believe they were on the same page, like they had a lot in common. He hated it at first, flipping through pages, speed-reading just to get through it and be able to mention a few points, but he eventually fell in love with those pages because in the creases of those books was where Bella's deepest secrets dwelled. The parts that made her laugh, the ones that made her cry, the characters she hated, and the book boyfriends she fell in love with all gave him a roadmap to the rugged landscape of her heart. He had promised her. They had made plans. He was supposed to get to the door, and he had fucked up. There wasn't a doubt in his mind that he was going to jail, and the thing that hurt most was the thought of saying goodbye to Bella Okafor. Henny was trying to be hard. He had zipped up his emotions for three days but, sitting in Bella's dark room with the scent of peonies he had bought her floating from the vase on her nightstand, and the thought of never seeing her again, pulled that zipper south, sending his emotions spilling out. What could he say to her? What could he do? His actions and stupid decisions had already spoken clearly and loudly. He moved closer to the head of the bed and touched her shoulder gently.

"Hey, Boog," he whispered.

She frowned, coming out of her sleep slowly but when he noticed her eyes go wet under the glow of her dimmed lamp, Henny leaned down to kiss her on the cheek. The salty taste of her dried tears against his lips surprised him. She had cried herself to sleep.

"You're out," she said without lifting her head.

"Yeah, Boog, I'm out," he replied.

"Why would you do something so stupid?" She asked. "Scoot over," he said. Bella moved over and Henny pulled the cover up over her body and then laid on top of it. If Ethic came into the room, he wanted it to be clear that nothing was going on. Bella was under the duvet, while Henny was above it. No contact, but he had to be near her. He was willing to risk Ethic's wrath when it came to Bella, but he knew his limits.

He laid beside her.

"What happened, Henny? I thought we had plans," Bella said.

"You have plans. I'm still trying to catch up. Thinking about us ten years from now is easier than actually living what's in front of me every day, Bella. You don't understand cuz yo' daddy got you put up in this big castle, but I'm still in the gutter. I can come here and get away from that when I'm with you. I can make my little money at your daddy's spot. I'm learning from him. I swear I am. Everything he says, I'm like writing the shit down in my head because I know I'm going to need it one day, and you asked me to go to school. I'm doing that too, but between classes, between highlighting chapters, and studying for tests, I've got to make some real money. Not no hourly shit either. Do you know how much it cost to go to Clark? Thirty-nine thousand dollars a year, Boog. That's not even counting a place to stay, food, none of that. How you think I'm gon' keep up with that? I know this sounds crazy, but I picked up the work to keep you, and I know you don't like it, so I didn't tell you."

He waited for her reaction, for her anger, because Bella was a little mean-ass when she wanted to be, but all he saw was sadness.

"If I knew you felt pressured by me, I would have never asked you to go away to school with me. I didn't know it would end up like this," she replied. "What if you go to jail?"

"It'll be my fault that I lose you. I don't deserve you, Boog. I never did, low-key. That's why it's so hard to meet you on your level because I'm way beneath you. I'm down at the bottom."

"No, you're not," Bella whispered. "You're one of the best people I know, Hendrix. I'm scared."

"Can I be real with you, Boog?" he asked. They may as well have been sharing lungs because their faces were so close that they recycled oxygen. His nose to hers. Forehead to forehead as they held hands.

"If you can't be real with me, don't say anything at all," Bella answered.

Hendrix's chin gave away his angst as it shuddered. "I'm scared than a mu'fucka too," he said.

"Promise me that no matter what happens, we'll always stick together," Bella said. "I saw what time did to Mo and Messiah."

"Time didn't do that," Hendrix replied. "We're not them, Boog. We'll never be them."

"Promise me that no matter what happens, we'll never become strangers," Bella said.

"On everything, Boog. I promise."

"You're going to break it. Whatever you're promising, you're going to break it because you're going to be dead and dead men can't keep promises. There's a chair and a bed in this room. Picking the bed, you had to know you'd likely die, no?"

Henny sat up quickly as light flooded the room, and Bella scrambled out of her covers, standing on the mattress, running across it, and leaping off as she ran across the room to Ethic.

"Daddy!" She bawled when he received her into his arms.

"My baby," Ethic said, picking her up off her feet.

It was the purest form of love Hendrix had ever seen. He had never felt jealousy over anything before. He didn't covet what others had, even though he had watched others have more than he did his entire life. Henny had never been a hater a day of his young life, but as he looked at Bella and her father, he was envious. Not of Ethic, but of Bella. The love she had from a parent was beautiful, and he wished he had a father to love him that way, to hug him that way. Henny had never been hugged by his father. He didn't even know his father but watching this exchange of devotion made him wish he had one.

"Are you okay?" Bella cried.

"Daddy's fine. Everything's going to be fine," he soothed. Henny knew that Bella believed Ethic. He could practically feel her worry for her father dissipate. It was like magic the way Ethic handled his family. Whatever ailed them, whatever hurt, whatever brought them anxiety, it all went away when Ethic walked into the room. It was like he took on all their pain, just to keep his family happy. Henny had seen it happen time and time again under this roof. From Eazy to Bella, to Morgan, to Alani. Ethic did that for all of them. He silently wished for someone to be that for him.

Boog got no idea how lucky she is, Henny thought.

It almost ripped emotion from his chest as he stood there feeling out of place.

"Get some rest. Henny will be in the basement. You will be in your room. You got me?" Ethic asked.

Bella's nod was enough for Ethic.

Trust.

They were a father and child who had love and trust. Henny was hustling for all that Bella had been born with, and it didn't seem fair. Hendrix Outlaw was just as enamored with Ethic as he was in love with Bella. This family had their problems, but the love they shared had never existed in Henny's world.

Bella turned to Hendrix and hugged him tightly. Hendrix kept his hands up as Bella held him tighter.

"I'm so mad at you, Henny, but I love you. You don't belong in jail. You belong here with us." Bella said it boldly, loudly, so her father could hear it, and Hendrix closed his arms around her back. Ethic flicked his nose in irritation, but Henny couldn't let Bella go as his eyes teared. He gritted his teeth, his jaw tensing as he fought the feeling Bella was giving him. The feeling of consistency, of understanding, of empathy, of friendship. He promised himself right then and there that he would marry her one day, not soon, but one day when he deserved her and when he could take care of her the way her daddy did. Henny would make Bella Okafor his wife. He wondered how she knew that he needed this hug. Had she been able to tell that he was green with envy watching her and Ethic? Did she sense his loneliness?

"A'ight, Bella," Ethic said. "It's late. Get to bed."

Henny let her go and walked out of the room. He and Ethic walked downstairs in silence until they got to the basement. Ethic pulled out the extra linens that Alani kept down there in the closet for him. Ethic tossed a pillow and blanket to Henny.

"Tomorrow, we'll know more," Ethic said. Henny had never heard Ethic sound less than confident. Tonight, there was something more in his tone. Regret. Remorse. Uncertainty. Even with the best of lawyers, Ethic was unsure if Henny would walk. Doom overcast the room and hollowed Hendrix. On many days, he felt wise beyond his years, but today he felt juvenile, like a child that had defied his elders only to find out fat meat was indeed greasy.

Henny sat on the couch. He nodded.

"You ain't got to pretend, OG," Henny said. "I know it ain't looking good, but I'ma get back to her one day, right? They ain't gon' take my whole life from me, are they? I ain't got what she got. I ain't got parents that give a fuck. Nobody cares but her. I just want to make it back one day."

"Somebody cares," Ethic said.

Hendrix watched Ethic walk up the steps and waited to hear the door close before he allowed himself to break. He sniffed away tears that eventually drowned him, coming out in the form of sobs. He was going to jail. Ethic's glimpse of caring proved it. No way would he be this nice after catching Henny in Bella's bed unless he was taking it easy on him. Henny was going away for a long time, and there was nothing Ethic, or anyone else could do but love him through it.

CHAPTER 8

I can't reach Morgan," Aria said. "Have you spoken to Meek or Messiah?"

"They gon' take care of Mo. I got to take care of us. Don't worry about her, Ali. Mo's covered," he said. They had been driving for hours. "I got to find out what the fuck is going on and pick up this bread so our pockets straight until we know what's what," he said. Isa had taken the money from his safe at home, but he never kept much there. It was a hundred thousand max in his possession. The storage unit in Michigan was a no-go. He didn't know enough about the heat on them to pull up there to retrieve what was stashed there. It would be just his luck that the cops would be sitting on it, waiting for him to come. It was the predictable move to make, so instead, he abandoned the money and hit I-75 South. What the police didn't know was that he had storage facilities all the way from Michigan to the tip of Florida, just collecting dust with product inside. As long as Isa had dope, he could make money. As he pulled up to the storage facility, he entered his code and slid through the electric security gates.

"Get out," he said. They hadn't done much speaking. The entire way had been filled with silence as the unknown occupied their thoughts.

Aria climbed out of the car, and Isa unlocked the storage unit.

He pulled the cover from over a lime green and black Yamaha motorcycle, climbing on and starting it.

"What are you doing?" she asked.

"I'm sending you South with the dough. My people down there gon' set you up real nice," he said. "You got the number to the new burner. Only call if it's an emergency. Otherwise wait to hear from me, a'ight?"

"What? You're not coming with me? I'm not going to Miami alone." She was panicked. He could hear her fear.

"I've got to go to Vegas, Ali. The nigga Hak we working with? We into that nigga for a lot of money and ain't no pushing product on our blocks right now. With the police on us, we got to shut all that shit down, but he's going to come looking for us. It ain't no calling time out in this shit. He's gonna want his money. We owe the nigga too much paper to get ghost until shit calms down. He's coming to collect on that and what you think happens when we tell him we ain't got it?" Isa asked.

Aria was terrified. Life was so accelerated with Isa. Everything was fast. Orgasms. Wedding engagements. Shootouts. And now this. Now running. From the law, from the life. The exhilaration that came with being with a man connected to the streets was glorious but this fear, this fear of kissing her man goodbye one night to wake up to news of his demise was absolutely terrifying. It reminded her of those nightmares she had at night. Someone else she had loved had kissed her goodnight only to be gone by morning.

"Isa, my brother can help us. If we have to post up anywhere for a little while, we can go there. He's a big deal in D.C. Nobody's touching us under his protection," Aria said.

"If you want to go home, Ali, go home," Isa answered. "You don't need my permission."

"I want you to come with me," Aria pleaded. Isa avoided eye contact as he began to pull plastic-wrapped bricks of cocaine from oil barrels.

"I don't need your brother. I been with the street shit. I ain't never ran from no wars," Isa said. "Your brother can't do nothing I can't do for you, but I ain't stopping you. If you want to go..."

"I don't want to go!" Aria argued. "But I don't want to run alone either. You're talking about sending me to Miami by myself while you do what? Where are you going? Somebody sent shooters into a dance studio because of this Crew shit. What if they come back and you're not there? What if this Hak person comes and you're gone? Ain't nobody in Miami going to protect me."

"Hak's not coming after you," Isa said.

"How can you promise me that?" Aria asked.

"Because I'm going after him," Isa answered. "I want you in Miami, so you not in the way. So my mind ain't on you. I want you out of sight so I can go crazy, Ali. So I can cut a nigga head off without terrifying you. You scared of monsters, Aria. I got to become a monster, baby, and you can't handle that."

Finally, some truth. When Aria had first met Isa, he was just a fine-ass nigga with some money. She had never imagined the goon that lived inside him. The Crew was different. Reckless.

Mean as hell. Almost inhuman when it came to their murder game, and that part of her man was like standing in front of the boogeyman.

"You want to be down, Ali, but you ain't built for this shit. You want to go on runs with a nigga. You want to be a part of the plan, but you can't. I need bust downs around, and I know you don't like it, but I ain't thinking about them. I ain't fucking with them like that, but they put in good work for a nigga when he need it."

"Fuck them bitches," Aria said, temper flaring. When she got angry, Isa would swear on everything that she grew ten feet. She was the only person in the world who intimidated him.

"You jealous and a nigga love it, but you can't do what they do. You not supposed to. I don't need my bitch in the field with me. I need bitches that I don't give a damn about. That bitch you worried about could get her head blown off right in front of me, and I wouldn't flinch. Wouldn't feel bad. Nothing. The play would remain the same. Y'all not the same."

"But you used to fuck her, Isa!" Aria protested.

"I did. I ain't gon' lie about that. I used to fuck lil' mama good," Isa said.

Aria swung on him, and he wrapped her up, hemming her arms next to her body as he continued to speak. "You dick a bitch down good long enough and sprinkle in some paper, she'll do whatever you want. I ain't fucking her no more, Aria. I fucked her so I could control her, but I was never fucking with her."

Aria was so blown. Hearing the way Isa handled women, the way he thought regarding women. The misogynistic bullshit and toying with emotions for gain had her feeling like she was just another means to an end for him.

"One thing about niggas, they gon' nig," she scoffed, shaking her head. "You playing with these bitches, and you want me to do what?" She challenged. "Watch and root you on? You mindfucking these girls is the same as you cheating; not to mention, it's fucking disgusting."

"She know what it is, and right now, it's just business. Ain't no victims in this shit. It's about the paper, Ali. These bitches got just as much game as these niggas. She knows your position and she gon' respect it as long as I respect it, and I ain't sniffing behind no bitch for no pussy. Only time I'ma fall in some new shit is if it's *with* you, Ali, cuz a nigga dying to see you get that pussy ate up again," he said. "Shit was sexy as fuck, and you wouldn't even let me get none."

Aria knew this was a twisted-ass love affair. She had every reason to take his head off, but instead, she gave in as he kissed her and slid his hand down the front of her leggings.

"You gon' let me get a threesome, Ali? After yo' nigga handle his business? I just want to watch."

"Absolutely, you deserve it, boy," Aria said as she butterflied her legs around his waist. Isa leaned her weight against the hood of the BMW and snatched at her pants, pulling them down.

"Word?" he replied in shock. Aria nodded. "I get wet just thinking about it." She circled her clit and then dipped two fingers inside before glossing his lips with her essence. "See."

"Yeah, a nigga see that," Isa said as he buried himself in her neck. "Give me a reason to stay alive, Ali."

"You just have to let me choose the nigga," Aria said.

Isa pulled away so fast he knocked over one of the barrels sending oil spilling everywhere as bricks of cocaine poured out with it.

"Fuck!" Isa said. "You be on bullshit, Ali!"

"What?" she asked, feigning innocence. "So, wait. No threesome? Cuz I thought you were dying to see it? You just wanna watch, right?"

She snatched up her leggings and slid them back on as Isa fished the bricks out of the oil. He pointed a finger in her direction.

"I'ma fuck you up. You real funny, Ali," Isa said.

"Stupid contests, stupid prizes," she shot back.

Their attitudes filled the storage unit with silence as Aria waited in the passenger seat for Isa to finish loading the product. It wasn't until he was done did they speak.

"I got to go, and you can't come with me, baby," Isa said.

"So why didn't you just leave me behind? I could have stayed in Flint," Aria said, sadness dripping from her voice. It wasn't the fact that he was leaving, it was the fact that she had known all along that he would leave, that this fantasy of a life together was just that— a dream. She had known better than to trust him. Her heart had fought her for loving him. Now, it was breaking.

"Because niggas know how to find you there. If the streets didn't touch you, the police would, and I can't see you handling either without me," Isa said. "You talk tougher than you are. In Miami, you're safe. Shooters are in place, and I'm coming back for you."

"I'll be just as safe in D.C.," Aria said, and I'll know somebody.

"I don't need your people in my business. You go running home and what that look like? You gon' be proving that nigga right. I set us up in Miami. You'll be safe there until I get back. I need you down there, waiting for me, baby. I need something to make it home to."

Aria nodded, reluctantly giving in as he pulled her into his arms.

"Where will you be?" She asked. "How long do I have to sleep without you?"

He remembered her nightmares. The thing they had in common. The only time they achieved peace was next to one another. They had some turmoil-filled days to come because circumstance was separating them.

"The nigga, Hak, has a hotel in Vegas, off the strip in Henderson. I'ma be around those parts," Isa answered truthfully. She was the only person who would know. Not even Meek or Messiah knew the power move he was about to make. "I'ma rob him and then kill him, Ali. When I come back, you ain't got to worry about nothing but spending this money and looking pretty. I'ma take care of you."

"Then you're out? After this, you're out for good?" She asked.

He paused. The game was about more than stacking paper for Isa. It was his kingdom. It was where he held power. He wasn't sure if he'd ever leave the shit alone, but to spare her in the moment, he nodded. "Yeah, Ali, after this, I'm out."

A car's headlights interrupted them, and Aria tensed.

"Relax. It's my people," Isa said. "This is where we part ways."

"What?" Her eyes misted before she could stop them.

"You can't ride with me in a car filled with drugs," he said.

"Isa..."

"Trust me. I know you scared. I know you don't want to go, but trust me," Isa said. One kiss. Then two. Then his tongue invaded her mouth. It was like their last kiss. Aria was too attached, and she hated it. Her heart thundered, aching, bleeding at the thought of the moment their lips parted because she would be heading one way and he would be heading another. He leaned her back on the hood of his car. Neither cared that they had an audience.

"I love you, Isa," she whispered. "Like, for real. Don't die on me."

"A nigga got a girl who love him waiting on him. I don't plan on doing no dying. A lot of killing, no dying, though. Keep that pussy to yourself until I get back. Be good. Save lives," he said.

Aria smiled, and her face warmed. Isa was her headache and her heart. He walked her to the waiting car, and a man with wild hair opened the door.

"What up, bruh bruh?" The man greeted as he met Isa in front of the headlights. They shook like gangsters do.

"Good looking on everything. It's only temporary, but it's necessary," Isa said.

"You know y'all solid down our way. She's in safe hands."

"Ali, this my nigga, Miami Mo. He gon' take you to my spot in his city. It's on the water. When you get there, enjoy yourself. Spend a little money. Do a little dancing. Get out in the sun. Get ya homie, Nick, down there with you or something so you won't be bored. I'ma catch up with you, a'ight?" Isa said.

Aria nodded. "Yeah, okay." She was still so unsure, but this was happening whether she wanted it to or not.

"Don't forget your clothes," Isa said as he passed her the duffel full of money.

Aria nodded, and he tucked her into the passenger side of the car.

"I'ma call you when I make it."

CHAPTER 9

Messiah knew it was a risk going back to the city, but if he left without speaking to Morgan, without explaining, a second time, there would be no coming back from the abandonment she would feel. Even in the tumultuous state of their relationship— or lack thereof— he couldn't just blow town. He owed explanations and not only to Morgan. If he left without giving Bleu a heads up, he feared even she would give up on him as well. And if Ethic didn't hear from him at all, he would assume the worst. Messiah could barely see out of the one eye that wasn't swollen shut as he maneuvered the steering wheel with one hand because the other wrist felt broken. His entire left shoulder felt like it was dislocated; at least, that's what the pain was telling him. It was blinding, radiating through his entire body, threatening to shut him down. Somehow, he found his way. He couldn't even fathom how he had gotten himself all the way back to Flint, but he threw the car in park right in front of Bleu's house. He was so beaten he laid on the horn. He was too injured to climb out, so he popped open the door and put one foot on concrete while gripping the steering wheel. The police had done a number on him, and he hadn't slept for days. He needed a minute to make it to her front door. "Messiah?"

Bleu's voice was near. He heard her front door slam as she came out onto the porch, and within seconds, he felt her hands on his face, lifting his bowed head. "Oh my god! What did they do to you?" She said, voice trembling. "I'm good, B," he groaned.

"You're not good," she protested as she helped him from the car. He threw one arm around her shoulder, and she put an arm around his back as they struggled across the lawn and into her house.

There was no making it upstairs. He found the couch and flopped down on it, crying out in excruciating pain.

"The police did this to you?" She asked frantically as she rushed to the kitchen for ice. She came back and kneeled before him. "Perks of having a boy. You always have a first aid kit handy," she said softly. She took the ice pack and placed it to his swollen eye.

"Where my kids, B?" "Morgan came to get them, Messiah," Bleu said. He was silent. Uncomfortably so, as if he didn't know how to react to the news of them being gone. Did he miss them? Before three days ago, he hadn't even known they were his to miss. Now them being away felt unbearable. A sudden attachment put disappointment in his heart at the revelation that they weren't within arm's reach.

"That's probably better anyway. I had them for a few hours, and the fucking police ran in my crib. Were they fucked up? Did I fuck them up? I should have never taken 'em. I don't know what the fuck I was thinking. I just spazzed so hard when she told me. Like they mine. I don't even know how I didn't feel the shit before when homie told me his name. Messari..." He shook his head as Bleu cleaned up his cuts and bruises. "...and Yara," he whispered. "He's so damn bad, man, and Yara. She's beautiful. I've never seen a more perfect human being. She's deaf, B. My daughter's deaf." He bitched up at the thought of that. He had so many questions. Was she born that way, or had something happened? Was she in a special school that taught her to sign? Had there been surgeries? Had major decisions about her care been made in his absence? Or was it just hereditary? Messiah lacked so much information, but he wanted to know it all.

"They're beautiful, Messiah," Bleu said, her tone soft, but it held pain.

"What shorty say? I know she was on her bullshit, probably got my kids laid up in that fucking castle with that bitch-ass nigga she running around here gaming."

"Mo had a lot to say, actually, but nothing bad about you. She seemed scared. Worried," Bleu said. "And pissed off that I had her kids."

"They not just her kids," Messiah said. "Now she knows how the fuck I feel. Having them around these niggas."

Bleu withdrew her hand. "So, is that what this was? You called me to your house to help with them so you could play tit for tat with Morgan? You wanted to make her mad by having her kids around another woman?"

Messiah realized his misstep too late. The look of disgust on Bleu's face was a mixture of confusion, disbelief, and aching he had never seen before.

"No, B. It ain't never like that with you," he answered truthfully. "I'm just saying she ain't got no room to be mad at you for having them."

Bleu sighed. "This is exhausting, Messiah. I'm literally burnt out. You hurt me so bad, and I don't even think you realize that you're doing it."

She handed him the ice pack and went to stand, but he pulled her back. "Whoa, hol' up. What u mean, B? Cuz I ain't never with that. The hurting you is a no-go."

"Don't worry about it," she replied. She dismissed her feelings. This was the routine. Always catering to him and disregarding what she felt. Bleu put all of Messiah's burdens on her back. Every time. Whenever he crossed her threshold, whenever he climbed in her bed, whenever she woke up to him on Saviour's floor or her couch, she took on the responsibility of his care. Caring for him. Loving him. Being his friend. No matter what fucked-up shit he did. And yes, he did the same for her, but she appreciated him, she showed him her appreciation all the time, every day, while Messiah took Bleu for granted. She was tired.

She tried to move again, and he pulled her back.

"I'm worrying about it, shorty, so start talking."

"I'm the last person you have to worry about. This is the last thing you should be thinking about. You already have so much on your shoulders. Why did they arrest you? What's going on?" Bleu asked. She was the queen of deflection. Whenever Messiah got too intense, she switched the focus to avoid the elephant in the room. Lately, they had been more intense than ever before. Avoidance could only last so long.

"It's a lot, B. You know the rules. Crew rules say we disappear when we come up on police radar. Isa and Meek already in the wind," Messiah said.

"Wow. Meek left?" she asked.

Messiah nodded but didn't speak. He knew what she didn't say. *Meek left without Mo?* That's what she wanted to say. That's what he wanted to ask when he had seen Meek. He didn't know what it meant, and at the moment, he didn't care. Morgan and her betrayal, her plot to conceal his children, and the sting in his eyes that came whenever he thought of Bash raising them... made him not give a fuck about Morgan Atkins... or it made him care so much that this disappointment turned him bitter. He didn't quite know which one yet. Messiah was always thrown into a fire, forced to feel everything at once. Shock was usurped by deceit, and that was stolen by overwhelm, which was replaced by confusion, then fear. He had felt all these things back-to-back in a three-day time frame, and Messiah just wanted to put it all down, just for a moment.

"And you're leaving?" Bleu asked.

"A nigga back against the wall," Messiah said. "I can't give them what they want me to give them in exchange for my freedom."

"Which is what?" Bleu asked.

"Ethic," Messiah answered.

Bleu sighed because she knew if Messiah had to choose to sacrifice himself or honor his mentor, he would fall on that blade every time. That's how deep his love ran for the Okafor's.

"I know you love them, Messiah, but when is someone going to sacrifice to make sure you're okay? That's all I care about. You being okay," Bleu said.

She took the ice pack from his hands and held it in place for him.

"I'm going to miss you," Bleu whispered. He examined her, staring deep, past the outside and into her soul. He knew her well, had taken the time to learn the languages she didn't speak verbally. She tenderly traced his face with her finger, touching his bruises lightly. Messiah felt those touches all over his body, so much so that he tensed to stop the ticklish sensation. His dick firmed, and the spit in his mouth became hard to swallow as she brought her face close to his eye. "This is bad. You might need stitches," she whispered. She reached for the first aid kit and removed peroxide, cotton balls, and Band-Aids. "A fist did this?" She asked. "It's deep."

"A gun," Messiah corrected.

Bleu's eyes fucking teared. She didn't know how much more she could take. Seeing the agony he was going through. His mental was beaten, his body had been through hell, his heart drug through the mud, and now the police.

"Hey," he said, taking the stuff from her hands. "I'm good."

She nodded. She was struggling to plug this hole in her emotions, so she was nodding, but the tears weren't stopping. She sat there bobbling like a fucking bobblehead, unable to look at him, unable to get control of herself because she was so damn bruised. From the twins reminding her of their dead son to him being snatched in the middle of the night by the cops to the thought of him disappearing before her eyes again. Bleu hadn't slept since his arrest, and her heart felt like it had been torn out. Bleu was worn. She was worn like somebody's favorite shirt. Messiah had tried her on again and again, not really caring to follow the instructions on the tag because it was just a throw-around garment that he would reach for whenever he needed to, tossing it in the corner when it wasn't suitable enough for a special occasion. Meanwhile, he treated Morgan like designer, hanging her carefully, washing her delicately, making sure to treat it with concern so that it would last. Bleu was ragged. She was his favorite, maybe, but not his most prized, and her soul was injured.

"Yo, B, these tears ain't it," he said softly. His hand to the side of her face only made her cry harder.

"I'm sorry," she sniffled, wiping her eyes. "You got to go, Messiah. If you're going to leave just leave already. Just stop coming back and just go." She made it halfway across the living room before Messiah caught her hand, pulling her into him.

"Stop fucking running from me, B. Stop acting like everybody else. We don't do that. That ain't even how we get down. So just talk. Say what's in your fucking head cuz I ain't no mind reader," Messiah barked.

Bleu pushed him. "Get out my face, Messiah!"

"Fuck, B!" Messiah shouted, feeling the blow reverberate throughout his body.

Bleu's glossy eyes softened his temperament. She was so fucking strong. Delicate and beautiful but strong. The way her bottom lip trembled made Messiah pull it into his mouth, kissing her. He felt her entire body shudder as he pulled back.

"What are we doing?" She asked.Messiah lingered there for what felt like forever. His eyes on hers, and then the space between their lips closed again. He wasn't sure if he kissed her or if she kissed him; all he knew was that she tasted like caramel candy, the kind the school counselors used to have on their desks on the days he did go to school and got sent to the principal's office for fighting.

The kiss was slow, timid, like Bleu would stop it at any second, so he kept her pace because he knew she was scared. Hell, so was he, but the storm in his chest, banging the shutters of his heart, the lightning striking, the rain pouring inside of him, had to stop itself because Messiah hadn't felt this alive in years. It was the way Bleu kissed him that kept him pulled in. The way she sucked on his tongue made him feel like she was sucking dick and Messiah's body was begging him to go further. He had never been kissed with such need. Bleu was swallowing his soul. He felt it lifting out of the darkest corner of his heart and transferring to her with every intrusion of her tongue. A conqueror. Bleu was a conqueror of men. Her vibe was unmatched, and since the day they had crossed the line, Messiah had craved this very taste on his tongue. Her flavor was like a specialty that you could only get once a year when you vacationed to your favorite place. Like Mackinaw Island fudge. You had to drive four hours North and pass an entire lake to the upper peninsula to get that shit. It took effort to get a piece of that shit. Bleu was like that, except she tasted better. He wasn't even with the kissing shit with most women. He had kissed a few, enough to know that it wasn't his thing. The spit swapping, the not knowing where women had been with their mouths, turned him off. Except with Morgan. He had kissed her for hours, and now, with Bleu, he could stay here doing this shit all day. Messiah pulled Bleu's body closer, pressing her into his need. Damn, how he needed her. She felt it. He did too. Incredible hunger between a man and a woman. Messiah wanted to lay Bleu down, right there in the middle of her living room. Through all the pain, both emotional and physical, he wanted to feel something more. He wanted to fuck her, and the way her tongue hungrily filled his mouth, he knew she would oblige. He remembered the last time. He recalled it often. Messiah had played that shit back in his head like a game-day tape. The shit had been phenomenal. She was wetter than any woman he had ever had, and he had been with more than a few. Bleu had something between her legs that made niggas shoot it out over her, fuck a fair one. He couldn't believe she was offering her body to him again. He had chalked it up to a one-time event between friends who were reacting to extraordinary circumstances, but this was different. This repeat would hold some significance. She would let him get it. He knew it, but he couldn't take it, however. Even though he wanted it bad as fuck, he couldn't lay Bleu down again. He took this moment for what it was because he was unsure if she wanted more. Hell, did he? He pulled back, but their foreheads pressed together as heavy breathing filled the space between them.

"Open your eyes, B," he said.

"This is a mistake, Messiah," she replied, frowning.

"Is it?" he asked. "Yeah," she gasped. "You'll do this because you're vulnerable right now. You only come here when you can't have her. So yes, this is a mistake. You should have let me leave with Iman, Messiah. You're so fucking selfish."

He disconnected this time. Her anger threw him off. Every time he put pressure on Bleu, she pulled back.

"You know what I think, B? I think you use Mo as an excuse to turn a nigga away. You don't know what the fuck I'd do because you always put the brakes on. You take away my options cuz you pussy," Messiah said.

"Or maybe I just know you won't choose me!" Bleu shouted.

"Fuck you talking about? I choose you every time I come over this mu'fucka when I got other shit I could be doing!" He barked back. "Messiah, can you change my furnace filter? Messiah, my tires need rotating! Messiah, I hear noises in the basement! Messiah, can you come to my meetings? I pull up eer'time, so don't act like them ain't choices!"

"You're right. We've blurred a lot of lines, and if you hadn't gotten sick, we would never have slept together. None of this would even be an issue. Sex complicated us and I just want to make it uncomplicated again because this is too much for me. When I saw Morgan, I was jealous of her, Messiah. Me. Jealous of a fucking 21-year-old girl!" Bleu said it like it was ludicrous. "Envious, not because she's better than me, smarter, classier, more capable, but because she has the attention of your rock-head-ass."

"Fuck you, dawg," Messiah mumbled, sucking his teeth at the insult and staring off because Bleu was on some bullshit. "You ain't got shit to be jealous of, shorty."

"I've never been anything but supportive of you and her and now this gray area makes me feel like I'm in competition with her, and it's a competition I can't win, so stop asking me to play myself!" Bleu shouted.

"It ain't no competition. There's you, and there's her. It's separate. Before the shit with you on the beach, I never even thought to look at you like that, B. Like, I saw you, don't get me wrong. You're fucking everything. You're beautiful, and I don' ran off plenty niggas who don't deserve you, but I wasn't trying to slide on it," Messiah explained.

He hated to even do that. He had never been the type to run down the reasons why he moved the way he did. He had said fuck it to many who chose to misunderstand his logic, but for Bleu, he was airing it all out.

"Because I wasn't good enough. You met me at my worst, and you've looked at me that way ever since that day," Bleu said.

It pained Messiah that Bleu thought that. It was the worst of her that he appreciated most. Her imperfections made her the same as him. Her wins gave him hope that the possibility for him to win existed.

"That's bullshit; ain't nobody holding that shit against you. I just wasn't supposed to be on it like that with you," Messiah said.

"Why?" Bleu asked. "I've seen you with plenty of women before Morgan. You would go out with them in public and then come here to chill at night. Like you didn't want to be seen with me. Like I wasn't good enough, and some of them I couldn't even understand what you saw in them!"

"Nothing! I ain't see shit! I was just fucking them girls, man, it wasn't like that," Messiah defended. "I ain't even know you was paying attention."

"Of course, I paid attention, Messiah!" She shouted. This was a lot of back and forth between best friends. If they were comfortable lying to themselves before, they could no longer hide behind ignorance now. They were too passionate about one another to call themselves just friends. Neither knew where they stood with the other, but they knew they had passed the friend exit two years ago on that beach.

"You weren't mine, B! You belong to Noah and I ain't been able to shake that shit since. I know he gone, but the way you love that nigga, man. I can't follow him up! I'ma fuck that up every time! He was the type of man you deserve. I ain't half as good. I just wanted to protect you, like he was supposed to. I respect you, and I love you, and Noah left, and I just wanted you to be good. Good like you were when you were with him, and you started looking at me the way you looked at him and the shit felt like something I needed. You know? Like natural. Like water. I ain't know love back then. I ain't know what it looked like, what it felt like, what it spoke like, none of that. Fucking with Mo made me realize I felt it before. In my friend, B. You gave me a lot of love over the years, and if I was a better man, I would have recognized it sooner, but I couldn't. I'm fucked up, and I couldn't see it. I never thought I was good enough for you, Bleu. That's the truth. It wasn't never because you came second. There ain't no seconds; it's just two girls that I care for in different ways, but I ain't fucking with that no more over there. The shit Mo be pulling is unforgivable," he said. "So, if that's your excuse, that ain't a good enough reason to run scared. I can't even look at her right now, man."

"And that's why you're here," Bleu said, sadly. "Because you're mad at her. It has nothing to do with you actually wanting to be in this space with me. Let me ask you something, Messiah. You're leaving. I can guarantee you I'm not your last stop. Where you going when you leave here?"

His silence was his admission.

He blew out a breath of frustration and took a step back.

"It ain't like that," he said.

"It's exactly like that," Bleu said. It was her tone that crushed him. It was like he deflated her.

"You should get some rest. I can tell you haven't slept. If you're going to get on the road, you should sleep first. You know where the guest room is."

Bleu walked by him, and Messiah felt like he was suffocating.

"That's it? End of conversation?" Messiah asked.

"End of confusion," she said. "I don't want to lose my friend, and giving in to anything that makes me a threat to Morgan makes me lose you. Eventually, that's where you're going to end up, and I don't want her to have the power or a reason to take you away from me. So, I just want my friend."

"If I knew the last touch was gon' be the last touch, I would have put my lips somewhere else," Messiah said.

Mannish. This nigga was hella mannish, and Bleu was taken so off guard that she blushed.

"Just friends, though, right?" He was making sure, giving her one last chance to make a different choice.

She nodded. "Make sure you tell me goodbye before you leave this time. You just left last time, and it ruined me," Bleu said. "All this shit, all the hurt, the confusion, all the things you came back to repair... it was a mess you made. You're just cleaning up your own shit, so stop blaming everybody else."

She walked upstairs, leaving Messiah alone with his thoughts. His mind was blown because the boundaries she had put up felt unnatural. Maybe he and Bleu had done too much. Maybe once lines were crossed, you couldn't backtrack. Messiah wasn't sure where they stood, and for the first time since meeting her, he wondered if he had placed her in the wrong position in his life.

CHAPTER 10

Morgan heard her babies in her mind but opening her eyes was impossible. She was so damn tired. Groggy. Her head felt foggy, like she was driving through an empty city block at dawn after a cold rain and her headlights were out.

"Why won't her wake up?" Messari asked.

"She's just really sleepy, kiddo," Bash answered.

Morgan groaned as she felt little fingers touching her eyelids, lifting them, forcing her eyes open. Yolly came into vision and then disappeared as she felt her daughter's fingers release her eyelid.

"I'm going to be sick," she groaned.

"Why don't you take Yolly downstairs to find Ms. Christi? It's snack time for you two," Bash said, referring to his mother.

"No," Morgan said. She tried to push up from the bed, but her arms felt weak like they would break if she put too much weight on them. The room felt like it was upside down, and she couldn't determine which way was up. Even the sun peeking through the blinds felt like knives as it met her eyes. "Ssari, baby, get Yolly and come to me. Come to me, Messari!" Morgan said weakly, reaching for her son.

"Come on, bud, let's go," Bash said.

"No, Messari, get over here with Mommy. Now! Get your sister and come here!" Morgan said with as much urgency as she could muster.

Messari's eyes welled, thinking he was in trouble, and Bash intervened. "It's okay. Mommy's just tired. Come on. Let's give her some time to rest." Morgan imagined the worst when he walked out of the room with her kids. Her entire body ached, and when she pulled back the sheets, the red marks on her thighs made her sob uncontrollably. Morgan felt like she would be sick. He returned without the twins, and Morgan struggled to her feet.

"What did you give me?" Her accusation was laced with disbelief and resentment.

"Sit down, Mo," Bash said. "You just need to calm down and sleep it off."

This nigga drugged me, she thought.

He went to touch her, and Morgan almost took his head off.

"Don't fucking touch me!" She shouted, swinging, fighting him. He absorbed a weak jab and took a step back, gritting his teeth as Morgan's legs screamed *enough*, forcing her to sit. She cried so hard she couldn't breathe. *This can't be happening.* Morgan felt violated. He hadn't needed to be violent to rape her soul. Her body felt different. Invaded. She hated that it was something she had felt before. Morgan had never thought she would be taken advantage of again. Not now. She had a voice, she could speak, she could say no, and the anger inside her was fuel for her to fight anyone who dared think the thought. Somehow, Bash still had. *He did, right?* He was acting so blasé about it that she questioned if she was losing her mind.

"You need to calm down before you scare the twins," Bash said.

Morgan shook her head, scoffing. This nigga had the audacity to talk about preventing fear when he had shaken her to her core. The mention of them made her close her eyes and lower her chin to her chest. Morgan was ashamed. Ashamed of last night. Ashamed of putting herself in a position where she felt trapped and her children were in jeopardy.

"You aren't a victim, Mo. We had a good time last night. It doesn't have to be bad. I think I know what went wrong with us. I let you behave like a friend while I behaved like your man. It's time for you to act like my woman," Bash said.

"I said no and you took it anyway." Morgan felt like ants were crawling all over her body. She was so disgusted.

"No? You never said no, Mo," he replied. Morgan frowned in confusion. He spoke with such conviction that her judgment clouded. She remembered saying no. She remembered fighting. *I said no. I would never say yes to him. I fought this time. God, did I?*

Dread filled her. He had all the power, and Morgan had none. She couldn't clear her mind enough to know what was real and what was fake. Bash was changing the narrative.

"Can I please have my babies?" She cried. "Please, Bash. I just really need them."

Bash paused at the door and looked back at her. There was pity in his stare, sympathy, and a bit of remorse.

He walked out without saying a word.

"You talked to Mo?" Ethic asked as he looked at his phone.

"Not since court. Why?" Alani replied.

"She's not answering my calls, and I want her and the twins home for a little while until I can figure out what's going on," he said. "I got a feeling shits going to get worse before it gets better, and I don't need them out of my possession."

"Well, she's with Bash if that makes you feel any better," Alani said. "She's not with Messiah or Ahmeek, so for once Bash and his squareness helps. It doesn't get more removed from the streets than him."

Ethic nodded. "Yeah, maybe you're right," Ethic said. "Corny nigga won't have a target on his back from any of this."

Ethic had no idea the enemies that lurked in close proximity, hidden by the shadows of improbability.

"I'll go by though if that makes you feel better," Alani said.

Ethic shook his head as he lifted from their bed, stepping into denim jeans and tossing on a tapered, fitted, V-neck, white t-shirt that cost more than some people's rent.

"I don't want you to do anything but stay right here in this bed and rest. Matter fact, I want you on the phone spending my money on the most expensive gender reveal you can plan in a week," he said.

"Wait, what?" She asked, smiling. "The baby is almost here. You can wait four more weeks."

It was the smile on her face for Ethic. That smile was the one he would freeze in his mind if prison ever separated them. It was the glow of her skin, the width of her lips as they parted with her grin, and the pull of the corners of her eyes that would bring light to the dark days that he silently feared were near. If he ever had to spend time in a cell, this image of her, with messy hair, life growing inside her, and this smile would be the poster he hung in his head. God had created women exactly like this for them to be the object of man's affection.

"I can't," he replied. "So, start planning." He reached for the nightstand where his wallet laid and pulled out a platinum Amex then placed it on the bed. "Get to work, Mrs. Okafor. Get your midwife over here to help you or something." He left her mind in a good place as he walked out the door, praying he would return.

Messiah sat inside of the funeral home, staring around in disbelief as he sat on the countertop of the receptionist's desk. It was a humble piece of the rebuilding of his life. It was the first thing he had put back together since his return and he couldn't even be happy about it because the girl he had done it for had switched up on him. He watched Ethic walk into the building, and he hopped down, opting to remain across the room.

"They did you bad," Ethic stated.

"It's a part of the game. Cops hate niggas. Niggas hate cops," Messiah replied.

"You weren't arraigned," Ethic said.

Messiah shook his head. "I know you got every reason not to trust me, but…"

"I only need one reason to trust you," Ethic said, cutting him off. "You're family, Messiah. That old shit is old shit. We gon' leave it there. I know the games cops play to bring down organizations. I also know I taught you to listen twice as much as you speak. So, what you hear? While they were interrogating you, what did they say?"

"They said a lot, OG. They got bodies. Niggas I dropped, the nigga, Lucas, and the little girl," Messiah said.

Ethic was unmoved by every word except the last two. Messiah saw the shift. It was clear as day. Talking about murder was something Ethic was immune to, but talking about that one murder, the one that permanently dwelled in his mind, that one was an affliction. "I don't know how but they know. I'm not sure what kind of proof they got but I wasn't careful with one of 'em. I beat the nigga who raped Mo to death. It won't be hard to put DNA on a nigga and send me away for life. If I don't give them something on you, they gon' take me away from my kids."

"Where the fuck is this shit coming from?" Ethic asked. Messiah knew better than to answer. Ethic was questioning twenty years' worth of moves, running back the game tape to figure out who he had left alive that had come back to haunt him.

"I got to leave again, man, and it's gon' kill me this time," Messiah said. "If I don't leave..."

"I'ma bring you back, Messiah," Ethic said, voice solemn. "You just met your kids. I'ma make sure you make it back to them."

"I asked you to deliver a message to Mo last time. You didn't owe me shit, and I'm sure you didn't tell her, but OG, this time, I'm leaving for you. I'm leaving because the only other option is to give you up, and as much as I love shorty, I ain't loved her as long as I fucked with you. Tell her I didn't leave by choice this time and them babies, man," Messiah paused and flicked his nose as he sniffed away emotion. "We got a lot of shit wrong between us, but that's the one thing we did right. Them bad mu'fuckas are beautiful, man. Tell her thank you."

Ethic and Messiah stood there, staring at one another for a beat. They were two, traumatized, Black men trying their best to make life livable. Ethic had found his way. Messiah was still lost.

"Tell her yourself," Ethic said. Messiah's confusion wasn't missed. He understood the rules. He had played his position long enough to know that the king had to be protected. Everybody else on the board was sacrificial except the king and the queen— Messiah included.

"You've missed a lot of time, Messiah. I won't ask you to miss more. If this goes bad, I'ma need you in place with my family. You get your head on straight so you can be right for your kids, and so I can count on your gun if I'm ever not around to protect the people I love," Ethic said.

"They gon' lock you up, man," Messiah said.

"Maybe," Ethic answered. "But if I'm going to go away for this... if they gon' lock me up... I need you to stop living in the chains your mind put on you. Stop being a slave to your past, Messiah. I can't be in there if you not really free, cuz you gon' fuck it up out here. Find somebody to talk to. Somebody for real. Somebody, you don't know."

"I ain't crazy, Big Homie, I don't need no shrink," Messiah said.

"And that's where the problem lies. Grown men dealing with trauma we can't handle and giving the shit to the women we love like they the ones supposed to fix it. That's why you hurt her, Messiah. That's why you'll keep hurting her. That's why the nigga, Meek, got her questioning where she supposed to be. Got her thinking she should just stay put with somebody she don't even love rather than choose between you and him."

"The choice shouldn't be that hard for shorty. We was different. She forgot how it felt when it was good," Messiah said, resentment lacing his heart and tone.

"Because your love comes with a lot of bullshit, a lot of pain. Mo got her own shit mentally, emotionally. All women do, but we're men. Men got to lead. Men got to protect. How she gon' know it's safe to let you back in if she don't see that you're different? How she gon' heal if you constantly re-injuring her? New hurt open up the old shit, and ever since you been back, it's been turmoil between you and her. You got to heal your shit. The abuse, the insecurities in your manhood..."

"Ain't no insecurities in my shit. I'm good." Messiah was defensive; his entire countenance changed, hardening as he held up his head slightly, arrogantly.

"Are you?" Ethic challenged. "Because I wouldn't be. Years of molestation, of beatings, of mental manipulation as a kid. You couldn't defend yourself, couldn't ask for help. No man would be secure with that until he addresses it. Until he understands that those weren't choices he made but a hell that was placed on him. You couldn't help that part, Messiah, and you don't have to prove shit to yourself. You can let go of the anger. That's why you are the way you are. Short-tempered, dangerously aggressive, reactive. Just put the shit down. Find somebody to talk to, and I guarantee you all the rest will start to fall in place. It's a lot of shit I can mediate between you and Mo if I'm free, but if I'm not, you're going to lose her. Don't depend on me, Messiah. Fix your shit. When you let all that shit out, you'll be able to figure out how to get your family back."

Messiah nodded and bit into his bottom lip hard before lowering his head as Ethic took a step into his space. Messiah's head hit Ethic's shoulder in disgrace. These boys that Ethic had somehow attracted over the years weren't just workers. They weren't just hustlers. They were more than soldiers. They had become reflections of him. Younger versions of Black men who had followed his path because it was the only example he had set. To be a kingpin. To be the boss. To sell dope. He silently blamed himself for giving them such a low bar to aspire to. He wondered if he was to blame for Messiah's troubles and Henny's brush with the law. He had tried to show Messiah how to navigate the streets smart, and for the most part, Messiah had mastered that life, but could there have been other lessons besides street code and money? Should Ethic have taught him about compassion? About forgiveness? About accountability? About masculinity and aggression? Ethic had missed a lot. He had withheld a lot, not because he didn't want to teach Messiah but because he didn't know. No one had shown Ezra how to navigate through manhood, so he made mistakes along the way as well. He hadn't been fit to be anybody's teacher, or so he thought. Standing there with a damaged Messiah, embracing him like he would his son, told Ethic he hadn't helped Messiah enough. If Eazy ever needed this type of affection, Ethic knew to be there, but Messiah hadn't had anyone. Ethic understood his trauma. A man so badly wounded didn't hurt others on purpose. It was all Messiah knew. Ethic pulled away and walked out without saying another word. They both knew that one of them had to fall on the sword. Ethic had already decided who it would be. Sometimes, the king had to concede to save the kingdom.

CHAPTER 11

Morgan sat in the clawfoot tub. She had soaked and drained the water three times, scrubbing her skin with the loofah so hard that it left red marks behind. Morgan had been in and out of a drug-induced sleep for two days. Whatever Bash had given her had tranquilized Morgan. Every time she awoke, she felt like her body had been misused. Morgan was a young woman whose intuition spoke a language of its own. In her silent years, it spoke loudest, and today, it told her that Bash had been inside her more than once. So, she scrubbed. She remembered a time when Messiah had been there to wash away her pain. He was gone now, and she feared she would forever feel unclean.

She stood and wrapped her body in a towel as she left puddles on the floor with every footstep. She stared into blank eyes as she looked in the mirror. She opened her towel, and the sight of her body made her stifle sobs.

I have to get my kids out of here, she thought.

Morgan plugged every emotional hole that she had, frantically wiping tears and clenching teeth with so much pressure they hurt.

She dressed, throwing on a sweatsuit and sneakers, underdressed for the standards of Morgan Atkins, but she looked the way that she felt. She rushed to the guest room where her twins slept and sighed in relief when she saw them sleeping soundly in their beds.

"Thank God," she whispered.

"I wouldn't hurt them."

Bash's voice sent Morgan out of her skin as he appeared behind her.

"Let them get their sleep. Come down for breakfast. We need to talk," he said.

"Have you seen my phone? I need it. I'm sure Ethic has called by now." Her voice trembled. Morgan hadn't been this intimidated since she was a child. Mizan would flip his switch between hot and cold in this same way. One moment he would be endearing, and the next, he would be slapping her sister into a wall.

Morgan didn't know which version of Bash she would get, and it pulled her right back to the most terrifying moments of her life. Trapped. Morgan was trapped. A moth to a flame, just like Raven Atkins had been.

"You'll get it back when we come to an understanding."

Morgan reluctantly left the room and walked down to the formal credenza where Christiana sat sipping from a crystal teacup. The room used to be one of Morgan's favorite places in the home. The way the sun came through the floor-to-ceiling glass windows and the dome of glass that formed the top made it feel like a place where she could come to reflect and grow. The flowers and open air just made Morgan feel like there was life in this massive mansion. Every other room felt like a museum, but this one felt peaceful. Today, it felt like a prison cell, like that one window in a cell that showed you an outside that you could never get to.

"I have good news; the wedding is in a month," Christiana said. "I was able to get St. Etheldreda's Cathedral to give us a quaint Sunday after service."

"I won't get married without Ethic," Morgan said. Morgan knew that resisting at this point would only make them treat her worse. She would have to play their game and figure out the rules to manipulate them to her advantage. She was shaking. She was so upset, and she wrung her fingers together as Christiana stared a hole through her.

"So, what do you have to do to make that happen?" Christiana asked. Morgan felt like she was selling her soul to the devil. "Sit."

She took the chair across from Christiana, and Bash cleared his throat.

"I'm going to give you both a minute. The twins will be waking up soon. I'll have the staff prepare breakfast. Chocolate chip pancakes for you, right, Mo?" He asked. She shook her head, unable to look his way. "I'm not hungry," she answered.

"Give us some time, Sebastian," Christiana said.

When they were alone, Morgan stared at Christiana in disgust. "Why are you doing this?" Morgan asked.

"Morgan, I will protect my son at all costs. Your children are still young, so I don't expect you to understand. One day you will do something that blurs lines to make sure your children's needs are met." "And I'm a need," Morgan said, scoffing in disgust. "Was Allison a need?"

It was like all the sun in the room had been sucked out the way Christiana went cold.

Morgan had hit a nerve.

"Who's Alli, Christiana?" Morgan asked.

Her heart had never beat this hard before. Morgan felt it in her bones that she didn't want to know the answer to that question, but she couldn't stop herself from asking. She had heard it subconsciously in her dreams as Bash had taken her body without permission. She had questioned if he had said it at all, but the look in Christiana's eyes told her that he had.

"Careful, Morgan," Christiana said. "Let's stay focused on the wedding."

"The only way I'm marrying into this family is if the charges are dropped against mine," Morgan said. She was bartering with her soul. She would sacrifice hers every time to save the people she loved. Morgan had gotten them into this, and only she could get them out.

"We can arrange to have the charges dismissed against your father," Christiana said.

"And the twins' father and Ahmeek and Isa and Henny and anybody else caught up in this bullshit," Morgan said.

"There are limits to our generosity," Christiana said. "Those thugs you've been chasing after are problematic. Now that you've revealed that the twins belong to one of them, that presents a conflict as well. The twins are a part of this picture. They complete the image required."

"Required for what?" Morgan asked.

Christiana ignored the question. "Your phone will be returned after the wedding. All calls will be monitored prior to. You need to call your father back. He and his wife have been calling nonstop for hours. A lot has happened in the past few days. You need to reassure them that you are okay but that you cannot be a part of their public scandal because of your ties to the monarchy."

"You want me to push them away," Morgan surmised.

"If you want to save them, yes."

Christiana held up Morgan's cell phone and Morgan reached for it.

Ethic (7)
Ssiah (5)
Meekie (3)
Alani (4)
Shooter (10)
Baby Sis (3)

Her missed call log was insane. All of her friends and family had been trying to reach her. Aria had called more than everyone. Morgan yearned for them all. The message previews on her screen tore her heart out of her chest.

Ssiah
I've got to leave town for a little bit. I'm not running this time. Believe me when I tell you I'm coming back, shorty. Don't hate me when I get back this time.

Morgan's heart sank. The idea of him leaving again was worse than the thought of him going to jail. Messiah being out in the world inaccessible was torture. She needed him.

Her kids needed him. Even if they never found "home" again, they had manifested family, and the abandonment that darkened her world when he didn't exist in it was crippling. She'd rather hate his presence every day than lack it peacefully. Christiana hawked her, ensuring that Morgan left the text message unanswered.

Meek
Let it go, love.

These niggas wanted her to lose her shit. Her eyes snapped shut as she processed what was happening. She loved them both, but if Bash had his way, she would never have either.

"I loved a man that deeply once," Christiana said. "And then I grew up. Call your father."

Morgan tapped Ethic's name and held her breath as the phone began to ring.

"Baby girl," Ethic answered. "I need you and my babies home. Where you been? It's a lot going on, and you're M.I.A."

"Umm, Ethic, I…" Morgan had to stop talking because if she didn't, her voice would crack, and he would hear her distress.

She felt Bash over her shoulder, and Christiana was glaring at her.

"You there, Mo?" Ethic asked.

Morgan cleared her throat. "Yeah, I'm here. I don't really have time to lock down my whole life just because you're going through legal stuff right now."

She knew how selfish it sounded. The line was silent, and she questioned if he had heard her. She knew he had. He was listening twice as much as he spoke. He was speechless, and Morgan could feel his confusion and hurt through the phone.

"Excuse me, Mo?" Ethic said without hesitation.

"I'm just saying. I have my own life. Nobody wants to be cooped up with Alani. I mean, I can deal with her, but no. I don't want to be all under y'all like that. I have stuff to handle in London anyway. I'm probably going back for a month or two. I got an internship at a hospital so..."

"Morgan, I'm not asking..."

"Ethic, I'm not a kid anymore! I'm not your daughter. I'm not your responsibility! I don't need you running my life and I don't want to be mixed up in more of your drama with a woman who you shouldn't be with in the first place," Morgan snapped.

Her tears fell.

"It's time you let me go," she said.

The line was silent. She wasn't even sure he was still on the phone until she heard him clear his throat.

"I thought we were past this, Mo," he said. "This resentment you have for Alani."

We are, she thought. Her heart crumbled.

"I'll never get past it. I hate her, and I hate you a little bit for marrying her. This whole arrest just opened old wounds. I hope it works out for you, Ethic, and I love you, but I've got to go my own way."

"Morgan, don't do this to me," he said.

"You did it. You chose her over me," Morgan cried.

"That's not the choice, Mo. I don't know how many ways I

have to explain it to get you to see that there isn't you versus anybody else. I love you with my soul. I raised you. I need you home."

"I'm not coming. Good luck with everything," she said. She hung up the phone and tossed it to the floor. "You happy now?" She asked, face stained with clear emotion as she sobbed. "Drop the charges."

She stormed out, snatching away from Bash as he tried to catch her hand. "You just took everything from me. I'm never going to forgive you for this," she said.

Fatigue chased Ahmeek down the highway as he drove West. Not even the sounds of Jay-Z kicking through his subwoofers were enough to stop his eyes from closing. He yawned and dialed his mother's number. He was far enough away from Michigan to make the call he had been dreading. He knew it would break her heart, and that was the last thing he wanted to do, but he couldn't stay. Meek had been locked away before. They had treated him like an animal inside. Telling him when to eat. Dictating when he could sleep. Keeping leashes around his wrists, his ankles, sometimes his neck. Spending months in the hole. It was the most inhumane thing he had ever experienced. He would never go back. He'd die before he went back. Leaving was the only option on the table, and those he loved couldn't come with him.

"Now you know better than to interrupt me while my stories on, boy. What you want?" Marilyn answered. Ahmeek snickered. He could hear the drag of the cigarette through the phone.

"I know you ain't smoking on them cancer sticks, old bird" he said. "Put it out."

"Boy, I'm your parent, not the other way around," Marilyn said.

"Now, Ma," he insisted.

"Fine." She knew it was better to listen than to object. Ahmeek would stop everything he was doing to go take the entire pack from her possession. "Damn boy thinks he's the boss of everybody."

Meek shook his head. He noticed the mile marker on the side of the highway. He was 30 miles from the Kansas state line. Her voice was enough to keep him awake until he crossed into another state. He was a long way from Vegas, but he was making his way. With a trunk full of money, a pistol on his hip, and one beneath the seat, he would eventually make it there. Miami had been the Crew's joint plan. Meek wasn't sure if that was right for him anymore. He had reassurances to provide to Hak anyway.

"You know I love you right, old lady?" Ahmeek asked.

"What's wrong, Ahmeek?"

It was just intuition. He hadn't even said anything out of the ordinary. There was no tremble in his voice, no fear in his tone. Still, his mother knew. She always knew. All those years ago, when he caught his case, she had known something was wrong before she even got the call from Messiah that Meek had dropped a body.

"Everything's everything, Ma. I just got to handle some stuff. It might take me a minute," he answered. "You remember what I told you? If I had to go away for a minute?"

Marilyn remembered. He knew she did. They had discussed this option many times before when he refused to get out of the game.

"Ahmeek Harris. I did this once with you, baby. I can't do it again. This phone is burnt. You made sure of it. Now start talking. Where are you, son?"

Ahmeek hated to take her through hell again. The first time he had gotten locked up, it had almost killed her. She had her first heart attack in her mid-thirties a week after he was sentenced. He had moved carefully with her in mind. Every step, every robbery, every ounce of cocaine he had sold that had eventually become bricks. He had mitigated the risks so that he wouldn't break his mother's heart again. Somehow, he hadn't done enough because here he was, tearing her apart.

"I don't really know much, Ma. Police picked up Messiah. He's out, but you know our rules. When the police come sniffing, we go missing," he said. It was one of his father's old sayings. Ahmeek hadn't had time to learn enough from his old man, but he remembered that. "I'ma ditch my phone in a bit. I'll call you from the burner when I pick it up."

"Be careful, Ahmeek. I don't want to say goodbye to my son. You be careful out there, boy," she said. He nodded, fighting something, disappointment in himself perhaps because he could hear her holding back tears.

"I will, Ma. I love you."

Meek ended the call and then went to throw the phone out the window. His screensaver stopped him. Morgan stared back at him. He hesitated a moment as their time together played vividly in his mind. So much love in so little time, falling for her and her kids had been the easiest thing he had ever done. Walking away was proving to be the hardest. He tossed the phone out the window and pressed the gas pedal harder. The Crew's plan was always to come back eventually, but Meek was unsure if he would. He had put enough bread up for his mother to live comfortably. Besides her, there was nothing left for him in Flint.

"The fuck, shorty!" Messiah said harshly into the phone. He hated to leave this on her voicemail, but she refused to answer his calls. "I got to talk to you, Mo. I need to leave. I just need you to answer my calls. I know shit's fucked up right now. I know this gon' feel like last time to you, but it's not. If you would just answer the phone, I could tell you that. I'm trying to do it different this time. This ain't desertion, Mo. I'ma come back and we gon' iron all this shit out and I'ma take care of you and my kids. Even if you don't like it. Even if you don't want me to. I'ma be there. Talk to Ethic. He knows why I'm leaving this time. Swear to God, it ain't with bad intentions. You need him more than you need me, so I got to take this L. I owe him, Mo. Owe that nigga my life. Take care of my babies, man. I ain't got to know 'em yet. I'ma forever love you for giving me them. I was gon' forever love you anyway, though, and as hard as you make it for a nigga, I know you know that. You know how a nigga love you, shorty. I'm coming home one day, Mo. Look up at them stars 'til I get back. I'll be looking too. This number won't work after this call. That's why I was trying to reach you. I'm sorry, Mo. For everything. I'ma make it right one day."

Messiah hung up, and he gritted his teeth in frustration as he squeezed his phone in one hand with all his might. Messiah had texted Morgan on repeat, and he had called so many times that his ego scolded him. This was not the way he wanted to leave, and he thought of taking her and his kids with him, but he and Morgan had too much to work out for it even to be a possibility. He loved her, but he was filled with a resentment he couldn't shake, and with whatever he had lingering in the background with Bleu, it made him want to leave them both behind in Flint. He needed time, and so did Mo, and he couldn't blame her for that. Their last encounter hadn't been kind, and after his house being raided with the twins present, he knew she had to be pissed. He wouldn't buck against her right now where they were concerned, not when he had no better options to present his children with at the moment.

Maybe they're better off with her right now, he thought to himself.

Despite his talk with Ethic, he couldn't see himself allowing the police to put him against his mentor. Ethic had been the most consistent man in his life. He was a gracious king, and Messiah had failed to protect him once before. He wouldn't make the same mistake twice, even if it meant sacrificing it all.

He sent Ethic a text.

> *Don't let my kids think their daddy doesn't exist. Let them know every day until I'm back. Bring me back, Big Homie.*

Ethic sat in the dimly-lit office awaiting his guest's arrival. It was a beautiful home. A family lived inside these walls. A wife had filled it with love. The pictures on the oak desk displayed the smiling faces of two children.

He hated to be in this position. It was so easy to revert to his old ways, but his life was on the line. He heard the sound of an engine as a car pulled into the driveway. The slam of one car door told him that only one person was entering the home. The click of a turned lock and then the sound of dress shoes against the wood floors.

Ethic waited patiently because he understood that every man had a routine when he walked into his home. When the steps grew fainter, and he heard the seal of the refrigerator door break, he leaned forward against the desk, steepling his fingers to his forehead.

"Fucking niggers."

The sentiment didn't surprise Ethic at all. Most men in this man's position felt that way. He listened to the echo of the hard-bottomed shoes come down the hallway. When the light switch flicked on, Ethic stared at the judge he had stared at less than 48 hours prior.

"What the fuck are you doing in my home?"

"We have exactly 48 minutes to get this right before your beloved Virginia comes home with little Steven and Marie," Ethic said.

"Do you know what happens when you threaten a judge?!" The man barked.

"Tonight, I'm the judge, the jury, and the executioner. Have a seat. You don't speak out of turn. Ain't that what you told me? That you were... what was it?" Ethic asked.

The judge eased into the chair across the desk. "I'm just doing my job."

"What did you say? You were what? My master. Is that right?"

Ethic's hand was wrapped around the handle of a shiny .9mm, and it rested on the top of the desk. He pointed it into the wood, stabbing it as he made his point. "I'm the master tonight," he said. "And I'm an unforgiving one. I ask one time; you answer with truth, or you die. And don't take too long..." Ethic checked his Rolex. "Now, it's 46 minutes. If we're interrupted, they die."

The judge was so angry that he was beet red, but fear stopped him from defying Ethic's command.

"Feels terrible don't it, to have your life in the hands of someone else and not be able to do shit about it," Ethic said.

"Tell me about the charges. Who's applying pressure from the D.A.'s office, and what evidence do they have?"

The judge sat stubbornly, and Ethic added, "I have no reservations about blowing your head off and leaving you here for your kids to find."

"I don't know," the judge said.

Ethic nodded.

BOOM!

The gunshot was muffled by the silencer on the tip of his gun. His shot was so precise it only took off the lobe of the judge's ear.

The scream the man let out was chilling, but Ethic knew it was more out of fear and shock than actual pain.

"The next one goes in your head," Ethic said. His calm was more terrifying than the weapon he held.

"I don't know! I don't know, okay?! All I know is I received a call in the middle of the night telling me to sign a warrant to search your property," he said.

"A call from who?"

The man nursed his bleeding ear as he stammered, "That's above me! I don't know! The call came straight from the governor at eleven o'clock at night. When you get that kind of call, you just do what you're told!"

It was worse than Ethic expected. This legal persecution was called from the top. This was no random discovery of guilt.

"Here's what we're going to do," Ethic proposed.

"I can't do anything! My hands are tied! This wasn't my

call! I'm just a man following orders," the judge said. "Please. My family will be home any minute."

"They won't actually," Ethic said. "If you call your wife right now, she's having car trouble. She's on the side of the road Downtown," Ethic said. "Her phone has no service because my people blocked the frequency from the cell tower down there. It's dark, and she's afraid to walk to the nearest gas station for help because she has two kids with her."

Ethic pulled out his phone. "A good Samaritan came to the rescue, of course," Ethic said. He held up his phone. A picture of a man helping the stranded family should have felt like relief.

"That man been sitting on your family all day. He's the reason the car broke down. Another man on your parent's house in Clarkston, another on your ex-wife's home in Ypsi. My men will stay in place until after my next court date. If anything goes out of my favor, they react. I don't want that. It doesn't have to go there."

"What do you want me to do?" The judge asked.

"Whatever you have to," Ethic said. "If my family has to watch them close gates on me, you'll close caskets on yours."

Ethic stood and tucked his pistol in his back waistline and stood. "Messiah Williams, Hendrix Outlaw, remember those names too. They belong to me. It would be a shame to mishandle them, no?"

He left without another word, but he was unsure if his threats were enough. This was political, and he wasn't even sure of how he had become a target. He had a feeling this was far from over.

I've got to prepare my wife and kids to do life without me.

CHAPTER 12

Eazy Okafor was the easy child. He was the one who didn't give his family much trouble. The baby. Well, temporarily the baby, because to his disdain, a new life was on the way, and in his soul, he wanted to be happy, but he was dreading it. He sat at the dinner table, doing his homework; his solemn was hard to hide because Eazy was all things except still. Today, he was a muted version of himself.

"Everything okay, Big Man?" Alani asked.

"Uh-huh," Eazy nodded without lifting his eyes off his paper. His head rested against the table atop of his hand. A lazy student but sharp as a whip, Eazy's pencil never moved, however.

Alani frowned and went to the refrigerator and removed a carton of ice cream.

"I've got a deal for you. How about you help me load the dishwasher, and then we can have ice cream while I help you finish your homework?"

Eazy shrugged and slid out of the chair. "I guess."

If Alani wasn't certain before, she was now. Something was bothering him, and after all that had been going on in their lives, she wasn't surprised.

"Come on," she said. They were silent as she rinsed each dish and handed it to him to place inside the machine. She might as well have hand-washed each one because she was basically doing a double job. Eazy would have pointed that out had he been in his usual spirits.

Alani was unsure of how to approach him. She didn't want to say the wrong thing. Ethic may handle this situation differently. She didn't want to divulge too much or sugarcoat where Ethic would pour truth. At the end of the day, Eazy was a Black boy who would grow into a Black man. He would be more cultured and privileged than most white men, and still, the world would view him the same. A danger. A threat. A thug. Her sweet Eazy was everything but dangerous.

Alani closed the dishwasher that separated them and held his face in her hands.

"You want to talk about it?"

He shook his head.

"Well, you know when you're upset it makes me really upset, Big Man. Can you ease my heart a little and just tell me a small part of what's wrong?"

"If my daddy goes to jail, you'll leave with the new baby, and me and Bella won't have anyone," Eazy said. "I hate that this baby is coming."

Alani wished she had braced herself for that blow. The thoughts that lived in this child. The fear of abandonment, even after all this love Alani had given on purpose, was great. It tore her up inside.

"Eazy," Alani whispered. "Come here, let's sit for a minute." She took a seat at the table and then watched him take the chair next to hers. She pulled his seat so that he was facing her. "I'm never going to go a day without seeing your face. It doesn't matter what happens in our lives; I'm going to be here with you, baby boy."

"You will have your own baby now. You won't have to love us anymore. When you get your own kids again, we won't matter."

"That's not how love works, Eazy. I'll love this baby so much, but I don't have to take any of my love away from you to do that. You're so important to me. You are my son."

"But not your real son. I'm not your real kid like this baby will be."

"You are mine," Alani reassured. "Nobody else in the world is able to hold my hand and tap their finger against the inside to the exact rhythm of my heartbeat, Eazy. You do that. You put ginger candies on my nightstand in the morning, but not every morning, only the ones when your stomach is unsettled because you say you can feel when I have morning sickness. You do so many little special things that let me know that God has brought us together. You are my son. I am the luckiest bonus mom in the world. Your mommy in heaven is relying on me to be your mommy down here. She's counting on me to keep you safe. I could never leave you behind. And Daddy is going to work this out, but if anything ever happens and he's not around, I will be. As long as God allows, I will be here for you, loving you so deeply and equally to your sister and Mo and the twins and this baby."

Eazy nodded, but he didn't hasten to speak.

"You know why having a baby with Daddy is so important to me?" Alani asked.

He shook his head.

"Because it makes me feel like I'm really a part of this family. The baby will share my blood and Daddy's blood. The baby will share your DNA, Eazy. So, it's like a mixture of all of our love all in one tiny person."

"Yeah, that part's kind of cool," Eazy said reluctantly.

"Very cool," Alani said, smiling.

"I tell you what. You can name your little brother or sister," Alani said.

The way Eazy smiled and rubbed his chin made Alani laugh aloud.

"Don't even think about giving this baby a weird name," she warned, chuckling.

"I'm going to give the baby the best name. I just need some time to think about it," he said.

"Well, think about it in the bed, kiddo. It's about that time," Alani said.

"Can I sleep with you?" Eazy asked.

Ethic cleared his throat, announcing his presence, and then said, "Not tonight, Big Man. I want to hug my girl tonight," he said.

Eazy practically toppled over the chair as he rushed to Ethic. It was the first time he had seen his father since the arrest, and Alani teared up at the way he ran into his arms. He was growing every day, but the way he poured out his emotions in this moment reminded her of the seven-year-old boy she had met years ago. He was afraid of losing his place, of losing the security of a mother he had come to depend on and love. She knew that if Ethic went to jail, their lives would never be the same. It would be impossible to heal from heartbreak like that. Giving birth to his child and then saying goodbye to him would shatter her but staring into Ethic's eyes as he held his son tightly, consoling him, she knew that she wouldn't have the luxury to give up. No matter what happened, she would have to piece herself together to take care of these kids. They needed her. Ethic needed her to be strong.

"I was just telling Eazy he could name the baby," Alani said as they broke their embrace.

Ethic looked at her in shock. They had gone over potential baby names for months, and never had she been this agreeable.

"You must be a special guy," Ethic said, rustling Eazy's head. Eazy's smile was all Alani needed to be settled in the decision.

"He's my favorite guy," Alani said.

Ethic placed a hand to his heart. "I been putting in a lot of work," he said. He bit his lip suggestively. "A whole lot of damn midnight shifts for that title. What this crumb snatcher doing to compete with that?"

Alani blushed, giggling. She was so grateful for a husband who still gave her butterflies. His love didn't have an expiration date. It didn't grow stale, and he was right. He had put in the hours. Between her thighs, every single night going to work with his tongue, with his fingers, with dick that she couldn't turn down. Ethic took care of his woman.

"What can I say? You can't compete where you don't compare. Eazy gets all the love for free."

Ethic nodded, amused.

"Come on, Big Man, let's get this homework and kitchen together, then go over some baby names before bed," Alani said. She winked at Ethic, and he mouthed, "I love you," before he disappeared upstairs, giving them time to finish whatever bonding they were doing before he walked in the door.

Alani didn't rush Eazy. She gave him all the attention he needed, leaving Ethic to wait until they were done. When he was in bed, she made her way to the basement, where she knew he would be. She thought he would be mid-way through his nightly ritual. Weights, then yoga and meditation, but he just sat on the edge of the couch leaned over, elbows to knees. He was so deep in thought he didn't look up at her when she entered.

"Mo broke my heart today, baby," he said.

"What happened?"

"I don't know," he answered. "We've made so much progress with her. I thought you two were in a good place."

"We aren't?" Alani asked, confused.

"She told me she's moving on from this family. I guess the arrest is hard for her. She feels like I chose you over her."

The sickness that invaded Alani forced her into the chair across from Ethic.

"Did y'all have words while I was locked up?" Ethic asked.

"No!" Alani said vehemently, denying whatever accusation was looming in his mind. "Ethic, Mo and I have been fine."

"That girl is going to break me," Ethic said, rubbing the top of his head in distress. "I don't know what to do here. Her distaste for you pulls her and both of them babies away from me. She put an entire ocean between us before. Those two years almost killed me, baby. Visits every once in a while, and FaceTime felt like a prison sentence all on its own. She's pulling away again. The way she talked to me." Ethic sighed heavily, shaking his head. "She doesn't want anything to do with this family."

Alani's eyes prickled. "Because of me?" She was so confused. She had tried everything to connect with Morgan. This rejection hit her out of the blue.

Ethic reached for her hand, but he never lifted his head. He was hurting. He was trying hard not to show it, but she felt it. The baby in her stomach reacted to the heavy emotions in the room, kicking so hard that she had to push out a long breath and brace herself.

"I can't keep begging for Mo's approval, Ezra," she said. "I've tried with her. I've loved her hard. I love the twins. They're my babies. I just don't know where this change of energy is coming from. I know your arrest brings up some stuff for Mo. It brings up shit for us all. She's not the only one hurting and I'm really, really tired of you making it seem like you understand where she's coming from. You make it okay for her to be offended by my presence."

Ethic looked up in confusion. "Come again?"

"You dote over Morgan like you have to apologize to her for being with me," Alani said. She was becoming emotional. Angry, in fact, because she had given her all to Morgan and the twins. She considered Morgan's children her grandchildren. Morgan had cried on her shoulder over the years, and Alani had completely fallen for the motherless young girl. She didn't understand how they had gotten back to such a dysfunctional place. Alani was hurt.

"If I do that, it's not my intention. I don't apologize to anybody for being with you. I'm going to talk to her," he said.

"I'm never going to be good enough to Morgan. She's always going to see me as the enemy. I can't prove myself any more than I have. When will I be good enough?"

Ethic pulled Alani into his lap. "You're too good," he replied, kissing her lips. "You're too good for us all, and I'm sorry if anybody makes you feel less than that. We don't deserve you, but we're grateful you chose us to slum it with. What's with these tears, huh?" He swiped them away with his thumb and then kissed her deeply. "I don't want to hurt you ever. Everything's going to be fine. We'll give Mo some time, get through these court proceedings, and then work it out as a family. We've made it through worse, no?"

Alani nodded.

"So, we'll make it through all this."

"What if we don't?" Alani whispered.

"We will, baby." Ethic's hand gripped her thigh. "A nigga stressed, Lenika."

"Take what you need," she answered.

He turned her, laying her back onto the couch. Placing her on her side because she was too far along to lie flat, and he remembered what their midwife had told him.

"Y'all like to get nasty, so you got to put her on her right

this late in the game. No missionary. Switch positions. Laying her flat will slow the baby's heart rate."

Ethic had taken heed. She slept on her side, exactly like this at night, but instead of the pillow that normally rested between her thighs, tonight, his head took its place.

"Ethic, what if I'm loud. You know my entire body is extra sensitive now that I'm pregnant," she whispered.

He was already lifting her silk gown. "Turn on some music," he whispered, kissing her thighs, working a path to her panties. He found her clit through the fabric, trapping it between his teeth gently, pulling it, waking it up, and then sucking on it. Alani just wanted the panties gone. She was soaking through them, anyway, might as well get rid of them.

"Alexa, play Softest Place on Earth," she said. She needed the music because she wanted to scream.

The humming of Xscape muffled Alani's moans as Ethic slid her panties to the side. He licked her like he was taking the first swipe at a soft-serve ice cream cone on a 90-degree day to stop it from dripping.

"Oh my god," she whispered.

Baby, won't you come inside. I'll take you on a fantasy rideeeee.

Ethic ate pussy to a rhythm as Alani lost her mind. Sex was different while pregnant. It had always been good between them, but with every nerve ending on her body intensified, the head Ethic was giving was otherworldly. He took his time.

"This pussy, baby," he said as he flicked her stiff clit. It was twice its normal size, and he enjoyed the swell as he sucked.

"Mmm." He was relishing this. He ate her pussy like it was his last meal, going buck on her, turning her over until she was on all of fours, then he ate her everywhere.

Ethic was deadly in bed, even in this moment when he handled her with extra care, he was a fucking assassin. One woman shouldn't know this much unbridled pleasure.

Baby, you can be the first, inside the softest place on Earth.

He was so focused on one spot, the right spot, a spot that she hadn't even discovered on her own body. How the fuck did he know where to find it?

"Cum." An order. He wasn't asking. If she didn't follow it, the punishment to come would be divine. She wanted to stall him out just to feel the pleasure he would torture her with.

"Oh, Ezra, baby, wait," Alani moaned.

"Mmm, mmm," he groaned, shaking his head slowly, going deeper. "Cum," he coached. Alani had never had a nigga eat her this satisfactorily. The way he was executing this shit, she wanted to put a sticker on this nigga's nose for being ahead of his class.

She screamed.

"Good girl."

Alani's face bent as she caught her wave, and Ethic released her clit, planting light kisses to it instead of the death suction he had just used. She quivered with every peck.

"Good fucking girl," he whispered.

She didn't know why she was spent. She hadn't put in any work, but she was exhausted.

"Lazy-ass," he snickered as he scooped her in his arms, the same way he had when he had carried her over the threshold of their home after they married.

He carried her all the way to the master bedroom, put her in the shower, washed every inch of her body, just once because he could see her fatigue, and then wrapped her in a towel, turning on the steam feature so she could relax while he finished his own body. She sat on the tile bench in their shower, mesmerized by her husband. Although he was trying hard to conceal his feelings, she could still see that he was bothered.

"I'm sorry that loving me complicates your relationship with Mo. Is it easier if I'm just not a part of that? Have I forced myself on her?" She asked.

"No," he answered. "That's not easier, baby. You haven't forced anything. The only thing you've forced is yourself to love me on days when I know you question if you should. I'm going to go see about Morgan tomorrow."

"But you're due back in court tomorrow," Alani reminded.

"After court," he answered.

"And if they revoke bail or something worse happens?" Alani was preparing for the worst. He could hear it in her tone. She was petrified.

"Stop worrying. About Mo... about tomorrow. Tell me about the gender reveal. What you come up with?"

Alani smiled softly. "Don't try to distract me, sir," she said.

"It's not a distraction. That's your job. That's your only job right now, baby. Bring my baby into the world. I got everything else."

Isa sat patiently outside the hotel. The Nevada sun was so smoldering that he could see the heat waves rising outside his windshield as the AC kicked out cold air on the inside. Learning Hak's weaknesses would be the hardest part of his plan. He couldn't just go in guns blazing. A man of Hak's stature had levels of protection. Isa would have to tail him, watch him, prey on him in order to pull this off. He wasn't the type of nigga to stick to the rules of a payment plan to make it right. The Crew had fucked up, but Isa didn't care. He wasn't a make amends type of nigga. He'd rather take it all the way and turn a mistake into intentional disrespect if he was going to be held accountable for it either way. The only alliance he valued was the one he made with his brothers in the sandbox. Outside of Messiah and Ahmeek, any other nigga could line up on the other side. Isa was ready to shoot 'em down like ducks, one at a time, and he would have to because it looked like Hak came with an army. Most people would notice the men in suits with earpieces first. Security. They were on payroll to protect Hak during business hours, but it was the men hiding in plain sight that Isa took note of. Wherever Hak went, there was a man dressed down, not far behind, and they never spoke. Isa would have to find the hole in Hak's schedule when guards were down in order to get in. He wasn't just coming to kill. He was coming to take first, so he had to be strategic to get to the bag.

Isa saw Hak climb into the back of a chauffeured truck, and before he could lift the foot off the brake, the passenger door was being pulled open and Ahmeek slid inside. Isa's gun was in his side instantly.

"Fuck, nigga! Fuck you doing out here running up on me? I almost popped you."

"Put your fucking gun away, man. Fuck you doing, Isa? Cuz it looks like you about to try homie, and that's a bad fucking idea, bruh," Meek said. "If I spotted you, you think his people won't? You think your one pistol can go against his reservation full of killers? Think, bruh," Meek barked in frustration, tapping his temple. "This ain't how we play this. The nigga ain't wrong. We fucked up the runs. We owe him the bread. Robbing and killing the nigga is out of bounds, bro, and we don't know the blowback that comes with that. You off this nigga, and we inherit a whole new set of problems. This ain't Flint. This nigga is next level. You don't come at a king without an army."

"Nigga, so strap up and let's ride on this nigga cuz I ain't paying him shit else, and what you think gon' happen when we late on that payment?" Isa asked. "How we making the money to pay that nigga with the police all over our backs? They arrested bro. You think we can slang dope while they got targets on our backs? No, nigga. We either gon' get locked the fuck up or not move enough work to pay this nigga and it's gon' be war anyway. So, we got to hit first and hit hard. Drop that nigga and run his pockets so ain't no mu'fuckas coming behind him avenging nothing cuz they know what they getting if they come this way."

"Drive this mu'fucka, man," Ahmeek said in frustration. "This ain't the move. You gon' get us all killed and by us all, I ain't talking about you and me. I'm talking about your girl, about my mama, about Mo and those kids, about Bleu and anybody else we have ever loved. You might be willing to take that gamble but I ain't with that shit. It's bigger than us."

"You sound scared, my nigga. Since when we move timid?" Isa said.

"And you sound stupid, bruh. You know how I get down. Get the fuck out of here, man. I'm not risking no lives if I don't have to. We went at a nigga on his level before, and we barely made it out last time. This nigga is Ethic level. Only nigga paid for that was me. I took a bullet. The time before that, I went to jail. I lost time off my life. You ain't have to answer for none of that. Messiah either. I'm calling this shit this time. It's a smarter play."

Isa was stubborn. He and Meek approached situations differently. Where Meek preferred reason, Isa got ratchet. He didn't need an excuse to go crazy on niggas, and he wasn't keen to search for one now.

"Look, you my mans, and I'm riding with you regardless, but I got a meeting with Hak tonight. We can iron this out like men," Ahmeek said.

"Or we can handle it like monsters and terrorize some shit," Isa said. He pulled away from the curb, headed to the hotel. "But we'll try your way first. If shit don't go accordingly, it's up for me."

If Morgan had ever thought she had experienced heartbreak before, she was wrong. Nothing had ever hurt her like disconnecting from Ethic. She didn't even breathe the same. The damage of losing the one man who had always been a constant in her world was life-altering.

"Mommy, when can we go home? I miss my teddy," Yara signed.

"Soon, baby. Very soon."

"Why are you so sad?" Yara's question took Morgan off guard. Her babies were only two. No way should they be feeling her solemn. She didn't want that. She remembered what it felt like growing up with tension in her home. She had suffered through many nights of Mizan and Raven's energy. It had made her shrink herself as a child. The realization that she was repeating that same cycle for her kids was devastating.

"Mommy's not sad, Yolly," Morgan signed.

"Papa Bash hurt you. Him put marks on your neck and make you cry," Messari said.

"Nooo, Mommy's Ssari. I'm fine. Everything's fine. Have you seen Papa Bash with Mommy's phone?" She asked. Morgan hated that Messari was so perceptive. He noticed everything, and the tension between her and Bash was evident. She hated that she was robbing her children of their peace. She remembered what it felt like to know something was wrong but not be able to do anything about it. She had known Mizan was hurting her sister long before she acknowledged it. If she could just get to her phone, she could call for help.

Messari shook his head but didn't pay her much attention as he continued to draw his picture. Morgan watched Bash from the upstairs window as he got into his car and pulled away from the estate.

"Us don't like it here, Mommy. We want to go home."

"We will, baby. I promise we will soon."

"Come on, follow Mommy," she signed to them.

Morgan had stayed out the way. She was grateful that Bash had let her be, but she lived in a state of anxiety because she had no idea what Bash and his mother had in store for her. She wished that Bash's father was around more often, but he was needed most in London these days, leaving his wife and son with enough freedom to terrorize Mo. Morgan made her way to Bash's office and ushered the twins inside. Her phone was somewhere in this house and if she could just get to it, she could call for help. Christiana was busy on the veranda with ladies from her social circle, and it was the perfect time for Morgan to snoop.

"You sit right here, baby boy, and don't move an inch. If you see anyone coming, I want you to start crying," Morgan said.

"But why, Mommy?" Messari said.

"It's just a game, baby. It'll let Mommy know somebody is near. Just cry. The loudest fake cry you can drum up, okay?" Morgan asked.

Messari nodded, and Morgan picked Yara up, carrying her to the end of the hall and disappearing into Bash's office.

"Where the fuck is my phone?" She whispered as she pulled open the desk drawer. Morgan's frustration grew the more she searched. She even walked over to Christiana's connected office, going through every drawer until tears burned her eyes. When she pulled open the file cabinet and flipped through the files a folder with her name on it stopped her in her tracks.

Morgan pulled it out and opened it.

Her heart sank when she saw the photos of her.

"They had me followed," Morgan whispered. Morgan flipped through the folder in disbelief. Pictures of her with Ahmeek in moments when they thought they were completely alone. There were images of her with Messiah on the merry-go-round, snapshots of her getting dressed, of her practicing with Stiletto Gang, of her lounging with her children. It was like they had a permanent lens on her life. She was shaking. She was so angry. She kept going through the files until she reached the back of the cabinet. A lockbox sat at the bottom of the drawer. Morgan pulled it out and then remembered a tiny key she had seen in one of Christiana's desk drawers. She took the box to the desk, and sure enough, the key worked.

"What is this?" she said to herself.

Papers with the name Allison Moran were folded neatly inside. *Is this a fucking autopsy report?*

Morgan had seen enough of them during her time in college. As a pre-med major, she had even shadowed as one had been performed so she knew exactly what she was reading. *He called me Alli the other day,* she thought. *Did she commit suicide?* Every internal alarm blared, telling Morgan something wasn't right, but when she got to the picture at the bottom of the stack, she felt sick.

The girl could be her sister. They looked so much alike that Morgan's hands began to shake.

When Morgan heard Messari's cries, she slammed the box closed and hurried across the room to put it back. She snatched up Yolly and rushed out of the room, bumping directly into Bash. She yelped in surprise, not expecting him to be the one to interrupt her.

"What are you doing, Mo?" He asked. "Yara wanted to scare me half to death and play hide-and-seek," Morgan lied.

"This house is big. It's a playground for kids," Bash said.

"Yeah, I see," Morgan replied. "You know we can't stay here with your mom forever, right? Like, we need clothes, the twins miss their room, they want to go home. I want to try to feel a piece of normalcy, Bash. We can't do that here. You and me… we can't even try to get on the same page as long as we're here."

"What do you expect me to do, Mo?" He asked.

"To not treat me like a prisoner," she answered. "Everybody's gone. I'm all yours, but these four walls are going to drive me insane. I need my phone, my friends; I still want to start my internship for school, I still want to dance. I can do all of those things and still marry you."

Bash nodded. "I never meant for it to get this far," Bash said. "You just make me crazy, Mo. I waited two years. The other night, I didn't force it. I was careful with you. It wasn't like those other guys. I was gentle, Mo," he said.

Morgan's eyes prickled. "I know," she said. So much hatred was in her heart, but she couldn't let an ounce of it show. This was a game of mental Chess and if Morgan could just get out of this house, she would have a better chance to win. "That's not what I want from you, though, Bash. I didn't want it to go down that way. I can't even remember it. I want to make love to you and remember what it feels like. It's not the same if we both don't enjoy it."

"You got to give me a chance, Mo…"

"In your mama's house? We can't do shit in here with her all over me. I feel like a science experiment the way she's picking my clothes, my food, watching me. It's uncomfortable. Let's just go to my place so we can have some privacy, and we can talk, and so you can touch me with permission, Bash. You have to know that how you did it is not okay," she whispered. Morgan was so close to him that she felt his dick react. "Say yes, Bash. Say I can go home."

He was holding his breath, and Morgan moved closer to his ear. "You want me to be awake this time, Bash. It's totally different."

Morgan had to will away tears because tears wouldn't get her anywhere. She had seen Raven cry every day for years, and the tears didn't stop Mizan from mercilessly degrading her sister. Morgan had done too much for Bash to care about her tears.

"Okay," he agreed.

Morgan turned to pack her things. She wanted to get out of there as quickly as possible before Christiana got wind and convinced Bash to change his mind. She knew the power of her persuasion would be stronger if she broke Christiana's hold on him. Morgan needed to distance Bash from his mom to gain the advantage.

He put a firm grip on her elbow, and she turned back to him. "Don't play games with me, Morgan," he said.

"I'm done playing games. I just want to figure out a new normal. I can't lie and say what you've done hasn't hurt me. It does," she admitted. "But I know what I did hurt you too. I'm sorry, Bash."

Morgan actually meant it. The college boy who she had met years ago was nowhere to be found. He had changed. So had she. Her deceit had destroyed his ego so much that he had turned cruel, and she couldn't see a way out.

"Bitch, explain to me why you're in Miami by your damn self. Where is our lil' light skin papi?"

Aria sighed in frustration because Whiteboy Nick was asking the same question that Aria had been asking herself for days. Miami was beautiful. Her Downtown condo was 35 floors up and overlooked the ocean. The entire city sparkled at night like a shiny new toy waiting for her to play with, but without Isa, it felt like a consolation prize.

"And who is that fine-ass man that keeps checking in on you? I bet money Isa don't know that pretty-ass thug is stopping by with food and asking if you need something, leaving money and shit behind. He want them panties, boo," Nick said.

"That's Mo," Aria said.

"Unt uh! Not another Mo! He a ho! We already know muthafuckas named Mo ain't got shit in they blood but ho! Run, girl, run!" Nick said.

Aria chuckled and shook her head. "Don't do that. My girl just in love and confused, okay; she's going to get it together. This one down here is probably a ho, though. You right about that part," Aria said, laughing. "And he's just being hospitable. If his name ain't Isa, I don't want him."

"Cuz, bitch, don't make me slide you over our man," Nick warned.

Aria shook her head. "Speaking of Mo, have you talked to her? This shit ain't right. After everything that's gone down, she would normally be the first person on my line. I've been calling, been texting. She'll hit me back on the text but responds with one-word answers. She real dry with it."

"At least you getting the one word. The queen, Morgan Atkins, hasn't hit me back one time," Nick said.

Aria was unsettled. She was away from too many people she loved, and she didn't like it one bit. Something about all of this just didn't feel right.

"Can you pull up on Mo for me?" Aria asked.

"Mo is a big girl. Maybe she doesn't want to be found right now," Nick said.

"Just check on her for me, Nick," Aria said. "If you don't, I'm hopping on a plane."

Aria's intuition was going haywire. If she didn't care about anyone else, she cared deeply for her friends, and Morgan was her absolute best friend. The scars that Morgan had left on her loved ones after her suicide attempt were still very real, and Aria had learned the hard way never to take chances with Morgan. If it felt like something was wrong, it usually was.

CHAPTER 13

Yay! We're home! We're home!" Messari shouted as they entered their apartment. Morgan felt that in her bones. Even with Bash trailing behind her, she felt safer in her own space.

"Are you happy to be home, baby?" Morgan asked. A small smile of accomplishment graced her lips. She had gotten them home. That was something. That was a step. They felt safe in that space, and it was Morgan's job to keep them there.

"Yes!" Messari shouted.

Morgan bent down and pulled off her kids' jackets. She caressed their faces and pulled them into her arms, kissing their chubby cheeks.

"Meet me in the room," Bash said.

"You can't wait until they're asleep?" She asked.

"Mommy, us not sleepy! Right, Yolly?" Messari said. He signed the words as well so that Yara could back him up.

Morgan's heart was so tender when it came to her kids.

"We not tired," Yara signed.

Morgan tapped their butts gently, nudging them toward their room. "Well, let's just try to rest our eyes. If you aren't asleep in twenty minutes, I'll let you stay up a little longer."

She bypassed Bash. "They won't last twenty minutes. I'll be right out."

When Morgan was inside their rooms, she locked the door and then hurried to their toy bin. Their iPads were tucked away inside.

"Please be charged," she whispered. Sure enough, the devices were dead. Morgan searched through the toy chest for the charger until locating one, and then she plugged it in.

"Messari, listen to me, okay," she signed. "I need you to be a big boy, okay? When your iPad charges, I need you to call Auntie Aria. Tell her to send help."

"Meekie's coming, Mommy?" Yara signed.

"He's coming, baby," Morgan signed back. Morgan wasn't sure who Aria would send; she just knew that the Crew would come. It didn't matter if it was one of them or all of them; they would ride for her. "But it has to be our little secret. If you tell Papa Bash, he won't let him come."

Morgan tucked the twins under their covers, and she put headphones over their ears. "No matter what you hear, I don't want you to get out of this bed," Morgan said. "Don't get up until I come back to get you. You understand?"

"But what if Auntie Ari asks to speak to you? Her your best friend. Her might want to say hi," Messari asked.

"You tell her that Papa Bash won't let me, and you tell her to send someone fast," Morgan signed. "I know this is a big task for you, baby, but I need you to listen. You know how to FaceTime her, Messari. Just hit her picture and wait until she answers. If she doesn't answer, keep trying. Whatever you do, make sure you whisper, okay?"

Her baby was so confused, but he nodded anyway, and Morgan laid them down and gave them the iPad before kissing them and walking out of the room.

Bash waited for her in the bedroom. He sat bent over onto his elbows, rubbing his hands together.

"We don't have to right now, Mo. Like, it's forced and..."

"That's what you like, right? Forced sex? I was unconscious before, and you wanted it then. Right? That's your thing? Is that what you did with Allison?" She asked. "Did she fight you? What happened to that girl, Bash? Cuz whatever happened, I don't want it to happen to me. I have two kids. So, if sex is what you want, you can have it." Morgan began peeling out of her clothes as she spoke through tears.

"Be quiet, Morgan," he said. His tone chilled her.

"I'm not gonna be quiet, Bash. I want you to know exactly what you're doing to me because you used to be my friend. I used to feel safe with you. Now, I just feel like you're just like everybody else. Here to take something. Here to force something. You're here to do damage. So, just do it. Since this is who you are, just do it. Take it. You felt comfortable taking it while I slept. So, do it now. Be the monster you are and take it. Is that what happened to your old girlfriend? I found her obituary, Bash. Did you hurt her? She didn't kill herself, did she?"

"She was unwell, Mo," Bash said.

"Was she? Did you trap her too? Did you isolate her? Blackmail her? Rape her? The way you did me?"

"I said shut up, Morgan!" Bash exploded on her, crossing the room and pinning her against the wall, wrapping hands around her neck, and then body slamming her onto the bed.

Morgan turned her head to the side as he ravaged her neck. It was like he could no longer help himself as he snatched at her leggings. Morgan kicked him off and swung so hard that his nose bled when her fist connected with his face.

"You're so bitch made!" She said, heaving as adrenaline stopped her from catching her breath. She shook her head in disgust. "You're a piece of shit! A nobody-ass nigga. Ain't got no presence about yourself, no real clout. You're a mama's boy who has to drug women to get pussy. You want it? You take it! Take it while I'm conscious enough to defend myself!"

Bash's backhand felt like it broke her neck. It disoriented her as a ringing filled her ear.

"She deserved it," Bash said. "Girls like that are a tease. Girls like you, Mo. When I saw you, I thought it was a second chance. You look so much like her, but you played the same games with me, Mo. Just like she played with me. I tried to be patient, to earn your trust, and wait for you to love me like I love you, but you let other people in. You let them distract you from what you had. Just like her. Putting other people first, other men. She learned, though. I showed her who was in control. You can give a girl the entire world, and she won't appreciate it." Bash spoke through clenched teeth as he choked her so hard her body sank into the bed. "Beg me, Morgan. Beg me like you beg your little thugs to fuck you. Is that what I have to give you for you to act like you appreciate what I've done for you? Huh? Huh? You're a whore just like your sister."

My sister?

Morgan didn't have time to think. She clawed at his fingertips, trying to get him to let a little air in her throat. Morgan brought her knee up with all her might, kicking his family jewels and forcing him to release his grip.

Morgan choked viciously as she sucked in air.

"Bitch!"

She crawled across her bed frantically, reaching into her nightstand.

She knew the gun wasn't loaded. She didn't keep bullets inside just in case the gun fell into the hands of her children. He didn't know that, however. She had brought him to her home for a reason. Home-court advantage meant she knew how to win. She reached for the gun, spun onto her back, pointing it at his chest, halting him mid-step.

"Get the fuck off me!" She shouted. He lifted both hands and took two steps back as Morgan scrambled to the other side of the room. Her mattress separated them.

"You killed that girl, didn't you? Allison Moran. I found the autopsy report in your mother's office! It said she died by suicide, but you did it. Because she didn't want you?" It was a question and an accusation, all in the same breath. His silence was his admission. "What is wrong with you?"

"It wasn't supposed to happen the same way with you, Mo," he said. "None of this was even about you at first, but you keep pushing me."

Morgan wished the gun was loaded. She wished she could do more than keep him at bay. She clicked off the safety. Red means dead. Where was Messiah when she needed him?

"Remember what I have on you, Mo," he said. "Put the gun down."Morgan sniffed away tears and clenched her teeth. "Let's talk about what I have on you," she said. "You brought me to my place. This is my shit, Bash. I knew how to incite you, I knew how to get to my gun, and I knew that everything in this house is recorded through my security footage," she said. Her mind went back to Ahmeek. The first time she had slept at his house, he had caught her spying on his iPad. After that, she had asked him to install the system in her apartment. It made her feel safe, and as soon as she had charged Messari's iPad, she had downloaded the app and made sure that it was recording. "Everything you just did and everything you just admitted to is on tape."

Morgan talked big, but her heart was racing. It took everything in her to hold the gun straight, but she did it because she remembered Messiah in her ear all those years ago, "Keep that shit steady, shorty. If a nigga know you scared, he might try to take that shit from you cuz he know you won't pull the trigger." So, she didn't shake. She didn't even breathe. "I trusted you, Bash."

"You want to talk trust?" Bash asked, snickering. "I took good care of you when you let me. For years you couldn't sleep at night. You found excuses to stay up. You blamed it on school, blamed it on dancing, blamed it on the twins when really it was you keeping them up because you were afraid to sleep. I stayed up with you, pretending like it was normal. I held your hand while you grieved another man, Mo, and I held you when you cried for hours. I didn't know what was going on until my mom told me about postpartum. We paid for you to see someone, the best therapist in London, and you told her everything. We didn't pay for you to see a therapist to help you, Mo. We did it to help us. You don't bring people into the monarchy without knowing everything. You weren't good enough, but you were my second chance to get it right this time. To make up for Allison. When I asked you about that night, you cried so hard you couldn't even speak. I knew I would marry you one day. Every man in your life had failed to protect you, even Ethic. So, I told myself I would keep your secrets, and we would build together. I wanted to give you a new life, a new start, like you gave me. Then, you let your past pull you back. It was a slap in the face. You're just so disrespectful, Mo."

"Do you want me because of me or because I remind you of her?" Morgan asked, mortified.

"A little bit of both," he answered unapologetically. "Every family has bones it's buried. Our bone is named Allison, your family's bones are named Kenzie and Lucas," Bash said. "So, what do we do now? Huh? Are you gonna shoot me?"

"We call it even, and you let me and my kids go, you call off these court cases, and you sign off the rights to my kids. They're mine. I struggled every fucking day to be strong enough to have them. You will have to kill me to take them from me," Morgan said.

"I've arranged more for less," Bash said sinisterly. "Don't overestimate your power."

"Don't overestimate yours. My security system is backed up on Ahmeek's account. He pays the bill. I have the password. Everything you said and did is on that tape. If you want it to stay there, get out of my house. If anything happens to me, he'll watch that tape. You know what happens then. He'll come. Ssiah will come. Ethic will come. It won't even matter if they go to jail afterward because they'll take their time willingly after seeing what you've done. The police will be the last thing you have to worry about."

Morgan could see he was fuming. The narcissist in him didn't like being beaten at his own game. The manipulation and extortion had been one-sided until now. Morgan had been prey in his family's home, but in this apartment, he was hers. She had outsmarted him and played weak until she could accumulate a bit of leverage.

He snatched up his jacket and nodded his head as he realized that Morgan had won this battle on this day. She wondered if she had won the war, however. Was it over? Or would he be back with more ammunition next time? She followed him all the way to the door and then locked it, adding the chain at the top when he was finally gone.

She rushed to her room, pulling the box of bullets from the top of her closet. Her hands were shaking so badly she could barely load the gun, but she wanted to be prepared just in case he came back. Now that Morgan had proof of Bash's abuse and insanity, she would use it as leverage to get away from him. The hardest thing would be admitting to Ethic that she had exposed him to danger, but it was a conversation she had to have, and the possibility of the fallout from that killed her.

"Shorty said what?" Messiah's face bent in confusion, and he pulled the phone away from his face, staring at it in disbelief as he tried to process Ethic's words.

"I'm trying real hard to give Morgan autonomy over her own decisions and her own life, but if she thinks I'm letting go, she's mistaken. This thing between her and my wife, it puts me in a bad way," Ethic admitted. "I've never handled Mo with impatience, but I'm iotas off taking her other options off the table. If she thinks she's running away again, she's mistaken. Not again. That's no way to live for a father. I'm not choosing between her and my wife. I'll wrap a royal in plastic before I let him take her across the ocean again."

Messiah knew how it felt to have torn allegiances, and every word Ethic spoke resonated in Messiah's soul. "Mo's wrong about Alani," Messiah said. "Alani ain't hurting nobody over there. From where I stand, she's been doing a whole lot of healing for the past two years."

"Yeah, let Morgan tell it, Alani is the worst thing that ever happened to her," Ethic replied. Messiah heard the sigh but didn't acknowledge it.

"Nah, that ain't what shorty would say," Messiah said sadly. He knew her worst moment because he caused it. Emotion tore through him, but he suppressed it, changing the subject.

"My ear been to the streets. I'm out the way but a nigga still listening, you know what I mean?" Messiah hadn't been able to abandon Michigan completely. He knew that he should, but the thought of leaving without speaking to Mo directly weighed on him. He was so guilt-ridden that he wondered why he hadn't allowed the same emotion to change his choices years ago. So much regret lived in him.

"This ain't come from the streets," Ethic said. "It's being handled. The next court date is tomorrow. I'll be in touch after that."

"Hurry, Big Homie. Shorty got something that belongs to me and it's eating me alive that I can't go get them. I swear to God I'ma kill that nigga just off GP. My kids think he's their father, man. Fuck type of shit she was on?"

"The type of shit that men who aren't present leave room for. Women settle for whatever feels safe for the sake of their kids. Mo played the hand you dealt her. Now, it's time to toss in the cards and deal again. Maybe this time, you won't fold on your queen."

"I don't know if I can get over the shit shorty did, OG. I just don't know about me and her. I just want to see my kids." Messiah had so much resentment towards Morgan. He remembered the moment they had planned those babies. It was a dream he hadn't even known he had. She had wanted to have his baby so badly, to create a family, a permanent ode to their love, and the way she had begged him, the way she assigned value to even the thought of sharing a child, had made him want it too. Morgan had given him hope that a piece of him would know peace even if he wasn't around to see it manifest. A child between the two of them would be nothing less than a blessing. She had upped the ante and given him two. Two souls, and then she removed him from the picture like he hadn't helped create them. He would have killed the next bitch for the same behavior, but with Mo, all he could do was agonize in silence. Killing her would kill him, so he was forced to endure her bullshit.

"I'm going to send you an address. I want you to go there. I'll text you the time and place."

CHAPTER 14

Are you worried?" Bella asked as she sat on the opposite end of the basement couch. Her feet were in Henny's lap, and he traced circles into her soles. He hadn't said a word. They were watching *Friday*, his favorite movie, and he hadn't even cracked a smile. They had watched this movie at least five times before, and Hendrix would talk her through the entire thing, teasing her because she had never seen it before meeting him. Today, she wasn't even sure if he was paying attention.

"Nah," Hendrix answered, trying to be hard.

"I am," Bella admitted. Hendrix finally looked at her, and she nodded. "It's okay if you are too."

Bella's heart had been in shambles for days. The arrest had rattled her. Worst-case scenarios ran through her head, but she held it inside because she knew that Hendrix had enough to worry about. Everyone had enough to worry about. Nobody had time to make her feel better about things. The threat of change loomed over her life, and Bella could feel it in her bones.

"If I take this to trial, they gon' hit me with a mandatory minimum," Hendrix said.

"What does that mean?" Bella asked.

"Fifteen years, Boog," he answered sadly. "I can't go to trial. They caught it on me."

"But it's not all yours. You can just tell them who you got it from, right? They'll cut you a deal if you tell them what they want to know."

The thought of Hendrix being removed from her life for the next fifteen years was numbing. It hurt so badly that she couldn't feel it. Couldn't think because if she had to imagine him in a cell while she was living free in the world, it felt like she would die.

"I can't snitch," Henny said.

"Hendrix, you can leave. You can go somewhere else, anywhere else. My daddy will help you!" She argued. "I'd rather you be away for two years than for fifteen, Hendrix. I can come to you after I graduate, and we can still do what we said we were going to do!" Bella said. The panic in her voice put a pit in Hendrix. He had disappointed Bella Okafor, and that felt worse than it all. She was the one person who had believed in him. She had put a fire in him that he now regretted because if she had never sparked the idea of possibility in him, he wouldn't be so terrified to fail. He would just walk down his time because he probably would have expected to be locked up one day anyway. Bella had fucked up his head and made him feel like he could be somebody only for him to prove her wrong.

"It don't work like that in my world, Bella! Ain't no fairy tale shit! This is real life! You don't get it cuz we not the same!" Hendrix shouted.

"What about the door?" Bella asked.

"Wasn't never no door for me! You was always walking through the door dolo! We don't belong together!"

He was crushing her, and Bella couldn't contain the damage. With tears in her eyes, she said,

"If you loved me, you would do anything to get to me, Hendrix. You're choosing to go away." Stubborn tears were now wetting her cheekbones.

"I did do anything to get to you!" Hendrix shouted. "Hanging around here with your family, playing like I fit in! Trying to keep up with your high-ass expectations! I should have never fucked with you! I would have never been out this way, man!"

Bella recoiled. "You think this is my fault?"

Hendrix stood and snatched up his jacket. "I'm saying, I got to do what I got to do and it ain't about you and that fake-ass door you been having me chasing."

Bella was livid, but she couldn't relate to Hendrix's struggle. For her, college was a natural progression. All of her dreams seemed attainable, and she knew exactly how to get to them. For Hendrix, they just felt like impossible wishes.

"You're giving up," she said, deflated.

"They finna lock me up, Boog," he said. He could barely choke out the words, and Bella watched helplessly as the boy crept out of this wanna-be man.

"We could run together," Bella said.

He turned to her, staring at her in awe as he shook his head. "You'd do that, wouldn't you?"

"Yeah, Henny, I would," Bella said. "Because you don't deserve this."

Bella looked up at him from where she sat, and Hendrix lowered, coming to his knees in between her legs so that he could look her in the eyes.

"I'd never pull you into no shit like that," Henny said. "That ain't love, and I really do think you're the first girl I ever loved, and when this ends, I want you to remember me right. I ain't leaving no bad taste in your mouth by asking you to make mistakes I know you'll regret."

"My heart will break if you go to jail," Bella whispered.

"I'ma be a'ight," Henny answered.

Neither knew if that were true. They would lock Henny away with grown men. He had some rough days ahead. They knew it. Unspoken fear filled the air with anxiety.

Bella put her hands on his face. "This isn't fair," she whispered. Hendrix leaned in slowly, admiring the details of her face causing Bella to hold her breath in anticipation. Her stomach fluttered as he kissed her. It did it every time. Bella had made plans for this boy, for their entire lives. She had it down to a science. He would take her to junior prom. He would get his Associate's degree from the local college and pursue credits until she graduated. Senior prom would be the night she lost her virginity. He would cheer her on at graduation and then they would drive down south and attend an HBCU together. They would backpack around the world on Summer breaks and spend holidays with her family. They'd be married after graduate school, buy their first house before she turned 30, and have their one and only baby by the time she was 32.

Bella could envision an entire life with him within the intimacy of this one kiss, and her tears flowed because nowhere in her plans had she made room for a jail sentence. It felt like she needed to squeeze everything in so he would know how much she loved him before he went away.

"Henny," she whispered.

Their lips disconnected, but he didn't pull back. Instead, he kissed her cheeks repeatedly, planting small tokens of love there, making the tiny hairs on the back of her neck stand.

"I love you so much, Boog," he said. "I hate when you're sad."

"You're going to miss so much," she said. "I was saving a lot for you. Saving myself because I thought we had time, and I wanted to make you earn it so that you would know it wasn't a cheap gift afterward, but we're running out of time."

Hendrix pulled back and stared into her eyes. "I'm running out of time. You still got your whole life," he said. So much melancholy was a sin for such a young couple. Their love language had never been this grim.

"There is no way I'm giving that to anybody but you," she said. "And no boy who will ever deserve it like you."

Hendrix was floored. He knew how important Bella's virginity was to her. Taking it in her daddy's basement while her parents were running errands wasn't what he had in mind. As much as he wanted to, as many times as he had thought about it, he couldn't.

He fingered her necklace, reminding Bella what it was there for. "Nah, Boog. You got to give me something to look forward to. You hold onto that for me. If it's still there when

I get out, I'll earn it again. The fact that you even feel like you got to rush means I don't deserve it right now."

Bella didn't know she was holding her breath until she sighed, and then she rushed into Henny's arms, crying inconsolably.

"We gon' be a'ight, Boog. You my girl, my best friend, man," Henny whispered as she fell apart. He was used to her being strong, so he knew if she was giving in to this emotion it was because she couldn't hold it back any longer. "I'ma come for you one day. It'll take me a while, and your life won't look the same; you probably won't even be the same girl you are now, but I'ma still come for you just in case there's a chance that you still want a nigga."

"Promise me, Henny," Bella said.

"We already made the pact, Boog. You know where to meet me if we ever lose our way," Henny said. "I'ma be there."

"And I'll wait. No matter how long they give you. When you get out, I will be there too. On everything, Henny. I promise."

He cleared her tears and kissed her. The way Bella's body reacted to him was like a flower blooming towards the sun.

She was a teenage girl, learning the ways a man's presence could influence her womanhood. She climbed into Henny's lap and moaned as she pressed into him. "I want to wait to do the big thing, but I want to experience the little things now," she whispered. Shock and a slight hesitation froze him. It was her nod of certainty that reassured him.

Henny's hands slid up her midsection, lifting her shirt with it until he discovered the lace bra beneath.

"You gonna have to tell me what's fair play, Boog," he said as he unhooked her bra, freeing pretty, perky titties. Her nipples were already tight, and he caressed them before putting one in his mouth while teasing the other. Bella bucked.

"That's fair play, Henny," she whispered, breathlessly. "It feels so good." He alternated between tongue kissing her and tongue kissing her breasts, and Bella had never felt anything better. Well, maybe one thing. He had put his tongue somewhere else one time before, and it had felt like bliss, but it had also felt like a sin. She was too afraid to let him go that far again.

"You can't keep asking me to test the waters, Boog; eventually, I'ma drown in you," he said. He slipped his hand down the front of her leggings, and her panties were wet. "See," he said, rubbing her clit through the fabric. Bella's mouth hung open. "You playing with me, Boog. You gonna give this shit to somebody while I'm gone."

She shook her head and bit down on her lip, arching her back because whatever conversation Henny's tongue was having with her nipples, they were speaking fluently.

"I won't," she answered, panting as she looked down her body as he kissed his way down her heaving stomach.

"Your skin is like soil, Bella," he said.

She lifted on her elbows, frowning in confusion.

"I'm dirty?" She asked, thrown off. He stopped kissing her and looked up over a creased brow.

"I can't explain it. I planted a flower one day when I was little. A Mother's Day project or something for school in like first grade. I played in that shit all day, spread it all over my desk; it was the softest thing I ever felt. Your skin is dark like that. Soft like that too. The prettiest flowers come from soil like that," Henny said.

She didn't even know why she was smiling. The compliment didn't even make sense to her, but she felt it. Whatever he loved about making that flower for his mom as a kid, he connected it to her skin, and she appreciated his attempt to communicate it.

"One day, you're going to be my husband, Hendrix. Does that scare you?" Bella asked.

He shook his head and resumed his kisses. He pulled the leggings down, and Bella tensed. "I won't go nowhere you don't want me to go. You tell me when to stop."

Bella nodded, and Hendrix started at her inner thigh. The most tender kisses to her inner thigh, and Bella cringed as she felt his nose cross her mound. She was young, untouched, and unshaven. Alani had taught her to groom her bikini line, but a full shave and wax were out of the question. It made her insecure because she wasn't sure if he thought it was nasty. She was a girl, nowhere near womanhood, and experiencing emotions so mature intimidated her.

"Boog, you're shaking," Hendrix said.

"I'm just," she whispered. "You've been with a lot of girls, and I don't know what I'm doing."

Hendrix nodded. "I've fucked other girls, Bella. I've only been with you. Should I stop?"

Bella shook her head, and Hendrix kissed her. Bella gasped and jerked so hard that she nudged his head backward. He looked up at her as he kissed her soul, softly, slowly, and Bella squeezed her eyes tightly because this was euphoric. "I'm sorry, Boog," Henny whispered as he kissed her there. "I'm gonna miss you so much the shit hurts."

"Hendrix, Hendrix, Henny, wait, wait, oh my god," she whispered. The way she touched herself had nothing on this. She trembled as Henny wiped his mouth and came up. They were face to face, and Bella blushed.

"I don't know if I want to wait," Bella said.

Henny nodded. "We got to wait, Boog. When we take it there, it won't be because we out of time. Our time gon' come. We ain't got to rush."

Morgan didn't know if the incessant knocking was the door or the banging inside her head. She hadn't slept. She was too afraid to close her eyes, so she watched over her twins, sitting on the floor of their bedroom with a gun at her side. Bash had taken her keys on his way out the door, and she hadn't built up the nerve to call Ethic yet. Nobody else was answering. Not Aria, not Ahmeek, not even Isa. She didn't know Messiah's new number by heart, and all of their social media pages had been deactivated. She felt stranded on an island without a boat. The only people left to call were her family, and with that came the admittance of her betrayal. She wasn't sure if her family could take anymore from her. She was always the one adding weight, bringing the dynamic of the Okafor connection down. After what Bash had made her say to Ethic, she wasn't even sure if they wanted her around. She knew Ethic well enough to know that he was letting her cool down before coming to see her. He had always been that way. Morgan would throw temper tantrums often as a child, and he would remain levelheaded and give her the space she needed to calm down. Once her emotion waned, he would knock on her room door and stay up all night talking out the problem. By morning, her heart would be settled, and the next day would be Ethic and Mo day. School nor business stopped it. Their bond disrupted everything. How she craved for an Ethic and Mo day right now. She needed him to make her feel safe, to make her feel loved, but she wondered if she had lost that forever.

The knock on her door sent her anxiety to the moon, and Morgan climbed up, releasing the safety on her gun. She looked out the peephole and pulled open the door so fast she startled the person on the other side.

"Bitch, I've been calling you!" Aria shrieked. The recognition of Morgan's undoing silenced her. "Mo, your neck."

Morgan shook her head in disgrace and wrapped her arms around Aria as she sobbed. "I need help, Aria."

"Oh my god, Mo," Aria soothed. "It's okay. It's okay."

Aria had known something was wrong, and the fact that she had left anyway put guilt on her that was almost too heavy to carry. Morgan wouldn't say exactly what had gone down, but the bruises on her neck and the way she had rushed into Aria's arms spoke loudly. Morgan wouldn't even close her eyes to sleep. She just laid there for hours. Aria hated to see what would have happened if she hadn't hopped on a flight to come home. This was heavy, and she needed reinforcements.

Aria paced the living room as she dialed Isa's number for the fifth time. She had been calling him all night.

"Where the fuck are you?" She shouted into the phone. "Isa, call me back! I know you're with Ahmeek and it's important." She left the voicemail and then tossed her phone onto the couch in frustration.

When she turned, Messari and Yara were peeking around the corner.

"Auntie Ari, are you mad?" Messari asked.

Aria turned to Messari and Yara, who sat coloring on the floor.

She went to them. "Noooo. No, boyfriend. I'm not mad. I'm just looking for your dumbass Uncle Isa," she whispered the last part. She picked up her phone and dialed him again.

"Answer, Isa," Aria whispered. She knew she was only supposed to call if it was an emergency, but if this didn't qualify as one, she didn't know what would.

"You better be sending a nigga a pussy pic or something cuz I know this ain't no emergency," Isa answered.

"I'm in Michigan, Isa. I had to come home because I

couldn't reach Mo. This motherfucka took her phone. You need to call Meek and Messiah. She won't tell me exactly what happened, but she's fucked up. She has bruises all around her neck, like he choked her, and Mo is terrified to call Ethic. Y'all got to come home because if that nigga steps foot in her vicinity, I'm going the fuck off."

Isa's silence was terrifying.

"Isa?"

Finally, he spoke. "We on the way."

CHAPTER 15

Messiah pulled up to the small office building and frowned in confusion. He double-checked the text message from Ethic.

"Fuck he got me at?" he said, brow pinched as he looked at the sign on the door.

Dr. *Khadeen Brown*, M.D.

The sound of high heels connecting with concrete turned him in the direction of the parking lot. A woman in clear-colored shoes, yellow suit jacket and small yellow shorts was walking in his direction. The yellow bralette she wore beneath exposed a dainty frame. In one hand, she gripped her coffee and a Maserati key. Miraculously, a large tote bag hung from the same arm as she dug through it distractedly.

Messiah didn't realize he was staring until she glanced up at him, forcing him to divert his eyes.

"You gonna get the door, or you gonna just stand there?" she asked.

"Pretty and rude, huh?" Messiah replied as he pulled open the glass door.

She frowned and challenged him with her stare. "Is that how you got beat up? Talking crazy to someone you don't know?" she said as she observed the sling on his shoulder and the black eye.

She walked inside, and the ringing of the office phone forced a sigh out of her mouth.

"You the receptionist?" he asked.

"I'm the doctor," she replied. "Have a seat. Someone will be with you."

"Nah, I think I got the wrong spot," Messiah said.

"Messiah Williams, right?" The woman asked.

The look on his face confirmed his identity.

"Have a seat," she repeated. "As soon as my late assistant shows up, she'll get you signed in, and we'll get started. I'm Dr. *Brown.*"

"This is bullshit, man," Messiah mumbled. He didn't know what kind of time Ethic was on, but he felt ambushed. He turned to walk out.

"If you walk out that door, you're going to be the same man, making the same mistakes, recycling the hurt that I see on your face," she said. His hand rested on the door. His back was to her. All he had to do was walk out. His feet wouldn't move.

"You don't know me, shorty," he said.

"Shorty," she repeated. "I take it you give women that nickname, and it flatters them. You flatter them. You're the type of man that doesn't really have to try too hard to attract anything into your life. You have a hard time keeping things, though. People. Shorties," she mocked. "You use the nickname because you don't want to attach yourself to people you can't keep. So, a woman becomes shorty. One after the other. You meet them, and you name them all the same thing so that way when you lose one, another is just waiting in the wings, and you don't have to deal with ever truly earning the presence of one person. It's Dr. Brown to you, not shorty."

Messiah took her in. She couldn't have been older than thirty years old, maybe younger, but she had read him like a woman with aged wisdom.

"I'ma pass on the psychoanalysis. It's just a name," he replied.

"Then why do you look down every time you say it? One of those shorties means something to you," she said.

Messiah thought about Morgan in that moment. Morgan meant everything to him. He couldn't identify a time when she hadn't. Even when Ethic would call him to plant eyes on Morgan when she was hanging out in places she had no business being, it was something about being the one looking after her that felt like an honor. When Morgan was in the room, his focus shifted. He immediately lost interest in the moment before him because his job became apparently clear... to protect her. He had gone from her protector to her lover against his will because she had wanted it, but he hadn't been ready, and the inevitable had occurred. His hurt had been transferred to her. Morgan had such an accepting heart that she had taken on his pain. He could see his pain killing her.

"A little time on somebody's couch might serve you well, Messiah Williams."

The burner phone rang, and Messiah answered it while staring the woman in the eyes.

"What's the word?"

He knew it could only be one of three people. Isa, Ethic, or Ahmeek.

"Where you at, bruh?" Isa asked.

"Around the way," Messiah replied vaguely.

"Get to Mo, my nigga. We got action. The mu'fucka, Bash, don' lost his mind."

Messiah didn't know what had occurred. He didn't ask another question. He didn't say goodbye to the doctor, didn't pause, didn't think, didn't pass go. He didn't even give a fuck about the police scare because he knew he was headed directly to jail anyway. If Bash had done anything in any way to hurt Morgan or his kids, he would never see the light of day again by choice.

He pushed out of the office and rushed to the car, pulling out of the parking lot so quickly he left burn marks on the pavement.

The worst assumptions ran through his mind. He had made so many decisions regarding Morgan since he had been back, and none of them had been made with her safety in mind. Morgan had seemed to be in control. Making big choices and backing them with arrogance and audacity. He had never considered her well-being. Not once did he think Morgan was in danger.

Ain't no way this corny-ass nigga don' hurt her, Messiah thought.

He had been so locked in on warring with Ahmeek; he hadn't seen the looming threat right in front of him.

"Fuck!" He shouted.

The miles between him and Morgan were torture. He had lived this before. The night of her rape ran through his mind, haunting him as he broke every law known to man to get to her.

Messiah hadn't been able to get that shit off his chest because Ethic had stopped him. Ethic had taken care of Lucas, and to this day, that was a score he wished he had settled. He wouldn't call Ethic this time.

Messiah felt like a tea kettle was inside him, reaching its boiling point, threatening to erupt. He had come back with one thing on his mind; to get her back. He didn't think she needed saving.

"Please, man," Messiah said aloud. He didn't even know who he was pleading to. He just knew he needed a little mercy. Messiah had never been given any. If there was a greater power at play, he just needed Him to show a little mercy. Not for himself, he knew he had done too much to deserve grace, but Morgan deserved it all. His children deserved the most.

Suddenly, it didn't matter who Morgan was with or what she had done. He just wanted to get to her.

"Mo, Messiah's here."

Morgan laid on her side with her back to the door. She just couldn't get up. She couldn't do another thing, couldn't think another thing, couldn't speak another thing. She couldn't look Messiah in the eyes, so she closed them when he rounded the bed.

"She hasn't said one word since I got here last night. She was sobbing, Messiah," Aria said.

Morgan could feel him in the room.

"I got her," Messiah said. "Where are my kids?" "They're in their room," Aria said.

Morgan opened her eyes, and Messiah was there, kneeling on the side of the bed.

"I'ma go see them, shorty. Just for a second, and then I'm right back to you," Messiah said.

Messiah bypassed Aria and whispered, "Let me holla at you."

Messiah didn't breathe until he got into the hallway. "Where is he?"

"I don't know," Aria said.

Messiah nodded. He walked down the hall where he heard the sound of laughter. It was foreign in this somber home, but it drew him near.

He headed toward their room and the way he bitched up when he saw them hovering over the iPad that sat in the middle of the floor made him feel like less than a man. He had no idea that it was the vulnerability for his babies that made him all man.

"Nigga, they don't bite," Aria said softly.

"How the fuck me and shorty make two perfect people?" He was taken aback at how breathtaking they were. "We so fucked up, and they're so pure."

"Mo's not fucked up, Messiah. You fucked my friend up, and you got me fucked up if you think I'm going to root for you when I know you'll fuck up again."

Messiah was shocked at her moxie, but at the same time, he appreciated the spot Aria occupied in Morgan's life. She was overstepping her boundaries with him because he didn't give a fuck about Aria and would turn her lights out without thinking twice, but he respected the way she stood up for Morgan. Morgan needed friends like that. She deserved a best friend who was ten toes down.

"No disrespect, but I don't know you enough for you to feel comfortable enough to have this conversation with me. Stop while you ahead."

"And that's the problem, Messiah. Two years is a long time. You don't know me like that because you haven't been around to see the bond we all have. I'm your kids' godmother. I'm who Mo calls when she needs to vent. She's my best friend, and you still think I'm the new girl she met on a humbug. You have no idea what you did to her when you played dead!"

"She moved the fuck on," Messiah spat back. "I was gone but I ain't replace shorty like she did me."

"She never moved on, Messiah! You weren't there. We watched her struggle to carry three babies for your disloyal-ass."

Aria's words froze time. His heartbeat stilled. "What?"

Aria closed her eyes. She had said entirely too much. Morgan would kill her. "Nothing. It's not even my place."

"Nah, you loud. Keep talking," Messiah said. "What you mean three?"

Aria shook her head. "Ask Mo."

"I'm asking you." When Messiah applied pressure, people cracked, and Aria was no different.

"You're pissed at Ahmeek for the way he is with Mo, but you should be thanking him. She was barely alive before him. You broke her, Messiah. She was carrying triplets, and after what you did to her on Bleu's lawn that day, she was never the same."

"Shorty definitely different than I remember," Messiah said.

"Don't do that. Don't try to play her like she's done you some kind of disservice. You can't go around hurting people and then decide how they react to it," Aria said. "She was too loyal if you ask me. She tried to give you her life. There were three babies, Messiah. One of them died. She tried to commit suicide after you left. Nigga, she thought you were worth her life. So, when you see her living now, smiling with Meek, having her cake, and eating it too, it's just her living. She's testing the limits because she's not even supposed to be here. Ethic pulled her out of a gas chamber she made in a running car."

Messiah backpedaled, and his back hit the wall, trapping him there. "Mo ain't do that shit, man. Shorty ain't do no stupid shit like that. She wouldn't do that," he said, shaking his head in denial. His face bent as the consequences of his actions stared him in the face. He slammed one fist against his chest like he was knocking on a furnace, praying it worked, jump-starting his heart. It didn't. It was failing him. This news, permanently breaking him.

"We all had to love on Mo a little more to make up for what you took away," Aria said, softer this time because she could see her words tearing through him. "So know that I got her back through whatever. You're a whole killer, and I'll go toe to toe with you over my best friend."

Messiah nodded his head as he fought to keep his emotions in control. He kinda-sorta understood how Isa had become so wrapped up in this girl. She was the right type. He had never been super fond of her, but he appreciated her in this moment. She was supposed to ride for Morgan. Nish had done differently. Nish would have been on her knees sucking him off by now, but Aria was proving to be uniquely loyal to Morgan above everyone.

Messiah gritted his teeth, forcing himself to swallow his feelings because he refused to let his insides spill before her. His jaw locked, and his temple throbbed. He was choking. This was too much to digest. Aria could see the pain all over his face. His eyes were fucking out of pocket because they teared at even the possibility of a Morgan-less world. Messiah was sick, nausea-filled, and mourning the 'what if' of it all. *What the fuck did I do?*

Aria shook her head hopelessly. "Fix it, Messiah, because if you don't, I'm always going to be team Mo, and if she decides to slice your tires and bust them windows out next week, I'ma be right next to her, and you better not shoot me."

Yeah, Aria was a real one, and he decided right then and there that he liked her. He understood how she had been indoctrinated into The Crew.

Aria sighed and turned to the kids. "Okay, Auntie Ari's about to go, give me some kisses," she said. Aria signed for Yolly, and Messiah was amazed at the dedication Aria had to his children. It wasn't an easy thing to learn to do. He knew firsthand. She had gotten a few signs incorrect, but she knew enough for Yolly to get up and scurry to her. Messiah bent down, taking the back of his palm to his wet eyes and sniffing away emotion, only for it to come right back as he stared into his daughter's ocean-deep eyes. He extended his palm to Yara.

"Hi, beautiful," he signed.

Yara looked at Aria for reassurance and then back to Messiah. She wrapped an arm around Aria's leg but waved shyly at her father.

"That's progress," he said, smiling sadly. The idea of a third little person that was missing weighed on him. He had left for two years, and in his absence, he had lost two babies. "What about you, playa? You got some love for your daddy?" Messiah asked his son.

"What happened to you eye?" Messari asked.

"I'm a'ight, man. It's just a little bruise. It's nothing to a giant," Messiah said, tapping Messari on his stomach gently.

"Did the po-wice put you in jail?" Messari asked.

Messiah hated for that to be their first memory of him.

"It was a misunderstanding, that's all," Messiah signed and spoke. "You want some ice cream? What if your auntie, Aria, took you to get some while I talk to your mommy?" Messiah pulled out a roll of money and handed Aria a few hundred-dollar bills.

"Mommy is sleepy. She no feel good," Messari informed.

"Daddy knows how to make your mommy feel better. I haven't been around to keep that pretty smile on her face, but I'm back now, and I ain't going nowhere ever again." Messiah was grateful for sign language because he could barely speak. The news of Morgan's suicide attempt had slid down the wrong pipe, and he was still struggling to get it down. The sobs he was holding were pulling his card, making a whole bitch out of him in front of Aria and his kids. He decided to give up on speaking altogether and signed. "So, ice cream sound like the move?"

Messari nodded, but Yara shook her head, making her little curls shake. She might as well had been shaking pixie dust into the air because Messiah was captivated.

"My mommy says no to ice cream," Yara signed.

"Well, Daddy says yes," Messiah signed back. "Daddy got some making up to do, so it's yes to everything."

"Really?!" Messari yelled.

"That's right," Messiah signed.

"Can we have a puppy?" Messari asked.

Messiah signed, "yes."

"Can you build us a carnival?" Messari signed.

"Daddy can make that happen too," Messiah answered, laughing because he was realizing that Messari was a "give an inch, take a mile," type of kid. He looked up at Aria. "Want to take them for a bit? Get the ice cream and stop at a toy store or something. Maybe keep them until I call you. I'ma need a minute with shorty."

Aria nodded and gathered the twins. "Take good care of her, Messiah."

Messiah was destroyed inside as he made his way to Morgan's side. It took everything in him to tether his aggression when he saw how she was curled up in bed. Whatever Bash had done, it had deflated her spirit. *Or maybe I did that,* Messiah thought.

Messiah's temper was raging. The only thing that would quench his thirst for blood was to put hands on Bash, but Morgan needed him more. Morgan needed to see a side of him that required him to be soft, not hard, and he was struggling with that as he rounded the bed to be at her side.

"Look at me, shorty," he said as he moved her hair from her face. Gas to fire. Seeing those fingerprints around her neck set off a grenade inside him. "Mo, I'm gonna murder me a mu'fucka. You know that, right?"

She didn't answer.

"He hurt you?" he asked.

Morgan closed her eyes, and tears leaked, because they were too heavy to hold.

"This is too much like the last time, shorty," Messiah whispered. "I don't really know what to do besides murder shit over you. I know I fucked up. I know I left. I know you're hurt, Mo, but until the day I die, I will murder a mu'fucka over you. I ain't never loved nobody like I love you. Nobody. I'm fucking itching, Mo," he said as he rubbed his fingers together. "You got to tell me how to love you right, shorty. Cuz I know I've been doing it wrong. Help me do it the way you need me to. That's the only thing that's keeping me in this bedroom with you and not at that nigga door."

Morgan opened her eyes. "Get him off me, Messiah," she signed. "Please, please, just get him off me. I've showered three times, and I still smell him on me." Messiah stood and scooped Morgan into his arms as he carried her to the bathroom.

He noticed that her body trembled like she was cold, but he knew it was fear seizing her.

He ran her a bath, struggling to stop up the tub because she was still in his lap as he sat on the side of the tub.

When he removed her shirt and saw her ribs, his nostrils flared. "Come on, let's get in, Mo," he managed to croak out. As soon as Morgan sat down, he dismissed himself. "I'll be right back."

Stepping out of her eyesight was all it took for him to break down. Messiah came to his knees in front of her bed and slammed his fists down before lowering his head on top of them. He felt like screaming. A cry was looming. His head hung in shame as his face contorted uncontrollably. Blood. He tasted blood as he bit his bottom lip.

Tighten up, he told himself silently. *She needs you.*

He swiped his face with one hand and blew out his angst before returning to the bathroom. His red eyes were every indication that he had left the room to cry.

Her body was exposed, and traces of Bash's trespasses were all over her. Morgan wasn't even shy about being naked in front of him. Her body had always been Messiah's expertise. It was her heart and soul she had to keep covered up with him.

She hugged her knees to her chest and rested her head on top. She closed her eyes as they sat in silence.

"I spent a lot of time just wanting to see your face, shorty. I know what this silence means and what happened to make you go dark. You ain't got to talk. I'll do all the talking, but just look at me, so I know you hear me."

Morgan opened her red eyes, and his forehead cinched as he got lost in the fantasies that existed behind her stare. She was the reason for his entire existence. She was the reason he had fought so hard to live, and he was the reason she had attempted to die. He knew that feeling. He had experienced it once in the hospital all those years ago. If no one understood her desire to not live without him, he did because living without her had almost made him eat his own bullet. He knew that Morgan had tried to manifest the hurt he had made her feel inside. He hadn't known leaving would be catastrophic. He had thought she would cry and then move on, but to abandon life behind his actions... Messiah was aghast. He had never suspected Morgan would take her grief that far. He had felt something was different about her, but never would he have imagined this. As he sat there respecting her silence, he realized her eyes said so much. Eyes so sad, they looked as if they had cried a thousand tears. He recognized it now, the melancholy inside her. He had thought her indifference to his return was cruel punishment for his abandonment, but he knew now that it was survival. Morgan couldn't love him like she had before because that love had almost ended her. She was terrified, and he didn't blame her. None of his actions since returning had proved that she would be safe in his care. The therapist popped into his mind. He decided then and there that he would go back, if not for himself, for Mo and his children. Plowing back into her life the way that he had was inconsiderate, and he acknowledged for the first time that it was selfish.

"You tried to kill yourself, Mo?" He asked. She looked up in stun when she heard the waver in his tone… like it mattered to him.

She didn't answer, but her body language was all the admission he needed. A flicker of embarrassment flashed in her eyes. She was mortified. It wasn't something she wanted the world to know.

"I ain't shit. I'm nobody, Mo. What I do don't determine how high your frequency vibrates," he whispered passionately. He was angry as he gripped her chin suddenly. "Don't ever do no shit like that," he said through gritted teeth. His face contorted, and his lip quivered. "Ever, Mo." His levees broke when he called her name, and he broke down. A cry forced itself from his lips. "Ever, baby. You're my baby. What I'ma do if you're not breathing, shorty? Huh? Fucking ever." He sobbed in front of her as he gripped her face, shaking her a bit to get the point through her thick skull. He wanted to murder somebody. He was so angry. It was the only way he knew how to expel emotions… to kill shit. He wanted to put his pistol to a nigga dome and curl a trigger. All because he had hurt this one girl. Messiah was almost inhuman… he was a beast, and she had loved him. He had been so undeserving. *I fucked this all up.*

Messiah washed Morgan's body for the second time after she was abused. It was his undoing. Flashbacks of his own torture at the hands of his father motivated him to move with extreme care. When she was clean, he held out a towel, and Morgan stepped into it. When he closed it around her body, he picked her up once more and carried her to the bed.

"Mo," he sighed while rocking her as he sat. "How we get here, shorty?"

Morgan looked up at him, and his tears shocked her. Messiah didn't cry, but the reliving of this trauma had him fighting ghosts she hadn't met yet. It would be the perfect time to divulge it all, but he didn't want to make her pain about him. Telling her about his cancer would feel like a sympathy play and telling her about Bookie would change how she saw him forever. A victim couldn't be her protector. Would she pity him? Would she judge him? Would she question his manhood? As badly as Messiah wanted to come clean to Mo, he wasn't ready for her to see him as a man who had been raped by another man. She would have questions. He knew her well enough to know that much, and he didn't have the answers. This was the closest he had felt to her since returning, and he didn't want to erase the intimacy of this moment with the trauma of his own. She wiped away his tears with the softest hands he had ever felt. He caught her hand and kissed the inside of her tattooed wrist.

"I'm sorry, Mo," he whispered. "For everything. We had three babies, shorty."

Morgan and Messiah cried together, mourning the loss of their child. It was a grief that Morgan hadn't been able to share with anyone else because she feared she would look ungrateful for the two babies that had been spared, but with Messiah, she could be free. She could acknowledge it because he felt it too. In their grief, they found common ground, and it felt like old times, like all they needed in the world was one another to make their dysfunction functional.

"Shorty got a nigga fucked up out here, man," he said as he tried to restore his hard exterior.

A ghost of a smile existed on her lips, one that took effort, one that she was putting on for him but didn't truly radiate from within. The sigh that followed revealed sorrow.

"I know you need me to be like this for you right now, but whatever he did can't go unpunished, Mo. I need you to tell me everything. It's bad. I can feel it. That's why you can't find the words. Sign it if you have to, but you got to tell me, Mo. Ever since I came back you been making it seem like you were on some snake shit when we were together. You may hate me now, but back then, shorty, you loved a nigga so right I didn't even breathe right when you wasn't around, so I kept you around. Ain't no way you were with him. How you end up with that nigga? Start from the beginning."

Morgan was hesitant until Messiah began signing.

"Use your hands. That's where you're comfortable at. I'ma follow you. I been practicing," he signed.

The fact that he had kept studying, kept signing while he was away, touched Morgan. On days when she had felt lonely, he was out in the world somewhere trying to get back to her. Practicing signs for a conversation that he hoped they would have one day.

As if he could read her thoughts, he said, "I was always trying to get to you, Mo."

Morgan averted his eyes as guilt sickened her. Had she given up too soon? Should she had waited for him longer? She blew out a breath of discontent. She had to tell someone because Bash was still a clear threat, and she had a feeling that he wasn't done with her yet.

Morgan told Messiah everything. She went through every day that she could remember since Bleu's lawn, even the parts that would make him angry, even the parts he wouldn't want to hear. The picture he had painted of her was worse than the reality. She hadn't just moved on. It had taken her two years. The fact that she hadn't slept with Bash this entire time told him that Meek was also more than a phase, but she was honest about it all, and he couldn't be mad at her for that.

"I messed up, Messiah. I messed up so bad. The reason everybody is in trouble is that Bash knows about Ethic killing Alani's daughter. He knows everything about that night, and he's using it to keep me from leaving. He wants you, Ethic, and Meek locked up so I will have no one but him. They also have legal rights to the twins," Morgan admitted. "I signed something thinking it was for my visa for school and my enrollment stuff. I was in a bad place back then. I didn't read it, and I signed it. Bash can take my babies from me. He's not just a corny guy. He and his family are powerful. They're royal, Messiah. They got you and Ethic picked up with a phone call. He's threatening to take everything from me. The threats started when I started messing with Ahmeek. He and his mother started threatening to recall my credits for my degree."

"And you kept fucking with him?" Messiah asked.

Morgan looked away. "I know you and Meek are on bad terms because of me, Messiah, but he took really good care of me. School wasn't worth me giving him up, so Bash took something else. He knows how much I love my kids and Ethic. He knows how much I love you."

"Me?" He said, shocked.

"You," she confirmed. "He knows. He's been ten times worse since you came back. He has my back against a wall because he knows I can't go to Ethic. He knows I'm afraid to lose Ethic."

"Listen to me, Mo. I need you to go home. Go to Ethic's and stay there. All this blackmail shit is a wrap. I'ma handle this nigga. I don't give a fuck how royal he is. I knock crowns off too."

"What am I supposed to say to him? Ethic has given me everything, and I put his entire life at risk. He's going to hate me. And Alani," Morgan said, sighing as she closed her eyes. "I know she hates me. I've taken them through too much."

"They're your family, Mo," Messiah said. "Time to woman up. I'ma take care of the big problems, but you got to handle the little one. All you got to do is tell the truth." Messiah knew he was a hypocrite to suggest something that he struggled to do himself, but Morgan had always been better than him. The truth was her natural love language, and the people she loved would forgive her. They loved her. He loved her. In every way. Through all things. He always would.

"How do you know they won't hate me?" She asked.

"Because I don't," he answered. "Anybody who ever loved you could never hate you."

CHAPTER 16

Ahmeek sat in the back of the room. He had never seen a classroom this big. It was like a stadium, and the students around him eagerly listened to the guest lecturer as Meek hung out in the nosebleed section. He had earned a degree in business, but his education hadn't been this fancy. He had studied from tattered books; in a 6x8 foot cell, under the glow of a flashlight, he had bribed a guard for. It was a piece of paper he had promised his mother he would get. Her first concern was his GED, and after that, she had pressed him to do something with his time instead of fighting and being thrown in the hole. She wanted her son to be a college graduate, and so he became one. His prison degree hung above her mantle in the house he had purchased her with drug money. Ahmeek hadn't used either a day of his life. He was a chip off his father's block when it came to his money and respect. He had a lot of both, and he earned them fast. He played the game smart and fair because he never wanted to go back to jail. As he listened to the instructor, he knew that today might be the day he gave up his freedom. It was a fate worse than death, but some shit was just worth dying for. He had tried to calm the storm that was brewing within him. He had sat through a four-hour flight trying to tuck his rage, but as he sat in the classroom watching Bash teach, he became even more certain of how the night would end.

"Aristotle lived by the golden mean. Can anyone tell me what that is and how they have applied it to their everyday existence?"

"It's the balance between extremes," Ahmeek answered. He sat tilted back in his chair, right arm extended across the desk, watch glistening under the dim lights as his Jordan-clad foot extended outward. When Bash landed eyes on Meek, fear saturated the air. Bash wasn't expecting Morgan to expose her hand because of what he had on her. Ahmeek had pulled up to his place of business in the most vulnerable atmosphere possible. Meek hadn't even thought about going to Morgan first. She had never seen him in this state of mind. The dynamic between him and Bash had always been tense because the disrespect was always high. Ahmeek had only spared him at Morgan's expense. The very girl who was keeping him breathing was the same girl he was mistreating. The audacity. "Aristotle thought that to be moral, you have to find yourself in the middle of an issue. Real-life would be finding yourself in a predicament where you can choose peace or violence to solve a problem."

"It would depend on the problem, right?" One of the students interjected.

"Okay, let's give them a problem," Ahmeek stated.

Bash was sweating bullets, loosening the top button of his shirt as he looked at Ahmeek in bewilderment. His malice was underhanded. His last name didn't allow him to air dirty laundry and nothing was more damaging than a public confrontation with a known felon and suspected drug dealer.

"There's a girl. Her fiancé is putting hands on her, on some real coward shit too because he's had plenty run-ins with a real man and he ain't want no pressure. So, he takes it out on her. The punishment for that, according to Aristotle, lies between forgiveness and murder. Those are the extremes. The mean is the action somewhere in the middle. Problem for the fiancé is this girl got people who love her. Got a whole army of mu'fuckas that's gang 'bout her. I operate in extremes, homie. When it's about her, ain't no golden mean."

The class went silent as they began to pick up on the awkward energy in the room. This was more than a hypothetical discussion. Ahmeek's stare was lethal.

"Well, without the golden mean, you would be wrong according to Aristotle," another student spoke up hesitantly.

Ahmeek's focus was Bash as he answered, "I'm okay with being the bad guy. Class is over. Unless you want to do it loud, I'm with that too."

Ahmeek could see Bash's ego raging behind his beady stare. He wanted to react. Meek was hoping the nigga jumped bad so he could lay him down where he stood.

He had assumed he was safe on Michigan State's campus. He had also assumed that Morgan would keep quiet and weigh her options. Both assumptions had been wrong. He hadn't measured the level of loyalty and recklessness that would come from offending a queen. Morgan may not acknowledge her crown, but the streets did, and they would avenge her disrespect.

The students looked to Bash who never turned his eyes off Ahmeek. "Study pages 122 through 200 for next week's class," Bash said. "Dismissed."

The students cleared the classroom, and Bash darted for the door near his desk.

Meek stood slowly. He wasn't in a rush to chase him down. This was happening whether Bash ran or came willingly.

Meek took his time getting down to the presentation floor because he knew Bash wasn't going anywhere. Isa eased Bash back into the classroom, keeping him tame with the barrel of a Beretta pointed point-blank to his head. Isa walked him right back to Meek. Meek grabbed Bash by the back of the neck roughly.

"Let's go," he said, pushing him to walk first and then jamming a gun in the small of Bash's back. "Walk, nigga."

"I don't know what she told you…"

"Stop fucking talking. Don't matter what you say. This shit ending one way. You put up a fight and I'ma push it to ya mama too."

"You don't know who you're fucking with," Bash said arrogantly.

The guard on staff had already been paid to disarm the cameras in the building and parking lot. They walked in silence, casually, until they got to the old-school box Chevy. It had dummy plates so that it couldn't be traced back to them. "Get that trunk, bruh," Ahmeek said.

Isa pulled out the key and unlocked the trunk.

Bash resisted, throwing his weight backward as he planted his feet.

"Help! Help me!" He shouted.

"Get yo' ass in the fucking trunk, nigga!" Meek said between gritted teeth as he pushed the back of Bash's head down, gripping his neck so tightly it felt like he would break it.

He grappled with Bash, slightly, stuffing him in the trunk, and when his frustrations boiled over, he aimed the gun and shot. Thank God for the silencer, or the campus would have been in turmoil. Bash howled as his kneecap shattered and blood poured from his leg.

"Shut up, pussy," Isa snickered, slamming the trunk as Bash's muffled screams echoed from inside.

Isa passed Meek the keys.

"You ain't got to take part in this, bruh. This personal," Meek said. "I'ma take my time with this nigga."

"Mo's family. We don't let nobody slide when they go against the family. This is personal for us all, my nigga. Her ass a fucking headache, but that's sis," Isa said. "I been trying to push this nigga shit back for a minute anyway."

"Call yo' mans and meet me at the spot," Meek said.

"Oh shit, we about to have a gangsta party, my nigga?" Isa asked, smiling like a kid in a candy store as he rubbed his hands together eagerly.

"Just meet me and hope he still breathing when you get there," Meek said.

Alani couldn't stop her leg from bouncing. Her nerves were eating her alive as Ethic drove to the courthouse. Alani knew that everyone in the car was lost in their thoughts. She didn't have silence in her world. There was always noise, always laughter, always bickering amongst siblings. Their lives were full of life, full of conversation. It was how she knew things were okay with her family. Today, they weren't okay. Today, Ethic and Hendrix would face their fates.

Ethic reached across the seat for her hand, and she held onto him for dear life. With his eyes on the road, he leaned to the side, a trigger that elicited a kiss, a simple one, one he delivered at least once a day. She wondered if that kiss would be the last as they pulled in front of the courthouse.

"Daddy, I'm nervous," Bella said.

"Everything is under control," Ethic said. "No matter what happens today, everything will be okay. Hendrix and I have spoken. He knows what to prepare for."

He glanced back at Bella and Henny's joint hands. Her hand rested on the seat, and his hand sat on top of it. Ethic would normally interrupt any kind of affection between them, but he let them have their moment today because he wasn't sure what would happen next. His lawyer stood waiting in front of the courthouse, and Ethic exited, walking around the car to open Alani's door. Henny followed suit, rushing to get to Bella's door before Ethic had a chance to open it.

Ethic stared at Henny in shock. He had been a good student. He was observant, he was obedient, and he had respected his daughter and his home. Hendrix was a sharp kid who had been handed a shitty hand.

Ethic reached for the tie around Henny's neck and adjusted the knot, frowning because he was irritated that Henny had weaseled his way into Ethic's village. Now, he felt responsible for him; now, it mattered to him that the tie was incorrect, and he wanted to teach him how to perfect a Windsor knot, the same way he had taught Eazy. Only he had no time. Henny was out of time because he was about to do hard time. Another boy under his care. How had he failed twice? Messiah. Hendrix. Neither had made it out. Ethic was beginning to think that being around him, seeing how he lived, admiring the power he had, only glorified the streets because no matter how much he poured into these boys, the streets still led them astray. With Messiah, he had made the mistake of encouraging it. He had been young, and Messiah was a perfect protégé. His ignorance had justified his teachings of grooming a gangster. With Henny, he had done the opposite, yet still, Hendrix had wound up here. Ethic ached a little over that.

"You got to keep your head up in there," Ethic said. "You don't ever avoid a man's stare inside. They will sniff the fear out of you, and once they know you're scared, they'll use it to their advantage. You're young. You're an easy target. Hold your own, though. You're still a man, you understand?"

Henny nodded.

"I got people on the inside that's gon' look out for you, but they can't earn your respect for you. You got to fight for that. We gon' walk it down, you hear me?"

Hendrix squared his jaw and blinked away his emotions as he took a step toward the entrance.

"Wait!" Bella called. "Can we pray?" She asked. "I just feel like we need God today."

"Yeah, little girl," Alani said. "We can pray."

Alani grabbed her husband's hand and the foursome positioned into a small circle. Ethic didn't bow his head or close his eyes because they were in the middle of Downtown Flint and he needed to keep his wits about him. Many men had been gunned down on their way to judgment simply because it was a known fact that you couldn't carry when going into the courthouse.

"Dear God, I know I ask for a lot, but You know me by now. We have a relationship. You are my most important relationship, and I need You. My family needs You. My boyfriend needs You."

"Your what?" Ethic interrupted.

"Ezra!" Alani warned, giving his hand a firm squeeze.

"Her friend, Big Homie. God, I'm just her friend," Henny added.

Bella laced her fingers between his, holding Henny tighter.

"God, protect them. We don't know what is going to happen, but we just ask for Your protection and Your mercy. We're asking. I'm begging You for forgiveness. I've seen You fix things that people would think are broken. You gave me a family. Please don't tear it apart. Please don't take my dad away. Please don't take the boy I think will become my husband away…"

"Her what!?" Ethic exclaimed. He released their hands and

began walking toward the courthouse.

"In Your name, I pray. Amen." Bella hurried the rest out, and Alani gave her a look.

"You gon' give your daddy a heart attack, little girl."

Bella shrugged, and Alani turned and joined Ethic, who was waiting for her at the door.

"You sure we don't want him locked up for life?" Ethic whispered in Alani's ear as she passed through the door he was holding open. She laughed aloud, giggling as they headed toward the courtroom. Only Ethic could make one of the heaviest moments of her life feel so lighthearted.

"The judge is ready for you first, Mr. Okafor. Hendrix is second on the docket."

Ethic paused, turning to Alani.

"You plan that gender reveal?" He asked.

"I planned it. Will you be there for it, is the better question," she replied.

"I love you," he said simply. "Never another. On the good days and bad. It's you for me, Lenika."

"Lenika?" She asked, frowning. "You might be going to jail for forever and you Lenika'ing me?"

"You mad at a nigga. You won't say it, but I can tell. You Lenika as fuck right now," he said as he pulled her as close as her pregnant belly would allow. "I'ma make all this up to you. Who love you?"

"You do," she answered. If anyone was watching, they were witnessing a love like they had never seen. "I'm so scared. I just want this to be over. I can't believe Mo isn't here for this. If you go away…"

"I'm not going away, and Mo and I will get back right. Stop worrying." Ethic went down on one knee, kissed her belly, and then stood and walked away with his lawyer.

"I got to go, Boog," Hendrix said.

Bella nodded, but she closed her eyes because she felt the tears coming. Alani felt Bella's young heart tearing in two. "You got to say goodbye, Bella."

Bella shook her head. "This isn't fair."

"I'm good, Boog," Henny said. "I'm yours. Time don't change that. Space don't either. I'ma come for you one day. The lawyer saying three years. We can knock out three years. You get a head start, and I'll catch up later. I'ma think of you every day. I'ma write you every day, Boog." Hendrix looked at Alani. "I'm in love with your daughter."

"I had this whole speech I wanted to say to you, Boog, and I'm so fucking scared I can't remember it," he said, blowing out a sharp breath. "Open your eyes, Bella Okafor. I want to see your eyes."

The pools of fear in her stare when she opened her eyes scraped Henny raw.

"Hendrix, it's time to go."

Ethic's voice was behind him. He and the lawyer had doubled back for him, but he couldn't turn away from Bella.

Alani put up a hand to halt Ethic, and Bella rushed into Hendrix's arms, bawling.

Henny didn't know what to say. He had rehearsed something. He had thought of this moment for days. He knew what to say but couldn't form the right words. The pit in his stomach was swallowing everything he wanted to express. The "goodbye" sounded too permanent. The "I'm sorry's" sounded pathetic. So, he held her close. She was falling apart, and Bella didn't fall apart. She was the strongest girl he knew, so seeing her like this disintegrated Hendrix.

Say something to her, stupid-ass, he thought, and then sang softly in her ear. It was the only lyrics he could remember right now. With his heart pounding out of his chest, he just couldn't make up his own goodbye.

"It's never a right time to say goodbye," he sang softly in her ear. "But I got to make the first move cuz if I don't, you're gonna start hating me. Girl, it's not you it's me. I got to figure out what I neeeeeed. We know we got to go our separate wayyysss. I know it's hard, and it's killing me. There's never a right time, a right time to say goodbyeeee."

He couldn't sing certain lyrics to her because they weren't true, so he skipped them. "I'ma come find you one day, Boog." He kissed her cheek and then squeezed the bridge of his nose and squared her shoulders before turning to Ethic and the lawyer. Ethic looked at Bella and then at Alani. "I've got her. We'll see you in there," Alani said.

Alani grabbed Bella's hand and led her to the bathroom.

"We can't control the actions of those we love, Bella. We can only control our reactions," Alani said as she grabbed a paper towel, wet it, and then used it to wipe the tears from Bella's face. "Right now, our reaction has to be strength. Even though we feel like giving up, even though it hurts. Hendrix and your father are strong, but they are weaker when they see our tears. If you love Hendrix, you have to stand tall, baby girl. Because what he's fighting is heavy enough. He can't be worried about hurting your feelings too. So, even if you're not okay, put on a strong face for them today. They need it. Sometimes in a relationship, it's the woman who protects the man, but there is no glory in that. They can't even know you're doing it because their egos won't allow it, but you know. You know that your struggle is wrapped in strength for them. Just hold my hand. When you feel like losing it in there, just reach for me. I'll always be there."

Bella nodded and took a deep breath. "I'm so mad at him. Why couldn't he just do right?"

"You can't make his decisions for him. He messed up. You also can't punish yourself. Your plans shouldn't change because his has to. I want you to know that," Alani said.

"I know," Bella whispered. But she was already rearranging her dreams in her mind because if Henny couldn't be there, they wouldn't fulfill her the same.

Alani and Bella made their way to the courtroom and took a seat behind Ethic and the defense table.

They stood for the judge, and Alani could barely do the up and down without holding onto something. Ethic was trying to distract her with this gender reveal when really, she was ready to pop. She heard the anxiety beating like a drum in her ear. Her pulse raced and she kept gulping in air only to blow it out.

"Mr. Okafor, please stand as I address you," the judge said.

Ethic stood, folding his hands in front of his body as he and the judge faced off. Ethic didn't speak, but his dominance filled the air. "In the matter of the State of Michigan versus Ezra Okafor. You know, some men think they're above the law. It is my sworn duty to uphold the fabric of the legal system in our great country and…"

The doors to the courtroom clanged open, and the unexpected sound turned the heads of everyone in the room to see who dared interrupt the court while it was in session. Alani forgot to release her next breath, and her temper flared as her eyes went from the door to Ethic. He met her there, in mid-air, their stares connecting as hers glossed over.

The judge stared at the woman in the back of the room and cleared his throat uncomfortably before shuffling paper.

"The state dismisses the charges against Mr. Okafor for lack of evidence and for violating the defendant's rights by conducting a search with an improper search warrant. You are free to go, Mr. Okafor."

"Baby," Ethic said turning to her. Alani stood to her feet and held onto every tear that threatened to make her crumble. She refused to cry. Not in front of all these people. Not in front of *her*. The motherfucking green-eyed bandit, a woman who had stolen Ethic's heart many years ago at *hello*. Of course, she was perfection. Of course, the fabric of her Dolce & Gabbana suit rode her perfect curves because she didn't wear anything off the rack; it was all custom-tailored. And despite the obvious upgrade in her life, Alani immediately felt like a coach passenger on a plane walking by the first-class snobs who were seated and barely made eye contact with the people who shuffled down the narrow-ass aisle to get to the back. The bitch was luxury from the top of her head to the bottom of her peep-toe Jimmy Choos. Alani instantly felt the blow of her presence because what the fuck… what the entire fuck… every late night Ethic had ever spent out since they had been married played in her mind. Was he cheating on her? Was this bitch still in the picture? How did she even know to show up? Did he call her? Was she his one call because he for damn sure hadn't called home when he had been picked up? Alani was ready to turn herself in because she was pre-meditating murder.

"Go to hell, Ethic," Alani said softly, deflated of all fight as she walked out of the courtroom.

CHAPTER 17

D addy! Hendrix is up next. We can't leave. Nobody else is here for him," Bella said.

Ethic ran a hand down his face, fisting his beard as he watched Alani walk out of the room. Disaya Perkins stood in the middle of the aisle. Silk, champagne-colored suit with ostrich feather sleeves and hem, tailored pants donned her body. A black, lace bodysuit lay beneath, and her stilettos bloodied the floor with every step. Her bobbed hair was parted down the middle. Ethic absorbed her entire essence in a glance.

What the fuck, man, he thought.

"What is she doing here?" Bella asked.

I don't fucking know, Ethic said to himself.

"I'll be right back."

"How could you not call me?" YaYa asked.

"Have you lost your fucking mind?" Ethic answered sternly, standing over her, chastising her under his breath. "Don't ever pull up on my wife." His warning sent chills down her spine.

"I see she's not fucking you right," YaYa said as she reached for his thousand-dollar suit and straightened his lapel. "You're mean when you haven't been fucked well. I'll be at our spot. There's something you need to know about this sudden police attention you're getting. Zya is stuck in Italy. She sent me with a message."

"Won't be no meet-ups, Ya," Ethic said. "And tell Zya I ain't with the blindsiding. You here to help, or you on some bullshit? Cuz you had to know your presence would complicate things for me."

"I haven't complicated things as much as I could. You should be more appreciative," Yaya said. "There are so many ways I can think of for you to show me you're grateful."

"You may not give a fuck about your marriage, but mine isn't disposable. And for that stunt you just pulled on my wife, we're done. Whatever respect I had, is gone." Ethic bypassed her as he headed for the door.

"Hey," YaYa said, realizing he was serious. "I'm not here to disrupt anything or upset anybody. I'm sorry, but did you really expect me not to come once I found out you were in trouble? You know how I feel about you."

Ethic was silent because he did know. He knew it would take a lifetime of discipline not to feel the shit they felt for one another. They had experienced bliss together, and it was something they could never tap into again because he had agreed to forever with a new love. He had no regrets, but he could see it in Disaya's eyes that she had many. YaYa closed the space between them. "The smoke came from the Frederick family," she whispered.

"Wait. What?" The information crashed into his psyche, wrecking everything that he thought he knew.

"That's who's behind all this. Zya says it needs to be a clean kill. You can't leave anything behind. They have to exist one day and then not exist the next."

"Are you sure?" Ethic asked.

"Positive," YaYa confirmed. "Good luck with everything. I know our season has passed, but it's like summer for me. It'll always be my favorite. I can see that you're happy. I'm really happy for you. Should I apologize to your wife for my intrusion? Get you out of the doghouse? Her name's Alani, right?"

"No," Ethic answered quickly. "You definitely don't want to do that, and her name is Lenika."

YaYa smiled. She was brilliant. She just shined everywhere she went, and Ethic knew he would have some work to do to convince Alani that this visit wasn't more than a warning.

"Take care of yourself, Ethic. You getting locked up would hurt a lot of people. I don't need you to be mine, but I do need you to be free."

She gave his arm a gentle squeeze before walking out, leaving her perfume in her wake.

Ethic walked out of the courtroom and looked around for Alani. She was nowhere to be found. Too many thoughts bombarded him at once. Morgan's involvement, Alani's safety, Hendrix's sentencing hearing, Bella's first heartbreak, his unborn child, Eazy's feelings. It was all stacking upon his shoulders. His chest tightened as he took the steps that led to the outside. When he saw her getting into the black SUV, and the glowing Uber sign in the front window, his soul left his body. His pregnant wife, who had put up with so much already, was leaving, and there was nothing he could do but watch solemnly from the top of the steps as the driver pulled away.

"Hendrix Outlaw, would you please stand?"

Henny glanced back at Bella and Ethic before rising to his feet.

"How do you plead to the charge of possession of a controlled substance with the intent to distribute?"

"Guilty, Your Honor," Hendrix answered.

"And the charge of possession of a firearm?" The judge added. "Guilty."

"Would counsel like to proceed to sentencing?" The judge asked.

Hendrix felt like his life was ending. The plea was the smartest move in his position. There was no erasing the evidence the police had discovered on him. *Three years. I can do three years.*

"Yes, Your Honor."

Hendrix kept telling himself that he could endure the next three years of his life. It would only be 36 months, only 1095 days.

"The court sentences you to 84 months in state custody with eligibility for parole in 60 months. The officers may remand the inmate into custody."

"That's seven years," Hendrix said in disbelief as he looked at his lawyer. "Aye, man, that's seven years! You said three!"

Hendrix heard Bella's cries and Ethic's protests as he was placed in cuffs but couldn't look them in the eyes. If he did, they would see the terror in him.

"Wait, man! Wait!" Hendrix shouted. "Ethic, man! Help me!"

He was pulled out of the courtroom, and as Hendrix was thrown into a holding cell with other inmates awaiting transport to prison, he knew that his life would never be the same. He was the youngest and smallest behind the wall. He'd have to have the heart of a lion to survive.

To go to Morgan or go to his wife. The way his heart was tearing in half was manifesting into physical distress.

"I like YaYa, Daddy," Bella whispered as she stared out of the window as they drove away from the courthouse. "But I love Ma more."

"I know, baby girl," Ethic answered. "Call her again."

Alani wasn't answering Ethic's calls, but he knew she wouldn't ignore Bella's. Ethic had to go to Morgan, but he needed to hear Alani's voice. He needed to reassure her, apologize to her because he knew the shit that was going through her head.

Alani answered for Bella on the first ring.

"They gave him seven years, Ma!" Bella cried into the phone.

"I'm so sorry, Bella," Alani said.

Ethic heard the sadness in her. Her voice shook, and she was breathless as she spoke. She always hyperventilated when she was upset. She would cry so hard that she could barely sneak in a breath, and he heard her on the cusp of an emotional breakdown.

"Baby...."

Before he could get out another word, she interrupted. "Bella, baby, I'll see you when you get home, okay?"

"Alani-"

CLICK.

Alani hung up before he could get a word in.

At least she's home, Ethic thought, finding some relief in that. His wife would be mad as hell, but she would be under his roof when he got there. As soon as he walked through the walls of her kingdom, he would make it up to her, but first, he had to go see about Morgan.

Messiah sat beside the bed where Morgan slept. He had promised Morgan he wouldn't close his eyes even for a second so that she would agree to get some sleep. The amount of restraint it took to not run out on her was monumental. He had been grateful when she closed her eyes because he could make the calls he needed to regarding Bash. Everyone had underestimated him. Thinking of the damage Messiah would do made his dick hard in anticipation. He had been wanted to ring this nigga's bell. He would lose all self-control because, from the very first kiss he had seen Bash give Morgan, Messiah had made plans to kill him.

Aria had kept the twins because he didn't want them around while he was in a murderous state of mind. He was already a stranger to his kids. He didn't want them to meet the murderer before they had a chance to really meet the man. He could tell they felt safe with Aria, so he let them remain with her.

The knock at her door pulled Messiah out his seat. While Morgan had been terrified for Bash to return, Messiah invited his arrival. He had been waiting... been ready. Pulling open the door and finding Ethic was a surprise he wasn't ready for.

Ethic's shock at finding Messiah there was quickly replaced by relief as he walked in without a formal greeting.

"Mo?" Ethic asked, but it came out more like a demand, like he wanted Messiah to make her appear out of thin air.

"Big Homie. Something happened with her..." Messiah paused, trying to pick the right words. "To her while she was with that nigga. I'ma need you to walk real light on shorty. You taught me to be quick to listen and slow to respond. I need you to remember that."

Ethic deadpanned on Messiah. Messiah realized he couldn't make the rules for Ethic, not where Morgan Atkins was concerned. Messiah might love her now, but Ethic had loved her long, and for the first time, Messiah realized how that trumped any other relationship in Morgan's life. He wondered if it trumped all in Ethic's life too. "Mo. Now."

Messiah held his tongue and nodded as he turned for the bedroom.

"Mo," he whispered as went to his knees on the side of the bed. "Shorty. Wake up." He ran a finger down the bridge of her nose and then traced her lips, causing her to stir. He hated the sadness he saw when she opened her eyes. They were empty, and he just wanted to fill her. He wanted to make her heart beat the way that she made his race. Just the thought of Morgan had brought a dead man back to life. The thought of him had brought a beautiful life closer to death.

She trapped his hand and wrapped her fingers around his so tightly that she transported him back in time.

Her swollen eyes were like a knob on a stove, turning his flame up and burning him.

"Ethic's here," Messiah said. "You know what I got to do, shorty. I got to go. I want to stay, but I got to go. I got to get this off my soul, Mo. You got to get it off yours too. You got to tell Ethic the truth."

"When you leave, you never come back," she signed. "I need you here. I can't tell him by myself. I need you to love me more than you hate him, because I'm terrified right now, Ssiah."

Messiah's frustration was apparent. Morgan always wanted him to exist in the most uncomfortable of states.

"I can't, Mo. Not this time."

He had let Ethic talk him out of dealing with Lucas. No one would talk him out of dealing with Bash.

"Come on," Messiah said. He took her hand and pulled her until she was sitting. "I need you to be strong, shorty. My babies need you to be strong. Aria is watching the twins. I need you to pull it together for them. The one person they've always had is you. I know that ain't fair, but you're their entire world, shorty. I'm so proud of you for the way you have loved my kids."

"It's hard," she signed. "It's been hard protecting them, making choices that benefit them, breathing for them."

"I know that nigga took your power. I'm about to go get it back."

She stared off, shaking her head because Messiah just didn't get it. He was willing to war with everyone over her. He would move mountains if one hair was out of place on her head, when the person she needed him to re-align was himself.

"He didn't take my power. I gave it to you, and you never gave it back," she signed.

"Nah, shorty. You got the game fucked up. If you knew how much power you had, you would never let anyone who didn't deserve you in your space. You got all the power, Mo. Everything moving on your say so and you ain't even said shit. One tear and niggas got that corny nigga tied up somewhere about you. I'm late to the party. I got to go, Mo."

Messiah went to her closet and pulled out clothes, a cropped t-shirt and jeans, then helped her dress before walking her out to face Ethic.

When she saw Bella sitting at her dining room table and then looked to Ethic and saw his stern face soften at the sight of her, Morgan broke down.

"Daddy, her neck," Bella gasped, eyes wide in horror. Morgan felt so exposed. Like two years' worth of lies were on display, and everyone in the room was gawking at her.

"I messed up really bad," she cried. "I didn't mean what I said to you."

"I know you didn't, Mo," Ethic said. She crossed the room, and Ethic received her as if she hadn't done anything wrong a day of her life.

"Shhh," he consoled. "Come here, baby girl; she needs all the love we got."

Bella embraced Morgan from behind, and Ethic wrapped his arms around both of his girls, absorbing the pain of two broken hearts. He had no idea there would be a third heartbreak to come, because what Morgan was about to admit to would wreck him.

"Did he rape you?" Ethic asked.

"I don't know. I think so. He just did what he wanted, like how I told you men would in the hospital that one time. He did that. Is that rape? Or is that just what happens to women, sometimes? Because I really can't tell if it's okay to say no anymore. Why don't they ever hear me when I say no?"

The conversation played back in Ethic's mind repeatedly as he sat in his Range Rover, gripping the steering wheel. He held it so tightly that his palms burned as he twisted his fists around the leather. He gritted his teeth, nodding as his chin shook, violently. He had never felt anything quite like this.

"It was me, Ethic. I told Bash about the murders. I'm the reason all this is happening. I really didn't mean to mess up this bad. I'm so sorryyyyy."

Ethic heard her cries so clearly, it was as if Morgan was sobbing right beside him. He had put her and Bella in an Uber to send them home, so that they wouldn't witness his undoing. Morgan was the most celebrated part of his heart. She was the one who required the most from him. She was the most cherished connection in his life. Still his sweet Morgan had betrayed him. Bash had used Ethic's freedom as leverage to keep her enslaved, while he abused her.

Ethic was murderous in this moment, but above all, his soul ached. Morgan's deceit injured him so badly that he couldn't do anything but break. It was like someone was pulling the seams of his insides apart. His heart was wide open. Morgan made him vulnerable in a way that made him weak. He could barely look at Morgan without anger and resentment protesting inside him. He was pushing it down, being strong, trapping it inside so that it wouldn't come out. But keeping his disappointment to himself was torture. It was trying to seep out, like poison; forcing itself out of his eyes in the form of tears, trying to push out of his stomach, knotting his gut so tightly he could barely breathe.

He had taken care of Morgan for almost her entire life. She would have been the last person he expected to set him up. The unlikely suspect was the guilty party, and Ethic was struggling. The inside of his vehicle was the only the place he could put his pain on display. He hung his head, shaking it in disbelief because Morgan was the last person, he would have ever suspected to do him dirty. In the forefront of his mind was her rape. How he had allowed her to be hurt not once, but twice, was pure failure. He hadn't honored Raven or Benny very well. Her abuse felt like a direct reflection of his fatherhood. She should have never been touchable.

Her hurt was preventable. He would have saved her. If he had known. When had he and Morgan drifted so far apart where she didn't come to him when she was in trouble? The disconnect was crystal clear and he was realizing it too late. What he thought was allowing freedom to choose her own path, was detrimental to her health. Now he wished he had been overbearing. He wished he could go back and force his wants on her. *She should have never been in London,* he thought.

Ethic would do anything for Morgan, and she had almost taken his life. He knew he could never speak on how he felt. He would have to tuck it away, where he concealed the pain of Raven's memory, so he got it all out, right here, under the crescent moon in the black sky.

Men had taken advantage of his sweet, deaf girl. They had turned her into a person who hurt other people and Morgan had done the unthinkable. A part of him knew he carried some blame. Murder was a heavy secret to keep. It wasn't her responsibility to carry a burden so weighted. He was supposed to do better at protecting her from shit like that, but the murders that threatened to send him to jail... the murders she had divulged to someone who could use them against him… those murders were committed as retribution on Morgan's behalf. Ethic was having a hard time digesting the logic she used that convinced her to ever speak on that night. Knowing where they were all those years ago. Remembering the jealousy and disdain Morgan had for Alani back then, made him feel like this was strategic, like Morgan's animosity had led her to act out. What she had told him was different, but the circumstance carried a plot all on its own and it was one that haunted Ethic because he didn't know if he could trust Morgan to tell him the truth. This was the hard part of parenting, facing such great disappointment that it split your heart in half. Morgan had hurt him, but as Ethic gathered himself, swiping a hand down his face, and blowing out a sharp breath to recover, he knew he would love her anyway. He had to. She was his soul, his gift, and his heart. He had to do what went against his ego and forgive Morgan because she was his. He started the car because there was still a debt to pay for the trespass. Despite how he felt about Morgan's actions, he would never allow anyone to hurt her and get away with it. Bash had violated her. The price to pay would be his life. Ethic would figure out the rest later.

Ahmeek wiped the sweat from his brow as he threw powerful body shots to his target. The sound of the gloves as they connected echoed throughout the gym. He stood in the middle of the boxing ring in the abandoned gym.

It was now Crew-owned. The deed said Ahmeek Harris, Messiah Williams, and Isa Jones. He remembered the days from his childhood when he would come to this very place to train with local legends. The OG's used to host boxing camps in the summers and on weekends to keep kids occupied instead of in the streets. He had rocked many niggas to sleep within these ropes. His chin had been checked a few times too. The memories flooded him as he circled the target, throwing practice shots. It was the way he kept his aggression at bay. Even when he had been locked up, instead of letting niggas bait him and ending up with additional time for misbehaving, Ahmeek boxed on the yard at rec time. His hands were nice enough for niggas to know not to try him. He had only had to make a couple of examples before the other inmates opted to leave him alone. He was winded. His fatigue told him that he was out of practice. Bottle service and nightclub lamb chops three times a week had him slipping. He used his gun more than his hands these days, but this time he needed to feel the aggression surging through him. He remembered the old man who used to own this gym. *"If I can't hear the bags, you ain't hitting hard enough. Make 'em sing, Murder Meek."*

So, Meek serenaded the room, delivering deadly blows so heavy that he felt them through the gloves. If he hadn't put them on, his hands would be broken; he was swinging so hard.

The doors to the dilapidated gym clanked open and Ahmeek dropped his hands.

"Damn, bruh, is the nigga still breathing?" Isa asked as he entered the building. "How we supposed to turn up if he half dead?"

Ahmeek turned to Isa as Bash hung from the heavy bag harness, acting as the recipient to the blows Ahmeek had delivered. There was no heavy bag, Bash had been at Ahmeek's mercy for close to an hour. Ahmeek peeled off the old gloves, revealing swollen knuckles. Bash's face was bloodied, swollen. Isa stepped over teeth and came close to Bash's face, inspecting the damage.

"Goddamn, boy," Isa said, grimacing at the devastation that had been done. He checked Bash's pulse and then looked at Ahmeek, stunned. "You broke his ribs."

"He can barely breathe. Feels like he's breathing through a straw. He don't deserve to go fast," Meek said as he bent down to arouse Bash back to life. He patted Bash's cheek with a heavy hand. "Hey, we ain't done yet."

Bash groaned weakly and lifted his head as Isa sat down the duffel bag he carried. "You knew Mo was Crew," Isa said, bending down to unzip the bag. He pulled out a bottle of Pure White Hennessy. "Now, you invited to a gangsta party, my nigga." He tossed the bottle to Meek and then delivered a crushing blow to Bash's face. Ahmeek had already shattered his jaw. It was hanging grotesquely. Isa's blow dislocated it so badly that he grimaced at the sight of it. "Wake up, pussy. This yo' party. You're the guest of fucking honor."

Messiah entered and stood at the doorway as Meek stared at him from the center of the ring.Messiah pulled up on the ring and took in the evidence of Ahmeek's rage.

He had seen him put in work before. Ahmeek had bodies on his gun that people would never speak about, but this was different; this was a punishment motivated by passion. Messiah both respected it and detested it. *He love her,* Messiah thought.

The shocking sound of laughter filled the gym, and the Crew turned their attention to Bash.

He was barely conscious, but the titter that fell from his privileged lips was taunting.

"Morgan and her thugs." Even in the most vulnerable of positions, his arrogance bled through. "Ask Messiah how he ended up in custody. If I don't make it home, my mother already has the blueprint for locking each of you up for the rest of your lives."

Ahmeek scoffed. "Your mama tied up somewhere too." That one statement clipped Bash's arrogant wings.

Isa gripped his face, and Bash howled in agony from the manipulation of his broken jaw.

"You gon' die tonight, college boy," Isa sang in an antagonizing tone.Messiah stepped into the ring, and Bash laughed hysterically as blood leaked from his mouth.

"Is this a joke? The one who fucked her over more than anybody is here to save the day? We're the same," Bash snickered, as blood continued to leak from the side of his mouth. He spit it out only for more to leak. "I tainted her real good. You don't want her back now. I fucked that pretty mouth of hers. She took it in every hole. I loosened her up, and she took it like the whore you both made her."

Messiah nodded, and out of nowhere, he shot Bash in the groin. "You fucked her where?" Messiah was seething as he grabbed the bloody flesh that used to be Bash's manhood. Bash's screams would have made the average person grimace, but the sound was music to Messiah's ears.

"You gon' pop the top on that Henny or you babysitting it, nigga?" Messiah said as he squeezed the blood from what remained of Bash's sack. He turned to Isa and Ahmeek, "Cuz we about to have fun with this shit."

The Crew hadn't come to this gym in a long time. They reserved it for special occasions, special kills, when it was personal, when they needed to take their time with it. They cracked a bottle and let the most devilish sides of themselves free for a night when they brought niggas here.

"Got to bless this shit," Meek said, tapping the top. Isa tapped it next, and Messiah stared Meek in the eye before following suit. Meek removed the cap and took a long, hard, swig before blowing out fire and passing it to Messiah.

"Ms. Marilyn gon' kick yo' ass for bringing her cruise ship Henny," Messiah said, smirking because ever since they were boys, Ms. Marilyn was the Black mama who got her groove back on some island once a year and came back slinging bottles of White Hennessy like her life depended on it.

Isa snickered before taking the bottle to take his shot. "No bullshit, I bought this shit from her last time she went out of town," Isa said. "Auntie taxed me too." He snickered. "Who up?" Isa asked.

Isa reached in the bag and removed a large filet knife. He passed it to Meek.

"A nigga got a whole bag of tricks in this bitch," Isa said. He took out a bottle of lighter fluid. "Let's see if this mu'fucka flammable, bruh."

"Open your mouth." Isa gritted his teeth as Bash resisted, turning his head left and right while howling in protest. Isa put a grip on his broken jaw that pried his mouth open like he was an unruly dog. "Swallow that shit, pussy! You put what in her mouth?"

Bash gagged, vomiting as he tried to stop the lighter fluid from going down his throat.

Isa pulled a blunt out of his back pocket. The flick of the lighter came next. Isa took a pull of the blunt and then passed it to Ahmeek.

"Helpppppppp!"

The bitch came out of Bash at the threat of being set ablaze.

"Remember that shit you was talking at the birthday party?" Isa asked.

"Hold up," Messiah said. "Why Mo?" He asked.

Ahmeek frowned. "What you mean why her? You talking like he targeted her?"

Messiah hesitated in his response. "He did. He too invested for it to be random. You wanted her isolated. You took her to London, but that didn't work because she came back. You want Ethic gone; you want us out the way. You want to put her on an island alone. She don't fuck with you like that, so why her?"

"Fuck you," Bash croaked. "She's a whore! Just like her sister and mother! You think this makes you safe? Fuck you."

"Nah, nigga, fuck you," Ahmeek said, finally speaking up. He hit the blunt, pulling smoke into his lungs, and tossed it at Bash. The tip of the blunt ignited against the lighter fluid instantly.

The Crew was unfazed by the animalistic cry that came from Bash as the fire slowly took over his face. Messiah watched the flames slowly flicker, charring skin, as Bash writhed wildly on the heavy bag chain.

Meek took his time exiting the boxing ring and walked into the small office. He snatched the fire extinguisher off the wall and then tossed it to Messiah. A slow death was an understatement. The punishment for laying hands on Morgan Atkins was torture. Messiah let Bash simmer a little longer. He would have let him burn to death if it wasn't for the order that came next.

"Put the fire out."

The Crew turned to Ethic as he walked into the gym. Messiah sprayed the extinguisher leaving Bash in excruciating pain.

"Please, just kill me," he cried. There was a level of pain that human beings couldn't endure. This surpassed that. There was normally a level of pain that human beings couldn't witness. The Crew didn't give a fuck.

Ethic stood back and observed the scene before taking steps toward the mayhem.

He climbed inside the ropes and took the small stool in the corner of the ring in one hand, placing it directly in front of Bash. He sat.

"You've been around for years," he said. "You've been around those twins for years. You hit them too?" Ethic asked.

Bash could barely answer. It was like everyone in the room was holding their breaths in anticipation of the answer.

"You drugged her?" Ethic asked. Bash only cried. "Raped her."

"I was gentle!" Bash sobbed. "I was careful."

"With raping her? You were careful raping her?" Ethic grilled sinisterly.

"She was asleep," Bash sobbed.

"You threatened to take her kids? To lock me up if she left," Ethic said. The questions were rhetorical. A reading of sins before judgment. Death was a guest in the room.

Ethic's stare went to Messiah, then to Ahmeek, and back to Bash.

"You killed Jacob!"

Ethic froze. He hadn't heard that name in so long that he had almost forgotten it. Years ago, back in Kansas City, he had gotten Raven so high they had gotten into a car accident. His temper had been uncontrollable back then. It was a kill that nobody knew about, a stain on his soul that he had acquired willingly. He had issued one warning to Jacob to stay away from Raven, but when the nurses told Ethic that Jacob had come around to visit, Ethic had taken the act of disobedience as disrespect. He laid Jacob down quietly without remorse. He had no idea that those old ghosts had come back to haunt him. That was the risk of the game. Karma might miss you and hit those you love. Ethic bowed his head, nodding, as the weight of Morgan's trauma fell on his shoulders. Maybe it was time to let her go. Maybe holding on too tightly had not only enabled her emotionally but endangered her physically.

"Who was he to you?" Ethic asked.

"Family," Bash answered. "My cousin."

Ethic's bullet silenced Bash, and he stood. The second bullet was for good measure. The third and fourth revealed Ethic's pain. This kill was personal. Just thinking of the ways he had violated Morgan, grooming her for some sick obsession and family revenge plot made Ethic feel like death wasn't enough. He had wanted to brutalize Bash, but he worried that his soul wouldn't return to Alani the same if he did, so he opted for a bullet. "Brick him up and throw him in Devil's Lake. No teeth, no fingerprints," Ethic said. "And then get to the house. Morgan and those babies need you."

His stare shifted from Messiah to Ahmeek to Isa. "Can I trust this?" The question was for Messiah. To leave witnesses behind to a murder he committed was risky. It didn't matter that they were Crew. They could identify him at the scene of this crime.

"We're complicit," Ahmeek said. "So, the question is can we trust each other?"

Ethic felt a disdain for Ahmeek that bordered on jealousy. It burned through him as he deadpanned on Messiah.

"Yeah, you can trust it OG," Messiah confirmed.

"Clean it up," Ethic said before turning and walking out, leaving behind a fractured yet united brotherhood.

CHAPTER 18

M a, where are you going?" Eazy asked as he stood in the doorway of the bedroom. Alani packed the clothes inside the suitcase.

"I'm not going anywhere, Big Man," Alani said.

"Then why are you packing?" Eazy asked.

"I'm just getting ready for the baby to come," Alani lied. "I'll need some things packed just in case we have to go to the hospital. Have you come up with more baby names yet?" She needed to distract him. Hell, she needed to distract herself. The betrayal she felt was overwhelming.

She had loved Ethic unconditionally, going against her every instinct to run away from him; now, she wondered if she had been foolish. She had painted him as a man that existed above the mediocrity of other men. She hadn't worried about other women, about cheating, or lying, because he was so damn perfect in the way he loved her. Now, she knew that he was simply perfect in the way he lied. The finesse was impeccable; the man was full of shit. It took everything in her not to burn his whole damn house to the ground.

"I was thinking of something cool like my name and your name altogether," Eazy said. "That way, the baby will know I'm always with her." "Her?" Alani asked curiously.

Eazy nodded. "I think it's a girl. In my dream, Kenzie and Love are playing with a girl, but I chose a name that can fit a boy too, just in case."

Alani smiled. Eazy and his dreams made her heart flutter. He shared them with her every morning. Sometimes he couldn't remember them exactly, but he would always remember how they made him feel, and they talked about that too.

Alani zipped the luggage and moved it to the floor, and then flipped the covers for Eazy to join her in bed.

Eazy climbed inside, and Alani turned on the television, turning to one of their favorite shows, "I Love Lucy." They watched the old black and white show faithfully.

"Let's hear the name. It better be a good one," Alani said.

Eazy removed one of his pillows and placed it behind her back because he knew she couldn't lie flat now that the baby was almost there. He had seen his father do it every day, and it was instinct for him to fill the role of her protector when Ethic wasn't home.

"I was thinking Ezani," Eazy said. "Eazy and Alani."

Alani couldn't help but smile. "Well, Daddy and I were considering True," Alani said. "True Ezani Okafor sounds beautiful to me. What do you think?"

"Yeah, that's a cool name," Eazy said. "For a boy or a girl."

"A cool name indeed," Alani said.

They laid there for hours, watching television as Alani tried to pretend that she wasn't unraveling inside. Eazy was good medicine, however. He reminded her that she was loved and valued, despite the insecurities swarming in her head.

When the alarm system announced Ethic's arrival, Alani climbed out of bed. When she made it to the door, she paused in shock as Morgan and Bella walked inside holding the twins.

Bella ascended the steps as soon as she spotted Alani. She ran to her, burying her face in Alani's shoulder as they embraced. It had been a long day for Bella. She had said goodbye to Hendrix and discovered Morgan's abuse all in one day.

"Oh, Bella," Alani whispered. She took Yara from Bella and held onto Bella tightly with one arm. Tension filled the room as Alani's eyes met Morgan's.

"I'm so sorry, Alani," Morgan said as she stopped a few steps below her. Morgan looked defeated. Alani saw the bruises and noticed the careful steps Morgan was taking. Morgan was a center of attention kind of girl. Even the way she entered a room was noticeable. Morgan's demeanor was timid in a way Alani had never seen.

"Who hurt you?" Alani asked. "Mo, who did this to you?"

Morgan shook her head and shrugged, her face bleeding into emotion as she stifled her pain. "I should get them to bed," she said.

"Okay," Alani whispered, taken aback at the damage that she was witnessing. She passed Yara to Bella. "Help Mo, baby girl. Get showered and ready for bed. I'll be in to talk to you in a bit."

Alani's eyes went to the door, expecting Ethic to walk in next.

"Where is your father?" She called after them.

"He sent us home in an Uber Black. He had to go handle something," Bella said.

Alani's spirit left her body, and she grabbed the railing of the staircase and sat right in the middle of the step. *He went to her,* she thought.

Ethic couldn't go back home in the state of mind he was in. He had to shower. He had to buy new clothes. He had to get rid of all the evidence on his body and soul that made him guilty of murder. He checked into a hotel, showered, and then waited for Messiah to bring him something fresh to put on. Then, they took everything they had worn to the funeral home and incinerated the items. As Ethic pulled into his estate, he looked in his rearview mirror at Messiah tailing him. It was truly a shame how the young shooter had switched up on him years ago. Messiah was a gangster with a flawless track record for putting in work. Even with the indiscretion on his jacket, he was one of Ethic's most valuable hitters. He couldn't explain the level of love he had for Messiah. Many might call him foolish for keeping him around, but he was family. Messiah exited the car and met Ethic at the porch.

"How do you go in there and be a father after shit like this? How do you love them so well, man? That shit scares the hell out of me. Thinking I'ma mess up with them, the way I messed up with Mo," Messiah admitted.

"Difference between your children and a woman, those children are you. You'll never get that wrong. But if you remember that those children are also her too, it'll remind you to love her right because if you injure her, you injure them. Kids can feel when you ain't done right by their mama. The women who carried them are forever connected to them. They might not say shit, but they can feel when you disrespect their life-giver. It's why you see children who are just as resentful as women when shit don't work out in a relationship. Men think kids take their mother's sides or that their baby mama is poisoning the kid against them, when really they just feel the shit. They are them. They felt everything that went on inside that woman from the moment of their conception. That bond don't end at birth. You hurt the mother, you hurt the child. If that ain't motivation to get it right with a woman, I don't know what is. Wild shit is, Bella and Eazy feel Alani that way, and she didn't even carry them. She's a fucking superwoman, and I'm never fucking that up. You and Morgan created life. No matter what, you're one."

Messiah nodded and followed Ethic inside.

There she was. At the top of the steps. She had been there for hours, overthinking, imagining what he could have been doing at this time of night. He knew what type of time she was on, and she hadn't said one word yet. Alani Lenika Okafor was about to give him hell.

Her bags sat at the bottom of the steps, perturbing him because they looked heavy, and she shouldn't have been carrying anything in her condition. He expected her anger. He hadn't anticipated her departure.

"Come," Ethic said.

"Messiah, get your ass up or downstairs cuz I promise you don't want to be in the middle of this," Alani said, ignoring Ethic.

Messiah's brows lifted in surprise, and he fought the smirk that was threatening to come out. Anybody who had ever been around Ethic knew that nobody bossed up on him. Anybody who had ever met his wife knew who the real boss was. She just had a way of getting her way. Messiah bit his bottom lip and walked up the stairs.

"I need to go grocery shopping tomorrow to get food for the gender reveal. Will you be available at around 11 o'clock?" She asked. Messiah stopped a few steps below Alani and looked back at Ethic.

"If I needed him, I'd ask him, Messiah. Eleven o'clock?"

He nodded. "Eleven o'clock it is," he said.

"Big Homie in trouble like a mu'fucka," Messiah mumbled, amused as he bypassed her.

Ethic rubbed the back of his neck, grimacing because he had walked right into some bullshit. He didn't even deserve this cold shoulder, but he knew better than to express that. It would only make her reaction worse. Her anger was warranted. He understood that her perception was the reality that caused her to pack her bags. She was about to unpack them mu'fuckas, but he would go through the motions. He was in the doghouse. He could accept that, but no way was she leaving him. Not over this. Not after all they had been through.

Fuck Ya, he thought.

Ethic took a step in her direction.

"I'ma take your head off if you come up these steps, so you might want to stay right there," Alani warned.

He kept coming.

"Can we talk? Without you raising hell? Cuz I know you been waiting to raise a nigga blood pressure all day," Ethic said.

"No hell to raise. There was an action. This is my reaction," she said.

"You not going nowhere," Ethic said sternly.

"You're right," she said. "I'm home with my kids, in my house. The bags are yours."

Ethic didn't mean to laugh in her face, but he chuckled.

"I'm not playing, Ezra. Get out. You can leave, or I can leave," she said.

"Where I'm going, Lenika? Where you going? You days from giving birth," Ethic said.

"You should have thought about that before your side bitch decided that today was the day to be seen," Alani said, eyes burning.

Ethic blew out a breath of frustration. "You gon' let me explain, or you want to keep assuming?"

"There is no explanation. That's the same bitch. The one you were hanging onto before me. Meeting up with once a year. Sending money too. You told me that was done. Clearly, it isn't," Alani snapped.

"It is done," Ethic reassured.

"Nah, no, it ain't," Alani said stubbornly. "I don't find amusement in lying about my dealings with a woman. If

I were in it, I would tell you I was in it," Ethic replied. "You're so fucking arrogant," Alani answered, shaking her head in disgust. He had a way of making his truths come out like disrespect. "It doesn't matter what you say at this point. There should be no space in your life that she occupies. The fact that she feels significant enough to be at your arraignment tells me all I need to know. Now get out."

"I built this bitch. You got a little authority, but you don't run this shit," Ethic said.

"Fine," she said, moving around him. Alani rushed down the steps so quickly she didn't see the remote-control car Eazy had left there. It was the same car she had asked him to put away a million times before. She lost her footing and tripped down the wooden staircase.

"Ezra, oh my god, oh my god," Alani whispered.

He was at her side, scooping her from the floor in a millisecond.

"I know, I know, baby," he said, seemingly reading her mind because he knew the fear she felt. The commotion pulled everyone from their rooms.

"Oh my god!" Morgan exclaimed.

"We're going to the hospital," Ethic announced.

"No!" Alani shouted. "No. I can't go back to where Love died, baby. I can't. Bella, call Nessa. You have her number. Tell her it's an emergency."

Bella rushed to grab her cell phone, and Ethic carried Alani to the living room couch.

Morgan and Messiah stood in the threshold in silence.

"Ow, Ezra, ow! My ankle; be careful," she cried. It was the same one she had shattered in the car crash. She was sure she had re-injured it in this fall. "Okay, baby, okay," he said. He kept repeating it. "You're okay. Can you feel kicks? Is my baby kicking?"

He was on his knees between her thighs, palming her belly, praying for life, for evidence of a heartbeat as she rubbed the top of his head gently. They would not survive the loss of another child.

"She said she's on her way!" Bella shouted.

"Bella, get Eazy," Alani said. "Wake him and bring him. Hurry, baby girl."

"Oh my god," Morgan whispered.

Messiah found her pinky and wrapped it around his. A little bit of strength on an impossible day.

The room was dire. Still. Somber until a sleepy Eazy walked into the room.

"What's wrong?" Eazy asked.

"Nothing, Big Man," Alani said, holding out a hand to him. "Nothing's wrong. Come here." Eazy reluctantly walked over to Alani and sat next to her.

"You know how you talk to the baby and he goes crazy?" Alani asked.

"Yeah. Ezani likes it," Eazy said unsurely.

"Ezani?" Bella piped up. "Is that the baby's name?"

"True Ezani Okafor," Eazy said proudly.

"Can you talk to the baby now, Eazy? Just to make sure True is listening in there," she said, eyes full of fear and anxiety.

Eazy rubbed his sleepy eyes and nodded.

"Ezra, you've got to make room for Eazy," Alani said.

Ethic looked up at Alani. He didn't want to move, but he stood as Eazy leaned down. "Hey in there; it's me again. You're probably sleeping because I was too, so I'm sorry about waking you up," Eazy started.

"Anything?" Bella asked.

Alani put up a finger to stall Bella out as she took a deep breath. The doorbell rang and Morgan turned on her heels. "That's probably the midwife."

Please kick, Alani thought. *Just kick. You always kick for Eazy.*

Morgan reappeared with Nessa, Alani's midwife.

"Whoa, it's a party going on in here, huh? I heard you had a little accident, and I can see by the looks on all your faces that you're panicking," Nessa said as she entered the room. She rolled up her sleeves and bypassed them all, headed to the laundry room down the hall to scrub down her hands. She returned and gave Ethic a gentle smile. "Breathe, Dad."

"Our son, Love, didn't make it because of a fall. He was stillborn. So we're all a little rattled," Alani explained.

"More than a little," Bella added in.

"Okay, well, we have to remember that while we look like we're super delicate while we're pregnant, we're tougher than we appear. The body is made to absorb a little shock while with child. This nugget is probably just sleeping like all of you should be."

"Who wants to help check for the heartbeat?" She pulled the at-home monitor from her bag, and Eazy quickly moved to assist Nessa. "You remember how to do it?"

ASHLEY ANTOINETTE

"Yeah, I've got to move it around her stomach until I hearrrr..." Eazy paused when he heard the steady hum of the baby's heart. "Found it!"

"You're a natural!" Nessa said.

"So, everything's good?" Alani asked.

"I'm going to examine your cervix and rub you down, but everything seems all good, Mama. The fall probably scared you, and the baby isn't moving much because Baby Okafor is asleep. You were right to call me, though. You'd rather be safe than sorry," Nessa said. "We might want to clear the room and give Mom and baby a little more privacy for the exam."

"So, she's okay? The baby is okay?" Ethic asked.

"Yes, papa bear, your queen and your cub are fine," Nessa reassured.

"Everybody can go back to sleep. I'm okay," Alani said. "Bella, take Eazy upstairs."

Eazy leaned down and kissed Alani's stomach. "Hurry and get out of there. You're making everybody crazy," he said.

Alani's body jolted as a strong kick took her breath away.

"Did you see that?" Eazy asked.

Alani nodded. "I did," she replied.

"It's a little creepy. Like a little alien moving around in there," Eazy said.

Bella headed for the stairs. "Come on, weirdo," she said, reeling Eazy in as everyone retired.

Ethic stood over the midwife's shoulder, watching intently as she spread Alani wide and inserted two fingers to check her cervix.

291

"Cervix is closed," Nessa announced. "Everything's good. Your balance will be off these last few weeks. Be CAREFUL, Alani."

Alani nodded and watched as the midwife packed up. She walked Nessa to the door, hugging her goodnight.

"I got the gender reveal invite. You guys are late in the game, aren't you?" Nessa asked curiously.

"It's just something fun. We've had some stressful family moments lately. Gives everyone something positive to look forward to," Alani explained.

"Well, I'll see you in a few days then," Nessa said. "Goodnight."

Before she could turn away from the door, Ethic had her trapped there, breathing in her scent and pressing his lips into the back of her head.

Alani sighed because she loved this man. She loved him too much. She hated that his touch healed every broken part of her, even pieces he had shattered. She almost forgot why she was upset. She turned and stared up at him.

"I don't need to stress during the last weeks of this pregnancy. I shouldn't be worried about you and your ex. I shouldn't be crying and anxious over my husband's actions. You need to leave. If you want me to make it to my due date, you need to get out."

"I didn't ask her to come," Ethic said.

"I don't care," Alani answered.

She moved around him and ascended the steps, and Ethic could feel the distance. Each step felt like miles. He wanted to put up a fight, but she was right. It wasn't worth the stress

ASHLEY ANTOINETTE

it would cause the baby, and Ethic wanted nothing more than for his child to be safe. He conceded despite his ego telling him to fight her on this because he knew it was best for her in this moment. For one night, he would give her space.

"I'm never not going to be here with this baby," he said when she made it to the top. "With you... but I'ma let you cool down because I can't see this getting anywhere, and I'm not with the yelling and fighting."

He felt her sorrow without even being able to see her fully. It was in her body language. In the subtle slouch of her shoulders like he had taken her confidence away with one indiscretion, one he hadn't even committed. Still, her perception plus YaYa's impromptu visit equaled betrayal in her eyes. In the court of Alani, he was already guilty, and it was disheartening to realize how fragile their trust was.

He climbed into his Range, looking up at the castle he had built his family, and with reluctance, he pulled off into the night.

CHAPTER 19

Y
ou want to pull up, don't you?" Isa asked.

"Nah. She's with her family. That's who she needs," Meek answered. His mind was so damn cluttered, all he wanted to do was shut it off. "He fucking raped her, man." Meek sat behind the steering wheel in Isa's driveway as they passed a blunt back and forth. "The nigga blackmailed her. Lame-ass nigga was so pressed he had to drug her. How fucking low is that, man? So much shit makes sense now."

"Mo should have said something," Isa said.

Meek shook his head. The weight of this discovery would sit on his soul for a while. He had never understood why Morgan wouldn't just leave Bash. Now, he understood that couldn't and wouldn't were two different things. It made the moments they spent together even more valuable because she was risking it all just to be with him. *I should have been killed that nigga.*

"We gon' have to lay low. Let shit cool down for a while. That mu'fucka kicked up a lot of dust," Isa said. "Hak is still a problem."

"Hak is my problem," Meek said. "The debt is strictly on me now. I made sure of it. So, no more rogue trips to Vegas, bruh."

"Yo' problems is my problems, so fuck you. Ain't about to save me like I'm yo' bitch," Isa said, snickering.

Meek chuckled as Isa climbed from the car and disappeared inside.

Thoughts of Morgan occupied his mind. What niggas confused as anger, Ahmeek identified as hurt. He felt all of it, and the thought of what she had been through sliced away at his manhood. He had been intimate with her. He had been between her legs more times than he could count, yet he hadn't paid attention. *How the fuck didn't I notice?* Meek wondered if he and Mo were the opposite of what he thought. She had him open, and they had fallen into something forbidden at the speed of light, but he now wondered if it was all physical. If he had missed something so important because he had been blinded by the wrong things. Life had been much simpler when he had kept things casual with women. Investing in women, falling in love with a woman, especially one as unavailable as Morgan Atkins, had put a level of conflict in his life that disturbed his peace. Morgan bothered him, and he was losing his mind because he craved her disruption. Ahmeek was a hustler interrupted. The level of focus repaying the Hak debt would take left no room for her. Still, he kept checking his phone, even though it was a number Mo didn't even have. He had revoked her access, and although it was the right decision, it wasn't an easy one to make, especially knowing she was hurt. He wanted to go to her, but the conflict between him and Messiah weighed on him; the conflict between his past and his future reinforced his decision to let it go. He had told Morgan he would be leaving the game, but with Hak's new demands, he would be going harder than ever before. The time he had given her, the attention, the loving through the night and lounging all day just to absorb her essence, would be limited now. Morgan Atkins couldn't be his if he were still married to the streets. What they had done had made him crave normalcy. Morgan had a way of needing a nigga that made him want to level up his entire approach to living. She needed him, so he was there. She depended on him, so he didn't slip. She used him for a reason to smile, for a reason to cum, for a reason to laugh, for a reason to dream, and my God, the way she called his name gave him a reason to do the shit over and over again every day for her to keep her satisfied. Her satisfaction mentally and emotionally meant his fulfillment in all ways. Meek had applied for a job that hadn't even been meant for him and mastered that shit. Letting go wasn't as easy as he would have liked for it to be. His soul was firing off warnings that he was getting ready to venture into a place where he wouldn't return from.

Ahmeek was known as a womanizer. Women from all over the country followed him, flirted with him. They were in his inbox, on his line, on his dick. It was nothing for him to fly a pretty girl in to see him for a night and then send her on her way. It was his way of balancing the hard with the soft. The streets had shown him some vile things. They were wicked. Women were pure. They were a retreat. They were a mental vacation from a war zone of hustling and killing. Morgan was more than that. She wasn't supposed to be but when he walked in her home, when she waited up at night for him to pull up and he stepped into her world, she felt like the prize at the end of a marathon. She was that first sip of water after the race. He just didn't know where they stood. He had made such a habit of seeing her daily that not seeing her was a tangible ache. He hated the shit. He didn't know how he had let her burrow so deeply under his skin.

"What the fuck, yo?" He muttered. After mayhem in the streets, Meek fucked. That was his routine. It was like he poured all his sins out in the purest thing on earth... pussy. Morgan had no idea how many times he had sought refuge in her bed. Tonight, the absurdness of his self-induced deprivation of her put him in a mood. It wasn't one he would soon shake. She wasn't a craving that would pass. Morgan Atkins, with her vibrance, her smile, her innocence despite her need to prove otherwise, would be with him for a while. His mother had told him that some women simply weren't replaceable. He had never understood the sentiment until now.

Bella's world felt like it was upside down. As she looked at the college applications piling up on her desk, she felt dread instead of pride. She couldn't believe things had turned out this way. Hendrix had given her companionship and intimacy in the most freeing way. Their plans didn't seem so scary because they were pursuing their dreams together. She had a feeling that she wanted the dream a little more than Henny.

She had always known that he was doing it for her, but she just knew that once he saw the campus and they embarked on the road trip together to visit the school that her dream would become his focus too. The streets had trapped him first, and it felt like they would never let him go.

Her phone rang and her father's picture popped up on the screen.

"Hey, Daddy. Where are you? Why didn't you just call me on the intercom?" Bella asked. Ethic's home was too big to yell when he needed one of his children, and he valued his peace, so he had an intercom system installed throughout.

"I'm not home, baby girl," Ethic said. "Where's Lenika? She's not answering her phone."

"I'll go get, Ma," Bella replied. "Can you find out how I can visit Henny? And what does he need, Daddy? You know he doesn't have anyone. He'll need stuff in there."

"Henny's commissary is already taken care of, baby girl. I'm not gonna forget that he's in there. I got him. It's not your job to hold him down. You're a teenage girl, Bella. Remember your worth."

"I know mine," Bella answered. "I just need to remind Hendrix of his. He doesn't belong in there. Can we visit? Please, Daddy. I just want him to know that we won't forget about him. I want him to feel like he has support."

"Support and blind devotion are two different things, Bella. I need you to keep your eyes forward. Always forward, baby girl. Henny made some choices that's caused him to lag behind you. You don't look backward for nobody. The minute you look backward is the minute you lose your pace.

When he gets out, if he's worth what you think he is, he'll work his ass off to catch up to you. You don't slow down for him. I'll see about the visit, but I need you to hear me clearly. My daughter isn't riding or dying for nobody's son."

Bella's spirit was broken. She didn't respond because she didn't want to hear what her father was saying. *He just doesn't understand,* she thought.

When she got to her parents' bedroom, she knocked and waited for Alani to invite her in before pushing open the door.

"How are you feeling?" Bella asked.

"I'm okay, my sweet girl. I'm just a little sore," Alani whispered.

"Your husband wants to talk to you," Bella said, passing Alani her phone. "I'll come back for it."

Alani held the phone but refused to give Ethic her full attention.

"You ready to listen?"

She took her time acknowledging him, carrying the phone to the bathroom with her and brushing her teeth for three minutes of torture him, and then taking another two minutes to floss while Ethic waited impatiently.

"You on your bullshit, no?" He asked. "What do you want? I have stuff to get for the gender reveal," she answered, tone loading into her verbal chamber like bullets.

"I want to wake up next to my wife, rub her feet, I know they swollen. You know they hurt," Ethic said, smirking.

Alani's feet were aching, but she stubbornly replied, "You know everything except why that bitch keeps popping up like she's fucking you."

Kill shot. Alani's aim was stellar. Her words were hollow points.

"I'm not fucking anyone except you. You know that," Ethic said. "Ain't loving nobody else either, Lenika."

"Bye, Ezra," she said.

Her finger was milliseconds off the red button.

"Don't lose your mind," Ethic said.

She paused. He was big on respect. Commanded it without effort. She looked at the FaceTime and her heart fluttered. He hadn't even climbed out of bed yet. Shirtless, his chocolate skin rested on pure white hotel sheets while he held the phone up above him. The band of Versace boxers peeped from beneath the lower half of the wrinkled bedding. They had made love all night on sheets just like those. She was angry that he was so damn fine. He hadn't even brushed his teeth yet or climbed out of bed for a morning piss, and he was still the most handsome nigga in the world. Flaws and all, Ethic Okafor was just the one. She wondered if he was "her one," however, or if someone else was occupying his bed. Had Little Miss Green Eyes slept there last night? Her logic said no, but her hormones and insecurities were whispering a different story in her ear.

"That was a bad fall. How are you today?" He asked as he rubbed his waves down and frowned. Damn it. Why was he so sexy? "My baby kicked today? Cuz if you ain't felt no kicks, we need to try to get some movement. You know she kick like crazy when I kiss it, baby. You want me to come home and eat it up?"

You motherfucka, don't bite your fucking lip, Alani thought, screaming on the inside. He knew what he was doing, and he knew her body was crying for him because, by this time, she would have already had his lips wrapped around her clit by now. He mitigated her stress with orgasms every day of her pregnancy. Even when he didn't get his, Alani got hers, and she was dizzy thinking about it.

Alani wanted to tell him to kiss her ass, but when his tone changed, she saw the genuine concern.

"Nah, for real. You felt kicks?" He had been up all night worrying about her. She could see the fatigue in his gloomy eyes and wrinkled forehead.

"I'm sore and bruised, but we're fine. She kicked," Alani said without enthusiasm, giving him a little relief.

"She?" Ethic questioned. "You been team boy this whole time, now you saying she? I miss a memo or something?"

"Eazy says it's a girl, so it's a girl," Alani said. "I got to go."

"I ain't got too many more nights in a hotel in me, Lenika," Ethic said.

"I ain't got too many more pop-ups from your side bitch in me," Alani shot back. "Goodbye, Ezra. I'll see you in a couple days at the reveal. Wear white. Be there at the park at 2 pm."

"You think I'm meeting my pregnant wife at my child's gender reveal like I'm some bum-ass father?"

"No, I expect you to act like a bum-ass husband who can't control his side bitch. We're not going to the gender reveal together. We might not even be together after this. I'm hanging up now."

Alani ended the call and sucked in a deep breath. She had a strong poker face, but her heart was bruised.

"Just get dressed. He married you. Stop letting that bitch see you sweat."

Morgan slept through the night, the entire next day, and the following evening. She was mentally and spiritually depleted, and when she finally awoke, the first thing she saw was Messiah, sleeping in the reclining chair in the corner of her room. Messari was asleep in his arms, and Yara was sleeping at the foot of her bed, lying sideways like her guard dog.

She had so much to face. She almost missed Bash's imprisonment because it was her excuse to not face those she had hurt. In Messiah's case, she had avoided facing the man who had hurt her. She climbed out of bed and picked Yara up, smothering her with love as she awakened her with soft kisses. "Everything's going to be better now," she told herself as she rocked her toddler gently. Yara rubbed her eyes and gave Morgan a grumpy frown as she cuddled against her chest and went back to sleep, despite Morgan's interruption.

"Pretty-asses."

Morgan looked up to find Messiah watching.

"You're so hard with her. She's a tough cookie, but she love her mama," Messiah said. "I still got to get used to all this, but I want to get used to it, shorty. This lil' nigga all up on me like I'm his personal pillow. Baby Killa over there don't give me much of a chance. She break a nigga heart every time she pull away from me for someone else."

Morgan felt shame for that.

"Let me ask you something, shorty. Did you know you were pregnant before I left?" He asked.

"I found out on the most normal Thursday ever. You were getting ready to ride out with the Crew and I was settling in to watch Grey's. I was so excited. I remember my hands shook for two minutes straight until those lines popped up on the test. I wanted to tell you, but I didn't want to send you out on a run with news that big on your mind. It was the most normal fucking Thursday. By Friday, normal didn't exist anymore. By Friday, everything changed. Your side bitch came to your house with a baby, Messiah. A baby we still haven't even addressed. Then, you left town. You promised me a family and then left me and got ghost with another bitch. You made me look crazy on Bleu's lawn. I fought so hard to get you to hear me that day, to get you to see me, and you were cold to me. You told me you didn't give a fuck, and then you left. It was too much. I've lost a lot of people in my life, but all those people loved me until the end. I've never been betrayed the way you betrayed me. Thinking we were one way and then discovering it was all a lie… Then, trying to process you being related to Mizan…" Morgan shook her head. "Nothing has ever hurt like that. I meant to tell you and I was going to tell you, then you became my enemy."

"You should have told me," Messiah said.

"When?" Morgan scoffed. "When you had a gun to Ethic's head? Or when that bitch showed up with your baby? Exactly when was I supposed to tell you?"

"Any of those fucking times, shorty! They mine! I would have never left had you opened your mouth."

"Because they were the only ones worth sticking around for?" Morgan was beyond offended.

"Quit putting words in my mouth," Messiah snapped.

"Somebody needs to because you ain't been saying shit! You want so much clarity, Messiah. Where's mine? Where have you been? Where is your other kid and the bitch who showed up at your house? Why would you take me through hell just to come back and raise hell when you realize I'm happy with somebody else?"

"Yo' miserable-ass ain't fucking happy! If you was happy, I would let it be. You confused. You want niggas to make you feel what I make you feel, shorty, but they can't," Messiah mumbled. "You love a nigga, and you hate it. Ain't none of these niggas giving you what I give you. You cap out here."

A soft knock on the door silenced them both.

"Mo? Can I come in?"

Morgan's shaky reply urged Alani to enter. She was seconds from tears. Angry ones because Messiah and his half transparency drove her insane. "Messiah, I'll be ready to go in about an hour or so," Alani said.

Messiah stood, picking up Messari and transferring him to the bed.

"I'ma shoot a move and get yesterday off me. I'll be right back. Have my shorties dressed. They can spend the day with me while you get your head right," Messiah said with an attitude. M&M was like oil and water sometimes. They were lovers yesterday. Today, they were adversaries. Conversations of the past had pulled them right back to Animosity-Ville. Still, his want to have his "shorties" with him made Morgan feel pure happiness for her children. It wasn't what she had pictured forever ago when she had begged him for his children, but it was still worthy of appreciation, even if she was left out of the frame.

"Are you okay?" Morgan asked.

"Are *you* okay?" Alani shot back.

Morgan shook her head, but then she changed her answer and nodded. "I will be."

Alani was silent as she took inventory of Morgan's bruises.

"How long was he hurting you?" Alani asked.

"Honestly, I think I hurt him more than he hurt me," Morgan said. "I wasn't innocent."

"Don't justify his actions, Mo. I don't care what you did. He's a man. He should never hit you," Alani said. "Did his parents know? I never liked that fucking mama of his."

"Can we just not?" Morgan said. "I mean, I want to. I trust you, but I just can't. It's too soon."

"Okay." Alani headed for the door.

"I know Ethic probably told you what I said. Bash was..." Morgan shook her head. "He wanted me to push Ethic away. I knew the way to do that was to go against you. He loves you. He'd never choose anyone above you. I didn't mean any of it. I know I've treated you hella unfair, Alani, but that's not where we are now. At least, I hope that's not where we are."

"We're good, Mo," Alani said. "I knew something was not right about that family. You were too…"

"Too what?" Morgan asked.

"Polite," Alani said.

Morgan couldn't help the laughter that took over her. Alani gave in to her own as she grabbed Morgan's hand.

"Am I that bad?" Mo asked.

"Oh, Morgan Atkins, you are hell sometimes," Alani said, chuckling. "I'm gonna pee on myself. Wait, wait."

Morgan shook her head and said, "I'm sorry. I don't mean to put you and Ethic through hell."

"You're a hell-raiser, but you're family, Mo. We love you. I have this incredible bond with Bella and Eazy. You and I have gone slower. We've spent a lot of time feeling one another out. I want you to feel like you can trust me, like you can talk to me. Because I would have been mopped that snobby bitch, Christiana, up for you."

Morgan smiled. "I do trust you. I was just scared to tell the truth."

"Yeah, well, there's a lot of that going around," Alani said. "You've been through a lot. Messiah has been through a lot. Maybe you should talk to Nyair. Ezra and I would not be together today if it weren't for him. I'm not trying to play matchmaker. I know you have a lot going on. I know you love Ahmeek too. I can see it all over you."

"I miss him," Morgan admitted. "I love Messiah so much, too much sometimes, but I miss Ahmeek."

"You're lucky, Mo. You have two men who love you. I don't know if there is a such thing as choosing between them.

None of the answers sound right. What I do know is that you have two children to think about. You and Messiah have to get things right with one another because the twins need to see that you trust their father and that he protects you. They need to see that love created them. That doesn't mean you got to be with him. I actually think you need to do some self-care before choosing either of them, but you and Messiah are family regardless. The twins deserve you both at your best. You should take Messiah to counsel with Nyair."

"Messiah not going for that," Morgan said, sucking her teeth.

"Neither was Ezra, but here we are," Alani replied. "Mental, spiritual, and emotional clarity can make you see life clearer, Mo. You don't know which one you want because you don't understand why they want you. You both have a lot of healing to do. You should try it."

"I'm just so stupid for him," Morgan whispered. "I shouldn't even want him around, but the what-if is torture. What if we had, had a chance two years ago?"

"Love isn't intellectual, Mo. We go against our minds every day as women. We love men who are undeserving every day. It's the gift and curse of femininity," Alani said. "Even if Messiah doesn't want to talk to Ny, you should. You've been through a lot. Don't feel obligated to be strong when it's healthier to be weak and let it out."

Morgan loved her time with Nyair. She almost didn't want to share him, but if he could help Messiah in the same way she had watched him transform Ethic, it was worth a shot.

"This some bullshit," Ethic mumbled as he rolled out of bed. He sat on the edge of the bed, leaned over, rubbing the back of his neck. "This fucking woman gon' be the death of a nigga." He didn't know if he was talking about Alani or YaYa. His wife wasn't wrong. YaYa had crossed a line, and he understood her anger. It was her inability to listen to reason that annoyed him. There was nothing worse than being accused of something you didn't do. His phone rang and he saw Disaya's number pop up on the screen. He let the voicemail pay her some attention and then lifted from the bed. His dick rose with the sun every morning and today was no different. Strong thighs and heavy steps led him to the bathroom. *Damn woman got me living outta suitcase.*

She had provided him with a home for two years. The sounds, the scents, the rituals of her love were all over their estate. The sterile and impersonal five-star suite he had holed up in last night wouldn't do.

He didn't even know how to begin to make this right because he hadn't done anything wrong.

Ethic had half the urge to call Zya and let her know that YaYa was not his concern any longer, but he knew the information Zya had needed him to receive couldn't be spoken over the phone. It had been important, and he understood why YaYa was her messenger. In the past, that one message would have led to months of lovemaking. YaYa was a rabbit hole of lust and luxury that he had left behind when he said, "I do."

Ethic dressed and headed to pick up his kids. They all seemed to need him at the same time for different dependencies, and he had an obligation to try to fulfill them all. It was hard sometimes, impossible at others, to balance fatherhood between three different children, but he was committed to being there. It didn't matter how old they became, how minuscule their problem may be, or how abhorrent their behavior, Ethic would always be present for their journey.

His phone rang again, and Ethic accepted the call this time.

"Grand rising, G," Nyair said. "I'm headed to scoop Mo. You at the crib?"

"If you ain't on time, bro," Ethic said, sighing a bit. Nyair had stepped up in all ways of brotherhood. He loved on his nieces and nephew real well. It was a genuine connection that Ethic hadn't known he needed until he discovered it existed. "I was on my way to grab the kids, but Mo needs a little more, if you n'ah mean."

"I got her. I'ma always have her," Nyair said. "I'll see you tomorrow at the thing. Alani went all out, apparently. You good with Pop and Zora coming?"

"Yeah, that's cool. Zo be on the move, but she took the time to come to my court dates. I never got the chance to thank her. Looking forward to it."

"And Pop?" Nyair double-checked.

"Man, that's yo' daddy," Ethic said, stubbornly. They were still figuring out their way. "It's his grandchild. He can be there."

Nyair chuckled a bit. "A'ight, bro. I'ma holla."

Ethic rode across town with his gun in his lap, an old habit, and he placed it in the hidden dash compartment when he arrived safely home. The sight of Alani's car gave him a little relief. He climbed out and went to open the garage door that led inside. When his key didn't turn, he frowned.

"I know this crazy-ass fucking woman ain't lost her mind." Ethic was blown. He pulled his phone out his back pocket and dialed Bella.

"Hey, Daddy," Bella answered.

"I'm at the garage door."

"Here I come," Bella said. When Bella pulled open the door, Ethic pushed inside, headed straight for the family room.

"Where's Alani?" he asked.

"Her and Messiah went to the grocery store," Bella said. "Something about getting food for the reveal."

Ethic nodded. "And Mo?"

"She went with Uncle Nyair. The twins and Eazy are with Alani. You ready?"

"Yeah, wait for me in the car," he said.

Ethic ventured to the basement and opened the fuse box. He disconnected the main fuse, turning all the power out in the house. He knew she would be too stubborn to call him at first. She would try to flip the switches, but she wouldn't know to reconnect the main source. Either he would be at home, or they would be in the dark.

"Changing the fucking locks," Ethic mumbled before walking out.

"Outlaw, on your feet."

Henny stood and braced himself as the guards buzzed him out of his cell. He hated the sound. To some, it meant that they could get out. To Young Henny, it meant someone could get in. He hadn't been there a week, and he had already been targeted by a gang of Beecher boys, a rival hood to the block Henny claimed. Henny had held his own. He had focused on one nigga, beating him with a food tray until he was bloody on the chow line. Ten inmates had stomped him out, but that one nigga who he had caught knew not to fuck with him again. He had shown heart, but he knew they would test him again. The sound of these locks releasing made him feel like they were coming for round two. The men behind these walls were predators, and Little Henny was fresh prey.

"Relax, kid. It gets easier in here. You got friends inside, but you got to look like you earning your keep," the guard said.

Henny's face revealed his confusion. "You got a visitor."

Henny didn't trust the guards too much either. He had seen them sneaking contraband inside, some even held the inmates in precarious positions and then demanded sex or blowjobs just for basic rights like food, water, and safe cell placements. Henny was trying to stay out the way. He had a long seven years in front of him. He hadn't slept in days because he was afraid of who might catch him slipping or sneak into his cell once the lights went out.

He followed the guard out of the cell and down B-block as men hooted and hollered, taunting him, baiting him. It was like the fucking zoo. His heart had never beat so fast.

I got to get a shiv or sum'n up in this bitch ASAP, he thought. Henny walked with his shoulders strong, head up. Ethic had said to keep his manhood, to stand his ground. He felt sick inside, though. He wanted to go home. He wanted to see his mama, shoot the shit with his potnah, Emil, and most of all, he wanted to see his girl. When he got to the visiting room, he looked around until his eyes landed on a familiar face.

"What you doing here?" Hendrix asked as he stood at her table.

Bianca sat, looking pretty in her Louis print dress and ones on her feet. Her fit was fake but it was fly. She put her shit together well, even when she rocked the knock-offs. She was a fakeittil-youmakeit type, but if you didn't know the brand extremely well, you wouldn't be able to tell. Henny knew her well; that's how he could distinguish. She played the part of a made chick real well.

"Just checking on you. The whole hood heard what happened. It kind of messed me up. I'm sorry you got caught up out there in the 'burbs. You don't belong out there, and you def don't belong in here," Bianca said.

Henny nodded and reluctantly pulled out a chair.

"The hood gon' miss you," she said, half smiling. A discreet tear slid down her face, and she brushed it away. "I'm gon' miss you too."

"Mannn, you ain't gon' be thinking about me. Yo' ass hell out here," Henny said, snickering.

Bianca laughed. "If niggas hell on me, I give it back. A nigga ain't finna treat me any ol' kinda way," Bianca bragged.

"I hear that; that's real shit," Henny replied.

"I got a job waiting tables at the club. I put a little something on your books," she said. "Just a little love. I know ya mama got her own shit you know. Just wanted to look out. Susan hood. We all we got."

Hendrix nodded. "That's solid, Bianca. I 'ppreciate you."

"Don't fold in here, Dris," she said, calling him the name niggas around the way used sometimes. "I'ma write your big-head-ass sometimes... if I feel like it. You know, make sure you still know how to read and ain't getting dumb in here."He put a bawled fist to his mouth, smiling.

"Ohhh, you got jokes. Okay, a'ight, mu'fucka. You got it," he returned.

"I got to go. My mama gon' be home soon, and I got to beat her there. You know my address. Use some of that commissary to buy some stamps and send me a kite sometimes. Maybe I'll send you some books or something since you stay reading now."

"Who knew you was watching. Fedass," Henny joked.

She laughed and then grew silent as a somberness misted her eyes.

"I've never really lost anybody, Henny. Like you been around since I was little. We literally been playing together since we was kids out here, and now you're locked up. It just don't feel right. I just thought you should know we miss you at home and we gon' hold it down until you back on the block where you belong."

Henny nodded, and Bianca stood. "Bye."

CHAPTER 20

I sat with a psychiatrist," Messiah said, randomly revealing it to Alani as they browsed aisle ten.

She knew better than to give a drastic reaction, but she felt it. Her entire stomach sank as she grabbed the macaroni shells off the shelf. By the time she spun to face Messiah, her shocked expression was normal.

"That's mature of you," she said.

"It was Ethic's doing," Messiah answered.

"What ain't his doing," Alani quipped, rolling her eyes.

Messiah chuckled. "You really mad at Big Homie, huh?"

Alani didn't answer.

"Yo' granny gon' kill your Pop Pop," Messiah signed to Yara, who sat in the front of the cart he pushed. Eazy pushed Alani's basket and Messiah pushed his own. One for the groceries. One for the twins.

"Umm, no," Alani said with a pointed finger. "I am not a granny. I am their La La."

"Sound like a dressed up nickname for granny to me," Messiah shot back.

Alani laughed.

Messiah grabbed a bag of chips off the shelf and opened them in the middle of the aisle, handing one to Yara.

"How about you?" he asked Messari who was at the bottom of the cart playing with Messiah's phone. He held up a chip for his son and he took it. He sucked on it, not even taking a bite, just letting his spit soften the chip.

"Here, Daddy. Me gonna share with you," Messari said, holding his little hand up in the air. The look of disgust that crossed Messiah's face sent Eazy up in stitches.

"Eww, Ssari, man. It's all soggy," Eazy said, laughing.

"It's good!" Messari said, hand still raised.

Alani watched as Messiah grimaced but accepted the chip from Messari.

She smiled and kept strolling.

"See, him like it!" Messari said, proving Eazy wrong.

Messiah could barely scarf it down, but the pride in Messari's voice put a little pride in Messiah's chest. He would eat a whole bag of soggy chips just to have Messari feel connected to him.

"I still can't get over them, man," Messiah said, amazed as he bent down so that he was eye to eye with Yara. He kissed her round cheeks and a temperamental Yara pushed his face away with her small hand.

"Yo, she strong-arming the fuck out of me," Messiah laughed. "Why is she this mean?"

"Cuz you're mean," Alani answered.

Messiah gave her eye contact and then kissed Yara anyway, despite her little hand protesting.

"I love you, Baby Killa," he signed.

He pulled another chip from the bag and gave it to her. She accepted that. She still pushed his face out the way, and he shook his head.

"You hurting Daddy's feelings, lil' mama," he signed.

"She'll come around. Give her time," Alani said, sympathetically. "Mo will too. So, therapy? You gonna go back?"

Messiah shrugged. "I don't want to fuck them up, man. I look at Mo and I see a perfect girl. Literally, the girl of my dreams, but she been let down over the years. She been hurt, abused. It's like no matter what good shit happens to her, she gon' always feel the bad stuff that happened first. I don't want to be the first bad thing that happens to them. So, yeah, I'ma go back."

Alani scoffed and shook her head as she strolled. "You are Ethic's son," she said.

"Huh?" Messiah was lost. Ethic didn't even look at him the same, and he damn sure wasn't trying to father him. Messiah would have turned out much differently if he had.

"I got all the faith in the world in you, Messiah," Alani said. "You're going to be an amazing father to them. Love and time are really all they need. You give them that, and you'll pass every test."

"Sometimes, I fuck up the love part. Like, I love my people too hard, and it hurts them, and then they think the shit came from malice," Messiah answered.

"Daddy said you got to feel safe to be soft. He told me it was okay that I didn't want to fight this kid at school who was bullying me because it just meant that I was used to being safe and that I hadn't learned to be hard yet. He says being hard comes from having hate in your heart. Who do you hate? Maybe if you try not to hate anyone, you can be soft for the twins? Right, ma?" Eazy said.

Alani and Messiah didn't even realize Eazy was listening. He was watching YouTube on his phone distractedly, pushing the buggy along, but his ears were open. The things that came out his mouth floored them.

Messiah hated his father. Even still, beyond the grave, the hatred burned so furiously he had walls around his entire heart.

Alani stared at Messiah, but she replied, "That's right, Big Man."

There was a sense of peace that came with being home for Morgan. The sanctuary that Ethic had created was one that she had missed. She was grateful and shocked that Ethic had forgiven her. He had done it with ease, without thinking twice. He hadn't even asked her why. He just listened to her pour her heart out, kissed her forehead, and put her, Bella, and the twins in an Uber to go home. It was the gloss in his eye as he listened to her confession that broke Morgan's heart. He was hurt by what she had done. He just wouldn't say it. Knowing that didn't sit right on Morgan's soul. She didn't even deserve the kind of love Ethic gave her. It was the definition of unconditional, and Morgan knew she had put many conditions on the table. She wasn't easy to love, and she realized how complicated she made his life.

"You hella quiet over there, Mo?" Nyair said.

"You hella secular over there," Mo replied, a defiant smile breaking through her melancholy, temporarily lighting up her face like lightning striking through a storm-filled sky.

They rode in silence as Drake provided the soundtrack to their tour around the city as Nyair delivered produce from the church garden to single mothers who were members of the congregation.

"I kept asking myself why you just left town on me when you first went to London. We spoke every day and then you dipped, like nobody here even existed," Nyair said.

"It wasn't about you. I just couldn't pretend anymore. Everybody here, everything here…" She paused. "I just needed to leave it behind for a little while."

"Guess you didn't realize you did to all of us what your child's father did to you," Nyair said casually. His words captivated her full attention. His hand gripped the steering wheel of the Audi, and the Piguet on his wrist gave him a feel that no pastor should have. Nyair had been her confidante since the day she had met him. She hadn't thought about how he would feel when she left.

"I didn't know you would care," she said.

"Yeah, well, I cared, Mo. I care. Those bruises on your body, the look in your eyes. I think about losing my religion every time I see you," Nyair said. She was speechless. "Why didn't you tell me, Mo? You know you can trust me with it all. I would have handled that for you."

"By the time it got out of control, I was too embarrassed and afraid of what everybody would think of me if I asked for help. I thought I could handle him," Morgan admitted. "And somewhere deep down, it feels like I deserved what Bash was doing, Ny," Morgan said. "I just feel dirty. Like I'm washed up. Who's going to want me after this?"

"Mo, it's crazy to me that you can't see what other people see. I get it, though. The whole butterfly thing. They don't see their own wings either. You're beautiful. I'm not talking about your face, or your body, because you know that much. You use that shit to your advantage, got these niggas on your line, so you know. I'm talking about the way you are. The way you believe in love after all the bullshit you've been through. The way you laugh even when you feel like crying. The way you pretend to be okay so that the twins will be okay. The way you crave family. All the little subtleties that make you, you. You're probably the most vulnerable person I've ever counseled. Most people put up their guards after the world beats them up, you just continue to live, you go for the gusto like you ain't never lost. That's why it hurts so bad when you're let down because you really want one thing to pan out, just once, cuz you giving this life thing you're all. That's beauty. That's resilience, Mo."

"Or stupidity. Naïveté," Mo countered.

"Nah, Mo. Women are the architects. You know exactly what you do. You just haven't learned the impact of your power. We all feel it. Sometimes, it feels good. Sometimes, it hurts."

Morgan looked out the window. "I'm done hurting people I love."

"Does that include yourself?"

Morgan's silence was his answer.

"Name the top five people in your life," Nyair said.

"What? Ny, no, this ain't therapy. I'm not tryna..."

"It ain't therapy. I'm curious. Who do you love? Humor me."

"I love you, but right now you on my nerves, so you def not in my top ten," she quipped.

He chuckled as he pulled into the church parking lot. They got out of the car and Morgan followed Nyair inside.

"What are we doing here again?" Morgan wasn't ready to put her list together in her head.

She didn't even know who would be on it. Or rather, who needed to be removed from it. Evading the question was easier.

"I just got to unlock the banquet hall for La. After the gender reveal at the park, she wants to have a celebration dinner here," Nyair said. "You really love her. How do you watch someone you love, love somebody else?" Morgan asked.

"I used to love her, but time did what it's supposed to, Mo. It grew us up. Now, I love that she's loved well by Ethic. By Bella. By Eazy. By the twins. By you," he paused. "Well, not always you. You like to give her a hard time."

Morgan lowered her eyes as they stepped inside the sanctuary.

"I do love her, though. She's grown on me," Morgan said.

"Point is, we don't always get to keep people we love. You put a person in a position and then expect them to play they part, but sometimes over time we change and their position changes too. The love changes."

Morgan's entire body felt that. "Change is terrifying."

"Change is inevitable. The more you try to fight it, the more damage you do," Nyair said. "I'll be right back. Let me let these mother-"

"Yeah, you're super secular right now," Morgan interrupted, giving up a genuine smile. Nyair just made her feel better, like she was capable of healing. "One day, you have to tell me how you became a minister because it just doesn't make sense in my head."

"I lost someone, decided I needed to save myself and then I wanted to save everybody else. That don't make me perfect, Mo. Just a servant. That old part just dormant. It ain't gone," he replied, winking. "I'll be right back. Think about what I asked. Who are the five people you love most, Mo?"

Morgan watched him walk up the aisle, and before he pushed out of the doors, she gave her answer.

"My kids, Ethic, Eazy, Bella..." she paused at the fifth spot. She didn't know who to place there. Messiah was on the tip of her tongue, but Ahmeek's name floated through her mind. Instead, she identified someone she would love forever, but never see again. "Raven."

Nyair turned to her, one hand in his pocket, one hand on the door. "And that's the problem."

"Loving my family is wrong?" She asked.

"You didn't mention yourself."

"Tell me about the eye." Ethic surveyed Hendrix as a table separated them.

"Small problems, OG," Hendrix replied.

"Shouldn't be no problems. You not alone in there. You have muscle," Ethic said, leaning forward and lowering his tone.

"I'm not on my block yet. It's overcrowded. It'll be a few weeks. I'm maintaining until then. I'd rather take an ass whooping and hold my own than walk in here and let it be known you holding my hand. We both know I won't make it seven years like that. I need to make my own name. Earn my own respect. Even with your stamp, I need to be able to stand on my own two, just in case I'm caught slipping when your people ain't around."

Ethic nodded. He understood the need to survive on your own. Hendrix's own mother hadn't ever protected him. The young kid didn't expect Ethic to stick around for his entire sentence.

"My people gon' be around, Hendrix. For seven years," Ethic assured.

Henny gritted his teeth, the stress of his situation pushing out of his jaw as it pulsed. He wanted to cry. He couldn't. He wouldn't be safe to show that type of emotion for a long time.

"Keep your head. Niggas watching," Ethic said. "The only place the tears won't show is in the shower. That's your time. Not here. Breathe."

Hendrix fought his fear and took a deep breath, sighing away the anxiety bubbling in his stomach.

"Your commissary come through?" Ethic asked.

Hendrix nodded.

"Good."

"Good looking out," Hendrix said. "Is she here?"

Ethic's silence filled the space between them, making Henny shift uncomfortably. Ethic was the ultimate girl dad. He didn't like any of his daughters' suitors, but if he had to choose one to tolerate, Henny was the one. He had done a good job proving his intentions, ensuring that he didn't taint Bella with his street mentality. He was respectful. Ethic had built up a reluctant hope that maybe, just maybe, Hendrix would make it out of Flint. Now, he was staring at an inmate. He hated this for Hendrix but most of all he hated it for his child.

"She's afraid for you. She feels for you. How do you feel about my daughter, Hendrix? I think I know, but I want to hear it from you," Ethic said.

Hendrix froze.

"She's the most important person to me." Hendrix thought about downplaying what he felt, but he couldn't, not when Bella was the subject.

Ethic raked his beard as he sat back in his chair. "I believe that, but you can't be the most important person to her. Not while you're in here. Bella's a year away from college…"

"I fucked this up bad," Henny interrupted. "They gave me seven years." His voice cracked as he thought about the time he had in front of him." He quickly cleared his throat, shifting in his seat, and then flicking his nose. His body language screamed terrified.

"Control yourself," Ethic said as his eyes bounced around the room. "Niggas in here watch everything you do. If you act scared, they gon' terrorize you. Self-control. Be aware of the way you move, the way you walk, the way you eat, the way you breathe in this mu'fucka," Ethic said. "Head up."

Henny nodded and lifted his head and closed his fist because his hand was trembling.

"I know Bella not built for this. Some girls you expect to wait cuz you the only thing they got going. Bella was the only thing I had going, OG, but I was lucky to even be in the room with her. Bella always had options. She could have chose better friends, better ways to spend her summers, her time after school, a better boyfriend..."

"A better what?" Ethic put a pin in Hendrix right there. His daughter didn't have boyfriends. He refused to believe it. "You swimming out real deep, lil' nigga."

Hendrix half-smiled, fighting disappointment. "I want to love my daughter the way you love yours one day. It's the most solid shit I ever seen. Your family. Like, I legit ain't never seen no man be there for they kids like that. I ain't never seen no man be there for his wife. Not without no bullshit in the game. You don't creep out on them, ain't no spending time with another bitch across town. You just there for them, and they know it. They trust you to be there. I ain't seen the nigga who made me. I wanted to be a part of that real bad, Big Homie. I wanted to prove myself, to her, to you. I love Bella, but I want to be like you."

"You a real slick mu'fucka, Lil' Henny," Ethic said. "Finessing-ass." Hendrix had finagled his way into Ethic's tribe. Now, he was family, and if Ethic didn't do anything else, he protected his family.

He shook his head in distress.

"While Bella's growing, you can grow too. Different soils, but nobody asks about the kind of dirt two roses came from. They don't care about the weather it endured, as long as it blooms. If there was anything that could have been done, you know I would have done it, right?"

Henny sniffed away emotions that couldn't change anything. He knew. Henny had put himself in a position so detrimental that no one could save him. Ethic couldn't erase evidence that had been confiscated directly from a car that was registered to Henny. He couldn't do shit. Henny had to do his time. "Can I see her one last time?"

Ethic knocked on the table regrettably. He was having a hard time walking away from Hendrix. Not just Hendrix, but boys like Hendrix. Messiah too. He used to be just like them. He was the Benny Atkins to their Ethic. He had admired Benny in the same way, so he understood their allegiance to him. In many ways, his love for Raven and Morgan had come from wanting to be a part of Benny's family. He understood Hendrix and Messiah's displacement more than they would ever know. "Bella ain't my excuse to come check you out. She ain't the only reason you have to call the house. You understand?"

Henny did. He was losing Bella, but he got to keep Ethic. He didn't know who the prize was and who was the consolation.

He loved Bella, but he enjoyed his time with every member of her family as much as he enjoyed spending time with her. It felt like Ethic was the Okafor he needed right now.

Ethic stood from the table and walked out. Hendrix felt like he was sinking as Ethic disappeared behind the door; but Bella, God, Bella was the loveliest replacement. She reminded him to breathe. Her high, messy bun and baby hairs were so pretty. Not just to him but to every inmate she passed because they all turned to glance at her as she walked by.

"Nigga, fuck you looking at?" Hendrix snapped as Bella passed the table next to his.

"Don't talk no shit, new blood," the man answered, focusing back on the visit with his kids.

"Keep your eyes on your own paper then, nigga," Hendrix replied. By the time Bella got to him, he was standing, and she ignored every rule and ran straight into his arms.

"Inmate, no touching!" The guard yelled.

But he could feel her shaking and he couldn't let go.

"Inmate!"

The second warning forced them to release each other, and Bella moved nervously to the other side of the table.

"What did they do to you?" she asked, disturbed by the sight of him. "Are you okay?" Bella asked. He could tell from her sunken eyes that she had spent her time crying, too much time. One tear was too expensive a price for Bella Okafor to pay over a boy.

"I'm good, Boog," he said.

"I miss you so much," she whispered, looking around with

unease. Souvenirs of her love for him reflected in his eyes. He would remember this look, the way she gazed at him, because every day that passed, her love would dwindle, her memory of him would dilute. "I've been looking up programs closer to home. Michigan has some good schools. I printed the applications to U of M so that I can stay here so that I can visit. Seven years isn't as long as it sounds. By the time I'm out of college, you can be up for parole if you have good behavior. And even if you have to do the full seven, I can focus on grad school. By the time I'm done, you'll be out. We can still do this, Hendrix. And there are programs that you can take in here…"

Hendrix stared at her, and it was like she was muffled. The gloss of her lips was so pretty as she spoke, but the shit she was saying was ludicrous. It made him feel like shit. Ethic knew his daughter well. Bella had rearranged the dreams she had been dreaming for eight years to accommodate his failures. Bella didn't belong anywhere near Flint. She deserved to see the world. To backpack around the world like she planned to during summer, to pledge Delta at an HBCU, to vacation on spring break in Cancun. She had included him in all those goals, forcing him to make corny vision boards and reading college admissions essays to him. Her hopes had been high. Hearing her lower them for him put a vise around his heart, an invisible hand around his throat. He felt like bawling. His eyes fucking betrayed him as he wiped away a renegade tear.

"I ain't fucking with you like that," Hendrix blurted out, cutting her off.

"What?" Bella's confusion was valid. She looked at him like he had grown a second head, like he was speaking a language she hadn't learned yet.

"Don't come back here. You in here talking about college and shit like that matters. You naïve, man. This is the end for me, Bella. Only door I'm walking through is the door of a cell. A dark, fucking cell, Bella! We're over," Hendrix said, standing.

"Hendrix, sit down! What are you doing?" Bella protested.

"Ayo, Guard!" Hendrix said, turning away from her.

"Hendrix!" Bella shouted.

The guard came for him, putting handcuffs on him.

"Wait! No, please, just wait! We aren't done! We still have more time left! Just let me talk to him for a minute," Bella pleaded. "Henny, wait!"

Hendrix looked over his shoulder and then lowered his head. He couldn't respond because Ethic was right, niggas were watching him, and he had to keep his head up. If he said one more word, he was going to fall apart.

"You got thirty minutes left. You sure you're done?" The female guard asked as she looked at Hendrix.

"If you walk away, I'm going to let you," Bella said. He knew she meant that shit, and it scared him, but he had to do it. He had to be unselfish. His stubborn teenaged girlfriend would become a tenacious fucking woman. He knew she would, but not if he let her do what she wanted to do. Not if he reduced her to a jailbird, flying back and forth to see him instead of focusing on her goals. The world needed Bella, a girl who took more pictures of the world around her than herself when she discovered a place that intrigued her. The girl who absorbed more books than TV shows. The girl who studied shit just to know more, not because she had a test. The world needed more girls like that. These bars would shrink her, and Hendrix just wanted her to grow.

"I ain't make it, Boog. We both got to know when to let go. Go to college. Don't come back here. Ever."

Hendrix was escorted back to his cell, and he could feel her walking out of the prison. It was like her energy was leaving him. Envisioning her free on the outside of these walls broke him down. He was grateful when the doors clinked closed. He let out a scream that sounded like a song of torture in A minor and sat on the edge of his concrete bed and sobbed. Hendrix sobbed, letting it out for the last time before accepting his fate. She was gone, and he was empty. He would remain that way for years... she was free to find the sun. He had let her go. He just hoped she allowed herself to *BLOOM*.

CHAPTER 21

E thic almost regretted his decision to encourage Henny and Bella's breakup. He noticed the change in his daughter's aura as soon as she walked back out to the waiting area. The way she had held in her tears tightened his stomach. He could feel her, fighting them now, keeping her eyes closed as she rode shotgun because if she let one leak of emotion out her eyes, she wouldn't be able to plug the hole on the rest. True love. First love. He recognized it, both on Henny and within Bella. His baby girl loved a boy, and Ethic hated it. He could protect her from everything except love. Love was a sneaky invader, breaking entry when you least expected it and robbing you of everything. Logic. Sanity. Selfishness. It was a complete mind-fuck, and Bella was its latest victim.

"Love you, baby girl."

It used to be enough. Today, it wasn't nearly adequate. This first scar on her heart would be visible for a while. It was an unavoidable rite of passage into young womanhood. Somebody's nappy-headed son had disappointed his pride and joy. And not in the traditional sense. Henny hadn't been caught with another girl's phone number in his pocket. He hadn't taken some other girl on a date or flirted with someone around the way. Those heartaches Ethic could triage. Henny had gotten himself trapped in a modern-day slave system. Bella had watched as a symbolic "Massa" put chains around his wrists and ankles and carried her first love away to the plantation. She didn't know if she would ever see him again, and the thought of what he was enduring was torture. His baby was heartbroken, but she was Ethic through and through because she was holding that shit. He didn't want that for her, the numbing of her emotions. If she didn't unpack this baggage, she would carry it around with her for years. He gripped the steering wheel with a strong hand, leaning against the door slightly while playing in his beard with his free hand. Carefully. Ethic was choosing his next words very carefully because if he said the wrong thing, his teenage daughter would shut him out.

Maybe a motherfucking boy is the move, he thought, thinking of his unborn. These girls would be his undoing. *Crazy-ass wife. Love-sick-ass girls. Big Man and I need another member on the team cuz this shit is fucking insanity.*

He glanced in the rearview mirror at the one little strand of gray that existed in his beard. That one had come from Mo. He hadn't even fully processed her poor decisions yet. He didn't want to because he had some anger lying dormant in him with her, so he waited. He waited until he could speak from a place of love instead of just reacting and regretting it later. He was sure Bella was the curator of a second. It was only a matter of time.

"I know you like I know myself, so I know you don't want to talk about it," Ethic said. "You don't have to talk, but I want you to hear me clear. There will be many boys. Some will lie. Some will cheat. Some will be removed from your life by things you can't control. You're still Bella Okafor in every circumstance. You hear me?"

Bella nodded, opening her eyes and leaning on the armrest so that her head could rest on his shoulder. "And I'ma be here in every circumstance."

His phone rang, and Ethic answered it, anticipating this very call.

"I need you to come home. The power is out, and I came downstairs to try to fix it, but I can't, and it's a lot of stairs, and my hips hurt, and I don't feel like climbing back up."

"So you want a nigga to come home?" Ethic asked.

"To fix the lights, then you can leave," Alani answered.

"I ain't really plan to be that way today. I got business…"

"Ezra!" Alani whined. Ethic's amusement was her irritation. He was already pulling onto their street, but just the thought of something coming before her ignited her disposition. He had spoiled her well over the years.

"If I pull up, I ain't pulling off," he warned.

She went silent and he knew her stubborn-ass was contemplating staying in the dark just to prove a point.

"You not sleeping in my bed," she said.

"That's fine," he answered. He didn't have plans for sleep tonight anyway. "You can do a lot of other things in a bed."

Alani hung up the phone as Ezra was pulling into the driveway.

He exited the car and walked around to Bella's side, opening her door.

"Can you still make sure he's okay?" Bella asked.

It was in that moment that Ethic wondered if Bella and Henny were designed to be more than puppy love. Even through misunderstanding and heartbreak, Bella wanted Henny to be taken care of. It was a mature reaction to an immature stage in her life. Bella was an old soul. He was sure she had been here before because the way she loved was wise beyond her teenage years.

"I will, baby girl," Ethic replied, kissing the top of her head and pulling her in for a hug. When they walked inside, the sound of life filled his heart. Eazy occupied the twins, letting them climb all over him as he destroyed the living room décor, knocking pillows all over the floor.

"Hey dad!" He greeted without missing a beat.

"Pop Pop, helpppp usss!" Messari shouted at the top of his lungs as Eazy spun him around like a rag doll.

Ethic laughed at the rambunctiousness and his heart stilled a bit when Eazy let Messari go and tossed him into the mountain of pillows.

When he went to pick up Yara, Ethic pointed a finger at his son. "She bet not get hurt, Big Man. Be careful."

"I'm the one getting hurt! These babies are crazy!" Eazy wailed as he picked Yara up, and her little hands immediately pulled on his ears.

Ethic laughed and kept his stride toward the kitchen. Alani had made it upstairs and was putting away groceries. A vision. Pregnant, swollen, and all, Alani made his pulse race.

Ethic came up behind her and took the orange juice she carried from her hands. "Sit down."

"I can't sit down. The reveal is tomorrow," she said. The hostility in her voice wasn't missed.

"You changing locks now?" Ethic ignored her question and posed his own.

She turned to him, eyes burning with a false story of betrayal she had written in her warped mind. "Did you fuck that bitch last night?"

"No." Simple answer. No hesitation. She took it as truth.

He saw relief cover her.

"You keeping me from my baby. I ain't feeling that," Ethic said.

"This baby ain't even born, Ethic. A day won't hurt you," she countered.

"You, Lenika. I'm talking 'bout you," he replied. "Don't ever lock me out."

His tone was filled with abandonment. Her actions had hurt him. He wouldn't say it but she knew.

"I need her to not be a factor in our lives. Unless there is a reason she's a factor in our lives. She moves in and out of your life like she has a right to, but you're not single anymore. You're a married man. My man. I'm not fucking having it. It makes me feel like she's around. Like you're with her. Or like she has something of yours, your son. Is her child yours?"

His entire body tensed.

"He is, isn't he?" She asked.

"What the fuck, Lenika," Ethic said, taking a step back and swiping his waves with both hands. "You like to be unhappy, no?"

She recoiled. "Don't evade the question," she snapped. His blatant refusal to answer rang out like a smoke detector and where there was smoke there was normally fire.

"No, Lenika! No! The fucking kid ain't mine!" he shouted.

"I want to sit down with that bitch. Until I do, me and you..."

"Me and you what? You're my wife. This ain't no on and off shit," Ethic said it calmly but damn if it didn't sound like a bark from the most vicious breed. "Get your hormonal-ass out your feelings and let this go. Cuz, wherever you are, is where I'ma be. Let the shit go. She showed up because we're affiliated with the same organization. That organization knew where the heat was coming from. They sent Ya..."

"Nigga, you better not finish that bitch name. Ain't no Ya, no nickname, no cute little situationship..."

Alani was fucking certifiable. Loony. Crazy. Ethic was so turned on that his dick stiffened. He loved her crazy-ass. Any other woman who had ever tried this with him had immediately turned him off. Alani Lenika Okafor, he had made her his wife. Her crazy was like the meter he measured her love for him on. It wasn't logical at all, but she made his world livable, made his heartbeat.

"If you weren't days from dropping my load, I'd fuck sense into you, Lenika," Ethic said as he advanced on her, trapping her against the kitchen counter. His lips were too close to her ear, and she gasped as he licked her ear, then her neck, kissing her cheek and stealing her lips. "Stop letting people get in your head. You're my wife. My queen, Lenika. It's only you. Ain't no hidden babies, no affair, nothing. It's me and it's you."

"I hate your stupid-ass," she whispered weakly as he sucked her bottom lip into his mouth. He stole her next insult because he put her tongue to work with a deep kiss.

"You what?"

"I love you," she whispered, kissing him back.

"You gon' act right?" He moved to the other side of her neck. Alani's hormones were out of control, and it all felt like ecstasy.

She had to put her hands against his chest, create a boundary to clear her head.

"When I get my sit down," Alani said. She moved around him. "And turn on the lights. I know your ass turned them off, so I would call you."

She stomped out of the kitchen and disappeared up the stairs leaving Ethic's head spinning.

He walked down into the basement and was surprised to find Morgan lying in the dark. He tensed. So did she. Their energy was awkward because so much had been left unspoken since she had come home. He fixed the fuse box and then took a seat on the sectional beside Mo. She didn't say a word, but he heard the heavy sigh as she leaned her head on his shoulder.

"I know we haven't talked," Ethic said.

"Because you're mad at me," Morgan answered. He was. He didn't want to admit it, but he was human, and he hadn't been able to reign in his anger with Mo, so instead, he avoided her.

"I'm confused, Mo. I'd give you the air in my lungs. I love you in ways that I can't even make sense of, and you just fed me to the wolves. They were going to have me locked up, and you didn't say one word," Ethic said. "I'm having a hard time with that."

"I know," Morgan answered. "Now that I'm out and he's gone, I can't really see what kept me there, but when I was in it, I just couldn't see a way out. I was afraid of losing you, afraid of being disowned if you found out I told someone."

"I would never give up on you," Ethic said.

"I've already made so many mistakes. I'm the problem child, and it just felt like I was on my last leg. I've taken you through so much. I just wanted to stay there to keep the peace. If I had just given Bash what he wanted, he would have never taken it so far."

"You've got to stay in counseling, Mo," Ethic said.

"I know."

"You worry me. You worry me like your sister worried me, and that's enough to kill me, Mo. I need you to be okay." Ethic spoke so passionately that Morgan shuddered. "I'm never going to unlove you. You will never not be a part of me. No matter what you do. No matter how many mistakes you make, but I need you to be accountable. From now on, you can't just do what you want without thinking about how it affects the people around you. I could have lost my life, Mo. Bella, Eazy, my wife, my unborn child. You. The Twins. I would have been out of here. You understand that, right? You know what would have happened if Bash and his family got their way?"

"We wouldn't make it without you. I know," Morgan said, wiping tears. "I thought of all that. I thought I was safe with

Bash. I thought it was far enough from everyone for me to not be broken around y'all. I didn't want my brokenness to break anybody else I loved. I was in the way here and everything here just hurt so bad. I just wanted an escape. To feel normal, somewhere far, with someone who couldn't possibly hurt me."

"And look what happened. When you run and don't fight, you feel like prey forever. You got to stop running, Mo. From Messiah. From Meek. You got to stand up and fight for yourself. When you're strong enough to say what you want and what you need, you'll have a clear mind to choose who you want. You got to be strong, Mo. Stronger than Raven. I can't watch another Atkins girl self-destruct."

Morgan nodded.

"Do you hate me?"

"Never," Ethic answered. "Come here."

Morgan melted into him, sobbing as the ghost of Benny Atkins reached through Ethic to console his daughter.

Ethic felt like he was suffocating in this house. So much estrogen filled the air. He could feel the moods of the women in his life lingering in this space. Alani was angry. Morgan was traumatized and Bella was drowning in disappointment. Ethic's world seemed to be spiraling out of control and for a man who was used to dictating everything, he was struggling with the chaos.

He hoped he wasn't bringing new life into a home that was falling apart because it felt like his foundation was cracked. It wasn't anyone else's responsibility to keep his family together but his. He had to figure out a way to make his wife happy, keep his daughters uplifted, and make Eazy feel as important as he was, all before his new child was born.

Eazy stood outside Morgan's bedroom door. The twins stood at his side, following him like they followed no one else all over the house. Nobody could maintain control of the Atkins twins like Eazy. He was their favorite person in the world, and they were his.

He knocked on her door, and when she answered, he could tell she was upset. Morgan was always upset. In fact, he had seen Morgan cry more times than he had seen her smile. It was why he always loved on her. Whenever she was around, he would deliver random hugs and kisses to cheer her up.

"Ma says she needs you to remind Messiah to pick up the twins' team outfits and shoes for the gender reveal," Eazy said. "She says he'll forget."

Morgan nodded and scooped Yara into her arms. "Okay. I'll call him. Thanks, Eazy."

He nodded and then turned to leave. He quickly changed his mind and spun to face her. "Are you sad, Mo?"

The question caught her off guard, and she looked at him curiously.

"Sometimes," she answered.

"It seems like you are sad a lot," Eazy replied. "I've only ever seen you happy a few times. Can I help make you happy?

It's hard to be happy when you're around because I feel bad for feeling good things when you feel so bad."

Morgan put Yara down and leaned down to grab Eazy's shoulders. "Nooo, Eazy. No. Never feel like that. I'm okay. You don't have to pretend not to be happy, Eazy. If you feel happy, you should look happy. You should smile and laugh. You deserve that. Your mom would want that for you."

"She wants that for you too," Eazy replied. "She says she wants her stank to find happiness."

The hair on the back of Morgan's neck stood up. Eazy had never heard anyone call her "Stank". It was a nickname that no one had used since Raven had been killed.

"How do you..." she paused, looking at Eazy in amazement. "When did she tell you that?"

"When I'm sleeping. In my dreams. She says it's okay to be happy."

Morgan nodded. "She's right you know. It's okay to be happy, even when other people aren't, E. So do me a favor and never hide that part of you. Because you make all of us smile. Okay? I love you. You know that?"

He smirked bashfully. "Yeah, I know, Mo."

Morgan was blown.

"Hey, you want to come to the mall with us?" Morgan asked. "I'd like to hear more about your dreams with your mom."

Eazy shook his head. "Can't! I'm going to Nannie's today! See you later, Mo! Love you!"

"I love you too!" She shouted the words at his back because he was down the stairs and on his way in seconds.

She made a mental note to be better around Eazy and then picked up her phone to call Messiah. She didn't know why she was afraid to dial him. Things were just uncertain between them. He had saved her, yes. That part came naturally for him. He always would. She knew that much. If someone ever trespassed, Messiah would enforce punishment. Perhaps that came with the territory of having his children, or perhaps it was just love and protectiveness he would always have for her. But it was the hard conversations that came afterward and that they had yet to speak that kept them at odds. Messiah blamed Morgan and Morgan blamed Messiah. Two souls torn apart by decisions that nobody wanted to be held responsible for. Every time they tried to sift through the history of their heartbreak, resentment led them to disagreement. Fuck the same page, they weren't even in the same book. She stared at his children and blew out a deep breath.

Just call him.

"What up, shorty?" Messiah answered almost instantly.

"Alani asked me to remind you about the twins' outfits for the gender reveal," Morgan said. It felt so awkward, asking for something so simple. There were days when Morgan would just dip into his stash and peel off thousands of dollars for whatever she wanted. Now she was asking for shoes for their children. It felt unnatural.

"I'm a little busy but I got it. They don't need 'em 'til tomorrow, right?" he asked.

Morgan immediately felt defensive. *Busy?*

Morgan hadn't had the luxury to be "busy" since her kids were born.

"What do you mean you're too busy?" Morgan asked.

"Don't add context to my shit, shorty. I said busy, not too busy. I got them. I don't need no reminders when it come to them. Whatever they need, I'ma handle it."

"Well, the reveal is tomorrow so..."

"Mo," Messiah said. "I got it." Messiah sounded distracted like he was moving around and half-listening and Morgan was annoyed. As much as he claimed to want to come home, she would have thought he would jump at the occasion to spend more time with the twins.

What's more important than them? Mo thought.

"Messiah, you got my time and attention if you're ready?"

Morgan's brow lifted when the soft voice played in the background.

"I'ma hit you in a minute, shorty. Don't worry about the shoes. I'll be by there later," Messiah said.

He hung up so fast Morgan looked at the phone in shock.

Thoughts of Messiah spending time with a woman sent a shock wave through her body.

He wouldn't do that. He wouldn't dismiss my babies for a girl, she thought.

Her gut twisted, but Morgan pushed the thoughts from her head. Visions of Wozi showing up at Messiah's house haunted her. *He wouldn't put someone before them. He wouldn't choose her over me. He wants to come home. He wouldn't play me again.*

It was the fact that she hadn't expected him to play her the first time that fucked her up most. She didn't know what Messiah was capable of, and his eagerness to end their call played hide and seek with her intuition.

"Just get the clothes yourself," Morgan said to herself. She didn't even want to give him the chance to disappoint her because she knew it would feel monumental. She was terrified of Messiah dropping the ball again because she knew she would never put another one in his hand. This wasn't even about their relationship because she wasn't sure if she even wanted one; it t was about their ability to co-parent. The pain had crippled her before. She didn't want to feel that again. If she decided to love him and he hurt her, it would be her fault this time because she knew exactly what she was dealing with. She wondered if this was what she would be reduced to if she chose Messiah. A girl with two kids wondering where he was. Wondering if he was with the girl who had shown up in the middle of the night and ripped away her reality.

"Let's get out of here," Morgan said. "Ssari, who's the conductor?"

"Ooo… me! Meee!" Messari shouted.

"Then lead the way to the door, baby," Morgan said, baiting him to stay focused and walk a straight line to the door. If she didn't, Messari would run all over the mansion, giving out hugs and kisses before saying goodbye. "Come on, Sir Topham Hatt. All aboard!"

"All aboard!" Messari announced. "Come on, Mommy. Get on the choo-choo." Morgan thanked God for Thomas the Train

Morgan put Yolly down. "Let's follow the choo-choo, Yolly Pop!"

Yara shrieked in excitement and pushed Messari out of the way so that she could go first. Morgan followed her twins to the door.

Morgan couldn't help but compare Messiah to Ahmeek in that moment. If she had called Meek, he would have come to her. He would have dropped whoever he was with to fulfill her need because he would be able to tell in the tone of her voice that it wasn't even about the outfits. She just liked to measure her importance in a nigga's life, make sure she was still a priority. Ahmeek wasn't an option to call any longer, however. He had left her, and she couldn't even be mad at him because she deserved it. It didn't stop her from missing him. It didn't stop her from wondering if he missed her too. It didn't take away her need for him. The most selfish part of her wanted to find him. Her heart hadn't ever been taken care of with such precision, but she knew her situation was too complicated to give him what they had planned. She had been so close to having something; someone, love. She had been close to a love that didn't hurt, but it had never felt more unattainable than it did right now. She wanted a man she would never be able to have, so she suffered silently, even though she knew he had the anecdote that would take all her pain away. Morgan knew he would take it all out of her possession and keep it as his own. The type of love they had, would be an instant distraction to everything that kept her up at night. He was peace. She was turmoil. Oh, how she needed him, but she couldn't ask him to save her, not this time. If he put a Band-Aid on her wounds, she would never learn to heal herself.

"So, we're meeting on your home court this time. I was surprised you called." Khadeen Brown was fine as fuck. Smart as hell. And expensive. Her $135 per hour rate meant she was the best and Messiah knew he needed the best. He hated to leave Mo hanging, but he needed to do this. He needed to try. "A drug dealer with a mortuary. I have to say it's extremely smart."

Messiah didn't confirm or deny, he just sat at the conference table in the family receiving room and tapped one finger on the wood.

"You judge all your clients?" Messiah asked calmly, rolling his eyes away from hers and out the window. Crack heads on the corner were his view before dead panning on her.

"Most are trust fund brats with anxiety issues. You're my first d-boy," she answered. He couldn't tell if she was joking or not. Her face remained stoic, but he saw challenge and amusement in her stare.

"Fed-ass." Messiah was snarky. "I got somewhere to be man. My kids need me, so what up? You gon' do your thang, or am I up out of here?"

"What are you kids names?" Khadeen asked.

"Yara and Messari," he answered. "Two-year-old twins. I just found out about them."

"Twins," she said curiously, nodding.

ASHLEY ANTOINETTE

"What?" he asked, smirking as he leaned forward, folding his hands on top of the table.

"Nothing," she said, biting the corner of her lip.

Messiah shook his head, licking his lips because he could only imagine the mental assumptions he was making.

"And their mother kept them from you?" Khadeen asked.

"I honestly don't know if she kept them from me or if I kept them from me. I just know it's fucked up. Everybody know 'em but me."

Sadness filled him. He tightened up, knocking on the table and drawing in a breath before continuing.

"How old are they?"

"Two," he answered. "Ain't that like the bonding years or some shit? I missed two years. What if they never fuck with me?"

The question wasn't meant for her. He was simply thinking aloud.

"You know there have been studies on different species who were removed from their young. Some due to capture, some for scientific purposes, some for entertainment, you know…like when they put whales in captivity for Seaworld and all that jazz. Those animals always remember their parent. When they're reunited. The DNA is so strong that they sense their connection instantly. It's just nature versus nurture Messiah. The only way those two years will destroy your impact on their lives is if you let it and your offspring will never recognize another man the same way they recognize you. It's inside of them, like a magnet pulling them to you."

"Yeah well feel like my lil' mama pulling the fuck away. My shorty kind of dope though. He real soft with it though, like his mama. Soft ass feelings, but he fuck with the kid."

Khadeen smiled. "You like the idea of being a father," she observed.

Messiah nodded. "Shorty made me like the idea of a lot of shit that I thought I'd never do."

"Tell me about her. Your shorty." Khadeen frowned when she said the nickname.

"Your facial expressions shole be fucked up for you to be a therapist. Ain't you supposed to have a poker face or some shit?" Messiah asked.

"No. I'm supposed to feel and not apologize for what I'm feeling or try to suppress what I'm feeling," Khadeen said.

"And you not feeling the word shorty?" Messiah grilled. He was challenging her. He was aggressive even when he wasn't trying to be.

"I wouldn't want to share a pet name. There is more than one shorty in your life. So, tell me about all of them. Which one do you trust most?"

"Bleu," Messiah answered. He didn't even have to think about it. "She's my best friend but it's complicated. Real fucking complicated."

"Complicated normally means sex is involved. Are you the kind of man who has sex with his sister?" she asked, using air quotes as she spoke. Khadeen was intimidating to Messiah, although he would never admit it. She didn't look like a doctor. Today she was in retro Jordan 1's, hoop shorts, and a cropped baby t-shirt. Curly hair was in a ponytail on top of her head, revealing a shooting star tattoo that he had missed behind her excessively pierced left ear. She had five earrings going up the lobe of her ear. She looked like she belonged to stiletto gang not in a therapist's office.

"We fucked," Messiah admitted. It was the flashes of that night that went through his mind that made him lower his eyes. When he closed them at night it was on replay in his mind. He didn't know what Bleu had done or how she had done it, but she was constantly in his thoughts. Mo in his heart. Bleu in his head. His body craved both. A predicament of choices. Most men would run game. Messiah just wanted to call timeout and figure out what the next play should be because if he made the wrong move he would lose. The thought of losing her shook him. The question was...which her?

"You fucked?" Khadeen repeated, frowning. "What are you fifteen? You don't fuck grown women Messiah. Unless you do and if that's the case, you're a boy, not a man."

"Putting my head between a woman's legs and sucking on her pussy til' she real wet for a nigga then stroking it til' she explode on the dick ain't fucking? If that ain't fucking, what is it, doc?" Messiah asked.

Crass ass nigga.

He snickered when her face flushed. It was like he had turned the thermostat to hell.

"It's called sex Messiah. You had sex and if you're good and there's some emotions involved-."

"Emotions?" Messiah said, brow denting in denial.

"You know those fuzzy sensations adults feel when they

are interested in someone?" Khadeen rolled her eyes as her sarcasm pulled a laugh out of Messiah's mean ass. "If emotions are present, you'd be lucky to call it love making. So, which one was it for you? Did you have sex with your best friend, or did you make love?"

Messiah took his time answering.

"She had my son. If that's love making than yeah, I guess we did that," he answered. Her silence was his greenlight to continue speaking. "I went away for a while. Our son died before I got the chance to meet him." The words barely made it out his mouth. He cleared his throat.

"I'm sorry for your loss," she whispered.

When his eyes met hers she blinked away, but her words stuck with him. He had lost something. He hadn't really processed the grief or losing a child, two children because Mo had lost one as well.

"I fuck Morgan," he said. "I'm like addicted to her. The way she smells, the way she says my name. The way she tastes, but I fuck her…"

Khadeen's brow bent.

"My bad," Messiah corrected. "I have sex with her. I love her, don't get me wrong but I don't make love to her."

"And why do you think that is?" Khadeen asked.

"Shit, ain't I paying you? If I'ma answer the questions, I can save my money." He was irritated because he had just made an obvious distinction between Morgan and Bleu.

"I don't know if you love shorty number two at all."

"You got all them degrees and you still don't know shit then," Messiah countered. "Cuz I'd die for her."

"Will you live for her though?" Khadeen asked. "And I don't mean breathe. I don't mean obsess over. I don't mean possess because the way you describe her sounds like she's an object. I mean really live for her. Will you explore the complexity of your manhood for her? Will you let her see you weak? Afraid? Strong? Insecure? Focused? Distracted? Emotional? Will you show her your triumphs and losses? Your pain? Will you let her live a life with you? Because a full life involves many weak moments. Will you share those with her?"

"A woman doesn't want a weak man," Messiah said. "Especially Mo. I know who raised her. Everything she's searching for stems from him and there ain't a weak bone in his body. He's probably the love of her life. If I got to follow that up, I got to be strong."

"I'm confused is this man her father?" Khadeen asked.

"He's not her biological father. He raised her though and she idolizes him."

"And you want to be like him. You admire him too, don't you?" Khadeen asked.

Messiah rolled his head to the side dismissively. "Mannn I ain't no kid."

"You're on my nerves so I'm going to say this one last thing and then get going…"

Messiah's amusement couldn't be hidden. "Yo' you're a wild one," Messiah said. "What's the last thing shorty?"

"Aht aht!" she said. "Don't you even think about calling me that bullshit."

Messiah's smile made her smile, but he complied, nodding

as he raised both hands. "You got it. Got ahead Dr. Brown, pop your shit."

"You don't want to show Mo your weaknesses because you feel like you have to be infinitely strong. You want to be like the man who raised her, but his weakness is her. A father will forever be the weakest man in the room because his heart exists outside his body. You have twins and two deceased children Messiah, and you share these children with two different women. Your heart is all over the place. A piece is grieving with shorty #1 and the other parts are with shorty #2."

"Yo' quit calling them that. What's wrong with you?" he laughed, while finessing the side of his face and shaking his head.

"What?" she asked, smiling. "Messiah with all the women. That's you right?"

"Nah, not even a little," Messiah answered. "But you clearly got your misconceptions locked in. It's cool."

"Well, I'd like to clear them up, over time, if you agree to keep seeing me," Khadeen said.

"I don't want to sit on your couch, doc. Like at all. If we can do it here so I feel normal I can show up," Messiah said.

"Yeah, because therapy in a funeral home with dead bodies is the normal choice," she said sarcastically.

He smiled bashfully. "Bodies don't bother me. It's the ghosts that give me hell," Messiah replied with a serious tone that melted the smile from Khadeen's face.

She nodded. "Out of office it is," she said. "Maybe a park or coffee shop or something next time though. The bodies *do* bother me."

Messiah nodded in agreement as he stood to his feet. His body language told her he was ready to go. "My kids really make me weak?" He asked.

"They do," she said as she grabbed her handbag off the table. Hermes. At least twenty thousand dollars hung from her dainty wrist. Her clear painted nails were short. Professional. The lime green simple artwork on top told him she only rocked clear because of her job. She was unlike what he assumed a therapist to be. Relatable. Khadeen was relatable and just her drug dealer jokes told him she was from where he was from. "And there is nothing you can do about it. So, you might as well love women with the same heart that your children have softened. Call my office to schedule your next session. Oh, and nice place. Congrats. From corner boy to CEO," she cracked, laughing at her own joke.

"Never been a corner boy baby, but thanks shorty."

Khadeen stopped mid-step on her way to the door and turned to him.

"You call me shorty again and you'll be the first body you bury here," she warned playfully. "Toxic masculinity Messiah. Look it up. We'll bust it down next session!"

With that she was out the door, leaving Messiah with a lot to think about. More than he was ready to process.

Navigating through a shopping mall with two twins was never easy, in fact, the twins in general were a handful, but Morgan loved every second of the time she spent with them. There was something about their existence that made Morgan feel like whatever she went through to make them and receive them was worth it. Being their mother was a gift, despite the circumstances that created them. It wasn't what she had thought her life would look like, single mothering and all, but love seemed evasive. Whenever it came her way, it was always fleeting, and she was left with damage after it retreated. Still, she couldn't help but appreciate the sense of completion she felt when she was loved well. When Messiah was on point and they tapped into the essence that created their babies in the first place; or when Ahmeek stepped into shoes that weren't his responsibility to fill and made her feel valued. Those moments. That male companionship; the partnership of it all, felt right. Like she could be a woman because a man was being a man in her life and providing protection and stability. Two men. One woman. The math didn't math. It never would and she was stuck in the middle of two brothers. Morgan's head spun just thinking about it. She walked into the shoe store, eager to finish the errands so she could get her kids home before it got too late. Tomorrow was a big day for the entire family. They had been through a lot. The gender reveal would be like rays of sun peeking through the clouds. Yolly and Ssari were getting tired anyway. She could tell because Yara was getting whiney and Messari was meddling with everything in every store.

If I could just get some help in here, I can get them home, she thought as she held the small sneaker in her hand and looked around for assistance. She had been waiting for close to fifteen minutes and no one had even attempted to assist her.

"Mommy wook! It's him!" Messari shouted.

Morgan turned in surprise as Messari flew across the shoe store. Messiah strolled through the door with a casual saunter that let everyone in the store know he had the biggest dick in the room. Messiah's aura would always announce his presence before he spoke. King shit and he knew it. Despite the tension between them, seeing Messari's excitement turned Morgan inside out. Messiah Williams was the father of her children. No more secrets. No more lies. Her children had their father again, and the thought made Morgan emotional. She wondered if there would ever come a day when she wouldn't be moved by the thought.

"Daddy's big boy!" Messiah called out as he bent down to scoop him as he swaggered into the store. Morgan despised the attention he got as he entered. Black, Nike jogger set and fly, Nipsey Blue 97's graced his feet. Gold chains and a fresh fade, with Ray Ban's covering his eyes. Messiah was fine as fuck, and Morgan hated it. She rolled her eyes as the pretty girl in the referee, Foot Locker shirt bounced over to him.

"Hey, can I help you with anything?" The girl asked, smiling.

I been in this bitch for almost twenty minutes and she ain't said one word to me! Morgan thought.

"Nah, I'm good," he answered as he approached Morgan.

"If you're ever not good and I can help…"

Messiah's brow lifted, and he scoffed before finessing his lips. "I'm good, sweetheart," he repeated.

He closed the space between him and Morgan.

"I couldn't even get a hello when I entered the store," she said under her breath, shaking her head. "What are you doing here?" she asked.

"Alani told me you were at the mall. I told you I would get what they needed," Messiah said.

"You seemed too busy for us so-" Morgan said.

"I'm not too busy for them," he answered. "It's you I got issues with Mo."

Morgan took the blow because she knew she deserved it. Hot and cold. On then off. The unspoken things between them kept them at odds despite what they felt.

"Hey, Daddy's girl," he signed. Yara laid on Morgan's shoulder, but she didn't move to speak to Messiah. "Come here."

He reached for her, but Yara fussed, whining as she turned her head away from him.

Morgan adjusted her daughter, forcing Yara to sit up. "It's okay, Yolly. Go to Daddy."

Morgan tried to pass Yara off and Yara had a fit, crying so loudly that Morgan heated in embarrassment. She pulled away from Messiah, unfamiliar and unfriendly.

"Yolly!" Morgan protested. "Hey!" Morgan sat on the bench in the store and placed Yara on her feet.

"Stop it, Yolly," Morgan signed. "You don't act like that with him."

"Why would she act any different? She thought that bitch-ass nigga Bash was her daddy," Messiah spoke up. "Don't fucking blame her. She don't even know me, and that's on you." Messiah was fresh out of therapy, and it was like Khadeen had left the refrigerator door wide open because all of his emotions were spilling out. All of what he was giving to Mo wasn't deserving but some of it was and he couldn't stop the resentment he felt. Every time his children denied him, he felt a little disdain for Morgan. He couldn't help it. He loved Morgan but these new feelings of resentment toward her were strong.

Morgan looked up at Messiah in shock.

"Says the nigga that disappeared on me for two years. No, that's on you," Morgan said. She picked Yara up. "Give me my son, you can get the shoes. I got the rest of the stuff they need. Just bring it to Ethic's. I'm out."

Morgan reached for Messari. "Nah he good," Messiah said. "This little nigga belong to me. Her too. You can walk up out of here, but they ain't going nowhere."

It took everything in Morgan not to react. "Look, Messiah. Is this how this is going to go with us? We good one day and at each other's throats the next? I don't need a baby daddy. I don't need static every time we see one another. I know you're pissed, but if this is how it's going to be with us…"

"I'm trying to get out my feelings because I know what you been through, but I ain't never been this mad at you, shorty," he interrupted as he placed Messari on his shoulders. "I don't know how to fake like I ain't either. I love you but I want to ring your fucking neck when I look at you for this shit you pulled with my kids…" He shook his head, jaw locked. "If you were anybody else, you would be dead, Mo."

"Yeah, well, I'm not anybody else," she replied. "You can pick out shoes with your son. I'll take Yolly to the hallway to stretch her legs because her patience is non-existent, and mine is leaving. She wears a size 3. Ssari is in a 4." Morgan walked out. She was so sick of carrying all the blame. Neither had expected this to be their life. Separate. Fighting. Disconnected. But it was his actions that had caused them to end up here. Yes, she had allowed Bash to play a role in their kids' lives, to father them, but Messiah had given him the opportunity when he abandoned her. Morgan still didn't trust him. Still couldn't get over all the lies he had told and the choices he had made. They hadn't even addressed them. Avoidance and disdain were the energy that surrounded them.

Morgan placed Yara down. "How about we go get a treat while we wait for your daddy and Ssari? You want ice cream?"

Yara's face lit up and she jumped up and down. "Ice cream! Ice cream!" Yara signed.

Morgan laughed and reached down, grabbing her hand and her daughter's soft touch was enough to still Morgan's racing heart. Yolly held onto Morgan's pointer finger for dear life as they walked up the hallway. The connection they shared filled Morgan with everything she needed to get through every hard day, and Morgan couldn't even stay mad at Messiah because he had given her that. He had given her Messari and Yara.

Morgan took her favorite girl to the ice cream shop at the end of the hall and sat patiently while Messari shopped with Messiah.

"You know Mommy loves you, right, Yolly?" Morgan signed as she handed the cone off to Yara.

Yara nodded.

"I know you don't know Messiah very well, but he loves you very much. He wished for you and Ssari. You guys are his favorite people in the whole wide world. He's your daddy."

Yara's brow pinched. "What about Papa Bash?" She signed.

"He loves you too, baby. You have a lot of people who love you." Morgan wondered if her twins would ever forget Bash's existence in their lives.

"Like Meekie? Meekie loves me too," Yara signed.

Morgan had to look away from Yara. She wasn't even three years old, and Morgan had already introduced confusion into Yara's life.

"Meekie loves you so much, baby, but Meekie isn't your dad. Papa Bash isn't your dad either. They love you, but Messiah is your daddy. Nobody loves you like your mommy and your daddy. Daddy loves you like I do."

"He does?" Yara signed. The confusion was written all over her face; then, as if a light bulb went off, her face brightened, brows lifting in amazement. "Daddy loves me like you, Mommy?"

"He does," Morgan signed back.

"Is him nice, Mommy?" Yara asked. "Him look mean."

Morgan laughed.

"Daddy will never be mean to you," Morgan answered,

laughing. "He will always keep you safe. So, can you be nice to him? Can you show him how big your heart is, big girl?"

Yara nodded and Morgan sighed in relief. Her daughter was standoffish. She wasn't receptive to everyone. She felt everything. Her empath spirit made her a perfect reader of energy, and Messiah gave off vibes of danger. Yara's instincts were right when it came to Messiah, only she was too young to realize that she was the exception to his malice. She was his soft spot, but much like him, she was untrusting.

Yara nodded.

Morgan sighed in relief.

"Want to go find him and give him a chance?" Morgan asked.

Yara nodded while using her tongue to try to reach the extra ice cream that had formed a mustache around her lips. Morgan pulled her into her arms and smothered her ice cream-covered face with kisses as she tickled Yara's belly. Yara squealed and laughed uncontrollably. Morgan was all smiles as she stood. She took a baby wipe from her purse, cleaned Yara up, and then headed back to the store.

Morgan approached the Foot Locker sign, but when she saw Messiah walk out her stomach hollowed.

Morgan released Yara's hand and placed one hand to her stomach.

"Mo?" Messiah called.

"Take those shoes off my son," she gasped.

"Fuck you mean? You said he needed shoes, so I bought shoes."

"Messari, get over here now!" Morgan barked. She practically snatched her son's arm off as she took him from Messiah. Morgan bent down, hands trembling as she lifted his feet. "Take them off, Messari!"

"Noooo. I want to match my daddy!" Messari cried.

"Messari, no!" Morgan said, panicking as a large tear drop fell from her eyes.

"Mo, you bugging. Put my son's shoes back on his feet," Messiah said. "What's the problem?"

"He's not wearing these," Morgan snapped. "I said no. It matters. When I say no, it matters!"

The hair on the back of her neck stood and Morgan's heart went wild inside her chest.

Morgan was so flustered that she alarmed Messari, and he burst into tears, feeling like he was in trouble. Messiah picked Messari up and grabbed Morgan's elbow to force her to her feet.

He took her face in the U of his hand. "What the fuck is happening right now?"

"Lucas wore red Chucks that night," she whispered.

Recognition flickered in Messiah's eyes as he realized the significance of the shoes he and Messari wore on their feet. He wrapped his free arm around Morgan and pulled her into his chest. It was the smallest detail, probably the most insignificant one of them all, but it stuck out in her mind like a sharp edge, cutting through her healing in an instant. He had held her down by her head and her eyes focused on those red chucks the entire time she was assaulted. It was a trigger, and it sent her reeling. Morgan panicked, and Messiah was heartbroken.

"I'm sorry, shorty. I didn't know," he whispered. He looked down at Yara. She was a few feet away and watching everything closely. "They're watching, Mo. Wipe your pretty face, shorty. I got you. Get yourself together and then meet us at the food court, okay? I'ma make it better, but they don't need to see you cry. Everything you do, they watch. You're they hero. Take a minute and tighten up."

Just like that, Messiah and Morgan went from ice cold to blazing hot. They had just been adversaries, now they were allies. It was just the way their love emoted into the world. So much passion between complicated lovers. It was never perfect, but it was them.

He kissed the side of her head, and then Morgan turned to retreat to the bathroom. Morgan hadn't been triggered about her rape in a long time. Some days, it was almost like it hadn't even happened. She could smile and laugh and dance and fuck and study and drink and play with her kids and go about her life on most days. This one little thing… red shoes, it jolted her. Her chest was so tight it was hard to pull in air. She remembered days of counseling with Nyair. How he had taught her to breathe when she would feel like the walls were closing in on her. She needed him now. She made a mental note to call him when she could pull it together. She had pulled away from everyone over the years, including him, but she never forgot his words. Her broken pieces were beautiful. Anxiety ate away at her. It was like a hundred ants crawling up her back. Just when a bitch thought she was okay, trauma came and cut her down a notch. Morgan blew out a sharp breath, splashed water on her face and then walked out. She had never been so embarrassed. Messiah stood there. The twins sat on the bench behind him. On their feet were red Chuck Taylors; even Yara kicked her little legs to show off her new shoes.

"I was gonna return 'em, shorty. I was gonna choose something different, but then I thought about it. My shorty can't let a ghost scare her. Nah, not when you got your own fucking monster that'll terrorize shit. Can't have that. He went into the black and white striped bag and removed another box.

Messiah walked up to Morgan and bent down in front of her as he removed one of her shoes.

"The way I see it," he said, as he slid a brand-new sneaker out the box. Red Chucks. Morgan shook her head.

"Messiah, I can't get it out of my head," she whispered.

He slid the shoe on her foot. "Way I see it, Mo, I got to put something new in your head. So that when you think of red shoes, you don't think of that. I want you to think of me. I want you to think of me, Yara, and Messari. When you look at these shoes, I want you to see today…"

"What's so special about today?" Morgan asked as she swiped at her teary eyes.

He slid the other shoe on her foot and tied them both before hiking up his pants as he stood. He took her face in one hand and pulled her forehead to his lips. "We're together, Mo. For a long time, I was one place, and you were another. My heart was outside my chest and halfway around the world, shorty. You know how bad that hurt?

We're together. I ain't saying you mine. I know you feel your way about that. I know you confused on where you want to be, but I'm looking at you, shorty. I can smell you. I can touch you. I can see those pretty eyes. For the first time. Me, you, and our babies are in the same place. I got babies, man, by my Shorty Doo-Wop. You know how fucking happy that shit makes me, Mo? So, we gon' make today special. In our red kicks," he said, looking down at their feet. "So, when you see red shoes you think of..."

"You," she finished.

He bit his bottom lip and nodded as he smirked. "Think of Daddy, Mo," he said. He turned to the twins. "Who's Daddy?" He asked, yelling loud and proud as he signed.

"You!" Messari said, getting riled up. Messiah grabbed him and tucked him under his arm, holding him wildly. He bent down to Yara and held out his lips for her. Yara hesitated and then turned her cheek to the side. "Kiss on the cheek. I'll take it. It's better than the cold shoulder," he snickered as he picked her up too. Messiah swung them around wildly. "Who's Daddy?"

"You!!!" Messari shouted. Messiah walked up on Morgan and asked her again. "Who's Daddy, shorty?"

Morgan smirked and rolled her eyes.

"You are," she whispered stubbornly.

"That's where my daughter gets that shit from," he said, smiling. "Stubborn-ass. Can a real nigga get a kiss?"

Morgan mimicked Yara and turned her face to the side, and Messiah planted a kiss there. "Motherfucking progress with my girls. I ain't mad at it."

He turned, still carrying the kids like logs on either side as their little red feet kicked away. Her heart warmed and she shook her head as she followed behind them. It felt a lot like right.

CHAPTER 22

Tell me something, Meek. I can't figure it out. Why would you take on the debt for your entire crew?"

Hak asked the question as he stared out of the floor-to-ceiling windows of the penthouse suite at the MGM Grand hotel.

"Because it don't take three lives to repay one debt. It's on me, all of it. If I don't do what I say I'm gon' do, you can take it up with one man. No pointing the fingers. No blame game. Just me and you, sitting down like men, settling this business," Ahmeek replied. "But Isa is out."

"And Messiah?" Hak asked. "Is he out too? Because I know that he is the one that orchestrated the robbery of the truck. Tell me why I shouldn't believe it's an inside job and that you tried to have me robbed."

Ahmeek felt the steel of a gun's barrel touch the back of his neck as Hak's security applied pressure.

"Because I do shit that makes sense. I wouldn't sever the relationship with you over what's on the back of one truck. If I ever rob you, it'll be for everything you got, not one load," Ahmeek said honestly. "And if homie don't learn some manners, I'ma teach him some."

A red beam appeared on Hak's soldier's chest.

"Always strapped and never alone," Ahmeek said.

Hak scoffed. "Touché." He motioned for his man to ease up and Ahmeek stood to his feet.

"You're smarter than the others," Hak said.

Ahmeek frowned. He recognized the play from a mile away.

"No finesse lives here, homie," Ahmeek said. "I am them. They are me. Ain't no dividing and conquering. So just let me know what the terms of our agreement are, and we'll rock like that, but they're off limits."

"Why would you protect the one who got you into debt in the first place?" Hak asked, turning to stare curiously at Ahmeek. "Why not make him help you earn my money back?"

"He's needed elsewhere. This one's on me," Ahmeek answered.

Hak waved a finger. "You are different," he said. "Valuable. I tell you what. I'll erase the debt if you agree to be a part of my operation."

"Work for you," Ahmeek said with a dented brow.

"With me," Hak corrected. "Give me two years, and I'll make you richer than you've ever imagined. After the two years, you can walk away. We'll call it even."

Ahmeek knew how long two years would be. It was long enough for Morgan to have children and fall in love with someone else. It was enough time for Isa to catch four more bodies. Enough time for Ahmeek to take over the city and find a new connect. Enough time for him to cross the line with Morgan Atkins. So many things had happened over the course of two years. If he left, he could only imagine how things would change.

"And if I say no?" Ahmeek asked.

"Then you carry the debt on your back and pay me in three months plus interest," Hak said.

"And my people are off limits," Ahmeek stated. "Isa, Messiah, and everybody attached to them."

"Either way, if the business is square, your mother, your girlfriend, her two children. What are their names again?" Hak asked, snapping his fingers as he jogged his memory. "Yara and…

"Careful. I wipe my finger across my brow the right way and my shooter putting your brain on the floor. Don't finish that sentence," Ahmeek warned.

"Your people are safe as long as you do your part," Hak said.

Ahmeek arose from his seat. "I'll have your money."

"Consider the two years. It's a better deal. There's space for you in Vegas."

Ahmeek didn't answer. He walked out, hating that his back was against the wall. He had always been knee-deep in the game, but he would drown in it now because, with Isa and Messiah out, he would have no one to watch his back.

"You're out bro," Ahmeek stated. "You're clean. No debt. No connection to Hak."

"How you fucking figure, nigga? I told you I ain't letting you clean up shit for me," Isa asked as he hit the blunt. He passed it to Ahmeek, who waved it off.

"Take the out, bruh," he answered.

"What happened to not leaving anyone behind? Sandbox rules my nigga," Isa reminded.

"We grown men now. Rules changed," Ahmeek answered. "You wanted the debt gone; it's gone."

Aria and Whiteboy Nick walked into the living room, interrupting their conversation.

"Ooooh, it's a motherfucking gangster party," Nick announced as he entered.

"Boy, hush," Aria laughed. "Hey, baby." She leaned down to kiss Isa and as she lifted, Isa pulled her into his lap.

"You good right here," Isa said.

She settled into his lap as Nick took a seat.

"Hey, Meek," Aria greeted.

"What's good, sis?" he answered.

"Have you talked to Mo?" Aria asked.

"Nah, that's a wrap." He didn't offer more details, but Aria could see he was affected.

"She know that?" Nick cut in. "Because, baby, the way she swoons when your name is mentioned, I'm thinking she don't know shit about that."

"She's having a hard time, Meek," Aria said. Isa kissed her on the side of her face as she spoke.

"She's strong. She'll be okay," Ahmeek answered.

"Umm... have you met Mo? Cuz her ass is pretty, sexy, flirty, smart, and a whole bunch of other shit, but my good sis ain't strong," Nick said.

"She's my best friend, Meek. I worry about her, and I know she misses you. Last time she was this broken..."

ASHLEY ANTOINETTE

Meek shook his head, interrupting Aria. "Y'all don't know the Mo I know," he answered. "After the love I gave her, she ain't gon' fold."

Whiteboy Nick put a hand to his chest and stood up dramatically. "Bitch, I'm fucking the wrong kind of drug dealers!"

"That's my cue," Meek said, standing.

Isa was buried in Aria's neck. "Hit me, my nigga, before you leave town. Don't need nobody else playing disappearing acts. I want to know how to find you, you feel me?"

Ahmeek knew Isa was referring to Messiah. His leaving had tormented them for years.

"I got you, bruh. I'ma holla."

"You're leaving?" Aria asked.

"It's just business."

"You know she will want to say goodbye, Meek. You can't just be a part of her world one day and gone the next," Aria said.

"She don't need the complications, Aria. I'm trying to do the right thing here," Meek replied.

"For who exactly?" Aria countered.

"Fall back," Isa whispered in her ear. Aria huffed and lifted from his lap.

"I'm going to rehearse," Aria said. "I'll be in the basement if you need me." Nick lifted from his seat to follow her, and before she left the room, Aria added, "If you leave without talking to her first, you're no different than he is. Just another nigga who fucked her promised her the world and then didn't think enough of her to explain why you couldn't stay."

371

Her words hit Ahmeek in the gut. He never wanted to inflict more pain on Morgan. He didn't know how to love Messiah and love her at the same time. Staying out the way seemed to be both a problem and a solution.

"Yo, that nigga, Messiah, is my motherfucking brother. Ten toes in the sand. You know that, but Mo, she's family now too. Ali got her nose in your bi'ness but she ain't wrong. I get why you don' put distance between you and the situation, but I don't wanna see the blowback of you ghosting her. Nobody wanna see that. Bruh don't know what that look like on Mo. If he did, he wouldn't wanna see it either. I ain't on no sides, but what I do know is that both of y'all love the shit out of that spoiled-ass girl. You got to be careful with the way you put her down or she gon' break cuz she fragile as fuck. She gon' be at Seven Lakes tomorrow with the twins around 2 o'clock. Just in case you want to do something with that information."

Isa didn't know if he was wrong or right by sharing the details of Mo's whereabouts, but he had a feeling if Meek disappeared on her, all their lives would spiral again, and nobody wanted that. They were all connected to Mo in some way, and when she experienced pain, it always found its way back to them.

Alani groaned as she pulled herself out of bed. She was exhausted. She hadn't slept well since Ethic's arrest. Anxiety and heartburn kept her up at night. The energy she needed to make it through the day was non-existent.

"Ooh," she said, blowing out a breath as she sat on the edge of her king-sized bed. "Oh my god." She was so nauseous, and the pressure building in her uterus took her breath away. "Cut mommy a break today." It was gender reveal day. She should have been excited, but the knot of uncertainty in her gut and the empty space beside her disturbed her peace.

The knock at the door exhausted her even more. She didn't feel like smiling today. She wanted to lay in bed all day and sleep. Her body was preparing her for childbirth, urging her to rest now because she had a task before her.

"Come in," she called softly.

"Morning, sis!"

Nessa walked in with her normal cheerful mood lightening the air. Alani doubled over, putting her head between her knees.

"I'm going to throw up, Ness," she groaned.

"Aht, aht," Nessa said, moving to Alani's side and rubbing her back gently. "Head up. Breathe in through your nose and sharp breath out your mouth. Three times. Let's go."

Alani closed her eyes and followed the instructions.

"I just want this baby out," Alani cried. Real tears. She felt them leaking down her cheeks. She was just so overwhelmed.

"Aww, Alani. You're doing great, mama. You're almost there. Today will be amazing. Don't overthink it. Don't stress over it. Just enjoy the moments. You need help in the shower? Because we've got to get you dressed after I listen to baby's heartbeat."

"I got that part, Vanessa, thanks." Alani opened her eyes and stared at Ethic.

"Okay," Nessa answered. "Let me just take a few vitals then I'll get out your way. I'll meet you guys at the park." Nessa took the next ten minutes to perform vitals before exiting the room.

Ethic nodded at her on her way out then he crossed the room. Finger to her chin he craned her neck back, stealing kisses she didn't want to give. He took a knee and kissed her belly before standing again. "I've got an entire team downstairs for you. Hair, makeup, wardrobe."

"I don't feel like all that, Ezra," she said.

"Do it for me," Ethic answered. "I know you're tired and you know I love you just like this, but I want you to feel amazing today. I want you to feel like a goddess, baby because you are, and a nigga worship you, Alani. Can I spend a little money on you today? Make you feel better?"

She sighed, giving in. "Okay."

Alani spent the next three hours being bathed, massaged, receiving makeup, and getting her hair done before a professional stylist dressed her in a white and nude summer maxi. She wore white Chanel sandals to match. By the time she was done, she felt beautiful, and she was grateful for the assistance.

When she emerged at the top of the stairs and Ethic looked up, she took his breath away. He stood and went to the bottom of the steps. "Come." An order. She followed.

"Beautiful, baby," he whispered in her ear as she fell into his embrace.

"Thank you," she answered. "Where is everybody?"

"They're all headed to the park. You ready to find out what we created?" He asked.

She was still so mad at him, but today she would focus on their blessing. "I'm nervous."

"Me too," he chuckled.

He took her hand and led her to the car.

"Thank you for giving me life, baby," he said as he opened her car door. They drove the short distance in silence, and when Alani pulled up to the state park, her heart swelled. The décor was so tasteful and high-end. Pampas grass and florals were everywhere, creating a gender-neutral bohemian theme in the field portion of the park. The beach glistened in near distance, and the trees around them sang as the wind rustled the leaves.

"Oh my godddd," she squealed as she exited the car to a round of applause. Their entire family and close friends were present. No more than 30 loved ones gathered today. It was an intimate group, all eagerly anticipating the news to come.

It warmed her to see how everything had come together in practically no time at all. She turned into Ethic, hiding her emotions in his chest as the guest whooped and hollered at their arrival.

Eazy crossed the field and held out his arm for her. "Come on, Ma. I got you."

Ethic stepped back as Eazy escorted Alani to the action.

"You look so beautiful!" Morgan greeted, hugging Alani.

"Thank you, Mo," Alani beamed, dabbing at her makeup, so she didn't ruin it.

"How do you like everything?" Bella asked.

"It's more than I imagined it would be." Alani kissed Bella's nose and then gave her a tight squeeze before making her way to center field.

"Okay listen up, everyone!" Morgan announced, cupping her hands around her mouth so that everyone could hear her. "This is a game of gender softball! Bella and I are co-captains of team boy and Eazy is the captain of team girl. We're going to pick teams, and then Alani will throw the first pitch to Ethic, so they can't be on the same team. Got it?"

"We got it, baby mama. We know how softball go. Yo' cute-ass just wanna be seen. Let's go!" Whiteboy Nick shouted back.

The small crowd laughed as Morgan huddled up with Bella.

"I got Messiah!" Eazy shouted.

Messiah came out the dugout and crossed the field, carrying Messari on his shoulders.

"Me too! You got me too!" Messari shouted.

They were quite the tag team these days, Messiah and his son. It was heartwarming to everyone watching because they knew it had been a long time coming.

"Okay, we got Alani!" Mo announced. Yara was already clinging to Alani, so they were a package deal.

"I got Papa Zeke!" Eazy called out. Ethic and his father had a tumultuous relationship, but somehow Eazy had become the bridge that kept them connected. They spoke daily, and despite Ethic's abandonment wounds, he never took the option away from Eazy. If he wanted to know his grandfather, Ethic wouldn't stand in the way.

"Let's see who we want?" Bella asked aloud.

Before Bella could say anything Messari's voice broke through the air.

"Meekie!!! Look, Mommy, it's Meek!"

Messiah had never quite felt his heart ache like this. Morgan was completely blindsided as she watched Meek walk across the field. Nobody had ever made a Nike track short set look so good, and she wanted to run to him, but her feet felt like it was rooted in the dirt. Guilt pulled her attention to Messiah, and the rage she saw fluttered her heart. It was mixed with pain as Messari tapped his shoulder in excitement.

"Daddy! It's you best friend!"

Messiah put Messari down despite his jealousy and watched as he ran across the field full speed to Meek. Watching his son's adoration for his best friend gutted Messiah.

Yara was next, abandoning Alani for Ahmeek without thinking twice.

Morgan was breathless. She felt their excitement, understood their need for him, and her eyes went wet, but she didn't dare move in his direction. She lent Messiah apologetic eyes because she felt his discomfort, but the absolute healing she felt at just the sight of Ahmeek was undeniable. She wanted to run to him too, to be in his arms, because there was no other place on Earth like the place of peace he provided. She didn't move, however; she barely breathed.

"Alani," she whispered. She didn't have to say anything else. Alani began making her way across the field before Ethic could.

"We'll take Isa!" Bella called out, resuming the game as Alani greeted Ahmeek. Even Ahmeek interacting with Alani lit Messiah's flame. He was territorial over the Okafor's. Meek couldn't have his people. He had already intruded on his girl and his kids. Now, Alani was offering her grace to him too.

"We got Meek!" Eazy called.

"Boy, getcho ass out the way," Ethic muttered, yanking Eazy in by the back of his t-shirt and pulling him to the back of the team.

Morgan almost died. Both her niggas on one team. She felt like running away, but she couldn't. She had to face it. This web she had weaved was sticky.

"He has other places to be, no?" Ethic added.

"Yeah, I know I'm pulling up out the blue. I ain't realize this was a family thing," Meek answered. Isa had sent him right into a trap. This wasn't what Meek had been expecting. "I'ma break out. Congrats on your new addition," he said, speaking to Alani and trying to pass Yara off. She wasn't having it. Yara turned away from Alani, which was something she never did, but if she had to choose, she was staying put in Meek's arms. Messari clung to Meek's leg as if he were climbing a tree.

"No, him can't leave, Pop Pop! Him is here for us," Messari said. "Wight, Meek?"

Meek pulled Messari off his leg and bent down to face him, eye to eye.

ASHLEY ANTOINETTE

"Always here for you, homie, but I got to go. You're here with your family," Meek said in a low tone so that only Messari could hear.

"But you is us family too," Messari said, big eyes welling at the thought of Ahmeek being anything less.

"Aww, baby," Alani said, taking Messari's hand. "Of course, he's family."

"Lenika-" Ethic interrupted.

The look she shot Ethic lifted his brows, and he rubbed the back of his neck in distress. This was her day, her party. She decided who stayed. "This shit, man…" Ethic complained.

"There is room for everybody that's coming to the table with love. This family has been through hell. We don't have generations of love behind us. We're still building it and it's not always gonna be clean or easy or comfortable. We're figuring it out. Everybody who has love to give this family should be here. So, you're getting your Gucci sneaks dirty, Meek. Get over there with the losing team. You and Mo can talk afterward."

Morgan didn't know if she was relieved that he was staying or fearful of what might happen because of it. The tension in the air could be cut with a knife.

Ethic walked over to Alani. "This isn't the best idea you've ever had," he whispered in her ear.

"Yeah, well, look at the twins, Ezra. Look at Mo. She hasn't even seen him since everything went down with Bash. At some point, you also have to pick a side. Messiah or Mo? My decision today was about Mo. I'm always gonna be team Morgan. Doesn't mean I don't have love for Messiah.

He's family too, but *she* is our responsibility. Look at them, Ezra. She's a totally different person in his presence." They glanced at Morgan and days of gloom seemed to be lifted off her shoulders and she hadn't even spoken to Ahmeek yet. "He loves her better, Ethic."

"He don't love her more, though," Ethic said. He kissed Alani's lips and then strolled over to home base.

They finished picking teams, and Morgan went to the space between the pitcher's mound and home base.

"Okay! Opening pitch will be made by the mommy-to-be! It's a special ball, and it's filled with either pink or blue. After the first pitch, we will play a quick game. First team to ten wins, then we have food and a DJ and drinks for everyone afterward."

She looked to find Messiah, Messari and Eazy on one end of the bench and found Yara, Ahmeek, and Isa on the other side. They were keeping their distance because she was sure they were just as uncomfortable as she was.

Alani made her way to the mound, and she smiled at Ethic, who stood on home base.

"You ready?" She asked, taking a deep breath. "Why am I nervous?" She giggled.

"I'm ready, baby."

"Okay, count down with me!" Morgan shouted. "One!-"

"Two!" The crowd joined.

"Three!"

Alani tossed the ball, and Ethic hit it with all his might sending streaks of pink flying across the park as the ball cleared the fence.

"It's a girl! Oh my god, it's a girl!" Alani shouted. She ran to Ethic, and he lifted her into the air like she was a child, spinning her, making her dress flair before bringing her to his lips.

"It's a girl, baby," Ethic whispered. He didn't even hear the excitement of everyone around him. All he saw was her. He didn't miss the speck of sadness in her eyes. He placed her on her feet and pulled her close, hiding her tears from everyone else.

He knew where her mind went. Her daughter. She felt guilty for replacing her daughter. He knew that's why she had been rooting for a boy, to avoid those feelings of betrayal.

"Breathe."

She clung to him as she bawled right in the middle of the field.

"You're allowed to feel this baby," he said lifting her head as he cupped her face in both hands. She nodded, focusing only on him. "You're allowed to feel joy too."

"Eazy was right," she whispered in disbelief. "True Blessing Okafor," she whispered. "That's her name."

"That's what and who she is. It's perfect," Ethic said. "You're perfect, Alani. Hear me when I tell you I'd never jeopardize this for anybody. That never has to be your concern. I'd never put that on you. I'm sorry for everything that has made you feel like you're less than my only. It's us for me, baby. It's you."

She nodded, and he kissed her again before slapping her on the ass with a bit of aggression. "Now, gone over there so we can get in that ass real quick. We batting first!" He announced.

Ethic and Alani had been together for years and no one in attendance had ever seen them quite so lighthearted. It was like their smiles were wider, their inner glow brighter, their aura less heavy. They were so close to bringing life into the world together that they were riding a natural high. It was beautiful to witness, and Morgan admired it all. The light touches, the laughter, the stolen glances when they interacted with others in attendance. It all made her heart flutter. It made her lift eyes to Ahmeek. He chopped it up with Nyair and Isa, undoubtedly receiving "G" talk and being convinced to dedicate some time with Nyair in the community. He had a way with hood niggas because he was cut from the same cloth. It was interesting, watching Nyair give Ahmeek the third degree. She knew how he felt about Messiah. She wondered if Ahmeek would receive the same judgement. Morgan hoped Nyair wasn't preaching him to death. She couldn't help but smile at how easy the concern of a man meeting her uncle was. She was used to worrying about the big stuff, the life-or-death stuff. This felt normal. Butterflies danced in her stomach as she wondered what Nyair thought of Ahmeek. Ahmeek kept his distance, and she kept hers out of respect, out of uncertainty, but his presence made her heart race so rapidly she heard it in her ears. Then there was Messiah. Her Messiah. He was already in the hearts of her family. Already inducted as an honorary Okafor despite betrayals that should have cast him out. He fit in her life like a puzzle piece. Ethic loved him, and it was apparent by the way they spoke amongst themselves while sipping cognac. Stick talk among men. They were enjoying the festivities side by side, Ethic giving game that only Ethic could give, undoubtedly teaching Messiah how to remain calm with Ahmeek's intrusion. Messiah and Ethic even had the same mannerisms. Messiah just existed easily because he was family. Long before they fell in love, he had been family, and it felt good.

"Only you could pull off having two men you're dealing with at the same place at the same time," Aria said as she came up behind Mo, passing her a red cup.

Morgan sniffed it.

"It's vodka," Aria said. "And a little lemonade."

"How do I choose between them Aria? I mean, look at them. I have these memories with Messiah that are beautiful, and then there are the ones that haunt me at night, but he's alive. I went years thinking he was gone, and now he's in front of me, and it feels like a sin to not appreciate that I have a second chance to love him. To fix it, you know? But he won't talk to me. It's like he's a stranger who knows all my secrets, but I know none of his. I know he's hiding something. I don't even know where he was or where that bitch is he left me for," Morgan said.

"That's a lot, Mo. Does Meek even fit into that equation?" Aria answered.

"Yes," Morgan answered adamantly. She said it too quickly for it not to be true. "I can't unlove him. I'm trying. I'm trying as hard as I can to make him mean nothing to me again…"

"He never meant nothing, Mo. When you and Messiah were together, we were around them so much that we became a part of their crew. We were around they asses every day, laughing, smoking, drinking, clubbing, spending late nights. Sometimes, we didn't do anything at all, and it was still a vibe, still a mood with the five of us. But do you remember how Messiah used to be? While the fun was going on? He was there, but he wasn't at the same time. He wasn't at the card table with you. He wasn't on stage with you, he was always in the cut, laying low, probably in his head about the shit he was really sent there to do. Don't get me wrong. He loves the fuck out of you, but even when y'all were together, Meek was never nothing. These niggas are our people. Our fucking shooters and our best friends. There were no nights without them. I can't recall one. Even on school nights, they came through. We were the college girls with the bad boys pulling up on campus and it was a complete vibe. That's why you can't let Meek go, because if you do, he becomes nothing when we both know it was always something. It was friendship and a friend ain't gon' fold on you. Why do you think he's there for you like he is? It's not because he's fucking you. It's because he's loyal to his friend."

"How do I keep my friend and let the twins have their dad? How do I let Messiah be in their lives without taking over mine? I need them both for different reasons," Mo admitted.

"If you don't make up your mind soon, he might decide for you," Aria said.

"What's that supposed to mean?" Morgan asked. "Is he seeing someone?"

Aria shook her head. "Just talk to him."

"I didn't know he was coming here today, Messiah," Morgan said. "I wouldn't invite him where I knew you were going to be."

Messiah didn't answer. He was in his head, battling the darkest parts of himself because Meek's presence had put him in a mood. Ethic had told him to play it cool, to consider Mo's needs above his own and he knew that Mo needed Ahmeek. She had been through so much, and he possessed a healthier love to give Morgan, and she needed it all to contribute to her healing. It didn't stop him from wanting her to himself, however. He was on the outside looking in on his own family, and it put him in a murderous mood. Morgan had given him space and Yara was in Ahmeek's arms. The only member of his family that was on his side seemed to be Messari. Messiah regretted the day he asked Ahmeek to take care of Morgan because he had understood the assignment and had mastered a test that Messiah was still studying for. His disposition was poor. His patience, leaving him. His fingers rubbing as he tried his hardest to keep his temper at bay. When he had fallen in love with Morgan, he had never thought of the day he would have to watch someone else love her after him. It was torture.

Before Morgan could say anything else, the DJ dropped a song in honor of Ethic and Alani's momentous occasion. The guitar strings floated through the air, and Morgan felt the hair rising on the back of her neck. She steeled, a deer in headlights; the song took her back in time. She stood in the middle of the park as the words snatched the ground from beneath her feet. She remembered. He remembered too. She knew by the look in his eyes that he placed this song as soon as it started. *Best Part*. It was only fitting that the artist's name was H.E.R. because Morgan would forever be the one woman that represented *her* in Messiah's life. If anyone ever mentioned the woman he loved, *Her*, would be the answer. If anyone ever mentioned the one who got away. *Her*, would still be the answer. Morgan replayed every single second of that night back in her mind. Her eyes landed on Ahmeek, and she knew that he knew what she was feeling. Aria and Isa too. Ethic and Alani may have taken the dance floor, but this song belonged to M&M, and The Crew knew it. They had been there. They had witnessed love so passionate it had transformed into insanity and this song pulled her back there instantly.

Meek felt it; he remembered the ice skating, this song, Morgan singing her heart out to a man who would eventually break it.

Change the song, please change it, Morgan thought. Her eyes burned as she fought herself, willing her eyes not to shed tears. *Best part*. Messiah had gone from best to worst to nothing at all in her life, and she hadn't been given a say. Messari was his mother's keeper. He felt her discontent and ran to her. Messiah picked him up.

"Wook at Mommy," Messari said to Messiah. "Why her sad, Daddy?"

Messiah did what Messiah always did. He broke the rules, uncaring of those around them, of the appropriateness of their interaction as he stepped into her space. Messari reached for Mo, hugging her neck tightly and Morgan received him with gratefulness, squeezing him back. Oh, how she was grateful for her son's love. Her eyes closed, and she felt the wetness on her cheek.

If you love me, won't you say something;
if you love me, won't you-

"Daddy fucked up, man," Messiah replied.

"Him sorry, Mommy," Messari said.

"Sorry as fuck, shorty," Messiah whispered, pulling her and his son into his arms.

"This song, Messiah," she said softly.

"I know," he confirmed. "I took this shit for granted, shorty. No lie, I just want to go back to that night."

"We can't," she whispered. "Messiah, I can't."

The song ended prematurely, breaking Morgan's trance, and she looked toward the DJ to find Ethic there. He always knew what she needed. Freedom. He had freed her of the emotions of her past, instructing the DJ to change the record to something more up-tempo. He hadn't known why the song affected Morgan, but he had always been able to feel her, and she was glad he was there to intervene.

Ahmeek, she thought.

Morgan looked over Messiah's shoulder for him. The space Ahmeek had occupied was now empty. He was headed to his car. Morgan passed Messari off to Messiah.

"I'm sorry, Ssiah. I can't," she whispered. "Ahmeek, wait!" She shouted.

Fear that he would pull off without acknowledging her made Morgan pick up speed as she crossed the lawn. She could only imagine how he felt. She remembered a similar feeling. She had fought with Messiah like this over Bash years ago, and he had pulled off on her. She had broken her finger that day. She would never forget it. This felt like that. Like she was losing him, like he was angry. When he started the car, her heart plummeted.

She walked to the front of his car, standing directly in his path. He would have to reverse the car and go around her to leave.

Meek opened his car door and stood, half in, half out, as he looked at her, brow bent.

"Go back to your family," he said, tone cool, unbothered, despite the storm forming inside him.

"You're my family," she said. "You're my everything."

"Doing shit like that," he said, pointing toward the celebration. "Nah, Mo. We ain't on it like that."

All she wanted to hear was him call her *love*. Her own name was a weapon against her in this moment.

"It was just… the song… it…" she was grasping for an explanation, a complicated answer that would explain how she felt. "I can't erase my history, Ahmeek."

"Problem is that shit don't look like history to me, Mo," he said. "That's the present. I'm up. You be easy, a'ight? I only came here to let you know I'ma be out the way for a minute."

She approached him, and he looked down at her in disdain.

"What does that mean? Out the way?" She asked.

"I'm leaving town. Shits hot, and I got business elsewhere. I just wanted you to hear it from me. I know where your mind wanders when you're left with the unknown, so I wanted to say goodbye to you first."

"We found something in each other, Ahmeek," Morgan said. "You can't just pretend like it didn't happen and leave."

"Did we, Mo? Cuz if all it takes is a song to make you forget a nigga in the room, what we found wasn't shit," Meek answered.

"He will always be in my life, but you…" She paused and looked down. "I'm in love with you, and as fucked up as I am, you still love me too. I'm used, I'm abused, by so many men, Meek. I'm not the girl you can love proudly. I'm the one with a past, the one you have to defend because niggas talk about what I've done, what they've done to me, but you still love me. You still look at me like I'm brand new. Like I'm not a mess. I just don't want you to leave because I'm crazy about you. I know it's hard, figuring out how we exist in the same world as Messiah, but I want to exist with you Ahmeek. I'm sorry if I care too much about him. I can't not care about him. You care about him too, how can you expect me not to care?"

Ahmeek sighed as he lowered his head. Foreheads touching, they stood there. "I don't expect that." She was professing her love for him. Choosing him. The ways he loved this girl, he couldn't even explain, but the things he had to do to rectify the situation with Hak, was forcing his hand. "You tell a nigga the right thing at the wrong time, love," he said, scoffing. "I can't be what you need right now."

"Whatever you can be is what I need," Morgan protested. "What you have been is enough. I know you think I've been playing games. Bash held so many things over my head..."

"He's gone, nothing to talk about. There's nobody even left to whisper the nigga name," Ahmeek said, temple throbbing as he tensed at the thought of what she had endured. Bash, nor his mother or father would ever be heard from again. "You should have told me, Mo. I could have done something."

Morgan looked away, and he used both hands to force her eyes back to him.

"FaceTime," she whispered. "You're acting like you don't love me anymore. Why am I always so easy to leave?"

"You're the hardest to leave, Mo, but I'm leaving because I love you. I'm back on some street shit, and it's probably gon' get ugly for a minute, and I need to focus on that for a while."

"What?" She didn't understand. He had told her he wanted out. That she made him dream of a normal future. "What street shit, Ahmeek? Why would you go deeper? You were supposed to be done."

"Yeah, well the game ain't always done with you when you done with it," he replied.

"This just ain't for us no more. You owe it to yourself to settle the 'what-ifs' in your heart, Mo." He was giving her an out. A clean break.

"This is bullshit," Morgan said sadly. "This isn't fair."

"Morgan Atkins, you ruin a nigga, love," he whispered, eyes closed, head still pressed to hers. "I swear you're a fucking drug. Go back to the party. I'ma see you around."

"But I can't even reach you. I get you're leaving, but you want to un-know me?"

Her feelings were crushed. She couldn't even fathom the thought of that.

"Can't outrun the sun, Morgan. You're everywhere I go. If you need me, you know how to find me and you know I'ma be there. Don't you?"

It was the thumb caressing her chin that took her out. This man carried such finesse. His love and even his disdain was given out so gently. He was careful with her, and after being mishandled for so long, it only made her fall harder for him. Her breathing was shallow, and her eyes closed as that thumb crossed her lips. She nodded. She did know. Even without his number, she could reach out to his mother anytime. She had the number. She had never used it before, but it was seeming like her lifeline in this moment.

"Ms. Marilyn," Morgan said sadly.

"She'll take care of you well, love. When you need it. When you're lost. Whatever you need. She said she wants to hear from you sometime," he said.

Morgan gasped. She was so overwhelmed.

"Go back to your family." The forehead kiss delivered such finality before he lowered into his car and pulled away.

"He'll be back for you," she whispered to herself as she watched his car disappear around the block.

Alani watched Ethic, Zeke, Nyair, and Messiah carry in the last of their gifts as she sat cuddled on the sectional with the twins as Zora, Nannie, Bella, Morgan, and Eazy sat around the room. It had been a long, eventful day, and she could barely keep her eyes open.

"True Blessing," Nannie said. "Yes, this baby will be indeed."

"It's a little storybook, don't you think?" Eazy asked. "It doesn't even sound like a real name! Ezani is better."

"Ezani is definitely better," Zora agreed, nudging him in support.

Alani chuckled and noticed Bella was unusually quiet. "You okay over there, baby girl?"

"I'm fine," Bella replied. "Just tired. May I be excused? I think I'm gonna go to bed?"

"Of course," Alani said. Bella stood and leaned to kiss Alani, then Zora, then Nannie before heading up.

"She's taking her boyfriend's sentencing hard, huh?" Zora asked.

"Extremely," Alani answered as she rubbed her belly, groaning and grimacing as she sat up.

"You feeling okay?" Nannie asked.

"It feels like something is sitting on my chest," Alani asked.

"Eazy, baby, get some water," Zora said.

Eazy ran to the kitchen as Alani grabbed her belly. "Woo," she said.

"Zo, help me up. I just need to pee," Alani said. "And I need some Vernors. This heartburn is killing me."

Zora stood and hugged Alani around her back, using her

body weight to pull Alani to her feet. As soon as she stood Alani froze. "Ohhhh my god."

"La! Did you just pee on my damn Loubs?!" Zora exclaimed.

"That's not pee. I think my water broke," she said. "Oh my god. Oh. My. Fucking."

"Alani, don't you use the Lord's name in vain now!" Nannie interrupted.

"Eazy, go get Daddy," Alani said as soon as he walked back into the room. "And get Bella down here."

Ethic, Nyair, and Messiah came rushing into the house.

"What happened?" Ethic asked, panicked as he took Alani off her feet.

"The baby's coming," Alani panted. "Ezra, she's coming. Oh my god, she's coming. What if she's not okay? What if this is the same as last time?"

"She's strong, Alani. Our girl is gonna make it. She's going to breathe," Ethic said. He lifted his eyes to Nyair. "Bro, come pray over my wife and child."

He wouldn't say he was scared because it would scare her, but his heart was racing.

"I'm calling Nessa," Nannie said, moving slowly as her old bones carried her to the kitchen.

Bella and Eazy came racing into the family room.

"Is she okay?" Bella's voice shook. She hadn't told anyone how scared she was of this moment. She too remembered losing Love and she was fearful of this birth going terribly wrong.

"She's fine, Bella. Her body is designed for exactly this," Nannie said. "Nessa is on the way. She says to get Alani in the birthing pool and to clear the room."

"Ny, make it the best prayer you've ever prayed," Alani said, her discomfort showing on her face.

Nyair stepped up to Ethic and Alani and placed his hand on her belly. He felt True kick, and he pulled his hand back in amazement.

"Nah, G, there is life inside her womb. God has his hand on baby True. She's going to be just fine." He touched her belly again. "Father. My G. I come to You with the humblest heart in the most beautiful time because You are dispatching one of Your angels to Earth. As this family prepares to receive baby True, still their hearts Father God. I know this has been a dream of Ethic and Alani's for a long time, and You don't give dreams that You don't plan to deliver. Deliver baby True to those You have entrusted her with and let her and mom have a safe delivery. We thank You for Your covering, and Your mercy and Your love and Your grace, G. In Your name we pray. Amen."

"Amen."

"Mo, get everybody to Nannie's. We'll call when we have news," Ethic said.

"What? I get to stay, right? Alani said I could stay with her until it's time to push, " Bella said.

"You can stay," Alani said.

"Make sure they get there safely," Ethic told Messiah.

Bella rushed up the stairs to get the inflatable birthing pool filled, and Ethic carried Alani up the stairs to the room they had designed especially for their child's birth. The bohemian-themed suite had been filled with calming neutral colors, candles, and Alani's favorite music had been programmed.

"I'm so scared I'm shaking," Alani whispered as he placed her on her feet.

"You can be scared, baby, but I believe in you. We're going to be fine," Ethic said.

"Is this a mistake? Having the baby at home?" She asked as he undressed her. Bella assisted and retrieved Alani's birthing gown. Nannie had spent weeks sewing it for her. She slipped it over Alani's naked body.

"If this is weird for you, Bella, you don't have to be here. You can wait at Nannie's with the others," Alani said.

"It's not weird. I've seen your body do something crazy twice. I took the classes with you. I learned to listen to True's heartbeat. I'm not gonna bail on you now that the hard part's here. I've got you, and I won't leave you until my baby sister is here," Bella said, eyes misting.

Alani nodded and squeezed Bella's hand as Ethic helped her into the pool. The chill of the water made goosebumps decorate her arm. Ethic kissed the tiny bumps.

"You sure you don't want to do this at the hospital?" Ethic asked.

She nodded. She wasn't sure, but she wasn't bringing her daughter into the world at Love's death site.

The doorbell rang, and Bella dismissed herself.

"That's Nessa," Alani whispered. "Thank God."

Nessa entered the room, and the look of calm on her face made Alani's worries dissolve.

"You ready to bring your baby girl into the world, sis?" Nessa asked excitedly. She got washed up and gloved, then pointed to Ethic.

"Trunks for you, sir, and get in this water," Nessa ordered. Ethic went into the bathroom, changed, and emerged.

"Okay now, Alani we're going to scoot you forward so he can get behind you. He's your foundation. You pull your strength from him," Nessa coached.

"These contractions are coming, Ness. They shouldn't be coming this quickly; my water just broke an hour ago," Alani said, worried.

Nessa spread Alani's legs and checked her cervix.

"How have you been feeling today?" She asked. "Any cramping?"

"Yeah, some," Alani said.

"Those were contractions. Your cervix has been opening slowly all day, I suspect. This baby will be here tonight. You're already to nine centimeters. I'm surprised you weren't in pain."

Alani leaned her head back against Ethic's shoulder.

"Baby, you're gonna have to help me through this because I'm terrified," Alani whispered.

"I got you," Ethic said. Somehow, it was all he needed to say for her anxiety to leave because she knew it was true. "You're so strong. You're beautiful, Lenika. Breathe."

Innnnnn. Outttttt.

"Breathe."

Innnnnn. Outttttt.

Nessa motioned for Bella. "Go get changed, Bella. Remember what I said. Antibacterial soap, rinse well, glove up. You wanna be ready to catch when the baby comes out."

"Ohhhh, Ezraaaa, waitttt. Nessa, this one hurts," Alani cried out as a contraction ripped through her entire body.

"I know, baby," Ethic whispered, kissing her ear. "I would take it if I could, baby. Our girl needs you, though. Only you. Just get her here, baby. Get her out so I can see her breathing, and you won't ever have to do anything else." Another kiss to her temple. "Breathe."

"I can't do this," Alani said. "Ethic, what if she doesn't breathe? What if I do something wrong?"

"You won't," he said. He stared at Nessa, trying to gauge her reaction as she checked Alani's cervix. "Look at me, Alani."

She craned her neck to stare into his eyes.

"Do this for me. I've never wanted anything like I want my daughter. After so much loss, we need this. You said you'll do anything for me. Is that truth, or you just be talking?"

Bella re-entered the room.

"Over here, now, Bella," Nessa said.

Bella didn't hesitate to climb into the pool.

"It's truth, baby. I'll die for you."

Ethic looked at Nessa, who nodded her head.

"It's time," Nessa confirmed.

"All I need you to do is push. Push, Lenika, push for me."

He held her knees and pulled back as she pushed from her soul. Her cry was like a battle cry, and it sent chills down his spine.

"Keep pushing!" Bella cried.

Alani heaved as the contraction ended. She was exhausted and Ethic cleared her hair from her face as he planted kisses to her head. "You're doing so good, baby. You're doing amazing. You're so strong."

"Okay, shut up, shut up," Alani shouted, irritated.

Ethic burst into laughter. "You so motherfucking mean, Lenika," he snickered.

Nessa laughed, too, as she prepared for the next contraction. "Okay, a few more pushes. You're tearing a little, so we have to ease her out slowly, okay?"

"Tearing?" Ethic asked, concerned.

Nessa nodded. "There will be some blood. That's okay. I'm going to take good care of her. We won't cut her. I want to change positions, okay? It's gonna hurt, and she needs to look you in your eyes. So, Alani, I want you to get up and balance your weight on the side of the pool and get on your knees."

She moved so slowly that Ethic could tell she was in pain.

"Ethic, we're going to have you on the outside of the pool," Nessa said.

Ethic stood, and Alani placed her hand over his dick print because no, absolutely not. The water and the shorts clung to him like a second skin... she would take Nessa's head off. He snickered and was grateful his daughter was distracted by the impending birth. He got on his knees in front of her.

"You wildin," he snickered.

"That thing is what got me in this situation in the first place," she whispered weakly.

They shared a laugh, forehead to forehead, as she gripped his forearms.

"I feel another one," she said, voice shaking.

"Be my strong girl. Breathe and push, baby, push!"

"Arghhhh!"

Alani's nails in his skin made Ethic bite his bottom lip. He kissed her lips. "Good girl, push baby," he said. How the fuck was he turning her on during childbirth? He stuck his tongue in her mouth, sucking on hers, pulling her lips into his mouth, swallowing her screams. "Push," he coached. A peck. Alani roared as she gave it her all.

"I see her head!" Bella announced. She was crying.

"Almost done. You can rest in a minute. You're so powerful, Lenika. The power you have over me, baby. It's fucking incredible. Show me. Push. One more time for me. Give me everything you got."

"I can't," she panted.

Red blood filled the pool.

Nessa looked up at Ethic in alarm.

"Daddy?" Bella's tone reflected fear, and Alani looked at Ethic.

"What is it, Ezra? What's wrong?" Alani cried. "Something's wrong, isn't it?"

"Look at me. Don't look back, just look at the man you love. The man that's gonna make sure you're good. I'm right here," Ethic said. Forehead to forehead.

"Ezra, it hurts," she whispered.

"Nessa, you need to tell me something," Ethic said calmly. He was dying inside. He could see her pain, and the water was now red. It looked like too much blood to come from one person.

"Alani, push," Nessa said.

Alani's and Ethic were hand to hand, wrists crisscrossed for leverage, and he pulled so hard, bracing her that he lifted half her body out of the pool.

"You're strong, baby. You can do this. You're doing so good. I'm so proud of you," he said. He was losing his shit. Eyes burning like a motherfucker because his wife was on the brink of life and death. Men had no idea how women risked their lives, but Ethic had witnessed it twice in Alani, and he prayed silently for her life during this battle. He gripped the back of her head. "Alani Lenika Okafor," he whispered, voice trembling. "We can't bury any more babies. Push. Fucking pushing, baby."

"I can'ttttttttttttt!"

Alani felt her body rip in half as True finally passed the birth canal.

"I got her! Oh my god, I got her!" Bella sobbed. She was a mess as her emotions overcame her. "She's here!"

"That's my girl," Ethic said, bitching up. His gangster left him. He was simply a father, and he broke. He kissed her lips. "You did so good. Good job. Good job, baby."

"She isn't crying, Ezra," Alani said weakly. "She needs you."

Ethic was watching like a hawk as Nessa went to work on his daughter. Bella was bawling while looking at her father, shaking her head.

"Go get her, Ezra!" Alani cried.

He didn't want to let her hand go, but he went to the other side of the pool. He watched in dismay as Nessa covered True's nose and mouth with hers and blew air into her body. Ethic took his daughter from her hands and brought her tiny, bloody body to his lips. He covered her mouth and nose and blew. Thank God he had paid attention in Alani's childbirth classes.

"Come on!"

The desperation and fear filled the air. Death was present. He remembered the feeling from when Love was delivered, and his stomach sank.

He covered her mouth and nose once more and blew air into her lungs. When her cries filled the air, he bawled.

"She's breathing, Alani! She's-"

Ethic looked to Bella as she climbed across the pool, and his heart sank. Alani was laid over the edge of the inflatable birthing pool. Her arms were limp, and her head hung over the side.

"Alani! What's wrong with her, Nessa?!" He barked.

"Bella, call 911," Nessa said. "Go now!"

Messiah sat on Nannie's porch with his son in his lap. "Don't you want to go to sleep?" He asked Messari.

"Unt uh," Messari said while rubbing his eyes with little fists.

The glow of the porch light shone down over them. It was a quiet night in the hood, the only sound was the serenade of the crickets as they echoed down the block.

"You stubborn, man," Messiah snickered.

"No, I not, you stubborn," Messari said, snuggling his sleepy body closer to his father.

"You a good kid man," Messiah whispered. "My baby boy."

Morgan stepped out onto the porch, carrying Yara and she took a seat beside him. Morgan and Messiah were enemies and lovers. A complicated dynamic for two people who didn't know how to exist without their energy being exchanged.

"You heard anything?" Messiah asked.

"Not yet," she replied. "It takes a little time. When I gave birth, it felt like forever. It's not easy. We might not hear anything til' morning."

Messiah looked at Morgan with regret. "I'm sorry you went through that alone. You didn't make them by yourself you shouldn't have had to birth them by yourself. I wish I was there, shorty."

She didn't know what to say to that. She could tell the apology was sincere.

"I wish you were there too," she said quietly.

"If you would just show me who you are Messiah, I would love the real you. You know that right?" she asked. "If I loved the lies, imagine how I would love the truth."

"You don't want the truth, Mo. You love for a nigga to be the bad guy," Messiah answered. "It can only be one victim, so I let it be you."

"Stop with the double talking, Ssiah. Why can't you just keep it real with me?" Morgan asked.

"Would it even matter, shorty? If you knew the truth? You in love with another nigga, right? What the truth matter for now?" Messiah asked.

"It matters," Morgan insisted. Morgan shook her head as Messiah leaned back in the wooden rocking chair and swayed while rubbing Messari's back. Morgan's eyes drank him in.

"I really hate that you cut your hair," she said, sadness clinging to every word.

"I'll grow the shit back if you want, shorty," Messiah countered. "It's just hair."

"It wasn't just hair. It was a crown. You were my king," she whispered. "I've been so lost without you. You left me and I died. I came back. Alani brought me back, but I'm not the same. I'll never be the same again, Messiah. We're different people now."

"It don't matter how much you change, I'ma love the shit out of you," Messiah said. "Because that what people do. They love you anyway, regardless of the bullshit that's attached to you. I'm home, Morgan. Let me back in. Love me anyway."

"You're going to destroy me," she replied, shaking her head. So much mistrust kept her from accepting him as her own.

"I won't," he urged.

She nodded. "You will. I know you, Messiah. You will."

"I swear to God on my life Mo..."

"Don't do that. I've lived with the thought of you not being here. It was horrible. Not on your life. We don't swear on your life."

"You talking like you love a nigga," Messiah said, looking aside bashfully.

"My heart isn't as simple as it used to be Messiah. Life isn't simple anymore. You complicated it in a way that makes it impossible to get back what we had," she whispered.

"So you don't love me, no more, Mo?" Messiah asked. "You can honestly sit there and say that shit?"

She paused. If she answered this with a lie, would she be able to convince him that it was the truth? No. Never that. He knew her too well to not see through the charade. Not even her disdain hid what he knew dwelled in her. No point in falsehoods. Fuck it. Put it all on the table.

"I love you, Messiah but it's not just about me," Morgan answered passionately.

"It's about Ahmeek?" His chair stopped mid-rock and his face filled with confusion and agony. Shock wore him and it didn't wear him well. Her admission had snatched the bottom from his stomach. "You really love that nigga that much, Mo? This is me, shorty. You want to hurt a nigga cuz I hurt you. I get it. Game over. You win, Mo. You caught a little vibe from the nigga, but you don't love that nigga like you love me, man."

"I do," she said. "I do love him like that."

Morgan held their sleeping daughter tighter because anxiety filled her. There. She had confessed. To his face. Messiah had known before, but she was sure he had talked himself into not believing it. Here. Face to face. She had womaned up. She had told him directly. She should feel better. She felt worse.

"We thought you were dead Messiah," she whispered. "I don't love you less. I love you so much." She paused as tears filled her eyes and an ugly cry shook her bottom lip. "I just love him too."

"Get the fuck out of here," Messiah dismissed. No way was he taking this seriously. This had to be about 'get back.' It was her fucked up way of making him hurt. It was punishment for all the fucked-up shit he had done to her. He deserved it.

It was the only reason why he passed no judgement. He had this coming from her, but he was tired of playing, tired of the back and forth. It was time for them to get back right. Despite everything. Like Ethic and Alani, he just wanted to get it right and defy the odds.

"I'm not saying this to hurt you. I'm saying this because I need to be honest with you about what happened while you were away. If we are ever going to even have a chance to be anything to each other, you have to know what happened while you were gone. Things between me and Ahmeek..." she paused. She was terrified to openly admit this to him. "It's serious."

The words raced out of her. She didn't even mean to give them clemency, but they were already free. Already turning molehills to mountains inside of Messiah's head. His distress filled the air.

"You were engaged to a whole nigga, Mo! Fuck you mean it's serious? You playing with these niggas. Collecting hearts cuz you need the attention. I left and I get it. You wanted somebody to fill the hole. It took two niggas to make you feel half of what I did shorty. You ain't really fucking with him, Mo. You can't lie to me, shorty. Might can lie to yourself, but I call bullshit."

There it was. The aggression that Messiah couldn't control. It was bubbling in him like lava, threatening to erupt.

"He stepped up in so many ways. He was genuine with me. He was different for me. I've seen him with you in the streets Messiah. He's a monster out there, same as you, but he never brought that into my space. He never slipped up.

He fixed a heart he didn't break," her tone was small, timid even. "He doesn't lie to me. He doesn't hurt me. He wants me. He chooses me."

"Bitch ass nigga ain't choose you," Messiah said. He was tired of the façade Mo was selling. "I forced him. Nigga wouldn't even be fucking with you if I didn't tell him to, Mo. You were a chore. I left town and left the nigga with a job. Shit ain't real. The nigga done gamed you, made you believe in fucking fairy tales. He a fucking bad guy, just like me. Bet his ass ain't tell you that." There it was. That bite. It was vicious. It tore her apart every time.

The revelation hit Morgan like a slap in the face. "You're lying," she said. "He wouldn't…"

"He wouldn't what, Mo? Step to my fucking girl? You right shorty. He wouldn't. Not without me putting the play down. I called the play! Like always. Ain't nothing changed. Meek just executed the shot," Messiah said. "So get over that shit before I lose my patience with that nigga."

Morgan felt like she would be sick.

"So, you handed me down to your boy like I was something old you didn't want anymore?" Morgan asked. "And he let you? Why would you do this?"

"Because I was fucking dying shorty! I had stage 4 cancer! I was dying and leaving the girl I love behind with a lot of fucking damage. I needed him to make it right! That's why! Bet he ain't tell you that shit when he was acting like he was here to save you. Now what the fuck you got to say about that?"

TO BE CONTINUED IN BUTTERFLY 5!

Ash Armyyyyyyy!!!! Why is Messiah this wayyyyyy? We're going to hop on this ride one more time before we move on to Henny & Bella. Butterfly 5 will be the conclusion of the Butterfly series. Download the Book Lovers app to stay up to date on release dates and join me in the Ashley & JaQuavis Book Club on Facebook to stay in the know.

I do not have a release date for Butterfly 5. Pre-order is available, but books will not ship until the official release date which is still being determined. If you choose to pre-order, know that there will be a wait while I am creating. Pre-order reserves your copy. When it is released you will receive a shipping notification containing a tracking number when your book is on the way. B5 can be pre-ordered at www. thebooklovers.co

DISCUSSION QUESTIONS

1. Should Ethic let Morgan go? Was what she did forgivable?

2. Was Zya wrong for sending YaYa to Ethic's arraignment?

3. Did Henny make the right sacrifice, or did he deliver unjustified heartache to young Bella?

4. Is Isa too reckless? Is he biting off more than he can chew with Hak?

5. Should Ahmeek have taken on the debt alone?

6. Was Ahmeek wrong for leaving Morgan behind?

7. Will he come back for her?

8. Morgan and Messiah are connected so deeply. Why won't she just give in and let him come home?

9. Messiah and Bleu are so complicated. What are they to one another?

10. Is Messiah wrong for indulging in Bleu?

11. Can Messiah's therapist break through to him?

12. The Crew came together to kill Bash. Will they ever be the same again?

13. What is the current state of Messiah and Meek's friendship?

14. If Alani dies will Ethic resent baby True?

15. Now that Morgan knows about Messiah's cancer will she forgive him for leaving?

Come discuss with me on the Booklovers App today!

Made in the USA
Las Vegas, NV
05 August 2024

93379711R00246